Coffee, Shopping, Murder, Love

Coffee, Shopping, Murder, Love

a novel

Carlos Allende

2019
Red Hen Press
Quill Prose
Award

Red Hen Press | *Pasadena, CA*

Book design by Mark E. Cull

Library of Congress Cataloging-in-Publication Data

Names: Allende, Carlos, 1974– author.
Title: Coffee, shopping, murder, love: a novel / Carlos Allende.
Description: First edition. | Pasadena, CA: Red Hen Press, [2022]
Identifiers: LCCN 2021045473 (print) | LCCN 2021045474 (ebook) | ISBN
   9781636280356 (hardcover) | ISBN 9781636280363 (epub)
Subjects: LCGFT: Black humor. | Novels.
Classification: LCC PS3601.L4393 C64 2022 (print) | LCC PS3601.L4393
   (ebook) | DDC 813/.6—dc23
LC record available at https://lccn.loc.gov/2021045473
LC ebook record available at https://lccn.loc.gov/2021045474

The National Endowment for the Arts, the Los Angeles County Arts Commission, the Ahmanson Foundation, the Dwight Stuart Youth Fund, the Max Factor Family Foundation, the Pasadena Tournament of Roses Foundation, the Pasadena Arts & Culture Commission and the City of Pasadena Cultural Affairs Division, the City of Los Angeles Department of Cultural Affairs, the Audrey & Sydney Irmas Charitable Foundation, the Kinder Morgan Foundation, the Meta & George Rosenberg Foundation, the Albert and Elaine Borchard Foundation, the Adams Family Foundation, the Riordan Foundation, Amazon Literary Partnership, the Sam Francis Foundation, and the Mara W. Breech Foundation partially support Red Hen Press.

First Edition
Published by Red Hen Press
www.redhen.org
Printed in Canada

To my dear sweet friend, Mr. Christopher Touchton, who gallantly accepted to be my muse. May you never regret it.

Contents

Coffee, Shopping, Murder, Love

En Guise de Prologue

Traumatic incident from my childhood number forty-two—when I am as sad as I am now, I tend to reflect on the reasons for my failure: Mr. Oatley, my music professor, flinching as if he had just been cut open with a samurai sword at my attempts to reach a high note . . .

I cannot sing. I know that now. Why, I sound vicious when I speak: a really deep vocal fry that soon transforms into a wailing crescendo. When I sing, I sound as if a drunken harpy had married a southern gentleman—which is not far from the truth, Aunt Gaynelle has always referred to my mother as a drunken harpy because my mother, well, she likes her hooch, and she isn't always the kindest, while my father has a drawl so thick you could cut it with a knife and make yourself a sandwich. It makes you want to turn on the subtitles. But anyway, I digress. Where was I? Oh yes, sunk in the depths of despair, wearing these fabulous camo pants and these hyper-chic hiking boots from Salomon Quest (50 percent off at Neiman Marcus), but also without a lamp, on a very dark night, lost in the Mexican desert, wishing that I had never crossed paths with Jignesh, that I had never fallen in love with his wealth and with his ravishing South Asian skin color, then agreed to become his accomplice, and remembering, right after failure number forty-one—calling Mr. Connelly "daddy" in fourth grade—of the time when Mr. Oatley, that awful, awful, horrible, terrible old man, winced as if an eagle had been eating his entrails at my attempt to sing *Der Hölle Rache* so that I could be chosen for the school chorus . . .

You would have thought that by the tender age of ten-and-a-half winters, having been called a fag since pretty much my first day at pre-school, my self-esteem would have already developed a thick callus. Well, it hadn't. It hurt seeing him shudder. It hurt seeing my music professor dismiss me as if I had been some importunate beggar instead of a little girlie boy full of enthusiasm, dreaming of one day becoming the next Kate Bush . . . Mr. Oatley's rejection should have prevented me from ending my act with a swirl, but I was already in character. I forgot that half my classmates had relatives in the Ku Klux Klan . . . *Ouch!* I keep bumping into these stupid cactuses . . . *Sweet, Southern, baby Jesus*, I cry. Will this be my demise? Will I die of hunger and thirst, alone, or will a rattlesnake bite me first and put me out of my misery . . . ?

No, I should have neither spun nor attempted a gymnastic curtsy, but after a whole two weeks wondering what should I sing so that my peers would be so impressed that they would stop spitting on my food in the cafeteria, and a full hour of really practicing, I couldn't just drop the invisible gown from the Queen of the Night to the floor, stick my tongue out, and scratch the back of my head like Tommy did when he too was rejected. He looked incredibly manly, yes, but I had to do my swirl. It was part of the act. It was necessary . . . Oy, talking about what's essential, I think that Charlie—that would be me, Charlie Hayworth, from Leitchfield, Kentucky, at your service; I tried to go by Chuck in seventh grade, but it didn't go well. Boys didn't like it—I think that Charlie should stop here and take a rest. These boots are fabulous, but they aren't really my size. My feet hurt a little. Where would be a safe place to stop and die of infinite sadness?

Traumatic incident number fifty-six, I reminisce, snuggling my head on the sand: being shoved into the girls' room and once there, getting punched unconscious by Samantha Hogg . . . You would think that self-loathing doesn't help, but it actually does. Ask any gay person. It is as if, when you're terribly sad and disheartened, as I am right now, waiting to die, lost and forgotten, betrayed by the man whom you hoped would pull you out of poverty, something inside your own body soothes you. The more you feel sorry for yourself, the better it feels. There's beauty in sadness. Why else would we keep watching reruns of *Old Yeller*? It must have something to do with the chemicals in your brain. Self-pity is addictive.

Six months earlier . . .

1

Murder

I'm looking at Charlie's texts, still labeled as "unread" on my iPhone. *How's your Sunday going, Jignesh? Any plans?*

For God's sake. Our date was on Monday. If I haven't responded to your many texts in six days, I think, taking a slurp from my Frappuccino, it must be pretty clear that my future plans don't include you, Mr. Charlie Hayworth.

Here comes another one. *Let's meet again soon . . .*

I'm tempted to reply with a STOP! *PLEASE STOP BEFORE I KILL YOU!* but I'm afraid that acknowledging receipt will only encourage Charlie to text even more. He knows I'm alive. I made the mistake of accepting his Facebook friend request a minute before meeting him in person, and now he can track all my movements. I'm tracking his at this very moment . . . Good God . . . The things he posts . . . A video of Geena Davis's Oscar acceptance speech for *The Accidental Tourist* . . . A meme mocking Romney's attacks on PBS—I'll share that, we cannot lose this election—then another one of praise to Malala . . . I mean, as a full-figured gay man of color, I am a confirmed feminist. I know what women and members of minorities go through. I know of the abuse, the rage, and the injustice. I know what it is like to be judged and ignored. But just look at those fucking eyebrows. No wonder the Taliban wanted to kill her.

Charlie's selling a freezer too . . . Almost new, I scroll down . . . $650.

That's not a bad price, but I have no use for a freezer that size. I haven't killed anyone yet, I giggle.

I thought I had fallen in love with the little white boy from Kentucky, I sigh, looking out the window. I honestly did. Charlie had a nice little ass framed in a miniature swimmer's body. Blue eyes, a turned-up nose. I thought of putting him in my pocket, that cute he was—but his voice, dear Jesus! An ultra-feminine southern drawl with an insufferable nasal timbre. *Is Fran Drescher here?* I turned around, looking for the hidden camera. He starts really slow, but then gains speed and applies to his discourse a rather unsettling crescendo, full of highs and lows, and gasping and crying and sudden snorting, which make him sound as if he were either possessed or having a seizure. Charlie's aware of how bad he sounds and apologized a few times. As a matter of fact, he apologized every time he lifted his fork.

Anyway, that's all in the past. I toss my empty Frappuccino cup into the trash bin. Artists as sensible and well educated as I am have no time to lose looking for sex online. I have decided to delete my Grindr profile and remove myself indefinitely from the dating pool. Let's be honest. Middle-aged Indian fatties like me don't attract the best male exemplars of the species. Therefore Charlie. Even he couldn't hide a grimace of surprise when he saw me enter the coffee shop instead of the airbrushed and much slimmer version of me that I sent him . . . Now, winsome Celt women with a wispy mane of red hair like Princess Salmonella McFallog? They do. They attract the best male exemplars of the species. She's the heroine of my latest fantasy novel: *Catacombs of the Shining Fear.* I wrote the prologue last night and decided to come to the office this morning to write in peace the first chapter. Typical of every Sunday, my brother brought over his horrendous family to visit our parents. One cannot write in a house full of gaudy Indians, especially a *Highlands* epic like Princess Salmonella's . . . I'm so in love with her already! I reach for the cup I just tossed so that I can chew on the ice. Who wouldn't be? Who wouldn't love Salmonella? She smells of moss and wild berries.

She rides horses, has impressive archery skills, a golden pistol that she received from a visitor from the future, and—

"What are you doing here?"

I turn around, instinctively taking a hand to my chest. Nina is standing by the front door, downstairs, carrying an oversized backpack that makes her twig-like figure seem about to fracture. She's looking at me, sitting at my desk on the mezzanine, as if she had just discovered a turd floating inside a public toilet.

"What are *you* doing here?" I ask back.

It is Sunday, for God's sake. Nina's internship ended on Friday.

"I thought you had already left Los Angeles," I say. "Forever."

She had a farewell luncheon and all, the little bitch. Everyone brought her a present. Everyone, including Mike, our stupid boss. Everyone commented on how sad it was that our "best intern" was leaving. She said she would be going down surfing in Baja for a couple of weeks before going back to Germany. Everyone rushed to give her advice and warn her about how dangerous Tijuana is. Friday marked my eighth anniversary here as well. I am the Chief Financial Officer at this shitty vacation rentals company, for God's sake. Well, more of a glorified bookkeeper and assistant to whatever fuckery Mike devises. Still . . . no one remembered!

"I came to print my train ticket," Nina replies, dropping her bag on the floor.

"Don't you have a printer at home?" I ask.

She shakes her head.

"Well, you are no longer an intern here," I continue. "I'm afraid you cannot just come and use the company's resources. Go to a Kinko's."

Nina gives me the middle finger and walks under the mezzanine toward the end of the office.

The nerve. So much changed in four months. From attentive little helper to aggressive cunty witch.

"Print if you must," I say, raising my voice, "but mind that I have important work to do too. Don't interrupt me."

Nina doesn't answer. I hear her start a computer . . . So fucking distracting. I heave a sigh, then return to my writing.

Princess Salmonella looked at the Roman mercenary feeling a vivid rage run through her flawlessly boned spine all the way to her head crowned with the wavy, red curls. She hated that man. That Roman soldier with thick, toned arms and incredibly dark eyebrows was the reason her father had lost his kingdom—

I hear Nina turn on the printer . . . My God. It is so vexing. Okay. Relax, Jignesh. Be divine. Don't forget you're basically a Jedi. She'll be gone soon. You're an artist.

'I thought you were dead, Princess,' said Claudius Julius taking a strand of Salmonella's hair. Salmonella pulled back, defiantly. Her eyes shone with the intensity of hot fire coming from a volcano—

A sudden snort interrupts me. What is that twat downstairs laughing about? Deep sigh. Keep on, Jignesh. Just ignore her.

'You Roman pig,' Salmonella spat on Claudius Julius's face.

Oy. Is it too early to start with bodily fluids?

Another snort from Nina.

"What's so funny?" I ask, raising my voice.

No answer. Okay, just relax, Jignesh. Don't let that German witch twitch your creativity . . . Every straight man lost his head over Nina. I never thought she was that pretty. She's only young. Who isn't beautiful at that age? I bet she's just another malnourished girl back in Germany . . .

'I'd sooner die than let a Roman pig touch me!' Salmonella pulled out a silver dagger encrusted with red emeralds that she kept hidden inside her tunic.

My, this is good! This is incredibly well written. I may need to raise the age group of my audience, however. This is turning into fine erotica . . . Poor Salmonella. How can one hate and want a man at the same time so badly? She's falling in love with Claudius Julius, I can tell. They were supposed to be enemies, but . . . those muscled-up Roman soldiers. Wearing miniskirts in the British Isles. In the middle of winter!

"I know what you're doing."

I turn around. Nina has come up to the mezzanine and is standing next to me with a sheaf of papers.

I cover the screen with my hands. "I beg your pardon?"

"You've been stealing company resources."

"Pardon me?" I manage to turn off the monitor.

"I am going to show this to Mike," she holds up the sheaf of papers.

Oh, shit. What is she holding? What does she know? I must have left something in the printer. Something incriminating . . . Miguel Hildago's receipts! Is that what she's holding? Miguel is my little Mexican hero. An expensive handyman, but worth every penny. He fixes problems before they're even reported. He fixes problems that never existed at all! Our homeowners love him. I love him too. He's cheap, sends his invoices via email, and gets paid whenever I have the time. If he existed, I'd marry him. He doesn't. Therefore, it is me who has to cash all his checks . . .

Nina must have found the receipts. I must have left them in the printer's queue, and they must have come up when she turned it on. I need a glass of water . . . I need air! She knows I've been stealing!

"I don't know what you mean," I manage to calm myself and laugh defiantly.

I've always been a wonderful actor.

"You know what I mean, you fatso."

It cannot be that much. Can it? Those receipts weren't even a hundred dollars. But if Mike learns they're fake, he may then want to check all of the others . . . Why do I worry? Mike doesn't even know how to turn on a computer. Then again, he may ask the accountant to check . . . How much has it been this month? Six hundred? More like sixteen hundred. About eight thousand for the year so far. I got a little greedy . . .

"Gimme that!" I leap out of my chair, trying to snatch the sheaf of papers.

"*Nein!*" Nina laughs, pulling back.

"Gimme that, you stupid twat! Gimme those fucking papers!"

"*Nein!*"

Oh, she's laughing now. She's enjoying it. How can she be so beautiful and so heartless? I'll go straight to jail if I get audited!

"Nina, give me those papers."

"No."

She's at the edge of the stairs. I could just push her. It wouldn't be the worst thing I did to her in the last four months . . .

"Nina, I know we have had our differences, but let's be civilized. Give me those papers. They're important."

"No."

I throw my pencil cup at her. She acts surprised. What did she expect? I won't let her ruin me!

"Give me those fucking papers!" I roar in anger.

Nina runs downstairs. I sprint behind her. She trips in the last two steps and falls. I reach for the papers. She resists, but I'm at least a hundred pounds heavier than her and finally snatch them . . . They're not receipts. They're the first pages of *Catacombs of the Shining Fear.* I forgot I had tried to print them earlier. I feel so silly.

"*Princess Salmonella?*" Nina asks from the floor. "Really?"

Did she read the first pages of my novel? I'm flattered . . . *A reader! At last!*

"Don't you know that Salmonella is a disease?" She continues.

"It's a name, too," I reply.

Nina tries to stand up. She can't. Crap. I pushed the intern down the stairs . . . No, I didn't push her. She fell . . . While I was chasing her. But she's not an intern anymore. Can she sue us?

"Are you okay?" I ask.

"I hurt my wrist, you asshole."

"I'm terribly sorry this happened."

"You're a paranoid idiot."

"You threatened to show it to Mike."

"So that he learns that you're wasting company paper."

"You came to print personal stuff, too," I remind her about her train ticket. "And besides, you shouldn't have read what was obviously not meant for you. It is a first draft. I'm sure it must have a few typos."

"A few typos?" She laughs. "This is *Scheiße*."

"What would you know about first-class literature?" I laugh.

"More than you do. Justin lent me one of your books—"

Justin lent her one of my books? Now I'm confused. Justin knows that I write? Justin, as in my worst enemy? Justin, the guy who refers to me as a "she," the guy who photoshopped my face in a bukkake and posted it in the laundry room so that the cleaners could see it?

"—and it's embarrassing." Nina continues. "Your book was so bad, I almost felt sorry for you."

"Justin bought one of my books?"

Three of my self-published novels are for sale on Amazon. *Princess of a Lesser Kind* has sold four copies.

"He bought all of them!" Nina replies.

All of them? Including *The Sky Beyond Tomorrow?* My heart starts beating fast. I'm baffled. *Justin?* As in Justin *Fuck-that-shit* Kettler? I thought that he hated me. He's so arrogant and unpleasant . . . Could he be secretly in love with me? Oh, had I only known . . . Justin looks as if the Marlboro Man had used moisturizer. Tall. White. Twenty-nine. He looks twenty-seven. Maybe now that he knows my soul, he regrets the way he has been treating me . . . I must confess that Justin's brown curls and his intriguing blue eyes inspired Julius Claudius. He inspired me to create Al'Kzum too, the rogue and sexy criminal from planet Argentaria in *The Sky Beyond Tomorrow*, Book 1 in the *Beyond Tomorrow* series . . . Justin inspired all of the sexy and terribly mean villains in my books . . . and I am princess Salmonella!

"He never told me he loved my books." I finally say, with a gasp. "I could have signed his copies."

Nina starts laughing again. "He bought them as a joke!"

"*What?* Liar! He could have not disliked them."

"*Mein Gott*, Jignesh. You are as fat as you are arrogant and stupid.

What you write is shit. *Scheiße*. Nobody in his right mind would like your writing. It's fucking crap. You're nothing but a pretentious elephant dreaming of becoming a princess. You're a loser, Jignesh, that's what you are. A fucking loser."

Okay. I may have been making Nina's life miserable for the last four months, continually breaking the coffee pot and forcing her to go buy coffees for everyone, never reimbursing her on time, messing up the files she had been working on. I may have led my beautiful Clara and that shoddy corn girl, Gabrielle, to believe that Nina had caught an STD that one time she called in sick. "Nothing too serious," I said, "but she's on antibiotics." And probably it wasn't too nice either when I asked Nina to trim a ream of legal paper that I had bought "by mistake," into letter size, and she had to use scissors because I hid the paper cutter. Still, she doesn't need to be this cruel. I know I'm fat. I've been fat all of my life. I am reminded I am fat every day by the continuous look of disapproval from random strangers; by the kind words of advice from baristas that recommend me buying a fruit cup instead of a scone; by the men I dare to contact online, who aren't kind at all, and by my parents and siblings, who think that they're doing me a favor when they say that no woman will ever want to marry a man my size. As if. And I know I'm not popular. I've got more than my fair share of shame to remind me.

I know, however, that I'm a terrific writer. Nina cannot take that from me.

"You are jealous," I say, turning away to hide my tears. "You are jealous because I write, and you don't. You are jealous because I have talent and imagination. You are jealous because you're a skinny German witch with no tits and bad taste, and I am a true artist. Justin must have liked my books. I am sure he adored them."

For a second, silence. Then Nina starts laughing again. Not a forced, bitter laugh, not the one you would expect from a villain lying on the floor, defeated, but actual crystalline, girlie laughter, the innocent laughter of someone who's still a child—and a goddess. Even I find this despicable German witch charming. Her eyes are so blue, the skin is so even. Nina could be a model for a Pre-Raphaelite painting. And I am a fraud. I am not an artist. I am not a princess.

Nina is.

Nina is Queen Salmonella.

She's also every person that has ever mocked me, I realize, feeling the lower part of my body suddenly get cold while my face and chest are burning. She's every girl that ever made me feel unwanted. Every bully that ever smacked the back of my head, every white person who made fun of my name, my size, my nationality, and my skin color . . .

"And you're also a faggot," Nina insists. "A morbidly obese and pretentious fucking faggot. You should do the world a favor and kill yourself. Everyone hates you."

I sit on her face.

She beats me. I press harder. She kicks with her knees. She pinches my butt. She tries to bite me. I push harder. I stay on top of her, with my two-hundred and forty-five pounds of queer Indian fat, until Nina stops breathing.

2

Freezer

Well, Charlie, it is Sunday. Maybe it is time you accept it. Jignesh won't be replying to any of your texts.

Not that I wanted to see him again. As I told my friend Lucille—Lucille is my best friend and *confidente*. Ever since that year that we spent together in France in our early twenties, learning the language of Marguerite Duras and surviving on cheese and tetra-pack wine from the Super U on the *Rue des Hautes Marchés, nous avons été inséparables*—As I told Lucille, I didn't find Jignesh that attractive. Actually, I referred to him, and I read now, from my phone, as a *pompous sea monster from the depths of the Indian Ocean.*

Typical of her, Lucille texted back with a *you ruined it again, Charlie!*

I called her immediately and explained to her that no, that I didn't ruin it, that *Jignesh was a fucking whale*—I'm reading again—*at least fifteen years older than he had said he was and not at all like his picture hinted.* She asked me whether I had remembered to put a five-minute timer on my phone so that I would give others a chance to talk too, as she had recommended. I replied that I did set the alarm. Lucille didn't believe me. I finally confessed that I had forgotten. That led to one of Lucille's obnoxious harangues about my prolixity, a harangue that I had to swallow in its entirety and take notes on, for how could I argue with a woman who managed to trap a gorgeous biracial man like Marco, her husband, a man who works for SpaceX and drives a Lexus? But anyway, I digress . . . Lucille has a master's degree and, therefore, she can be a very difficult person. I don't even know why we are still friends. She's such a bitch. Anyway, the thing is that I find it extremely impolite that Jignesh hasn't texted back yet. And I know he's alive because I've been following his every move on social media.

Maybe I should text him again, just to be courteous. I've only texted him twice since our date . . . Well, no. More like forty-seven times, I see. It doesn't matter, my parents didn't raise an apple knocker.

Let's meet again soon, I type. As in never, of course, I'm not a masochist.

I thought he had money. Not that money is important to me, I am by no means a gold-digger. However, I am twenty-two thousand dollars in credit card debt, still five years away from paying off my student loans, twenty-five years away from paying off my underwater mortgage, and in a dead-end job making ten dollars an hour plus commissions at a call center. I thought that an Indian American working in finance would be a step up from my long list of romantic involvements with the down-on-their-luck men I meet at the gas station . . . I'm only kidding, I stopped doing that since I moved to the City of Angels, where you can pick up college graduates at museums. Anyway, I'm utterly broke, and I need to come up with $950 by the end of the month to pay my mortgage.

I serve myself a glass of Cinzano. I haven't had breakfast yet, but I need it . . . If only I liked pale skin. My chances to marry well would be better. My mother would be so happy. She's always been a tad racist. "My little Nancy-boy," she would say, clapping her hands and making her arms jiggle. "Dating a white southern Baptist with money . . . And he votes Republican!"

Not that I would like to see that vain hippopotamus from the Ganges ever again, I take a sip from my glass. Still, Jignesh could at least have sent me a text, something along the line of "I had a fantastic time. Thank you." We both would have known it didn't mean we had to repeat it. It is an unwritten code of gay chivalry. You write back to say thanks for a lovely evening, whether you had intercourse or not, but especially if you didn't, then block your failed hookup from your phone. Forever. Or you remain friends. I stay friends with all of my previous dates . . . Well, no, I chuckle, taking another sip. Sooner or later, they all threaten a restraining order if I don't stop texting.

The only person who texted me today was Kurt, my ex-roommate. He sent a picture.

Sup, Charlie?

That jackass. His girlfriend looks lovely, though. She reminds me of Melanie from *Jacki Brown*. I hope she doesn't get shot in the parking lot of a Macy's.

Kurt left me with three months of unpaid cable bills.

"But Charlie," he cried. "I need Showtime!"

"Kurt," I remember I said in my calmer voice, the one I reserve for rational conversations with highly emotional people, "we can order *Nurse Jackie* DVDs through Netflix."

"But the mail takes too long! And they never have the latest season!"

Well, probably the one who cried for *Nurse Jackie* DVDs was me. Kurt is quite manly. He would never cry. He probably burped his response to my hysterical claims that we couldn't afford to continue paying for cable, then blew out some air forcing me to smell what he had eaten for breakfast.

I shouldn't have given him back his deposit. I shouldn't have fallen in love with his perfectly round, straight ass either. The tattoos on his big, bulging arms and the waxed mustache were a clear sign that he wasn't honest. During that first interview, four months ago, when I asked him what he did for a living, and Kurt said that he worked the register at the Wienerschnitzel in Ladera Heights, I shouldn't have replied: "You do? How intriguing!"

No, I shouldn't have opened the doors of my fabulous two-bedroom, 950-square-foot craftsman in West Adams to that half-black, half-Japanese, one hundred percent stud jughead.

"I don't have AC," I remember I said. "Will that be a problem?"

I had to be honest about that. You cannot begin what promises to be a long and steady relationship with a man you're dying to fuck backward with lies, can you?

"When it gets too hot, I just strip to my underwear and open the windows," Kurt replied.

My, the vision of this racially ambiguous young man in his tightywhities opening the fridge on a hot summer day, then turning around to say, "we're out of beer, Charlie," as he scratched his left butt cheek, crossed my mind like the vision of a flying saucer saving humanity must have crossed Ron Hubbard's. The vision of Kurt lying on the couch watching TV, his boxers rolled up on his legs well beyond decency, his hairy chest, the musky scent of his manly armpits filling up the room . . . The vision of Kurt swiping left and right photos of chicks on Tinder while reaching inside his basketball shorts to stretch his penis . . . I didn't interview anyone else. I immediately deleted the ad from Craigslist, forgot about Kurt's credit check application, and begged the Good Lord that he would have enough money to pay a deposit or at least let me give him a blowjob.

It took Kurt two months to pay his half-month deposit, and I never had the opportunity to see him walking around in his underwear, barely a couple of times shirtless.

He never washed a dish. He never cleaned the bathroom. He ate my food, drank my booze, and used all of my beauty products. He's twenty-six and straight, for God's sake. Why in the world would he want to use my *La Mer rejuvenating crème?*

Many a night I spent pressing a pillow against my ears while he had sex with those stiletto-wearing sluts he picked up at the clubs in Hollywood.

The one time I brought home a trick, he dared to judge me.

"You guys are gross."

Still, when he gave notice, my heart bled a little.

"Where are you moving to?" I asked, brushing a tear before he could see it.

"Hermosa. This girl I met has a pad right on the beach. She wants the meat, bro," Kurt added, grabbing his crotch.

My eyes must have widened like Gary Oldman's did when he saw the blood on Keanu Reeves' razor blade in Dracula, for he started laughing. "What's a man going to do?"

I wanted the meat too. I wanted the whole pig, not just the sausage.

In addition to $350 in unpaid cable bills, Kurt left me a kit to grow marijuana using UV lamps, a box full of pamphlets, and a freezer that weighs a ton and occupies half my garage, which I bought online on a whim because Kurt suggested once that if he and I were going to work out together, I would need to start eating better, and who has the time to cook? He proposed cooking our meals in advance and freezing them. I agreed, thinking that one thing would lead to having showers together.

"Kurt, bro, what d'you think we should have tonight?" I imagined myself saying, drenched in sweat, wearing a band on my head, and my new hyper-expensive shorts from Lululemon. "Boeuf bourguignon or chicken piccata?"

We worked out together just once. Now Kurt is gone, the freezer is empty, and not a single person has replied to the ad I put on Craigslist and that I shared with all of my Facebook friends. I'm only asking $650 for it, but I'm afraid I'll need to lower the price a bit if I want to make enough money to pay my mortgage . . .

An hour later, the freezer is sold for $150. It hurts a little. They'll pick it up this afternoon. Now I'm only eight hundred dollars short of my mortgage.

I need to clear my mind. Otherwise, I'll start crying.

I refill my Cinzano. Then, I fetch a bottle of body lotion, open my laptop, and visit Pornhub.com. I type "twelve men orgy in an eccentric European mansion" in the search field. You may not agree with me, but pornography always reduces my tension. Then, before I can choose a video that'll suit my current mood—intense blue, in case you wonder, blue as the eyes of Chris Evans in the first *Fantastic Four* movie—the phone rings. The caller ID shows Jignesh's name.

"Jignesh," I answer the phone. "What a surprise? How can I help you?"

"I'm calling about the freezer that you're selling on Facebook." Jignesh bursts out. "Do you still have it?"

"The freezer?"

I haven't heard from Jignesh in almost a week, and now he calls asking about the freezer? I scroll down to check some more videos.

"I'm afraid I sold it," I reply coldly.

"You sold it?" He cries.

My, he sounds desperate.

"I had to, Jignesh. I'm sorry, but no one wrote, so I was forced to lower the price a little. They haven't picked it up yet, though . . ."

Jarek Fucks Christian . . . This might be worth checking out.

"I'll take it!" Jignesh replies. "I'll pay the full price."

"But I said to this man he could have it." *Oh, my.* Jarek is a rather big fella.

"I'll pay nine hundred."

"Nine hundred? Cash?"

"Check."

"I cannot take a check, Jignesh, I'm sorry—"

"I'll bring cash, Charlie, please don't sell it!"

I apply some body lotion to my hands. The Vaseline brand smells like plastic, not too sensuous. "But this man is picking it up at four."

"I'll pay a thousand," Jignesh insists. "I just need one hour to get the money."

"Well, in that case . . . I guess I'll call the other guy and tell him I'm sorry."

"It's a big freezer, right?"

"Oh, it's quite large. Large enough to hold a human body," I joke.

Sudden silence.

"Jignesh?" I ask. "Are you still there?"

Jignesh replies with a groan. I give him the address, and then we hang up.

Oh, my, *a thousand dollars!* Less than what I originally paid, but still pretty good. I won't be needing Jarek's video anymore, I think, closing my laptop. Then I open it again. Silly me. What else am I going to do on a Sunday morning?

Forty minutes later, Jignesh calls again. He may need an extra hour. He's renting a truck and picking up some guys at Home Depot to load on the freezer.

"Take your time," I say, focused now on cat videos. "As long as you're here before four, it'll be fine."

3

Home Depot

Fuck, fuck, fuck, fucketty, fuck. I killed a woman. I killed a woman. I killed an innocent woman. But I have a plan. I have a plan. I do have a plan, don't I? I'm panting. I'm driving and panting. I cannot breathe. Jesus, Mary, and Joseph, what God am I supposed to pray to in these situations? Help me, Lord Krishna. Help me, and I promise to never swear again by the name of a Christian god . . . Calm down, Jignesh, you have a plan. You're going to freeze her. That's a nifty plan, that's your plan, and it will work out. You're going to buy Charlie's freezer, and you're going to freeze Nina. That will buy you some time. Then you will make another plan. You have a freezer, you have a truck, now you just need to make it to Home Depot—Oh, Christ! What the fuck am I going to do with her body?

"MOVE THE FUCK OFF!" I honk at the car in front of me. Jesus Christ, I need to calm down. I'm driving at fifty-five in a residential area. Slow down, Jignesh, slow down, and relax. I should have popped something. Mike keeps an entire pharmacy in his desk drawer. "MOVE THE FUCK OFF!" I yell again.

What time is it? It's only 1:25 p.m. I have time. Plenty of time. Goddammit, I should have stayed on Lincoln. WHY DIDN'T I FUCKING STAY ON LINCOLN? I'm crying now, and my skin is so dry that the tears burn. I should have mapped it. Now I have to go all the way to Centinela.

At long last, I see the Home Depot. I'm not even going to park. I'll drive around and just pick up two strong-looking Mexicans . . . Where the fuck are they? I cannot see any. Where the fuck are all the Mexicans when you need them? It isn't that late. This place is typically full of them. Where the fuck are they?

"*Signore!*" I roll down the window when I finally find one. "*Tú a mi trabaja? Dinero?*"

"I speak English," the man answers, approaching the car.

Oh, thank God. I wouldn't say he does, with that accent, but it will make things much easier.

"I need you for one hour. *Una hora.* How much?"

"I charge a hundred for the entire day."

"No, no, no," I wag my finger. "It's easy. *Una hora.* I'll pay you twenty." I pull a bill from my wallet and show it. "*¿Veinte? Mucho dinero.*" These fuckers make nine an hour at the most.

The man makes a dismissive gesture. "I charge a hundred for the day."

"*Una hora,*" I repeat. "Twenty."

He shakes his head.

"Twenty-five? Half the day is gone. No one will pay you a hundred."

"Sixty, then."

"Sixty?" I lose my patience. "Sixty? What the fuck are you, a Mexican Jew? Sixty dollars for one hour? What the fuck you think I'll ask you to do? Do you think I'm going to ask you to drop your pants and bend over? I can get my dick sucked for twenty . . . Okay, okay, okay," I change my tone when I see him walking away. "I'll pay you sixty. Sixty, you see," I show him the bills. "*Tengo dinero.* Now, step in."

He shakes his head. "No, *pinche negro loco. Me subo y capaz que me mates.*"

"*Negro no,*" I say, pointing to myself. I didn't understand what he said, but I understood the words *negro* and *loco.* "Indian, from India. I'll pay you a hundred, you fucking greedy bitch. Get into the truck now."

He puts his tools in the back and gets in. I try to smile politely. He snorts. There's no one else here. We'll have to manage between the two of us.

"What is your name?" I ask.

"Manuel," he answers.

"Manuel," I repeat, "fasten your seatbelt because we're in a hurry."

4

Indian Food

I am so excited about the thousand-dollar deal that I made with Jignesh that instead of a shower, I take a bath, with the salts that Lucille gave me last Christmas and that I had reserved for a special occasion, such as this one. I know, I shouldn't be filling up the tub when there's a drought, but I shouldn't be doing a lot of other things either . . . Could all this be a sign? I look at my fairly extensive collection of shampoos and body gels. Each product promised a state of happiness that never truly arrived. But now, I think, gently scrubbing my shoulders with my bare hands, dwelling on my success, like Marlene Dietrich did in *Knight without an Armor*, I have sold the freezer. To Jignesh. Of all people! I'll have enough money to pay the mortgage this month and tomorrow—tomorrow will be another day!

Jignesh wasn't that horribly fat, I think, now in front of the mirror. I am the one who's probably too short and tried to blame on his size my insecurities. He actually came across as awfully smart and attentive. He complimented my . . . I'll be damned. I don't recollect whether he complimented me at all. Still, he must have given me some praise for I remember him as big, yes, but also as awfully kind, and sensitive, and extremely well mannered. Unless that's what I read in his profile description. I can't remember.

A little after two, I'm sitting next to the door, all gussied up and smelling pretty, drinking a cup of Earl Grey with lemon, as it should be, when the doorbell rings.

I turn a page of my GQ. I'll take my time, just as Jignesh did . . . *Tattersall checkered shirts and a striped blazer?* One must be rather bold. The editors of this magazine must be all Yankees . . .

The doorbell rings again.

"Coming," I sing, pretending to be further away from the door than I truly am.

I take a quick look around. I cleaned the house as best as I possibly could, which means I tossed all the junk into the second bedroom.

Jignesh rings the doorbell again. This time, he keeps his finger on the button. *Well, that's just rude!*

I stand up and open the door.

"Well, hello," I say, mellifluously. I can make a perfect interpretation of Alexis Carrington anytime, thank you. "Come on in. Are you helping Jignesh?" I ask his Latin companion. He nods, and I discreetly ogle his lower backside. "Can I fix you all something? Coffee? Water? Tea? A glass of champagne? Just kidding, if I could afford champagne, I wouldn't be selling a freezer."

Neither laughs at my joke. My, Jignesh is drenched in sweat. And he's so poorly dressed, in sweatpants from American Eagle, I can tell, and a nineteen-dollar H&M orange hoodie from the 2010 collection, if I'm not mistaken. That's a terrible sign. He seems mortified to see me too. Do I look that bad? I turn fast to the mirror above the fireplace . . . Nope—not a hair out of place, and no boogers. My fly is up. I'm wearing my comfy house shoes, but that's to be expected, I'm at home. Alone. I do look lovely. The silk scarf I put on is a nice touch . . . Is it my place? Well, what did he expect, Graystone Mansion?

"We can't stay long," Jignesh says.

"I bet you can't," I reply, feigning composure. "But isn't this a marvelous coincidence?" I pick up my tea. "We go on a date, I have a freezer for sale, then we coincide again. Must be destiny."

Jignesh stares at me as if he was about to cry. His friend looks at me as if I were the strangest person on the planet. My voice did go up in my last sentence, but I cannot be the first gay person he ever met, can I?

"I'm just kidding," I say, breaking the silence.

Neither laughs.

I take another sip of my tea.

"I prepared some hors d'œuvres," I say, turning toward the kitchen. "D'you all think you could—"

"We don't have the time," Jignesh stops me.

Oh, boy, his face is twitching now. This whole thing is weird. I shouldn't have killed myself doing baloney sandwiches.

I take them to the garage.

"Can you lock it?" Jignesh asks, gaping at the freezer.

"No," I reply, giving my negative the intonation of a question. "Why would you want to lock a freezer?"

"I need to lock it."

My, he looks pale too. Is he sick? I'm about to offer him a cup of chicken soup but then his Mexican friend, whatever his name is, intervenes:

"I can put a lock on the lid," he says, approaching the freezer and pretending to drill the top with his finger. "I brought my tools."

He's not a bad looking fellow, I leer after him. The thick mustache ages him, but he cannot be a day older than twenty-four. He could use nicer garments, though. Baggy pants are so 1995 . . .

"And where the fuck are we going to find a lock?" Jignesh cries, wiping the sweat off his face with the back of his hand.

Jesus Christ, Jignesh is about to lose it. He has a fat vein pulsating on his forehead, the type one only sees on men in Italian porn movies. I have to admit, though, that I find this version of Jignesh wearing sweatpants and giving everyone orders much less unattractive than the pompous butterball wearing green pistachio slacks from J. Crew and reeking of cheap cologne I met last Monday.

"At Home Depot," his friend responds.

"We haven't been introduced," I interrupt, extending my hand. "My name is Charlie Hayworth—"

"Home Depot?" Jignesh cries before the young man could give me his name.

The young man nods.

His name is probably Juan. Go figure.

Jignesh pays me, and we load the freezer onto the truck, Jignesh's friend and I holding one end, and Jignesh the other.

"I would have never guessed that below all those layers of fat there was some muscle," I whisper to Juan.

"You need to be strong to carry that much weight," he sniggers.

He has a lovely accent, this young man. Intriguing eyes and a beautiful skin color. I wonder if there's a Mrs. Juan or if he possibly—

"We'll also need help unloading it," Jignesh says, interrupting my thoughts.

"I can call a cousin," Juan offers.

"I could help," I offer.

What can I say? My southern upbringing.

Jignesh turns down my suggestion since taking me to his house means that he would have to drive me back to this part of town, so Juan calls his cousin. He isn't available, though.

I insist.

"You could pinch a disk. One time, my cousin's husband, Doug is his name, helped some coworkers of his lift a trailer. He hurt his back and ever since, he's been on disability, which has been atrocious for my poor cousin because she's only a cashier at a Cracker Barrel in Louisville and with three children—"

"Hop on," Jignesh interrupts me. "We need to go."

I continue my story on the way to Home Depot: "Doug got hooked on opiates, and then it got worse because Becca—I call her Mrs. Danvers after the Alfred Hitchcock movie, did you see it? Judith Anderson is just terrifying. Anyway, Becca found out that Doug had been cheating on her with a . . ."

I'm forced to stop for a second time while Jignesh and Juan rush into the Home Depot. Ten minutes later, they come out and Juan, or whatever his name is, installs the lock. I attempt to resume my story, but I'm kindly asked by Jignesh to shut the fuck up. Fine. He'll never learn how Becca's story ended.

We take the freeway to Jignesh's home in the Valley.

Apparently, Jignesh still lives with his parents.

He seems frightened. Or angry. Perhaps both. Juan, too, looks a little nervous. I start feeling a tad upset myself, sitting between the two of them, not knowing what to do. This is how Maribel Verdú must have felt in *Y Tu Mamá También*, I suppose, every time the two boys started fighting. The situation is so ridiculous, after a while I start laughing nervously. Jignesh glares at me as if I had just tried to stab him.

"What are you laughing about?" he asks.

"Nothing," I reply, with a coquettish smile.

"Then fucking stop it," he mumbles.

Well, that's just rude. One must admit, however, that Jignesh looks manly when he's angry. I have a brief vision of Jignesh making love to me, my legs in the air, his hand pressed against my face, the top of my head bouncing against the headboard, and Juan whacking off on a chair, looking at us . . . I know. I watch too much HBO . . . Besides, Jignesh isn't precisely the man to fantasize about. Unless you're into abusive men. Which, unfortunately, I think I am.

I know. It isn't healthy. My seventy-five-dollar-an-hour therapist with a twelve-dollar haircut from Fantastic Sams said it wasn't. Thank God I couldn't afford more than a couple of sessions. He would have been so worried if I told him that I've been Facebook-stalking this mean bully from third grade, Tommy.

One time, Tommy caught me looking at him, and I smiled. I couldn't help it. I wanted Tommy to invite me to his fabulous plantation-style house for a sleepover. You can't reply with anger when someone smiles at you, can you? Well, Tommy did. He and his friends chased me through the schoolyard, and when they caught me, they threw me headfirst into a garbage bin.

"Why did you do it?" the principal, Ms. Sebold, asked him.

"Because he's so faggy!"

"I know he's faggy, but that's no excuse."

Oh, Ms. Sebold. I know I was faggy. I still am, and I will always be, I'm afraid. I used to butch up my walk, pretending I held big pomelos under my arms, as I walked down the streets of Leitchfield, Kentucky, when I was a teenager, but ever since I moved to California I just flutter around, fabulously faggy indeed, throwing kisses and benedictions in every direction. Now I can laugh at your improper use of offensive words, Ms. Sebold, but back then, being called a fag by a teacher hurt as much as being thrown headfirst into the garbage bin had before. Maybe more. You don't tell a nine-year-old boy that he's faggy. You tell him that he enunciates well and keep quiet about the peculiarities of his demeanor.

Tommy got suspended for three days, and the school counselor had a talk with my parents. He suggested conversion therapy. My father proposed that I join the boy scouts. He thought that that might be enough to repress my effeminate mannerisms. I thought that that would be a fantastic idea and did a series of pirouettes to celebrate it. I loved the shorts, the cap, and the badges. And when I learned that the boy scouts uniform included a sewing kit, I almost fainted.

"We're going to do embroidery?" I asked. "Like the sisters in *Little Women*?"

My mother started crying. In one of her rare compassionate moments, she pulled me to her bosom, and, between sobs, she called me her sweetheart. She's the one that turned me gay, I suppose.

I felt incredibly disappointed when I found out that the regular sewing kit, the one that most cub-scouts carried, had only threads in four colors. Black. Gray. Military green, and white. Imagine trying to embroider a Strawberry Shortcake or a My Little Pony with only those four colors. You need blue. You need pink. You need purple! The sewing kit was but an emergency kit, meant not for doing embroidery but for mending rips and sewing buttons.

The meetings weren't that fabulous either. *Au contraire*, I got beaten, bashed, and insulted every time by those little barbarians. I got knocked unconscious, playing tag. Playing tag! Can you believe it?

Now, the pack leader, Akela, was this twenty-something, Black-Irish guy with a permanent stubble whom I found rather intriguing. I couldn't keep my eyes off the tuft of hair poking out above his collar. It was as if Tommy had killed me and I had been sent straight to faggy heaven. Akela liked me too. Or at least he felt sorry for me, I couldn't tell.

"Are you okay, buddy?" He used to say, extending a hand to help me stand up after one of the boys had tripped me.

"I'm all right," I'd reply, cleaning the blood from my nose, pulling down my shirt and offering him a smile that now I realize must have made me look as crazy as Vivian Leigh playing Blanche Dubois in *A Streetcar Named Desire*.

A year or so ago, Tommy came up on my Facebook feed as a suggested friend. He no longer goes by Tommy, of course, but by Thomas. He graduated from Brown University. He's married and has two girls. His forehead became more prominent, and he has a bit of a dad bod, but that only makes him more attractive. I was so in love with him, despite everything. Tommy was everything I would never be: wealthy, handsome, athletic, and manly. He's shirtless on his profile picture. He's on a boat, carrying a big mahi-mahi he has just caught. Seeing him laugh in that picture reminded me of that other time he caught me, dropped me to the floor, and while his friends held my legs and arms, he sat on my chest and forced me to open my mouth with his fingers. *Is he fixing to kiss me?* I remember I thought. I closed my eyes, only half horrified. When I opened them again, I saw a thick, yellowish phlegm coming down . . .

Life's so weird. I look now at Jignesh, glaring at the car in front of us as if he was about to ram into it. One can exchange all sorts of bodily fluids—the number of times I've eaten ass!—but that one time Tommy forced me to eat his phlegm, I cried in my bed for an entire weekend.

I'm sure that when Tommy remembers it, he feels guilty. He and his friends must giggle with embarrassment when they meet for a beer, and loser Charlie comes up in their conversation. "We were so mean to that poor bastard," they probably say, then finish their drinks and hop in their Lexi or their Bimmers or whatever expensive vehicle they drive now, and go home to their wives, watch TV on their sixty-inch flat screens and hope their kids don't grow up to be as awful as they were. I know they feel guilty because one of Tommy's friends apologized once, via Twitter, so my forty-two followers could learn what a loser I used to be in elementary school, and his three hundred and fifty thousand followers could see what a big man he had become. He received a lot of praise. I know because they included me in every reply. I tweeted something along the line of *thank you. It means a lot to me, #itgetsbetter* . . . *Way to go, Joe!* one of his followers replied. *So proud of you, Joe!* another did. *You're a big man, Joe, with a big heart, and deserve the best,* tweeted another.

Jignesh is definitely not as handsome as Tommy. Still, he looks just as mad as Tommy did that one time he chased me through the school-yard, and therefore, just as manly . . . Maybe I misjudged him. From this angle, Jignesh doesn't seem so vain anymore. If he lost some weight, say, two million pounds, he wouldn't be too shoddy. He's not entirely bad looking, either. Interesting nose, arresting skin color . . . Compared to the pretentious jerk I met for lunch last week, this mercurial Jignesh wearing sweatpants and an orange hoodie from H&M, I'm pretty sure, looks a lot better . . . I really don't know how I'd react if he suddenly smacked me against the dashboard and forced me to do all the things that a lady shouldn't.

Sweet Southern Baby Jesus, why do I keep falling for aggressive men? Is it because my parents never spanked me? I surely deserved it—all that time that I spent jacking off to pictures of Roman gods in the encyclopedia.

Anyhow, enough fantasy. We're now in fabulous Canoga Park . . . My, the streets here are so ample! Look at all those beautiful strip malls . . . Oh, and isn't that a lovely Victorian . . . ? Turned into a dental office . . . With a Walmart-size parking lot . . . Next to a car repair shop . . .

We turn into an alley and park behind a two-story building that seems an addition to the original front house. Jignesh gets out of the car and opens the garage door. Juan and I jump to the back of the truck and push the freezer to the edge. Jignesh tells us not to put it down until he makes some space inside. The garage is full of furniture.

Not knowing what to do, Juan and I stay in the bed of the truck, waiting for orders.

"What are you two doing there?"

The question comes from a young woman glaring at us from a window above the garage. I call Jignesh for help. He steps out and says something in Indian to the young woman. Hindi, perchance? I cannot tell. My knowledge of foreign languages is limited to the western part of Western Europe.

"No!" The woman replies.

Jignesh then says something that sounds a tad offensive, mixing a few words of English. The girl yells back at him, then disappears.

Jignesh gets back into the garage.

"Please hold this," he bawls at Juan.

At least he's polite. I jump off the truck and help Juan put away the big floor lamp that Jignesh gives him.

"Who was that?" I ask nonchalantly.

"My fucking sister," Jignesh answers.

I should have guessed. There was a *je ne sais quoi* of sororal love in her distasteful demeanor.

"She's pretty," Manuel ventures.

Jignesh snorts. "Sita? She's a fucking cunt."

Is she? I exchange a look with Juan, who chuckles. Sita sounded upset, but not that horrible.

A minute later, Sita comes down. She's a plump, tomboyish girl in her early thirties, wearing jeans and a dark lavender Brillo t-shirt. She's sporting a beautiful mane of curly dark hair that makes me incredibly jealous.

"You're not bringing more junk into the garage, are you?" She asks Jignesh, pointing at the freezer.

"It isn't junk."

"*Pitaa* asked you to have it empty so that I could use it."

"And I'll empty it. I just need to find a place to store these things first."

"You've been saying that for a year!"

"Why are they now speaking in English?" I whisper to Juan. "Maybe they think they are being polite by including us in the conversation, but dirty linen shouldn't be aired in public."

"You're not leaving this in here!" Sita hits the freezer with her open palm.

Jignesh takes a second to breathe. Then he says something in Indian, pointing at me.

Sita glowers at me.

"It's just temporary . . ." I venture, guessing that Jignesh has told her he's doing me a favor.

"This is not your house, Sita," Jignesh continues. "This is our parents' house, and this is our parents' stuff. Most of this stuff is actually theirs."

"IT IS YOURS!" Sita explodes. "You brought home all this crap."

"This isn't mine," Jignesh responds, raising a toolbox. "And neither is this." He lifts a painting of a multiple-armed man riding a tiger.

"And what about this couch? And these chairs? And this table? You've brought all of this, Jignesh. This is all the crap you've stolen from the houses you manage. *Pitaa* said I could use the garage as my studio!"

"I haven't stolen anything," Jignesh responds, then wipes the sweat off his face with his shirt, offering a not too flattering sight of his brown belly. I'm sweating too, I realize. The Valley is always horrendously hot. "And you will get the garage, Sita, once I find a place for all of this." Jignesh pulls his phone out of his pocket. I realize that since we got on the road, Jignesh's been checking the time every few minutes.

Sita glares at me again, then stamps on the floor and leaves with a growl.

"She's a lovely gal, your sister," I joke, after Sita leaves, trying to uplift the spirits. "Very pretty."

Jignesh takes it the wrong way. He grabs a box of Monopoly from a plastic crate and starts hitting it against a shelf. Cards, money, houses, and hotels fly around. Then he tries to split the cardboard in two with his teeth.

"I HATE MY FUCKING SISTER!" He ends throwing the box against the wall.

Oh, boy. Juan and I exchange a worried look. I start hating Sita, too, in solidarity. She was mean. I make a mental note to never again refer to her as lovely. Or pretty. She was pretty, though, if you're into plump, strong, tomboyish women.

We continue working in silence. A few minutes later, Sita returns, followed by an elderly woman who, I assume, must be Jignesh's mother.

"Jignesh, could you let me know what it is that you're doing?" The woman asks in English.

"He's letting his friend put his junk in the garage." Sita cries.

Jignesh's mother gives a nod, acknowledging Juan and me, then continues in Indian. Jignesh responds in the same language, pointing at the truck, then at me, then at Sita.

"It will be months," Sita snaps. "I know you, Jignesh."

Juan respectfully slips out of the garage, back to the street. I remain inside, trapped between the wall and a sofa. Jignesh says something that I infer mustn't be too kind, because his mother raises a threatening hand in response. Jignesh refuses to back down. He raises his voice, and so does Sita. Ultimately, his mother slaps him.

Then, a sweet-looking old man wearing flip-flops comes dawdling from the side of the house. Jignesh's father, I figure. He sees Sita first and asks her something in Indian.

"Jignesh said he would empty the garage," she replies in English. "But now he's putting more stuff inside."

The mother intervenes. She points a finger at Jignesh, shakes her head several times, and then threatens to smack him again. Sita is now weeping. Jignesh's father reaches out to comfort her. Then he acknowledges our presence with a small bob and a courteous simper.

He asks me: "Why are you doing that, son?"

The question surprises me.

"It won't be for long," Jignesh bursts before I could reply.

"You're full of lies!" Sita cries. "You're always lying!"

The mother mumbles something at Jignesh that doesn't sound too motherly. Well, I guess it does, depending on who your mother is. The father caresses Sita's head while he shakes his at Jignesh, then kisses her forehead. Sita calls Jignesh something that probably means asshole, for the father reprimands her with a soft cuff, but then he chuckles. The mother questions Jignesh again. Jignesh says something of which the only words I understand are "freezer" and "Charlie." He keeps pointing at me and moving his head funny. I smile politely. He's using me as an excuse, I can see that, but I'm not exactly sure what the excuse is. I keep grinning. More Indian. More screaming and tears but no Bollywood dancing, which I know is ludicrous to expect, yet, I somehow expected.

The fight continues. Every time Jignesh opens his mouth, he says something in a cynical tone, with a flair that sounds grandiose and not at all gentle. Something similar to the opening lines of Phoebe Cates in *Lace*, when she asks Pagan Trelawney and the other two actresses—I forgot their names, wasn't Maxine Pascal one of them? I can't remember—'which one of you bitches is my mother,' but in Indian. Every now and then, Sita and her mother look at me with intense hate. Not wanting to hold their sight, my eyes wander inside the garage. I pretend to be entertained by a pillow. But then I notice a huge white paper bag from

Bottega Veneta that must have contained something extremely expensive . . . My heart stops. What could it have been? A coat? A giant purse? The scene suddenly becomes 50 percent less vulgar. *Are these people rich?* Why, everything else points to the opposite.

"I'm sorry, sir," Jignesh's father eventually says to me, interrupting my mental review of the early fall 2012 women's Bottega Veneta collection. *What on Earth came inside that huge bag?* "But you won't be able to keep your freezer inside our house."

"Oh," I reply. I'm not sure if I should pretend to be mortified. I look at Jignesh. He hasn't lost the defiant air on his face, but his eyes now look supplicant. "It is me who should apologize," I say, running my fingers across the top of the couch. "I didn't want to cause any inconvenience."

Sita smirks, triumphant.

We're about to hop back into the truck when the father says something else to Jignesh. Jignesh replies with a loud cry, to which his mother replies with another slap. Some more Bollywood barking, then Jignesh slams shut the driver's door.

"We're invited to stay for dinner. You too," he calls Juan.

All this time we've been outside, Jignesh's elder brother, his brother's wife, and their two boys have been waiting inside the house watching television. Juan and I are introduced to everyone. I learn that the family name is Amin, that they are from Gujarat, and that the language they speak isn't Indian but Gujarati. They all seem to be charming people. I learn too that Juan's name is actually Manuel and that he comes from a little town outside of Guadalajara.

There's also an Asian girl, Kim, who must be a good friend of Sita's, for when we're invited to sit down, they sit next to each other. Kim reminds me of those rich skinny girls you often see on Abbot Kinney, wearing broad-brimmed hats and sunglasses, frequently accompanied by a young gentleman wearing rags who at first you presume must be homeless, but then you hear him talking about his plans for Coachella . . . I squint my eyes. Could Sita be playing the role of that gentleman?

There is not enough space at the table. Thus, Jignesh and the two boys sit in the living room.

The conversation takes place in English.

"How do I know Jignesh?" I say, in response to one of Mr. Amin's questions. "From a common friend," I say. That seems to satisfy him. Sita and her friend exchange a look of mutual understanding.

Jignesh eats and ignores everybody.

"This is a lovely house," I venture.

The father thanks me.

It is lovely, yes, if you're fond of pink walls, white-tiled floors, and furniture from Ashley's. There are some tasteful *Big Lots* pieces hanging from the walls and a tacky portrait of an Indian deity by the staircase. No Modernica in sight. No BoConcept. Perhaps one of those old chairs is from Restoration Hardware? Probably not . . . My, the things I would do to make this place more livable . . . For a start, I would burn all the furniture.

"How long have you all been living here?" I ask.

"Over thirty years," the mother replies.

"That makes sense," I reply.

Mr. Amin starts talking about how he and his wife got to buy this house, a story that makes him awfully proud, I can tell. However, no one else seems remotely interested. I try not to laugh at his accent. It is funny.

"These lentils are just fabulous," I say during the first opportunity I have to compliment the cooking. "What is the spicy aftertaste? Cumin?"

They have a few other properties, Mr. Amin lets me know kindly, including a small eight-unit building in North Hollywood.

"This young man doesn't need to know all that, Madhu," his wife interrupts him.

But I do, ma'am, I think, turning at her. *Especially if I will be seeing your son again,* which after learning someone in this house shops at Bottega

Veneta and that he may inherit rental property one day, has become a much less distant possibility.

I mean, just look at Jignesh's brother's watch. Amrit, that's his name. He must be doing really well. His wife is wearing a blouse that I could swear I recognize from an ad for Moschino. Never judge a house by the color of its walls, the nonmatching silverware, or the carpeted staircase . . . Sita wants to convert the garage into her studio. Isn't that a clear sign? Nothing hollers hidden riches like fostering your youngest child's creativity, especially when she, based on the way she eats, with her elbows on the table and occasionally cleaning her fingers on the tablecloth, lacks any true artistic talent . . . Never mind the curtains, either. This family undoubtedly has money. Raising a child the size of Jignesh must have been terribly expensive. Maybe he has a trust fund. After all, Gujaratis are the Jews of India, I saw that on Reddit . . . How much would a two-bedroom apartment rent for in North Hollywood? I'd say at least $1,800. Times eight units—how much is that? I discreetly open the calculator app on my phone to make a monthly estimation.

"Are you married, Charlie?" Mr. Amin interrupts me.

"Married?" I laugh, with my eyes still on the calculator. "Of course not, how could I be? I'm a practicing hom—" I interrupt myself, noticing Sita's fearful stare. Well, I'll be damned. I thought they knew, having two queer children. Can't you all tell I'm one of those *mauvais anges* living in a valley of bittersweet shadows? Jignesh's brother and his wife appear strained too, and while I cannot really see Jignesh's face from where I am sitting, his hunched back lets me know he's hoping I say the appropriate thing. "Horticulturist," I finish my sentence. "My professional life leaves little time for anything else. You could say I'm still waiting for the right person—girl, that is. I like girls. I like them pretty and big breasted, as one should, and those cost a lot of shekels, don't they? She will come. One day. I suppose." I start making a taco with an Indian tortilla. "I'm too young to marry anyhow. I just turned thirty," I lie.

"Jignesh here is forty-two," Mr. Amin intervenes, "and he still hasn't introduced us to any girlfriend."

Forty-two, huh? His profile said thirty-one. I wonder what else he's hiding.

"My husband and I went to *Guahaladara* once," Mrs. Amin says to Manuel.

"*Guadalajara*," Manuel replies with a grin.

"*Gualalahara*," she tries again. "I can't pronounce it," she laughs.

"*Guadalajara*," Sita intervenes, pronouncing every letter the correct way, which gains a little ovation from her parents. "Kim and I visited the original in Spain."

"Was that a school trip?" I ask.

Sita nods in response.

"Sita speaks perfect Spanish," her mother announces.

"She speaks English, Gujarati, Spanish, and German," the father adds counting with his fingers. "She's very accomplished."

Unlike her eldest brother, huh? Now I understand why some people hate her.

"This baba ghanoush is delicious, by the way," I praise whatever the fuck is that I'm eating, trying to get back the reins of the conversation.

"Baba ghanoush is Persian," Sita's friend corrects me. "This is *kadhi*."

"Oh, what a terrible *faux pas!*" I apologize with a guffaw. "I am sorry. I grew up eating country ham and hushpuppies. I never tried fresh vegetables until I moved to LA. So, how many units are in your North Hollywood building?" I add nonchalantly. "Are they all one or two-bedrooms?"

5

Road

"I can keep the freezer in my garage until you find a place, Jignesh," Charlie offers, as the three of us walk back to the truck.

I don't care to respond. I climb in the car and turn on the engine.

"I swear it won't be any trouble," Charlie continues. "I never use my garage."

I cover my mouth to burp discreetly. I overate. One would think that committing a crime would kill your appetite, but I was starving.

"What do you need the freezer for, anyhow?" Charlie asks.

"It's for my boss," I mumble.

"Can't he find a place to store it?"

"He has a sister too?" Manuel asks. He's sitting between the two of us.

Charlie laughs. I force a laugh too—fucking turds.

Nina's body is still at the office. I put her body in the bathroom, tucked against the toilet bowl. I start driving.

"Seriously," Charlie continues, "you can keep it at my place. I wouldn't want you to get in any more trouble with your family, who, by the way, are all lovely. I have to remind myself to send them a thank you note for having us for dinner. More of a late lunch to me, I hardly ever eat dinner this early. But I digress, I'm sorry . . . You already paid for it. The freezer is yours. You can pick it up anytime, whenever you need it. I could have you then for dinner. Do you have an appetite for French cuisine? I recently bought a Le Creuset, a real steal at only $179 at Williams Sonoma, and I make a fabulous risotto from a recipe that I . . ."

I let Charlie talk. At least, he's distracting. It's better to think about throttling his neck to shut him up, than on what I did to Nina . . . Oy, what I did to Nina was wrong . . .

We're already on the 10 when my phone vibrates. I pull it out of my pants pocket. It's a message from Mike.

What is the alarm code?

Oh, fuck. He's at the office!

I call him.

"Uh," Charlie begins. "Maybe you shouldn't use your phone while you drive, especially on the highway."

"Jiggy-boy!" Mike answers the phone. "My little brown calculator. I'm outside the office."

"What are you doing there? It's Sunday."

"I'm on my way to meet some friends for dinner on Abbot Kinney. I need to use the bathroom, though, and I don't know my alarm code."

Of course, he doesn't. Mike has never had to use it before.

"Can't you pee at the restaurant?" I suggest.

Mike giggles. "I need to go number two, Jignesh. What's your code?"

"I cannot give you my code, Mike. It's personal."

"Jignesh, I'm your boss."

"I'm literally two blocks away," I lie.

"Okay. Hurry up. I'll wait here."

I hang up and try to speed up. But the car in front of me is too slow, and there are too many cars coming from my left to change lanes.

"Uh, Jignesh," Charlie taps on my shoulder. "Maybe you're driving too fast? You're a tad too close to that Mercedes."

"I said two blocks away, didn't you hear me?" I snap. "It's at least four miles to my exit."

"Must be an Asian woman," Manuel ventures, referring to the car in front of us.

"Oh, that's an utterly sexist and racist assumption," Charlie scolds him. "They probably are Persian Jews, anyhow, since it is an old Mercedes . . .

Although the license plate is from New York . . . Probably they're Bubbe and Zayde visiting their grandchildren from Manhattan . . . Well, no. Only partially right," he adds when I'm finally able to change lanes and pass the slow car. "It's an old couple, but from the looks of their hair, probably they come from some bastion of protestant whiteness, like Saratoga. My, I hadn't seen hair as tall as that since Janice Dickinson appeared on the cover of Simplicity Magazine dressed like a bible-belt cowgirl. That happened long before her first surgery, of course," he taps Manuel on his arm, "when they still played 'speak softly, love' on the radio . . ."

We reach the Fourth Street exit by the time Mike texts me again.

Where are you?

I'm here, I text back. *I cannot find parking.*

There's plenty of parking here, Mike replies. *Where are you?*

"Should you be texting and driving?" Charlie asks.

Go to the Roosterfish, I text to Mike.

The Roosterfish is a gay bar.

So? I ask back. *Have you never been inside a gay bar?*

Mike rings me again. "Jignesh, I'm not going to take a shit in a gay bar. Give me the code."

"Okay, the code is . . . Police! I cannot risk a ticket," I hang up and put the phone in the cupholder.

It rings again. I ignore it. Mike tries one more time.

"Maybe it's an emergency." Charlie ventures.

I glower at him. But then I realize that if Mike can't reach me, he will try someone else.

"I'm literally one block away," I call again, then immediately hang up.

Five minutes later, I park in front of the office. Mike is no longer outside. I step off the car. Charlie opens his door to step out too.

"Stay there," I order him.

I open the metal gate between the building and the street and climb the five steps to the main door. The door isn't locked . . . I'm too late! Mike is already inside the office.

6

Eighty Degrees

"Stay here?" I say to Juan—I mean Manuel, Spanish names are so complicated. "It's eighty degrees!" I open the door. "Then again," I close it,
"Jignesh sounded rather severe. Let's just roll down the windows."

I do so on my side of the truck. Manuel stretches to reach the window
crank on the driver's side, and I catch a fast glimpse of his underwear
elastic. I'm somewhat disappointed to find out that the brand isn't Papi.

"What do you think is Jignesh's problem?" I ask.

Manuel shrugs. I adjust the side mirror so that I can check for rests
of food on my teeth. He's probably straight, I think, stealing a fast glance
at Manuel. And far too young for yours truly, although I bet he must
have had a few wild experiences. Haven't all straight men had a few? I
wouldn't be too offended if he suddenly drops his pants and insists on
showing me his willy. What do you know? Men from the third world
all fuck each other, my cousin Sheila told me, because women are too
prudish, she said. They insist on waiting till matrimony. She and her
husband live an alternative lifestyle. He's from a small town in Florida,
which explains a lot. They know well what twenty dollars can buy in
Puerto Vallarta.

"My Spanish is not as satisfactory as my French is," I say to Juan, I
mean, Manuel, moving the mirror so now I can check my neck. My neck
looks just as long as Cate Blanchett's in *Benjamin Button*. I wonder if
Manuel noticed. "I can read some Spanish, and I know how to say the ba-

sics: *Muchas gracias. ¿Cuánto es?* But not much more. What is the name of your town again?"

"*Tateposco—Está loco,*" Manuel chortles, responding to my original question. "Crazy."

"Jignesh? Yes, he is." I laugh too. "How old do you think I am, Manuel? Be honest."

Manuel puffs. "*Sepa,*" he replies.

Sais pas? Oh, how witty of him to reply to my question in French . . .

The gate to Jignesh's office opens, and a blond man in his midforties comes out. He looks irritated.

"You're an asshole," he snarls at Jignesh, who's following him closely.

"How did you get in?" Jignesh asks.

"I called Murat," the man responds.

"Where are you going now?" Jignesh cries.

"To the Roosterfish!"

"But didn't you go to the bathroom?"

"It's fucking locked from the inside, Jignesh!" the man yells.

Oops. Potty drama. How *ordinaire.* The man leaves, and Jignesh rushes back into the building.

Manuel and I exchange a look. I decide to step out.

"You wait here," I say. "I'm going inside."

"I'm going to have a smoke," he replies, stepping out too.

"Okay," I say, thinking that in Jignesh's absence, I'm in charge. "Just don't go too far, we may need you."

7

Bathroom

I commend myself to all the deities in the Ramayana, then turn the knob of the bathroom's door . . . *It's locked!* I sigh in relief. This bathroom locks itself all the time, and because Mike's never here, he doesn't know where the key is.

I reach atop the door frame, grab the key, and unlock the door.

"Who was that man?" I hear Charlie's voice behind me.

I hastily enter the bathroom and shut the door behind me.

"What's going on?" Charlie asks.

"What's going on about what?" I reply, staring at Nina's body. How on Earth did I think that this whole ordeal would take less than one hour?

"About all this," Charlie continues. "You, driving like a maniac. Making us wait outside. That man came out calling you an asshole."

"That was my boss."

"He's the one you got the freezer for?"

"Y-yes," I reply.

I need to pee, but how could I, next to Nina's body?

"He looked awfully mad."

"He probably was."

"Are you in trouble?"

"Charlie—do you mind? I'm in the bathroom."

"Oh, I'm sorry . . . I didn't mean to upset you. I apologize. I just thought that if I—Anyway, I'll shut up. This is, by the way, a fabulous office. I love the industrial look and the open plan design. Is it a converted loft? How much does it rent for?"

Please, Lord Krishna, enlighten me. I cannot pretend that I found Nina's body in here. I cannot flush her down the bowl, either. And I cannot take her out with Charlie here . . .

"—Or do you guys own the building?"

There's only one solution. I step onto the tub's edge to open the window. I pull the screen out and stick my head out to the service corridor. There's no one there. The trash bins are at the right end. The recycling dumpster is full of discarded cardboard boxes from the seafood restaurant. If I push Nina's body out onto the service corridor, I could then rush lickety-split and toss her body into the dumpster. That would buy me some more time until I can come back tonight. The vertical blinds are closed, so Charlie won't be able to see me through the sliding glass door, and Nina's so small, she should easily fit through the window.

8

Inside the Office

I wonder which one is Jignesh's desk, I survey the room. I open a drawer in the one closest to me . . . A bag of dry nuts and a hair donut . . . This mustn't be it . . . I open another in the next one. A calculator, post-it notes, and a half-eaten protein bar . . . Maybe he works on the mezzanine upstairs . . . There's a small kitchen. Full of dirty dishes, how *ordinaire*. I serve myself a cup of water. This place is a dump. My office is way nicer . . . Oh, they have an espresso machine!

"I see you have a nice coffeemaker," I say aloud. "How do you like working here?"

Jignesh doesn't respond.

"I said: This is a charming place," I add, looking up at the spider webs on the wire track lighting.

Jignesh still says nothing.

I knock on the bathroom door. "Are you still alive?"

"What?" Jignesh barks back.

"Oops," I chuckle. It sounds as if he's having a bit of a struggle.

"I said that I like your office. How many people work here?"

"S—six," he replies. "Plus the cleaners."

My, he is having difficulties in there. I'm not sure I'm ready for this level of intimacy.

I sit down and play with a stapler. Finally, Jignesh opens the door and comes out. He's covered in sweat.

"I didn't hear you flush," I mutter with horror.

"My bad!" he apologizes. He goes back into the bathroom and flushes the toilet. He doesn't seem mad anymore. He's actually giddy. Satisfied, I suppose. He washes his hands with the door wide open.

"Do you need to come in?" He takes an air freshener and sprays half the can inside. "It's ready."

"I do. But I think I'll wait for a few minutes."

"I have to go out," he says and rushes out through the sliding door at the back end of the office. The blinds are closed. I cannot see where the sliding door leads.

I mean to follow him, but just then, Jignesh's boss steps back inside.

"Who are you?" he asks when he sees me.

"Oh, I'm sorry," I reply, standing up. "I apologize. My name is Charlie Hayworth. I'm a good friend of Jignesh's. Nice to meet you."

"Mike Ferguson," he extends his hand. "Did he open the bathroom?"

"Yes, he did. I'm sorry I startled you."

"I had to go to the Roosterfish."

"I've been there before. It's a neat place. Mighty friendly."

"There's no door to the toilet stall," Mike continues.

"Oh. And the ceiling is covered in—"

"The biggest collection of hard-ons I've ever seen," Mike starts laughing.

I laugh with him. He seems to be a swell guy, this Mike Ferguson. A bit too white for my taste, but his teeth are beautiful. "It might not be the biggest collection," I venture. "I wager there must be a larger ceiling covered in penises somewhere else."

"Thankfully, the bar was empty."

"It's always dead," I reply. "I used to go to the Roosterfish every Friday, back when I lived in Culver City. Now I live in West Adams—It's not a bad place to live," I add before Mike can form any judgment. "It's in transition. I haven't heard a shooting since May. But I digress . . . Back then, I would sit at the bar at the Roosterfish and nurse a gin and tonic all night, with an eye fixed at the door, waiting for Prince Charming to make his entrance. He never came, and the gin got weaker and weaker. Anyways, we have your freezer."

"What freezer?"

"The one you so desperately needed. My, today has been such an adventure," I add, playing with an imaginary curl hanging behind my ear. This Mike Ferguson isn't ugly.

"Why?" He asks. "What is Jignesh doing outside?"

9

Dumpster

I pick up Nina's body from the floor and charge as fast as I can down the corridor to the back of the restaurant, then throw her body into the recycling dumpster. I pull out some of the cardboard boxes to make sure that her corpse drops to the bottom. "I'll come back tonight," I mutter to myself. "This is just temporary."

But then I look up and see Manuel standing by the gate at the end of the corridor, holding a cigarette. The expression of dread on his face tells me that he just saw what I did with Nina.

I need to stop him. How? I cannot jump over the metal gate and strangle him. My chest hurts. My neck feels as stiff as if I had on an iron collar. Maybe I'm having a stroke. Lord Vishnu, inspire me. Give me the strength I need to overcome these difficult circumstances . . .

I insert my right hand into my hoodie's pocket, then raise it, pretending I have a gun, and slowly walk toward the end of the corridor. Manuel falls for it. However, instead of standing still with his hands up, as I expected, he drops his cigarette and runs as if he had just seen the Devil.

10

Accident

"What is Jignesh doing outside?" I repeat Mike's question. "I don't have the slightest idea. He can be quite the extravagant, you will agree. I was about to follow him out the moment you came in."

Mike walks toward the sliding doors but, as he opens the blinds, we hear a car screech, followed by a hard pound, and then Jignesh screaming in horror. Mike opens the door and sticks his head out, then he steps back, to let Jignesh in, who darts across the office and out the front door.

Mike and I follow him. The three of us turn around the corner and discover Manuel's body lying in the middle of the street. A white Fiat is just behind, with a terrified young Latinx girl at the wheel.

"Oh my God," I cry. "Is he dead?"

Jignesh braces his head with both hands. He looks ghastly.

"What happened?" Mike asks.

"He didn't see the car coming," Jignesh mumbles.

The girl steps out of the car. She's shaking. Poor thing, of course, she's upset, I would be too. Her brand-new Fiat has a broken headlight and a long streak of blood on the hood, which, of course, is the lesser reason to be disquiet about. Manuel's neck is in such a contorted position, he can no longer be alive.

"Is Manuel dead?" I ask again.

"He came out of nowhere," the girl cries. She's holding a cellphone encrusted with fake diamonds in her left hand. Well, that explains it. She apologizes to whomever she had been talking to and calls 911.

Mike squats down to check on the body.

"He's dead," he says, not daring to touch him.

"I've never seen a dead person before," I say to Jignesh, grabbing his arm. He flinches. "Well, I did see Nana," I continue, more to myself and out of apprehension, "and Aunt Martha, but they don't count because they were lying inside a coffin, dressed up in their best gowns and with lots of makeup on."

"It wasn't my fault," the girl insists.

"You must have been driving incredibly fast," Mike scolds her.

"I wasn't," the girl shakes her head, making her multiple bracelets jingle.

Oh, my, she's crying so hard, I'm fixing to start mewling too.

Mike cannot stay, so he leaves. The police arrive shortly after. Then an ambulance, and two firetrucks. Two dozen people are now surrounding the body.

Jignesh cannot say a word. I, on the other hand, am too shocked to remain quiet. I give testimony to everyone willing to hear me, and then to those who aren't.

"I certainly didn't know much about Juan—I mean, what's-his-face? Manuel. I'm terribly bad with names," I explain to the parents of the poor girl that killed him. The mother is crying too. "Nevertheless, the couple of hours or so that Manuel and I spent together were enough to create a special bond. We were on a mission to deliver a freezer."

The girl's elder brother asks me to shut up. Well, that's just rude. He's on the phone talking in Spanglish to the family lawyer.

I apologize and return to Jignesh's side.

The girl is sitting on the curb, talking to a police officer. She ruined all her makeup by rubbing her face with her hands. God bless her.

"She's on the portly side," I whisper to Jignesh, "so I figured she was much older. According to the mother, she's only nineteen and in her first year of college. Now she'll have to get a teardrop tattoo that will forever remind her of today's unfortunate incident. I know because a distant cousin of Sherise, one of my coworkers, married a Mexican gangster. I feel terribly shaken about Juan—I mean, Manuel—but I cannot help feeling sorry for her too. And it's not only because she looks rich, don't think I'm racist."

"I caused this," Jignesh says, letting out a soft whiffle.

"Oh, don't be stupid, Jignesh, don't blame yourself," I reprimand him. "It wasn't your fault. Manuel crossed the street without looking . . . Now, I know this will sound incredibly selfish," I change my tone to a gossipy one, "but you have to stay positive. Maybe a TV crew will show up too and, well, with my fabulous way with words and us two as the star witnesses . . . What do you know? This could be our YouTube moment."

A police officer approaches and asks us whether Manuel had been running away from something. He's one of those sexy Asian bears you only see on underground Japanese porn sites. And in your dreams, of course. His arms barely fit inside his uniform.

"Well, I'll be damned. I don't really know, officer," I reply, all flustered. "Do you?" I turn to my Indian friend. He shakes his head rapidly. "We don't know. He just ran."

The officer leaves us.

"I felt tempted to confess I pushed Manuel," I whisper in Jignesh's ear. "If only to get handcuffed and have this hot officer take me to prison."

Jignesh glares at me.

"That's of abysmal poor taste, Charlie."

"You're right," I reply. "I'm sorry, I apologize. I shouldn't be making jokes when Manuel's body still lies on the pavement, I'm sorry." Nevertheless, I think, if that police officer asked me to accompany him to the station for a few routine questions and then asked me to take off my clothes so we could have a shower together, I would oblige willfully . . .

"We better leave," Jignesh says eventually. "I needed to return the truck before six. Can I still keep the freezer in your garage?"

11

Drive

I cannot stop shaking. Charlie's going to suspect. What is he saying now? Something about me looking as pale as Carla Bruni. I don't, I briefly check myself in the rearview mirror before turning on the engine.

"Could you stop talking for just one second?" I beg.

Charlie apologizes and remains silent for a brief moment. Then he apologizes again for being so inconsiderate. He gathers that people sometimes need silence to cope with loss. Does he remain silent, then? No. He mentions how much his father grieved when some redneck relative of his died, and then goes on and on talking about his Nana. I want to pull over and squeeze his neck with my bare hands, but that would make him the third person I kill today. No, I didn't kill Manuel. That was an accident!

"Do you think he was running away from something?" Charlie now sounds like Dolly Parton with a stopped nose. "Maybe he saw an immigration officer. Maybe he thought they were going to deport him, and that's why he ran without looking . . . Well, probably not. And it's wrong to assume that all Hispanics are here illegally, I know. The girl that killed him looked legal. I bet he was not. Are you a citizen, Jignesh? Besides, had Manuel been running from an immigration officer, the officer would have been the first to help, you would think. Unless it was an officer with no conscience. Or a special officer like the ones from *Men in Black* who had to keep their identity secret," he chuckles. "Maybe Manuel wasn't only an illegal alien, but an out-of-this-planet alien—probably illegal too."

I give Charlie a box behind the ear. "He just died, Charlie!"

Charlie's too surprised to reply. I seize the brief moment of silence to brood on my situation. What am I going to do?

"Well, I suppose I deserved that," Charlie resumes talking a minute later. "It's been too much excitement for one day, I reckon . . . Oh, that's a lovely house . . . Now, we need to take it easy, Jignesh, if you want my opinion," he taps me on the shoulder. "One step at a time. We need to remain calm, breathe in, and—OH, MY GOD, THEY OPENED A CAFÉ GRATITUDE IN VENICE! Have you been there already? I've been to the one in Los Feliz. That restaurant is utterly and absolutely fantastic! You always leave hungry, of course, but it's SO GOOD!"

I'm only this short of taking a hand off the wheel and smacking Charlie's head against the dashboard.

"Let's have a cocktail when we get home, after we unload the freezer," Charlie suggests, suddenly. "How does that sound?"

Alcohol? "A cocktail sounds relaxing," I hear myself say.

"Well, maybe not a cocktail. I had a bottle of Cinzano, but I finished it this morning. I only have wine. Do you like wine?"

"Yes."

"Do you prefer red or white?"

"Red," I mumble.

One glass will be nice. It will help me relax. With the police still there, I won't be able to return to the office for at least a few hours.

"It will have to be white, Jignesh, I'm sorry. Yesterday I finished the last bottle of Sangiovese that I had from this fabulous winery owned by Cathy Schembechler—you know who she is? She married Bo Schembechler, the football coach of the Michigan Wolverines. I only know who Bo Schembechler is because my roommates in college watched ESPN every night. They watched the screen, I watched them. To this day, I don't know how many points a quarterback is. However, I still savor the smell of beer, sweat, and Tostitos that reigned in that room. Somehow, the name of Schembechler became familiar. But I digress, I'm sorry . . . I meant to say that I had this fabulous red wine that my friend Jill brought me from Santa Barbara. She's doing a low-residency master's there and drives up every few months. What on? I can't recollect. Something about media and psychology. One of her roommates is this lesbian from Long Beach who, the one time I had them for dinner, told me that my barbecue sauce was delicious but a little unpleasant to look at because of its pink color," Charlie starts laughing. "Never had I felt more embarrassed. I had refilled an expensive-looking bottle from Bristol Farms with barbecue sauce from the 99 Cent Only Store!" Now he's gasping for air. "Anyways, I had meant to save the last bottle for a special occasion—that wine was insanely good, Jignesh. One sip alone makes you feel as if you were Sofia Coppola spending a summer afternoon at her father's winery in Sonoma. Today would have been that special occasion, as tragic as it has been, but last week I had one of those blue moments that one occasionally has which, you know, require wine, and I drank the entire bottle."

"What special occasion would that have been?" I ask.

"That we run into each other again, of course."

"That was a coincidence, Charlie."

"Oh, there are no such things as coincidences in this life." He puts a hand on my leg. "It was meant to be."

Is Charlie now flirting with me?

"We'll have white wine and some hors d'oeuvres," Charlie continues. "I must have some goat cheese leftover, but I'm out of crackers. There's a *Fresh & Easy* on La Cienega, though. There's also a Mexican supermarket on West Adams Boulevard, but there are always a bunch of black kids waiting outside at this hour, and, nothing wrong with that, don't think I'm racist, I have plenty of black coworkers and cousins through matrimony, some of my neighbors are black too, and I must say that some of those kids are rather fun to look at, especially one they call Tucker, he's so yummy, the things I would do to that African booty of his, but one is *petit*, and it's already dark and—"

"A man just died, Charlie," I remind him.

"Oh, shoot. Yes. I apologize, I'm sorry. It's not that I forgot about Juan, but one should make the best out of horrible circumstances, don't you think?"

"You mean Manuel."

"Jesus Christ, I did it again. I apologize. I'm so sorry. All those Hispanic names are quite complicated for someone who grew up in a little town in rural Kentucky. I never know if someone is Mexican, Portuguese, or Italian. We can order pizza too. Do you care for olives? There's a Little Caesars on Western if you don't mind a chain. That would take us out of our way, but the one off of Crenshaw isn't as nice and always smells a tad greasy."

12

Wine

Despite all my recommendations, Jignesh insists on unloading the freezer first, so we end up driving straight to my little craftsman in West Adams. He parks the truck in the driveway, I step down, and open the garage entering a code.

"Five, five, four, five," I sing aloud, then press the pound key. "I have this bad habit of saying aloud all my passwords," I explain to Jignesh. "I inherited it from my mother. One day I'll get my savings swiped after somebody hears me entering my debit card pin code." *The whole forty-three dollars,* I add to myself.

We cannot carry the freezer into the garage by ourselves, so we ask for help from my neighbors.

"I'm pretty sure they're drug dealers," I tell Jignesh after the two of them leave. "It may be my Southern upbringing, but two college-age Latinx men living together must be either criminals, students, or homosexuals. And again, I'm not racist, but those two don't look the type that could afford to be studying at USC and they often receive female visitors. Therefore . . . Well, I also receive female visitors quite often. Then again I haven't worn white tube socks since *Dynasty* ended, and believe me, Jignesh, if I could ask God for one wish—five, five, four, five," I repeat aloud the numbers to close the garage door, "it would be to vanquish white tube socks from existence. One could be tempted to ask God to end poverty or war, but if you had only one wish, just one wish . . . Anyway, I digress. They may or may not be criminals, my two neighbors, but one thing is sure: they're wonderful people."

I turn to Jignesh. His lips are moving as if he was repeating something for himself in silence . . . I'll be damned. Did he just memorize my garage door code? I can't decide whether that's creepy or romantic.

Jignesh notices the look of surprise in my face and immediately interjects: "Should we order the pizza?"

We enter the house. I take off my shoes and invite Jignesh to do the same. He doesn't. Well, that's not very Indian.

"Hold on a minute," I say, walking toward my bedroom.

"I cannot stay too long," Jignesh replies.

"Relax." This time, I'm scolding him. "Sit down. I'm just going to change into something more comfortable."

It's not that I'm trying to seduce Jignesh, but if we're having a glass of wine, I want to enjoy it thoroughly, and I just can't in these jeans. They're size twenty-eight, and now I'm more of a thirty. I feel like Nicole Kidman in that *Moulin Rouge* movie, squeezed into a tiny corset . . . I won't bother about underwear either; I'll just wear my pajama bottoms . . . So, much better! I pull off my socks too. The cold floor feels delicious on my tired dogs. Should I toss my skivvies into the laundry basket? I take them to my nose. They smell fine, and I only wore them for half a day. I need to save money. Each load is $1.25, so probably not.

"I'm back," I announce, coming out to the living room, and, partly because I'm trying to improve the mood, partly because that is the way I usually walk at home, I sashay my way through the dining room and into the kitchen.

"Maybe I should just go home," Jignesh says.

Poor thing. He's still sweating. *Like a June bride in a feather bed*, my uncles would say. I'm cleaning that up, of course. Not quite what I used to hear as a child in Kentucky.

"Juan's death upset me too, Jignesh," I say. "It felt almost as bad as when Vanessa Redgrave tells Anthony Minghella what really happened with Robbie and Cecilia in *Atonement*. It was an accident, though, and this will sound harsh, as most things coming from a friend do, but you barely knew him. Do what I do when all the news about the Syrian refugees get to my head: change the channel. There's no need to be so distressed, Jignesh. You didn't kill him."

Jignesh flinches at my last words. I motion to the couch, inviting him to sit down. My, he's worse than I thought. He's quivering like a bird with a broken wing. I open the kitchen cabinet looking for glasses. I cannot let him drive home in such a state, can I?

"Do you want a Xanax with your wine?" I ask. "I think I also have Vicodin."

I'm usually not this prodigal when it comes to prescription drugs, but Jignesh seems to be in dire need of some benzodiazepine, and I've had this bottle of Xanax that a friend left me for over a year now—it was his payment for three weeks of meals and lodging. I only take half a pill at the end of the month before Tunisha, the sales director at the call center, calls me into her office with that exquisitely manicured hand of hers, to review my numbers.

"No, thank you," Jignesh replies with a snivel. "How long do you think it will take the police to leave?"

"I don't know," I reply. What a strange thing to ask. "What does it matter? Are you hiding something?" I joke. "They need to do their work."

"One hour? Two?" He insists.

"At least." I open the fridge. "Oh, I forgot I had made baloney sandwiches for your visit this morning," I add, taking a bite from one. "Do you want one?"

"I'd rather order a pizza," Jignesh whimpers.

I close the fridge. Jignesh definitely needs something. I have never seen anyone sweat, babble, and shake in such a manner since George Bush left office. I pull out the bottle of Xanax from my medicine drawer, pulverize one pill, and drop it into his glass . . . Maybe another one, just to be sure . . . He's a big guy . . . Two pills won't kill him. Then I pour the wine.

"Here you go," I return to the living room and offer Jignesh his glass. I pop half a pill too. My neck hurts a bit. It's all the tension.

Jignesh takes a big gulp.

"They already know me," I say, while I wait on the phone for the pizza parlor to answer. "They always call me 'Ma'am' and I don't have the heart to correct them—Hi . . . Yes, I can wait—Do you want to watch something on TV?" I offer the clicker to Jignesh. He shakes his head. I turn on the TV. "Yes, you got it right, this is Ms. Hayworth." I wink at Jignesh. "Is this Holly? The usual, dear, a Sunflower with soppressata, but this time, make it extra-large. I have a guest who's a little bit hungry."

I check what's new on Netflix. Then I check HBO. Then I check Amazon, then I check Netflix again. I choose *Two Days, One Night* with Marion Cotillard.

"It has subtitles," I warn Jignesh. He simpers politely.

"I won't need them," I add. "Did I mention that I spent a full year living in France?" He nods. *Did I?* I don't remember. Maybe during our first encounter. "I absolutely adore Marion Cotillard." I continue. "I'm her number one fan since *La Vie en Rose*—or *La Môme*, in its original title . . . I couldn't be happier when she became the face of Lady Dior. She's so . . . Well, French! That's the only way to describe her. She reminds me of my days in Tours. I was so innocent.

Jignesh doesn't respond. He's staring at the TV as if expecting to be disappointed. Poor thing. He probably has never been to France. "I lived an entire year in France, did I ever tell you?"

"You just did," Jignesh replies.

"Well, technically it was only ten months," I take another a sip of my wine, "but that's a full school year, isn't it?"

"I wonder where this place is?" I add, looking at the screen, five minutes into the movie. "It definitely isn't Paris. Why, with all the times I went to Paris—at least, five, that I remember; the train was expensive—I am an expert in all things Parisian. I could say I am an expert in all things

French, but that would be an exaggeration, of course . . . *Montmartre. Saint-Germain-des-Prés. Printemps. Le Bon Marché. Le Dépôt. L'Entre Deux Eaux* . . . Those were beautiful days . . . I was so innocent."

Jignesh doesn't respond.

"This is definitely not Paris," I say again, fifteen minutes into the movie. "It cannot be the *Banlieue*, can it? It looks too provincial."

I turn to Jignesh to check if he knows what *Banlieue* means. He probably doesn't. I cannot tell for sure, though. He's too focused on the movie.

"Now, while I absolutely adore Marion Cotillard," I continue, "I am disappointed by the outfit she chose for this movie." She's wearing jeans and a pink tank top. "You can see the straps of her bra. Not that I hadn't seen that before," I laugh, "but this takes place in France, *n'est-ce pas?* not in godforsaken Leitchfield, Kentucky. Anyways, there were poor people in France too. Moi, for instance. I was so poor that I had to smuggle Kool-Aid into the clubs to pretend I was having a colorful cocktail . . . I wonder where this is . . . It isn't Tours . . . It isn't Lyon, or Orléans, or Champagne, or Marseille, or Toulouse, or . . ."

Jignesh must be terribly impressed with my knowledge of French geography.

"I don't think this is France," he suddenly mutters.

He seems more relaxed now that he's drunk most of his wine. He still looks sad, but at least he stopped trembling.

"Of course it is, you silly," I reply, almost a minute later. "How in the world would I not know it?"

I can feel the Xanax working on me too. I'm wholly against predatory capitalism, but thank God for big pharma's blessings.

"I think they're in Belgium," Jignesh says.

I'm about to refute Jignesh's obviously unfounded guess—Marion Cotillard would never, ever set foot in Belgian territory. But then I hear it. Someone says "*septante-cinq,*" instead of "*soixante-quinze,*" and my ears start bleeding. Jignesh is right. They're in Belgium. And in Liège of all Belgian towns, I soon discover. That whore Marion Cotillard is playing a Walloon! No wonder I disliked this movie from the very beginning. I hate Belgium, especially Wallonia. Les Ardennes are the European Appalachians!

"I don't think I'm loving this movie too much," I say to Jignesh, making an effort to sound unruffled. "Should we change it?"

He shrugs, then finishes his wine. "I'm enjoying it," he says.

I go to the bathroom. When I return, I notice that Jignesh has refilled both our glasses.

"I had this Belgian boyfriend once," I begin, sitting down. "From Liège," I add, rolling my eyes, then I stop. I cannot make myself continue. It's too painful.

We continue watching the movie in silence . . . My, Marion Cotillard wears one disastrous outfit after the other.

The pizza arrives. I serve myself one slice and leave the rest to Jignesh. I cannot eat, though. The movie is too upsetting.

"For fucks, sake, we know it's trashy Wallonia," I finally explode. "Couldn't she at least wear some makeup? This is a horrible movie, Jignesh, I'm sorry. I completely regret having chosen it. I apologize. Belgian French ruins French for me. I'm so sorry."

Jignesh says nothing.

"Never believe a Walloon when he says that he loves you," I catch myself saying next. "Make him say it in French." I brush off a tear and wipe my nose with the back of my hand. "If he can only say it in English, he's not being truthful."

"I didn't mean to kill her," Jignesh mumbles.

Oh, boy, now Jignesh's talking nonsense. Who did he kill? Ah, the pizza, of course. I still haven't finished my one slice, and he's already eaten all the rest.

"Do you want more wine?" I ask, noticing his glass is again empty.

"She had an entire life ahead of her."

I take that for a yes and refill his glass. Jignesh guzzles it.

"Well, yes. Poor Marion Cotillard. She will likely end up losing her job, and that's always stressful. Don't let that be a reason for getting the willies, though," I add, finishing the bottle. "She ends up moving to France and then wins an Oscar."

Now Jignesh is crying. That's what those stupid Walloons will do to you if you ask me. I cannot care less. I stopped watching the film long ago, and now I'm browsing Tumblr on my iPhone . . . The posts from *Assbootybutt69* are just fascinating . . . Beautiful peaches . . . My, is one supposed to believe that all these straight boys are merely curious . . . ?

"Oh, come on, Jignesh, it isn't *Titanic*," I say, ten minutes later, without lifting my eyes from my phone, when his bawling becomes as loud as if we had just seen Leonardo DiCaprio sink into the depths of the Atlantic Ocean.

Jignesh lifts his shirt to clean up his nose. Horrified, I return to my iPhone.

"Sweet Southern Baby Jesus! Look at this guy's thighs, Jig—" I turn to share a post from *cutestboyass* with Jignesh, but he's no longer sitting next to me. He's in the kitchen. He asks if he can open another bottle. I'll be damned, what's one to say? I say yes.

"I'm too upset," he says when he comes back, wiping his nose on his shirt again, "so I did have a Xanax."

Shoot. I must have left the pills on the kitchen counter. That would have been his third. Should I worry?

Jignesh sits down.

I watch him for a few seconds. Then I return to Tumblr.

"I did something terribly wrong, Charlie . . ." Jignesh begins, ten minutes later. "I just don't know if I could tell you."

Oh, boy. I drugged Jignesh, and now he's going to tell me about the one time he had unprotected sex with an Armenian bear in the parking lot of a Wendy's. Or about the one time he lost his ride home from a pool party in Burbank because he couldn't make himself leave the "designated area." Or about the one time he got banned from Hamburger Mary's . . .

"We've all been there," I say, taking a sip of my wine.

This will sound rather unkind, but I'm not really that interested in listening to another coming out story.

"I did something terrible," Jignesh cries.

"Honey,"—I am not someone who uses the word *honey* lightly, but some situations in life call for it—"we all have done things that we're not proud of."

As in the first time I stepped into The Bullet Bar, for example.

"I did something for which I could end up in prison," Jignesh insists.

"You did?" I roll my eyes. "I peed once inside of an ATM," I say, scrolling down to Tumblr's next picture . . . *Gold medal for best ass* . . . Jesus, I'd be quite happy with the guy who won bronze. "I was drunk. It was a dare. I was hanging out with a couple of straight guys in my sophomore year in high school, and I wanted to prove that I could be one of *them* straight boys. It's been almost two decades, but I still avoid any branch of Bank of America."

"I did much worse."

I raise an eyebrow, ready to hear how Jignesh got arrested for pulling a Pee-wee Herman at the Studs Theatre. *Who hasn't done that?* I'm ready to say, but then, Jignesh remains silent.

Whatever. I return to Tumblr.

Eventually, Jignesh says: "My parents never loved me."

Oh, God. Family drama.

"My mother has always said I'm a disappointment," he continues. "She's always comparing me to my brother. And to my sister. I heard her say once that Sita is more of a man than I will ever be."

Well, Sita looked pretty dykey.

"Oh, Jiggy," I say, now focused on the posts from *toploader*. "I wish I could say that my parents are horrible too, but the truth is that they have never had anything but praise for me. I mean, my mother's a drunk, and she can be a little bitchy, but she never compared me to my two sisters, who, by the way, are quite the overachievers. Jennifer married a restaurateur and moved to Knoxville; Gracie's husband owns a gas station in

Louisville . . . My parents know I'll never accomplish much." I reach for my glass. "Still, they encourage me to keep trying."

It is true. It is only because they love me with all their hearts that every once in a while, they remind me that I could always move back home and work the register at my uncle's hardware store.

I steal a glance at Jignesh. Poor thing. Forty-two years old and still in the closet. He must live in perpetual guilt. It's no wonder why he got so big. He looks as if he was about to faint too. Should I worry? I switch to Safari and google "Xanax and wine" on my iPhone . . . Oh, crap. The mix seems a tad dangerous . . . Well, no. A woman says here that she always takes a pill with a cocktail when she flies. Another one says that one tablet is fine, as long as one does it with no more than half a glass of wine. But that would be if the pill was 0.25 milligrams. Jignesh had three tablets, half a milligram each, and probably more than a liter of wine since I only refilled my glass twice, and he opened a second bottle . . . Oh, he's quite large. He'll be fine. It's me I should worry about. I had half a pill . . . I return to Tumblr. My, the things I would do if I were left alone with any of these young men . . .

Ten minutes later, Jignesh has fallen asleep. He's not too unattractive from this angle. I'm also feeling sleepy. I turn off the TV. I didn't care at all for the film, but I will give it five stars on Rotten Tomatoes since it had subtitles.

I walk to my linen closet and pull out a blanket for Jignesh. I check the clock. It's not even nine. I'll just take a short nap.

It's half-past eleven and Jignesh is still sleeping. I tried lying down in bed, but I couldn't sleep, so now I'm back watching TV next to my Indian friend, munching on dry baloney sandwiches . . .

Why is it that half the commercials on TV are about cars? The other half are about food or prescription drugs, which reminds me, I have to ask my doctor about Allebra . . .

Jignesh left his phone on the coffee table. Does he have a code? Not that I would dare to snoop in, I just wonder . . . Oy, he doesn't.

I take a selfie. Smile! *Click* . . . I look stupid. Another one . . . *Click*. This one isn't bad . . . Now one with him. *Click*. Would it be too bad if I peruse through his photographs? Of course, it would be, but how else would I know he isn't a murderer? He could be a North Korean spy, you never know . . .

Mostly boring stuff. Here's one of him shirtless. And here's one of his butt. Jesus Christ, any romantic interest for this man aroused by that Bottega Venetta bag has now officially perished. Then again, his family has a small building in North Hollywood . . . This one isn't too bad . . . He doesn't smile in any of his pictures. He should. I would be sad too if I photographed this bad, but showing teeth removes twenty pounds. Too much curry, my friend, I pat Jignesh's belly. Too much curry and not enough lentils.

I turn my attention to the TV. Teri Bratchet looks sad too. I wonder what happened to her. The poor thing is so skinny.

Jignesh has 128 unread emails.

I nibble on a second sandwich. I shouldn't be reading his emails, should I? Bah, we're Facebook friends, he's sleeping it off on my couch, and I already saw a photograph of his butthole. It should be all right . . . Let's see . . . *Apple. Atlantis Events. Equality California* . . . An invitation to attend the Church of the Nazarene, "where all are welcome." Why would anyone want to visit a church this century when we have malls and movie theaters? . . . *Michelle Obama* . . . CREDO . . . Doesn't Jignesh have any friends? Here's one from Chase about his bank statement. Let's follow the link . . . Now, of course, I would need to know his login and password to see his account balance, wouldn't I? What would your password be, my little Ganesh? Apple won't come up with iCloud Keychain until late 2013, and watching a 2014 movie in 2012 is enough anachronism for one chapter . . . Of course, I could always click on this *Forgot your User ID and Password?* little link and then check his email, couldn't

I? That would be a terrible thing to do, though. Besides, Jignesh would notice that someone changed his password the next time he tries to log in . . . Although he may come to think that he made a typo and locked himself out . . . It happens to me all the time . . . I just need to make sure I delete the email asking me to reset his password, so I don't leave any trace . . . Can one go to jail for this? He said he had done something awfully wrong before. Maybe he checked someone else's bank balance too. Probably that's what he couldn't tell me . . . Should I press on the link? What would Jesus do if he were a thirty-seven-year-old white homosexual from Leitchfield, Kentucky, wanting to know how much money the large Indian stud lying on his couch made last month? Jignesh didn't protect his phone with a code in the first place. I'll interpret that as a sign that Jesus gives his permission. Wives do it all the time. I suspect girlfriends do too, and I am something right in between . . . I'll go to the dining table, though, in case he wakes up . . .

Meh. The balance in his checking account is $1,386.52. His savings account has only twenty-nine dollars. How disappointing. Let's see his latest transactions . . . A transfer of fifteen thousand dollars to *Charles Schwab*. Then another for one hundred and twenty-three thousand dollars two days before . . . Oh, my God, now I have to check his *Charles Schwab* account. I'm gonna guess two hundred thousand the most . . .

HOLY FUCK! He has $743,412 in his brokerage and $17,462 in his retirement account . . . My, I stretch my neck to check on Jignesh, this man has suddenly become much, much less unattractive. About three-quarters of a million dollars less unattractive . . .

Not that you could buy anything bigger than a one-bedroom in a recently gentrified neighborhood with three-quarters of a million dollars in the City of Angels, but it's still impressive. Oh, boy, my heart is beating so fast I'm afraid he can hear it. I have never dated a man with money. Could we retire now? Assuming a 10 percent return, that's about seventy-five thousand dollars a year before taxes. We could perfectly live with that if we do certain economies. What am I saying, no man with a soul could live with just that! Maybe I could start working shorter hours, but Jignesh would have to continue working full time, especially if we wanted to go on long vacations . . . I've never been to Italy. I haven't gone on a real vacation in at least a decade . . . We could also pay off this house . . . Do some repairs. At least paint the kitchen and replace the old flooring. New curtains, too . . . Oy, three-quarters of a million dollars would last long and well in a place like Leitchfield, Kentucky, but not here in Los Angeles!

Now, Charlie, hold on. This isn't your money yet. You met this rather intriguing brown man less than a week ago. You cannot fantasize about marriage when it's not even legal in California . . . Is it in India? I'll have to google it. I go back to my phone . . . We could have a destination wedding! I always thought that I would prefer a small ceremony, inside a tiny chapel, no more than a hundred guests, but if we married in India, we could go overboard. A five-thousand dollar wedding there would be equivalent to a two-hundred-and-fifty-thousand-dollar wedding here. We could rent that white hotel, what's its name? The one you see in all the Indian movies. It cannot be that expensive.

13

Endeavor

"Time to wake up, sleeping beauty," I hear Charlie's horrifically nasal voice. "It's after eight o'clock. You've been asleep for almost twelve hours."

Twelve hours? I open my eyes. Where am I?

"Don't you have to go to work?" he continues.

I'm in Charlie's house!

"I'm late myself too. Don't worry. I called to say I had the stomach flu. Do you want coffee? I prefer tea in the mornings, but I can fix you a cup if you want."

After eight o'clock? In less than half an hour, my coworkers will be at the office.

I jump off the couch.

"Where are my shoes?"

"They're by the door," Charlie replies.

I put on my shoes, grab the truck keys, and dash out of the house.

"Don't forget your phone," Charlie calls behind. I turn around. He's standing by the door, wrapped in his bathrobe, holding my iPhone. I hesitate for a second, then race back and snatch it.

"Call me," he yells as I run back to the rental truck. "Or, better, why don't you come back this evening for supper?

I can make it, I say to myself as I insert the keys in the ignition. *I can make it*, I repeat as I turn right on Crenshaw. *I will make it*, I state, as I get on the ramp to the 10. *I will make it before anyone else gets to the office.*

But the 10, being the 10, has no mercy for incidental murderers. The 10 freeway is a miles-long parking lot as it usually is at this time of the day, on any given Monday. It takes me forty-five minutes to get to the office.

I find Justin listening to his annoying podcasts of Rush Limbaugh and Clara at her desk, going through her personal emails.

"*Buenos días, majo,*" she says when she sees me. "Why so early?"

I never show my face before ten. I mumble some silly excuse about having to make a payment then go straight to my desk. Justin doesn't bother to say hello or even take his eyes off his computer, but he lowers his speakers' volume.

I sit down and wake up my computer.

"Aren't you going to make yourself a coffee?" Clara asks from downstairs.

Coffee is the last thing I need. My heart's beating so fast I can barely breathe. I'm feeling groggy, nonetheless, and I have a slight headache. Must be the Xanax I took last night. I hate the world, too, I notice. A touch more than usual. I hate my desk, and I hate my computer. I hate the printer behind me, the dirty gray carpet, and the plastic mat under my chair. I hate every single atom in this office. I ordinarily hate Justin, too, but today, today I despise him.

"No coffee, *corazón?*" Clara insists, from the bottom of the stairs, holding a mug.

I even hate Clara's honeyed voice. I want to strangle her with my keyboard cord. I usually find her naiveté charming. I do need coffee!

I race downstairs. Thankfully, the coffee pot stopped breaking itself a while ago.

"I hope you find it strong enough," Clara says, following me into the kitchen.

I raise a hand to hide her obnoxious sight from me.

"Is it good?" She insists as I take my first sip.

It is. Of course, it is. I've yelled at my sweet Andalusian princess so many times before for making weak coffee that at long last, she learned how to make it . . . Oh, the comforting bitterness of strong coffee. Only morphine mixed with crack could feel this good, and I bet it doesn't. I immediately stop wanting Clara dead. I want to make her my wife.

"This is so much better than an orgasm," I venture.

"And sure, you know what an orgasm feels like, right?"

This last comes from Justin, who just entered the kitchen too to refill his water bottle. He couldn't help but regale us with his sarcasm.

I dare to smile. Smiling doesn't hurt. How odd! It feels almost natural. Must be the coffee.

"Thank you," I say to Clara, refilling my cup. "Excuse me," I add coldly to Justin, then return to my desk.

I no longer want him dead. Just tied up. Naked and defenseless.

Gross. I have over two hundred unread emails. Plus three credit cards to reconcile, and I better start closing the month soon if I don't want to start receiving threatening calls from our homeowners. I have so much work to do, leaving aside returning the truck, and getting rid of Nina's body. Now I'll have to wait until it gets dark. At least I know that the garbage truck won't pick up recycling until Tuesday.

Anyhow, first things first. Let's check how the stocks are doing. I may be rich by now.

You see, I've been investing some of the company's money in the stock market.

Since we do not pay our homeowners the money from the vacation rentals in a given month until that month is over, yet we charge our guests a 50 percent deposit the moment they make a reservation, I proposed to Mike that instead of leaving the funds producing nothing inside the trust account, we should put them into an investment account, then transfer back into the trust account only what we would need to pay our homeowners once the month is over. He agreed.

"If I make a few hundred dollars, that's good."

I, he said, without including me. How incredibly selfish. We're not supposed to earn any interest in the money we collect in advance from our renters.

I've been transferring most of the money into Mike's investment account, according to his instructions, but then some to my personal too, and then to my brokerage account to buy stock. I play it safe. Say, only a couple thousand dollars every month, hold it for a few days, stay in if it goes up, sell immediately when it starts going down. The following month the same. I made an extra two thousand dollars last year. This year, I got a whit more ambitious: I transferred three hundred and fifty thousand dollars at once in March. I made almost fifteen thousand dollars in two days! At the current 1% APR, Mike would have made less than three hundred dollars in his investment account for the entire month. Two months ago, when the trust account was the fattest because of the summer rentals, I risked a tiny bit more: one million dollars. I panicked, however, so I sold after two hours. But in those two hours, I made almost $2,400. And then the market kept going up. It can only go up since the great recession ended, right? Had I kept that money longer, I would have made a fortune. But then August ended, we had to pay off everyone, and our liquidity went down considerably.

Now it's growing fat again because of the holidays.

In the last two weeks, I've taken a total of seven hundred and twenty-five thousand dollars from the Trust account. I put nothing into Mike's investment account, everything went to my brokerage. I played it safe and bought only Apple. Now, I don't need more stress in my life at this moment, so even if Apple's price grew only half a cent, I'm going to sell everything and return the money . . .

Huh? *Charles Schwab*'s not taking my password. Did I do something wrong? *LiteraryBoy1234#* . . . It's not taking it. I guess I'll have to reset it . . .

Suddenly, the front door opens, downstairs, and in walks Murat, the handyman.

"Hello, hello!" he sings in his low baritone voice to the salespeople. He sounds like that talking dog from YouTube. "Look what I brought you!" He laughs, holding up a half-eaten pie and a vanilla ice cream container.

The ugly Turkish boar. As if leftovers rescued from a guest's refrigerator could win our approval . . . Well, apparently, they can, for Clara does a little dance in her chair and calls Murat *"un ángel del cielo."*

Traitor. She sometimes calls me that too.

Justin rolls a sheet of paper and gives Murat a fanfare. He then notices that I'm looking at them and gives me the finger.

"I still don't have your reimbursement check," I warn Murat from my desk.

I know too well that his next move will be to come up to demand money.

"It's been five days!" Murat cries.

"It may take three more."

"What? Do you think I shit money?"

Shit? Dear God, why must he always be so coarse and repugnant?

"I am incredibly busy, Murat."

I truly am. I have to get rid of a body.

"And please, watch your language."

"Fucking princess," I hear Murat mumble.

"Murat!" Clara chuckles with a mouth full of pie. "Stop it."

"What?" Murat cries. "She's a princess. Look at him, her fat majesty on her throne high in heaven."

Justin celebrates the offensive joke with a howling.

"Murat, please," Clara insists, still laughing. "No name-calling in this office."

"At least he acknowledges my noble stock," I mutter sourly, then return to the Charles Schwab site with a new password.

I'm finally in and . . . the stocks are down . . . I've lost over sixty thousand dollars!

"I need sugar," I wheeze, then start opening all of my drawers. Somewhere I must have a half-eaten chocolate donut, a granola bar—something. "Clara?" I beg. "Do we have any cookies?"

"We have pie," Clara invites me downstairs.

I didn't want to, but if I don't put something in my stomach right now, I'll die. I rush downstairs. Before I could reach the pie, Murat pulls it away from me.

"Where's my check?"

"Murat, I didn't have breakfast this morning, and I'm feeling quite fragile."

"No check, no pie," Murat replies.

"I have ice cream," Justin says, raising the container from his desk.

He does? Normally, I wouldn't take a good morning from Justin. On the other hand, I desperately need the sugar.

"Thank God, you do," I say, glaring first at Murat, then turning to Justin with a grin the width of the Pacific Ocean. One must pretend and be gracious, sometimes, for the sake of keeping the office's harmony. "It's very thoughtful of you, Justin," I add.

"Oops," Justin says, putting the entire last scoop into his mouth. "I ate the last bit."

"Oh, what a selfish, senseless brute!" I scream.

Murat starts laughing. I reach then for Clara's plate, but she has just finished her slice. I hurtle upstairs, take forty dollars from the petty cash, and leave the office. I'll plan my revenge later.

Oh, woe, Apple went down! Burning tears run down my cheeks as I gallop toward Abbot Kinney. And Nina, what the hell am I going to do about Nina? Oh, shoot, and the truck! I need to return the truck!

Murat, I type on my phone, waiting in line for a burrito. *Could you do me a big favor?*

By the time I return to the office, Murat has already returned the truck and parked my car in the basement garage. Gabrielle and a new intern the agency sent us are also there. The intern is a skinny Mexican hipster called Rogelio. He's wearing a New York Yankees ball cap with a Che Guevara t-shirt. Ironically, I suppose.

I feel slightly better, but still too upset to do any real work. I beg Clara and Gabrielle to take care of the child and set my phone extension on do-not-disturb. Then I warn everyone downstairs not to bother me with stupid questions. I'll spend the rest of the morning lamenting my luck and playing *Candy Crush Saga*.

Text from Charlie. *Did you make it okay to your office?*

Of course, I made it okay, you pint-sized twat, I think, looking at the screen of my phone, but text nothing. I better not answer this text, or Charlie will be texting me back all morning.

And now one from my mother. *Where are you?*

Shoot. I have thirteen missed calls from her. I didn't call home last night. I cannot call now; I don't have the animus. I set my phone on airplane mode and hope that a good excuse will come up this evening.

Every now and then, I turn my gaze from my game to check that the people downstairs aren't wasting their time on Facebook. From above, I can see everyone's screens, except for Clara's. And because of the open plan and adverse acoustics, I can hear all of their conversations too. The only true private spaces in this office are the kitchen and the bathroom. No one could have a private conversation where people poo, so when we need to have one, we head outside or into the kitchen.

I notice that Justin picks up his mug and walks under the mezzanine toward the back of the office. Then I see Gabrielle's blond hair following right after. They're probably going to the kitchen.

The office modem is in the kitchen too. The ethernet cable for the computers in the mezzanine goes up through a small hole in the floor. If you stick your ear to this hole, you can listen to any conversation taking place in the kitchen. That's how I learned that Gabrielle's roommate had had an abortion.

The problem is that the carpet is terribly dusty.

"Have you heard from Nina?" I hear Gabrielle ask.

"Not yet," singsongs Justin.

And you never will, I think.

Now, why would Justin be waiting to hear from Nina?

"Are you going to visit her?" asks Gabrielle.

"In Germany?"

"Yeah."

Why would Nina want Justin to visit her? Nina never invited me, and she spent most of her time at the office with me.

"If I can afford it," Justin replies.

I'll make sure then you can't, *Monsieur Dantès!* Let's see how it goes next time I do payroll. The dust is making my nose itchy. I have to raise my head from the floor. And now Clara is coming upstairs, licking a spoonful of peanut butter and, I assume, another of her stupid computer-related questions.

"I said I was busy," I bawl.

Clara doesn't even lose her beam. She simply turns around and descends the stairs.

I go back to my hearing hole.

"Will you miss her?"

"A little," Justin responds. "We weren't serious. We just went out a few times."

Justin and Nina went out? Not in my office! If I remember correctly, romantic relationships are strictly forbidden in the employee manual, and they are grounds for immediate dismissal. How do I know? Because I wrote it! That little German whore—and with my sworn enemy! I rise to my knees, open a drawer in the file cabinet and pull out a thick binder. It must be somewhere here, I browse fast through the pages. *Code of Conduct*, most probably. I remember well having written it. I remember planning to make an amendment, the first time I met Justin, for those at the executive level. That happened when I still found him attractive and before he started with his hurtful innuendos, challenging all my instructions.

"So, where in Mexico is she now?" I hear Gabrielle ask.

I lay down again to hear Justin's response.

"Rosarito? I have no idea. She wanted to surf. She'll call tonight. Or tomorrow. Or when she's back in Germany. I don't know. I sent her a text message this morning."

A text message? Justin will be expecting one back. And Nina's folks in Germany will be expecting a call too, I suppose. I would if my twenty-three-year-old was traveling alone down the Baja peninsula . . . Now I feel guilty. I put the *employee manual* back into the file cabinet. They will be dead worried for her. And if they don't receive a call, sooner or later they'll call the police, and the police will start an investigation . . . I need to get rid of her body before the police start asking questions. I cannot go on with that stupid freezer idea. I must take Nina's corpse and dump it as far as possible . . . Where? I can only think of the desert. I could combine it with a fast trip to Palm Springs. I could stay at one of the nudie resorts and see what those places are all about . . . Who am I kidding? I wouldn't dare with this life preserver around my waist. And with this heat, I doubt I would have the strength to walk far into the wilderness. Maybe I should dissolve her in acid.

I jump to my desk and open a private window on Safari. *Dissolve a body in acid*, I start typing. *Dissolve a body in hydrofluoric acid* pops up. *MythBusters proves 'Breaking Bad's Walt needs some more schooling'* is the first link. I click on it and start reading . . . Jiminy Cricket. Apparently, one cannot dissolve a body in hydrofluoric acid.

I go back to the list of results.

"Who are you planning to get rid of?" Mike asks behind me.

He gives me such a scare I let out a small fart.

"What are you doing here?" I reply.

"I work here, Jignesh, remember?" Mike replies, stepping back. He covers his nose and uses a folder to fan away the smell. "This is my company."

"I mean, so early?"

He laughs. "Sometimes I have work to do too, Jignesh. Are you okay? That was a bad one. You look agitated. Are you wearing the same clothes as yesterday?"

I haven't even checked how I look today, but, yes, I'm wearing the same clothes as yesterday. I assumed I look like a darker version of that painting at the Hammer Museum, Doctor Pozzi in his red robe. Handsome and relaxed, inspiring awe and respect. Then again, I'm wearing sweatpants and a very old hoodie. I'm full of anguish, and I just farted in front of my boss. I guess then, I must look instead like the painting of a beautiful damsel in distress . . . Which one? Medea, about to murder her children.

"You haven't told anyone about what happened yesterday, have you?" Mike asks, lowering his voice.

I shake my head.

"You better not," he adds. "I don't want the day to be lost in gossip. It was an accident." He walks to his desk. "You don't look good at all, Jiggy-boy. Why don't you take a break?"

I go downstairs and enter the bathroom. Fuck, I think, looking at my reflection in the mirror. I do look bad. My countenance wouldn't remind anyone of a painting. I haven't even washed my face yet today. I do so with cold water. I pull up my cheeks. I'm not getting any younger. Or any thinner.

Then, I hear someone opening the street gate to the service corridor, followed by the sound of a dumpster rolling over the concrete. I rush outside. A man is pushing the recycle dumpster down to the street. They weren't supposed to pick up recycling on Monday!

"Sir!" I yell. "Do not take that dumpster!"

The man turns at me but doesn't stop.

"Why not?" he asks.

"Because I . . ." *Because I what?* Because at the very bottom of that dumpster, you'll find the corpse of a young girl I murdered? I cannot say that. What can I say instead? That a girl fell inside by accident? That wouldn't do either. Oh, what would Lady Macbeth say in such unforeseen circumstances?

"Because some important documents are in there." I cry. "And besides, recycle day is tomorrow!"

"It's Mondays." the man replies.

"Since when?"

"Since ever."

"Could you please come back later?"

The man shakes his head.

"What's going on there?" Mike asks from his window upstairs.

"I cannot let this man take the recycle."

"Why not?"

"I may have dropped some important documents in."

"What documents?"

"Some . . . very . . . important documents."

"For fuck's sake, Jignesh. Fetch them out and let that man do his job."

"They may be at the bottom."

"Ask for help, then. Clara, Rogelio," Mike turns around, "go help that fat oaf outside."

"No!" I yowl, but it's too late, Clara is already out.

"What's wrong, *cariño?*" she asks with her sweet accent, still licking on her spoonful of peanut butter.

"I threw some documents into the dumpster," I mumble.

"What documents?"

"Checks."

"Clients' checks?" Mike yells from above. I nod, shyly. "For Christ's sake, Jignesh! If you fucking lost Alman's—" He interrupts himself and runs downstairs. "If you fucking lost the check from Alman's"—Clara moves aside, and Mike comes out of the door—"I'm going to ream your sorry Indian ass so bad—"

I can't be flattered. I very much doubt that rimming means to Mike what it means in my dictionary.

"What checks did you lose?" Mike insists, his face is red with anger.

"Blank checks," I reply. "I lost a full stack."

"Just void them."

"I need the actual checks to void them."

"Stop them, then. Tell the bank not to pay them."

"It'll be too expensive. It's thirty-two dollars for each one," I say, appealing to Mike's cheapness.

"Where is Alman's check?"

"I deposited it."

Mike makes a brusque gesture. "Get those checks—I'm sorry, sir," he turns to the trash collector, who's been patiently waiting for us to stop arguing. "Could you wait for a few minutes?"

"They're at the bottom," I repeat. "It may take me all day."

Mike rolls his eyes, exhales, and goes back inside. "I asked you to help too!" He barks at Rogelio, who hasn't yet moved from his desk, then climbs upstairs.

"Could you perhaps come back later today?" I ask the trash collector. "I'll make sure that we—"

The man lets go of the dumpster and leaves laughing.

"I'll get a chair to step in," Clara says, stepping back into the office.

"I won't need your help, Clara."

"If we hurry up, maybe we can still have them pick up the dumpster."

"No," I say, as dramatically as an offended mother would in similar circumstances. Rogelio is now standing next to Clara. Gabrielle and Justin are watching us, too, from inside. "It is a matter of pride, Señorita Clara. It's my responsibility. It was me who lost them. It will be me who finds them. I made an oath when I became a bookkeeper."

"But if we help you—"

"No!" I wail as if rejecting a helpful hand to the scaffold. "I can do it myself."

"Let him alone," hollers Mike from upstairs.

Clara and Rogelio return inside. I pull the dumpster back to its place, then climb inside.

And there it is, Nina, trying to guilt me, staring at me with her eyes wide open. How insensitive. The trash collectors would have found her body in less than one minute. How am I going to take her into my car? The only way to the basement parking is through the garage or the side door by the entrance. I cannot dart across the office carrying a corpse. Oh, dear God, I need a miracle . . .

"Whose backpack is this?" I hear Gabrielle ask inside.

Fucketty fuck. I forgot Nina's luggage!

"It's a guest's!" I cry. "Don't touch it."

Jesus Christ. Now I need to remove a corpse and a backpack. I cannot breathe. My whole body aches. I think I'm about to have a heart attack . . . Lord Vishnu, I pray, preserver of the cosmos, please help me. Dear Lord, you are full in all opulences, but I do not beg you for opulence. Please do something to empty the office. An earthquake. A tsunami . . . Mother Lakshmi, goddess of fortune, you and your son are the proprietors of the entire creation—empty this office, please! Do something that will make everyone gallop outside screaming. Lord Uttamashloka, may my ambitions be fulfilled by your grace. Start a fire . . . Yes! That's what I need, a fire! I could start one at the kitchen, have the sprinklers go off, rush everyone out, then pick up the body and cross the office at light speed . . . Oh, but if there's a fire, everyone would be waiting outside looking toward the building. They would see me come out with the body. I need a miracle, a real miracle.

I pray to Lord Brahma. Then to Lord Rama. Then to Ganesha. Soon I run out of Gods. There are three hundred and thirty million Indian Gods, but since I rarely ever pray, I can only remember the names of so many . . . The women that clean our homes always pray to the *Santisima Virgen de Guadalupe*. Would that work? It may. She's known to have made impossible miracles, Juana told me. I kneel down. Then I pray to *la morenita*.

Mother of all mercies, I begin. *Star of the Sea, Queen of Heaven . . .*

"It's coming!" I hear Rogelio sing suddenly.

What is coming?

"It's coming!" I hear people say, from other offices in the building. I see then excited faces stick out of the windows. Suddenly, everyone rushes out to the street. I step inside.

"The *Endeavor* is coming!" Clara shouts at the door, then steps out.

The Endeavor? The Endeavor, indeed! I clap—the last of the space shuttles, in its final journey to the California Science Center. The *Endeavor* is flying all over Los Angeles!

"¡Gracias, virgencita!" I exclaim.

I hurtle back outside, dive into the dumpster, and pull out Nina's body. She weighs as much as a thought—or is it me who has suddenly gained strength? She smells of cardboard, but nothing else yet. I enter the office. Everyone has left except Justin, who's on the phone, trying to catch a glimpse of the plane carrying the Endeavor through the front window. There's no way I can pass him and that he would miss Nina. I drop the body in the kitchen.

"Justin," I cry. "Hang up. You will miss it!"

Justin looks at me for a second. He has no reason to trust me. Then he hangs up and runs outside. I go back to the kitchen, pick up Lili Marleen, and dart to the front door. I step out, not even looking around to see if anyone can see me, then climb the three steps down to the basement door. The gate is locked. *Fucketty, fuck, where are my keys?* I left them on top of my desk. I look through the main entrance. Everyone is standing in the middle of the street, looking up to the sky with their backs at me. I go back inside, drop the body under Gabrielle's desk, then hurry upstairs.

Mike is still at his desk.

"I'm about to win this shit," he explains.

He's on eBay.

"I'm in the last two minutes of an auction," he says. "I don't want to miss it, but I can't go out before I win it," he complains.

Two minutes? I don't have that much time! The Endeavor will pass by, and everybody will come back in and see Nina's body.

"Go out!" I cry. "I'll win it for you."

"Will you?"

"For fuck's sake, Mike. Go! The Endeavor is more important. I'll win it, I promise."

He looks at me with a mixture of gratitude and discontentment, then runs downstairs.

"Don't bet more than twelve dollars!" he yells as he steps out.

I bid one thousand dollars. Hopefully, he wasn't trying to buy another farting bank, like the one he gave me last Christmas. I rush downstairs and pick up the body. *Oh, fucketty, fuck, I forgot to grab my keys!* I drop the body again, hurtle upstairs, look for my keys, they should be on my desk—where the fuck did Murat leave them? Where are my keys? I CANNOT FIND THEM!

"Murat," I call him, "where did you leave my car keys?"

"I kept them," he replies. "You give me my check, I give you your keys."

I hang up.

This is no time to have a fight. I grab Mike's keys from his desk, so that I can open the gate, go back down and fetch Nina, then climb down the three steps to the basement at once, open the gate and . . . it's empty, thank God! I drop Nina's body beside my car, go fetch an old AC motor that, about a year ago, Murat left by the space where we keep the bikes— I've been asking him to remove it ever since—and without hesitation, I smash the passenger window. It is only after I reach to open the door from inside that I realize that Murat had left my car unlocked and the keys in the ignition.

No time to get angry. I stick Nina's body into the trunk of my car, then return for her backpack.

"Where is it?" I yell, a moment later, coming out to the street as happy as a puppy.

Avoiding prison is well worth a broken window.

"Where is the Endeavor? I want to see it!"

People are running down the street, rushing each other, pointing up at the plane carrying the Endeavor. I turn in every direction but still cannot see it.

"Go to the beach!" Gabrielle urges me.

I charge around the corner and across Abbot Kinney, barely paying attention to the incoming traffic. *How much will it cost me to repair that broken window?* I'll charge it to the company. Then I see it, mounted on a Boeing 747, the pinnacle of human achievement: the Endeavor space shuttle. *Thank you, Virgin of Guadalupe,* I weep. *Thank you for this great miracle of science!*

14

Bear Dungeon Orgy

The day came to an end, and Jignesh didn't answer any of my texts. Well, that's just rude. Maybe something happened to him. Perhaps he died, or his phone ran out of battery. One shouldn't be too negative.

Let's check my email one last time . . . Nothing. Let's go to Instagram . . . If I had never been to West Hollywood, I would think that this level of anorexia is impossible . . . Baby Jesus, it's half past midnight, and I need to be at the office by 7:00 a.m. tomorrow. I need to get off social media and stop worrying about that odious blubbery man who didn't call. Alas, I cannot sleep. Should I take one of my dolls? I took melatonin already. I better not. If I take a sleeping pill, I may be too groggy to function properly in the morning. I'll need lots of coffee, and then I won't be able to sleep again, and I'll have to take another pill. Maybe I should just whack off. That helps sometimes.

I reach for my laptop, open Safari, and type "My." The MyVidster porn site pops up. And what comes up first? Twinks. Gut-churning. It's comforting to see that the white, skinny, and petit are in high demand, but I prefer the dark, the beefy, and the hairy. I type "Hairy Hunks" in the search field. Now we're talking . . . This one looks incredibly nasty. I'll click on it . . . Yuck. Super low rez. It's during moments like this when I regret canceling my membership at Nakedsword, but twenty dollars a month for movies that take forever to load is a rip-off . . . I type "Environmentally conscious straight college boy attending a bear dungeon orgy." If

I'm interested in establishing a steady relationship with Jignesh, I should start by becoming acquainted with the portly man archetype.

Nothing good on page one . . . Nor on page two . . . Let's try page number sixteen . . . Page forty . . . Page 363 . . . Nothing. This one looks decent . . . Beautiful bod, awful selection of bath towels . . . Let's go back to page 125 . . . Sweet Southern Baby Jesus, it's already after one. What am I doing? I should just take a sleeping pill.

I walk into the kitchen without turning on the lights and rummage inside the medicine drawer. I find something with the shape of a Benadryl that I pop into my mouth. Then I see through the window that the garage door is open.

Great. The door mechanism broke, and now it's going to cost me a fortune to repair it.

Then I see a flashlight inside. Jesus Christ, somebody broke into my garage!

What should I do? Should I scream? Yes, and then I should call the police. Where did I leave my phone? It's in my bedroom. Maybe I should grab a saucepan instead and hit it against the counter as loud as I can. They may think it's a gun like Corey Feldman said in *The Goonies*. But what if they have a gun and shoot back? Oy, is it they? How many people are inside my garage?

I see a man step out. My heart stops. He's rather large. He types a code, and the garage door closes. How does he know my code? *Sweet Southern Baby Jesus*, the man is Jignesh!

"What are you doing inside my garage?" I ask, coming out to the yard, my heart beating as fast as when my aunt Wilma caught me trying on makeup.

Jignesh starts babbling.

"Are you stalking me?" I ask.

Why, he obviously is . . . How romantic!

"I've never been stalked before," I say, resting on my bed next to Jignesh once our amatory session is over. "I must confess, though, that I have been a stalker a few times . . . I once met this Italian guy, Agostino, during my year in Tours. Big hands. Strong legs. He played soccer. After our first date, he never returned any of my texts—SMS, they called them in Europe—or any of my calls, but I kept calling him every day, twenty-five times a day so that I could hear his beautiful Neapolitan accent. '*Mi dispiace, non posso rispondere. Lascia un messaggio.*' That's all the Italian I know, but I know how to pronounce it correctly thanks to Agostino . . . Then there was Jesse . . . The one time I met a guy shorter than me who I actually found attractive, and I ruined it as well with excessive texting. And waiting on the stairs outside of his job. And introducing myself as his fiancé to all of his coworkers. And by calling his mother. Awfully nice lady, though. My call made her so happy. Jesse wasn't out to her, but she had her suspicions, she told me. She thought that I was a woman, and I didn't have the heart to correct her . . . And of course, there's the Belgian bastard, with whom I corresponded for months after a serendipitous encounter in Elysium Park. I sold all my possessions to be able to afford a plane ticket across the Atlantic . . . but that's a long and unpleasant story to tell now. I better not start, should I?"

Jignesh shakes his head. He looks as if I had just confessed I gave him the cooties. Oh, boy. Only a moron like me starts prattling with his new boyfriend about all of his previous love interests the first time they have sex.

I stand up to go to the bathroom. Intercourse wasn't bad, I just wish Jignesh had had a shower before, I think, reaching for my toothbrush. I didn't get to perform all my *repertoire* because of the odor.

I'm not saying I'm disappointed, I gargle a capful of *Listerine*, but the situation called for some lusty, lascivious action that we failed to have. I had imagined myself having to apologize to the neighbors in the back for all the moaning and groaning. Not that I fraternize much with them. I don't even know their names. It would have been nice to blush like a young Elizabeth Taylor in *Raintree County* when she tells Montgomery

Clift that she lied about the baby the moment they made a reference to the noises coming out of my room. Alas, there was nothing of that.

Anyway, the important thing is that Jignesh had a pleasant time, I spit. He's the one with the money.

15

Freeway

I left Charlie's house before dawn, and there's already traffic.

I hate this town, I weep. I hate it with all my heart. I hate the 10. I hate the 405. I hate the 101, the 710, and even the 90, which I rarely take but I still hate it, fuck it, I don't care, I wish they all died. I hate every freeway and every street in Los Angeles—except for Vermont, but I only like that track of Vermont between Prospect and Franklin, so fuck it too, fuck Vermont, and above all, fuck Santa Monica, and fuck Abbot Kinney . . . I should have had a cup of coffee before I left Charlie's house— where's a fucking Starbucks? I pull out my phone. "MOVE IT!" I scream at the car in front of me. I wish a horrible plague wiped out two-thirds of the LA population. That would be so wonderful. Can you imagine? All the streets empty of traffic. From Hollywood to Canoga Park in less than thirty minutes. Imagine a trip to Costco . . . Why is this shit not working? Oh, crap. I forgot I set my phone on airplane mode since yesterday morning.

The first ten texts to come in are from Charlie.

Why didn't you wake me up to say goodbye?

I already miss you, says the last one.

Oh, fuck you, Charlie. Fuck you a million times. Don't you ever stop talking or texting? Isn't it enough what happened last night? You robbed me of my dignity!

I left your fucking house not even ten minutes ago, I start typing, trying to keep an eye on the road at the same time. I stop short from hitting send, however. I need to be on Charlie's sweet side until I find a better place for the freezer.

I check all my other messages. Fifty-two missed calls? And here's yet another text from—oh, fuck, my mother.

Where in God's name are you?

Crap. I forgot to call. And I haven't been home in two nights. They must be dead worried.

405, I type. I'm actually still on the 10. *Home soon.*

I hope she hasn't tried calling the office yet, because I was planning to call in sick. I need to go home, get my passport, then drive all the way down to Tijuana. I'll take a few photos on Nina's phone and post them on Instagram. Then I'll throw away her backpack. That will buy me some time. I need everyone to believe that she made it across the border. But first, I need coffee.

How did I get into so much trouble? I brush a tear off my cheek. I don't even know how Instagram works. Nina posted all kinds of shit. Should I post a message in English or German? Probably German . . . Please, please, Google Translate, make it sound realistic. Although she made a few American friends, including that fucktard Justin, so I guess she could be posting in English too. I need to check whether she ever did.

I reach for her phone in the glove compartment, but then my phone vibrates with yet another text from Charlie.

BTW, what's in the freezer?

Crab, I type, one eye on the road, one on the phone. *Don't fucking disconnect it.*

Shoot. I shouldn't have cursed.

XOXO, I type. *See you soon, gorgeous.*

A moment later: *Want to come for dinner this evening?*

No, I don't want to come for dinner, you stupid dwarf. I am most thankful for the unsolicited rimjob from last night, but I only need a fucking place to store a corpse until I figure out what to do with it . . . I wish I could send that. Instead, I type: *Maybe. I'll let you know how my day goes.*

Call me, Charlie responds.

Meeting! Gotta turn the phone off.

A man gestures me to put down my phone. I give him the finger. I've been driving for almost twenty-five years, for fuck's sake. I can perfectly type and drive.

Where the fuck can I get some coffee? There's a Starbucks on Fairfax, which is the next exit. But I'm all the way over in the left lane. I look in the rearview mirror for the cars coming. I should look over my shoulder too, in my blind spot, but I'm too stiff, I didn't sleep well, my neck hurts and who am I kidding? I don't even use the right-side mirror. This is when one takes a leap of faith. *Please, dear God, protect me.* I take a deep breath, close my eyes, then turn the wheel right, and change three lanes swiftly.

Ten minutes later, I'm back on the freeway, enjoying a delicious triple black-eye Frappuccino with ten envelopes of Splenda.

I spot Angelyne's pink Corvette to my left. How cool is that? I love LA. I love this city so much, even with this horrible traffic. I wouldn't want to live anywhere else.

Fifty-five minutes later, I park in front of my house.

My dad's car is still in the driveway. He must be at home too.

My mother opens the door before I can reach the handle.

"You're going to send me to an early grave!" she yells before she starts hitting me with a slipper.

16

Supper

"He's a bit dry," I say to Sherise, showing her the messages I exchanged with Jignesh this morning. She nods, without lifting her eyes from the form she's filling in on her computer. I spend a lot of time at work with Sherise. She lets me play with her hair sometimes. She doesn't think it's racist. "But overall, he's utterly sweet." I continue. "Jignesh seems to honestly care. Couples aren't always all peaches and cream, you know that."

Of course, she knows that. Sherise's husband is an artist who hasn't had a steady job since probably 1990.

"Relationships are complicated," I add.

"So, you two now are a couple?" Sherise asks.

"Oh, the fuck we are," I laugh. Today, Sherise pulled her hair back in this super cute tall chignon, and I'm adorning it with clips and colorful rubber bands for lack of flowers. "We better be. Jignesh's a financial manager at this awfully grand, hyper-exclusive real estate company in Venice," I raise my voice, making sure that that bitch Jade can hear us from her desk. She's one of those odious Filipino women who loves to complain about white people's manners. Tunisha announced this morning that Jade was the top seller again for the fifth month in a row, and now no one can stand her. "He has three-quarters of a million dollars in his brokerage account," I say, then I bend down and add, to Sherise only: "Don't ask me how I found out—He wants this?" I raise my voice again, pointing at my compact yet awfully well-defined little body in my best interpretation of a sassy African American teen working part-time at the Fox Hills Sephora. "He better put a ring on it."

Maybe I shouldn't have said that to Sherise, I reflect, on my way to the Bristol Farms that evening. She and her husband didn't exchange rings. They got tattoos, instead. They're very down-to-earth people. She may come to believe I'm a gold-digger.

In a certain way, I am one, though. I'm a gold-digger. I step out of the car and grab the canvas bags from the trunk. Is that wrong? When one grows up watching Disney Princess movies and getting hand-me-downs from his better-off cousins living in Nashville, all one can dream of is achieving social progress through marriage. Perhaps if I had stayed home in Leitchfield—I wave hi to the security guard as I enter the supermarket; he already knows me—I could have caught a wealthy husband, like my sisters. What am I thinking? A husband? In Kentucky? A boyfriend alone would have gotten me killed.

I love coming to this Bristol Farms on Wilshire. It's a long detour, but it brings me good memories. For instance, the sampler tray by the cheese island reminds me of that blessed day I left for France. The coach section had been oversold for the first leg of the flight, between Louisville and DC, so the agent at the ticket counter asked me whether I would mind being upgraded to business class.

"Would I?" I turned to the person behind me in the line, a young man wearing a ball cap with the confederate flag. "I suppose it'll be fine," I turned back to the clerk, in my best interpretation of Bette Midler in *Beaches*. "This must be a signal from God," I turned back to the man behind. "I'll probably sit next to a rich diplomat, who may also be traveling all the way to Paris—I'm fixing to do a year-long residence in Tours, a small city south of Paris, France. That's in Europe," I explained. "Across the Atlantic." The man wore a *Camel Towing* shirt too, with the caption: *When it's Wedged in Tight, We'll Get it Pulled Out*, so I assumed he might have not known where exactly Europe was.

"You see?" I showed the boarding pass to my parents, waiting for me to say goodbye before going through security. "I'm glad I didn't listen to your suggestion of wearing more comfortable clothes for the long flight."

Alas, I didn't sit next to a diplomat in business class. My trip companion was an oversized fourteen-year-old brat full of pimples. He wore loose cargo shorts and a Red-Sox shirt or whatever basketball team that was, smelling of what a typical teenage boy his age smells like. This *Stanser Schafkase* at only $14.95 for half a pound smells just as bad. The boy's parents sat across the aisle, and his siblings just behind them. He spent the whole flight to DC talking about Kobe Bryant with his father.

It was fun to travel in business class, nevertheless, if only for a little over an hour.

"One day I will marry rich," I think I said to the kid, after my third glass of Prosecco. "Just like your mother did."

I was so excited, it was difficult to keep to myself. I kept looking at that child's mother from the corner of my eye during the entire flight, her big golden earrings, her perfectly round Dallas hairstyle, hoping she would make eye contact with me so that I could ask her directly: "How did you do it? How did you manage to catch a husband that can afford to pay for the entire family to fly business class?"

Unfortunately, life happens. I flew coach for the leg between DC and Paris. Then I came back from France, got my degree, and ended up moving to Los Angeles. Now I'm thirty-seven, still single, and I drive a Honda Civic from 2003 instead of a 2013 white BMW hatchback. Oh, the things I would do with a white BMW hatchback. I would never stop at any pedestrian crossing. I would change lanes without using the signal, I would take two parking spaces, and I would never, ever apologize for anything!

I cannot fuck it up with Jignesh. He isn't perfect, of course, but he's my last chance.

By 7:00 p.m., I'm back home. By seven thirty, supper is almost ready.

The water is boiling, and I only need to hear from my Indian Heathcliff to throw in the pasta. Fresh pasta from Bristol Farms takes only two minutes. I'm making this fabulous Fettuccine Alfredo that, according to a recipe I found in the Sunday edition of the *New York Times*, was Jackie Onassis' favorite dish at Elaine's, in Manhattan. It smells so good with all that butter and cheese . . . So yummy!

Are you still coming? I send another text to my Bollywood Valentino.

It's half-past nine.

No response.

I made a delicious dinner for you.

His loss, I decide, by the time the clock strikes ten. I go to the kitchen and put the water back to boil. A minute later, I put it off. Maybe Jignesh is driving, and that's why he cannot reply.

Are you driving? I type.

If you are, you don't need to answer. Send.

I wouldn't want you to have an accident, of course. Send.

I will stop texting now. Send

Your all right, right? Send.

I meant, "you're," LOL. I'm sorry. Send.

Did you read my other texts? I fixed supper for you. Send

Let me know if you run out of battery. Send.

I turn on the TV. I suppose I'll watch some episodes of Miami Vice until Mr. Saruman texts back. I mean, Mr. Hanuman. Isn't technology fabulous? I can re-watch all the series I grew up with just the click of a button. Now I can judge the value of 1980s television from a mature perspective . . . Tom Selleck's hairy chest gives me a warm feeling running up and down my spine. And look at Olivia Brown. She looks fabulous in those faux leather pants.

I grab the phone again.

I'm watching an old episode of Miami Vice. Olivia Brown looks ut-

terly fabulous in faux leather pants and a long sleeve, tube top straight out of Flashdance.

I should post that on Facebook too. And on Twitter.

Now, since I'm already on my phone, let's see what's going on on Grindr, just in case, just to see what's happening in this town . . . Someone in Echo Park is inviting me to a *menage à trois*. A proof of virility is required: *Why no cok picz?* . . . I browse the photos of my digital Romeo. That half a gallon bottle of lotion next to a box of tissue against a wallpaper that cries my mother last redecorated this home in 1972 isn't too inspiring. And couldn't he pick up his dirty clothes from the floor before he flexed? I've seen better photos from suitors living in rural Ukraine . . . *I don't have X-rated pics*, I write to him. I know this is Grindr, but not all of us are that ordinary. Some of us prefer to post pictures that portray what lies within our soul. Photos of a beautiful sunset, the cover of our favorite book, an illustration we made of Freddie Mercury kissing David Bowie in our early twenties . . . *Take one*, he types back. I suppose I could take a picture or two of my genitalia, but let's check your private collection before, not because I'm interested in dating a cloned white man with the most common tendencies but to satisfy a purely scientific sentiment of curiou—Oh, my fucking God. That must be a foot long. Holy shit! And here's one of the boyfriend. He's an Adonis! And they're asking me to join them? Me? Are they sure? Did they see all of my photos? Did they read my profile? Do they know how short I am, how I sound, the things I say, and the car I drive? Maybe they sent this message by mistake. Holly, shit, I need to send a dick pic at once . . . I pull down my pants and start working on my Peter Pan to make him more photogenic.

The phone vibrates.

It's a message from my Indian Romeo. He literally caught me with my pants down.

You didn't unplug the freezer, did you?

Oh, that stupid freezer. I wish I had never bought it in the first place. *I did*, I type. *I won't be wasting energy on an empty freezer.*

The phone rings, a second later.

"Well, hello sailor," I answer the phone, in my best interpretation of a June 1944 pin-up girl waiting at the bar of the Hollywood Canteen for someone to offer her a martini. "Look who's showing signs of being alive—"

"You need to plug it back!"

I let out a little coquettish laugh. "I was just kidding," I say. "I don't want my whole house to stink of rotten crab."

"What crab?"

"The crab you put inside?" I say, making my statement sound like a question. "You texted me that today." Oy, Tom Selleck is wearing shorty shorts on a kayak. "Are you still coming up for dinner?"

"I can't, Charlie. I'm too tired. I've been driving since early in the morning."

"You don't have to stay late. It's not even eleven yet. Besides, you owe me: I'm taking care of your crab. You wouldn't want me to disconnect that freezer, would you?" I giggle.

"I'll be there in twenty minutes," Jignesh says after a short pause.

Oh, I'm sorry for you, you naughty and more-than-well-endowed, sexy Caucasian boys from Echo Park. I have a more attractive prospect than a one night stand with a couple that may or may not be siblings, judging by the similar length of their beards and haircuts, and who may eventually require therapy to solve the problem of why they can't get off without sharing their bed with a third person. I can't risk catching an STD. You probably don't have a pot to piss in, anyhow, as the vulgarity of your surroundings suggests in all of your photos. Jignesh does—three-quarters of a million dollars to be exact. Besides, based on how all my one-night encounters end, with me falling in love with a man who can't love me back, you probably don't want me in your bed. Ta-ta!

17

Courtship

Dinner at Charlie's goes without much incident. We eat, he talks for about an hour, then I leave, claiming I'll have to be at work early the next morning.

That was one helluva trip to Tijuana. God bless social media. Nina had her Instagram account connected to her Facebook and Twitter accounts. The photo of a poor donkey painted like a zebra has already gotten ninety-eight likes, forty-two hearts, a few shares, and many, many many, irrelevant comments. Two guys even started a fight. I had to interfere and tell them to play nicely. That's what Nina would have done, I suppose. Now her whole social network thinks that she's alive and traveling across the Baja peninsula, with limited access to Wi-Fi but having the most fantastic time of her life!

I left her backpack at the beach too, in hopes that the Mexican police find it and conclude that she had drowned surfing or something.

I'm forced to return to Charlie's home on Friday. I cannot say no. He's guarding the corpse. We watch an episode of *Downton Abbey*. Charlie spends the whole show praising the women's wardrobe while I brood over my unresolved problem.

Maybe I could burn Charlie's house, I daydream, looking around, while Charlie clings to my chest and rubs his face against my shoulder. Tonight, he called me his "little pot of Indian honey." That made me laugh. He's such a weirdo! Now, if I torched the house, the police might still find Nina's body, and having it be found this side of the border would be a mistake. Then again, they may come to think it was this little chatterbox who killed her . . . How much benzine would I need? Maybe I could just turn off the oven pilot. Would a kitchen explosion reach the garage? Probably not. And I've been seen coming and going out of this place too many times already for the police not to be suspicious.

"I'm sorry," Charlie interrupts my train of thought. "I think I'm a little bit farty. I ate dinner too fast."

I reach for a magazine to fan away the smell. I have to admit, though, that cuddling with this midget doesn't feel bad. He's quite amorous. I enjoy pinching his butt. One starts to like him, especially on the rare moments he's capable of keeping his mouth shut for more than one minute.

Before I leave, Charlie gives me some bad news.

"Now, Jiggy—I mean Jignesh, you told me you don't like that name, I apologize, I'm sorry—do you think you could take the freezer with you by the last day of the month? I know I said you could leave it here for as long as you needed, I'm sorry, but I'm offering covered parking with the rent of the other room, and I desperately need a roommate. I cannot afford this whole place by myself."

"Do you have someone already?"

"No one for sure, I'm afraid, but this guy is coming to see the room tomorrow. Honestly, I don't have my hopes set too high. He said he's looking for a job too—another recent graduate from film school. 'Oh, Honey,' I should have told him, 'I heard that Target is hiring. They pay slightly more than McDonald's.' I shouldn't be making jokes, I'm sorry, but I'm so desperately broke that I would take anyone at this point. Do you perchance know of someone with a steady job, looking to rent a room in beautiful West Adams? $950 a month, shared bathroom, but includes the garage."

"How much do you need for a deposit?" I hear myself asking.

18

Gage Weston's Ballsack

I'm sitting on the living room couch with my legs crossed. If I smoked, now would be the moment to light up a Virginia Slim, take a deep drag, stare off into the distance, and then exhale with a whimper.

It's been two months since Jignesh moved in. I would be lying if I said I wasn't curious about his reasons to buy the freezer, first, then keep it in my garage all this time and forbid me to ever set foot inside, but with him taking care of a few outstanding bills, sending Murat to repaint the kitchen, and, of course, paying his rent on time, I completely forgot about it.

I mentioned it once to Lucille. She told me to be careful.

"He could have a dead body inside," I replied, then took a long sip of my pumpkin latte. "I don't care."

I really didn't.

You see, there have been many men in my life. Tall. Short. Kind. And abusive. Mostly abusive, and let's not forget about that miserable rat, the Belgian bastard, whose name I cannot pronounce without getting a bitter taste. Jignesh is the first one with money. I didn't want to ruin it with stupid questions about a freezer.

Was I curious? Of course, I was, but so were Bluebeard's wives, and I am no Jean Parker. Therefore, I decided not to give it another thought. Why, with Jignesh and I doing so well as a couple? We still have separate rooms. He said he didn't want to rush things, and I respected his decision. Yet every once in a while, with him feeling lonely and me always horny, we've been sharing more than the couch for watching TV. But then I returned home this evening, after having spent Thanksgiving at Lucille and Marco's, carrying more turkey leftovers than I could fit inside the refrigerator.

"I guess I will have to put the rest inside Jignesh's freezer," I sang to myself, in my best interpretation of Marcia Cross from *Desperate Housewives*, then sashayed my way to the garage. I was in such an excellent mood. Lucille, Marco, and I had spent the whole afternoon listening to Wilson Phillips.

Jignesh hadn't returned from his parents' yet. Therefore, I couldn't ask for his permission to unlock the freezer. I didn't need a key, anyhow, just a screwdriver to remove the latch. I felt so manly, setting up a ladder against the wall to reach the top shelf, taking down the toolbox, selecting the right screwdriver—did I need a Phillips head or a flat one? I had to go down and check twice. *If my father could see me now*, I remember I thought. "He'd be so proud," I laughed. I bet I snorted too. I always snort when I laugh. "He would think I mended my ways and stopped using cosmetics."

I'm certainly glad my father wasn't there to see me, though, because it wasn't frozen Alaskan crab what I found inside that darn freezer.

Well, I'll be damned, I thought for a brief second. *This isn't Alaskan crab. This is a human body.* Then I screamed louder than Nicole Kidman in . . . well, any of her movies!

I shut the lid and, following my first instinct, ran to the middle of the street where I tried to scream again. Out came only a muffled bellowing. I stayed there, gasping and mewling in pain for a few minutes. If anyone had heard me scream before, no one came to my rescue, #CityOfAngels. Eventually, I reckoned I wasn't in any immediate danger. Jignesh wouldn't be back till late. His mother is not like Lucille, who starts cleaning and packing up leftovers for her guests the moment she puts the pie on the table. I went back inside and searched for my phone, planning to call the police. I couldn't find it. Then I remembered that I had connected it to Lucille's stereo, so we could listen to music on Spotify, and realized that I probably left it there.

I sat down on the couch and cried. Oh, boy, did I cry. Louder and more crestfallen than a Mexican soap opera actress who suddenly discovers that the man for whom she left everything behind, including her father's fortune, is a cold-blooded murderer. I know, calling Jignesh my man is rather a stretch. The French would refer to our relationship as *plan cul*, which is but an elegant way to say that we have no real attachments. Still, I felt shattered.

Again, it's not that I didn't have my suspicions. Jignesh can be rough sometimes. He's arrogant and unkind and envious of other people. Then again, most men I talk to end up being rough, arrogant, and unkind too. I assumed that Jignesh was but an ordinary man with ordinary man urges. Forcing me to stay in my place felt like his manly prerogative.

I was about to go and call the police from the neighbor's, but then I looked at the *Men of Colt* calendar on the wall that Marco gave me as a joke for Christmas—the joke was on him; I actually liked it—and it reminded me that today is only November 22, 2012, barely two weeks after Obama's reelection. Jignesh never pays his share of the rent before the thirtieth. And the mortgage is not due until the fourth.

"What should I do?" I asked, looking intensely at Gage Weston's ballsack.

Just last Monday, Tunisha reprimanded me at work for prattling over the phone with a client about our wedding.

"We're going to elope to New York," I told Dr. Kurash. "Just imagine, a beautiful, sunny day in Central Park, with lots of children running around, a butch lesbian wearing a dark suit officiating the ceremony, and us two, wearing white matching suits from Dolce & Gabbana . . . No, it wouldn't be recognized in California, I'm afraid, but maybe one day, cross your fingers . . ."

Thank God that Jade had just sold Dr. Kurash a new membership and had asked me to make conversation with him while she finished the paperwork. Otherwise, Tunisha would have fired me on the spot.

Anyways, that was Monday. What I did today is return to the couch and whimper some more. And I've been here ever since, sobbing my soul away, flinching at the slightest noise, puzzling over whether I should go to the neighbors' to call the police or pretend I found nothing. I only stood up to go pee, play on the computer *Chi Mai*, which is the only tune that could adequately serve as musical accompaniment to my current state, so crestfallen, and help myself to a slice of pie. Lucille's pumpkin pie is so delicious, nom-nom. I wish I had whipped cream, nom-nom.

I wish I had asked Jignesh to pay in advance for the last month too. That would have given me some time. I'm going to keep Jignesh's half-month deposit. Of course I am. Why shouldn't I? He's been hiding a body inside my garage. He may have a lot of legal expenses once he gets arrested, though. He'll probably want it back, and other than bringing a dead woman into my house, he hasn't caused any damages. He may end up asking me to repay for all the expenses he incurred since he moved in. He paid for the liner to build the fishpond. Oh, and what if I get in trouble too? I raise my t-shirt to clean my eyes. What if he says I was his accomplice? I sold him the freezer, *n'est-ce pas?* His boss saw me the day we went to his office . . . Oh, no! Did Jignesh kill Manuel too? No, that couldn't be. That was an accident. Wasn't it? His parents saw us, too, trying to put the freezer in their garage. Maybe they know. No. That old couple is so sweet. I can't imagine them helping Jiggy commit a crime. Although you never know with foreigners. Maybe killing is considered a sport in West India. If I were to blame anyone, I would blame that horrible sister of his, Sita. Jiggy detests her . . .

"Oh, my God!" I stand up, horrified. "The body inside the freezer is hers! JIGNESH KILLED HIS SISTER!"

No, that cannot be. The woman inside the freezer looked white, I think, sitting back down. Although . . . Anyone will look white when frozen . . . I need to go and check . . . Oh, no. I cannot make myself open that freezer again!

I cannot stay here either. I start walking across the room and back.

"Did Jignesh kill his sister?" I ask Gage Weston's penis.

Now, even if I had the guts to go and check, I don't remember what Sita looks like. I've seen her once. That's all . . . Who's coming next month? I turn the page of the calendar. I don't know this guy's name, but he sure looks yummy. Oh, there's a special offer for 2013. Should I order the *Couples* or the *Butt Beautiful?*

Okay, Charlie, relax. Breathe in and breathe out. You need to calm down. This is what you're gonna do: You'll fix yourself a cup of chamomile first and pop a Xanax. Then you'll light a relaxing candle, sit down, turn on the TV, and pretend you saw nothing—just until Jignesh pays the rent. That woman is dead. A few days more inside the freezer can't hurt her. Then, and only then, you will call the police.

"Why did Jignesh have to be a crazy murderer?" I fall on my knees, crying. "Maybe we weren't meant to be a couple, but he was the perfect roommate!"

Gage Weston's magnificent hard-on remains silent.

I cannot stay here. I need to go. Where? I should call Lucille and tell her. Maybe I could stay with her for a few days. Where is my phone? Where did I leave my stupid iPhone? Oh, yes, I left it at Lucille's. I should go back to her house . . . Can I drive? I can't. I can't even breathe, how could I drive? I'll call a Lyft. Where is my phone? I walk through the house looking for it. Where the fuck did I leave it? I enter my bedroom. Where the fuck did I put that stupid cellphone? Oh, God, I left it at Lucille and Marco's. I'm not thinking straight . . . And what am I going to say to Jignesh? He still needs to pay his share of the rent. Maybe I could ask him to leave a check on the kitchen counter. Then I'll ask Marco to come and pick it up while Jignesh's at work . . . But what if Jignesh attacks him? Lucille would never forgive me.

I hear a car pulling into the driveway.

He's back.

It's not even seven yet. Jignesh must have gotten into another fight with his mother. Should I run? I can't. My legs feel so brittle . . . *Men of Colt, please protect me. Give me the serenity to pretend nothing happened.*

I hear Jignesh insert his key into the door lock . . . "How was your day, Jignesh?" I'll ask. "Mine was extremely nice. I didn't find a dead woman inside the freezer. How was my day, you asked? Well, I didn't find a dead person inside that old freezer I sold you, how was yours? Terrific. No, I didn't find any frozen body, why do you ask?"

Maybe he's armed. Maybe he has a knife. Maybe he'll kill me.

"Mr. Charlie!" Jignesh sings, coming in. He's carrying two canvas bags full of food. "My mother sent us a lot of leftovers. We won't have to cook for a week."

I must remain calm. I must pretend nothing happened. He doesn't need to know I found out . . . OH FUCK! HE'S GONNA NOTICE I UNSCREWED THE LATCH! I got so scared I forgot to screw it back. *Sweet Southern Baby Jesus*, I can't let him enter the garage! But why would he go? He doesn't have a reason to go. Does he? It's full of junk. He can't park inside. I'll scurry in tonight, reattach the latch, and pretend nothing happened. That's it. Sit down, Charlie, be pretty, and remain calm. Imagine you're Audrey Hepburn in that first scene of *Roman Holiday*, trying to put on that damn shoe while presenting a straight face to the public.

"Are you all right?" Jignesh asks.

"I'm utterly and absolutely fabulous, thank you."

I cannot pretend to be Audrey Hepburn. I feel more like Julia Roberts in that Dr. Jekyll and Mr. Hyde movie—what was the title? The one where she falls in love with John Malkovich. She didn't look her best in that film if I'm allowed to be unkind. She's not the young girl, full of dreams with that fabulous disheveled brown hair from *Mystic Pizza*—

"What?" Jignesh asks. "What are you mumbling about pizza? Have you've been crying, Charlie?"

Jignesh sets the bags on the coffee table. One of them must have a large glass container. I clearly hear the thud when it hits the wood. *Kulfi*, perchance? Two months living with an Indian have turned me into an addict.

Jignesh sits next to me. "Are you okay?"

"Never better," I reply, immediately standing up and walking toward the dining table, which is a fairly stupid move because if Jignesh's going to suddenly attack me, I won't be able to escape anywhere safe.

"You look miserable."

"I watched an awfully sad commercial," I reply. "It had a doggie."

Jignesh laughs. "You're hopeless, Charlie. I, on the other hand, am in terribly good spirits." He lifts the bags and enters the kitchen. "I had to go to the office this morning before heading home. Mike's taking December off and wanted to go through some last-minute instructions." He looks at all the food that Lucille sent and never made it to the freezer. "You also got food, huh? What are we going to do with all this?" He cuts himself a slice of pie. "We'll have to throw out half of it. Anyway, long story short: I got season tickets for the opera."

"The LA Opera?" I ask.

I have never been to the opera since I moved to LA. I have never been to the opera, period. Not even when I lived in France. I only took one photograph of the *Palais Garnier* because it was the nineties and film was too expensive . . . The Belgian bastard mentioned once he would take me to *La Monnaie* in Brussels. It never happened. I went alone to a *friterie* and paid for my own *mitraillette*, instead . . .

"Madame Butterfly is playing," Jignesh says.

"I know," I mutter. The posters along Wilshire Boulevard are a constant reminder.

"They're in the sixth row," Jignesh says, pulling out the tickets.

Sixth row? I have to hold on to the edge of the dining table.

"A client gave them to Mike as a present this summer," Jignesh continues. "And he forgot. He doesn't care much about classical music. I found them today at the bottom of a drawer and asked him if I could have them. He said he'd rather give them away in a raffle, among everyone that works in the office. 'To be fair,' he said. I replied that if he didn't let me keep them, I would call the State of California and denounce him for all the terrible conditions in which he forces us to work. So, he did. Yay!" Jignesh claps. "He gave them to me. I would have smashed the company's seal on his head if he refused."

"Who would forget they had season tickets to the LA Opera?" I dare to ask.

"Mike did."

"And who are you planning to take with you?"

"I was hoping to take you, stupid. Who else? I know how much you like music. And you've been awfully kind, as you say."

"I suppose I have been." I reach for my nonexisting pearl necklace. "When is the next performance?"

"December 1. It's a Saturday."

December 1? I could perfectly do that. Attend Madame Butterfly on the first, then call the police on the second. "And the last one? How long is the season?"

Jignesh pulls a leaflet out of his pocket. "The last performance is *Dulce Rosa* in June."

June? As in *June 2013?* That's seven months from now. I couldn't possibly wait that long. I wouldn't be able to sleep with the apprehension of knowing that Sweeney Todd is only a few feet away from my bed.

"Oy, they're performing *The Flying Dutchman* in March!" Jignesh exclaims, still checking the leaflet. "And Cinderella. And Tosca!"

Cinderella? I return to the couch. *Tosca? Could I endure this for seven months?* My eyes dart briefly toward Gage Weston's ballsack. Jignesh returns to the living room, sits next to me, and hands me the leaflet. I don't know much about opera, but as a young, white homosexual growing up in godforsaken Leitchfield, Kentucky, I often dreamed of attending a performance. Our appreciation for the *beaux-arts* is one of those things that distinguishes us from the bullies.

The LA Opera, the leaflet reads, *at the Dorothy Chandler Pavilion.* Oh, what should I do? What would Jesus do if a murderous gentile invited him to a performance at the Dorothy Chandler Pavilion? And these tickets are for the season. There's no way on Earth I could ever afford sixth-row tickets for an entire season. I look away, hiding my tears. I haven't made enough sales this month to even pay for my share of the mortgage . . . *What would you do in my place?* I ask to Gage Weston. I'm almost twenty-five thousand dollars in credit card debt, still five years away from paying off my student loans, twenty-five years away from paying off my mortgage, and in a dead-end job working for ten dollars an hour plus commissions at a call center. Even if I waited until December 2 to call the police, how would I find another roommate fast enough to pay the mortgage the next month? And who's going to move into a house where they found a dead body?

Jignesh takes my hand. "Do we have a date on December 1? I'll buy you dinner too. Somewhere fancy . . . Oh, Charlie, you look adorable when you cry." He pinches my cheek. "Did the doggie die in that commercial?"

I nod.

"I'm terribly glad I moved in with you," Jignesh continues.

"You are?" I ask.

"You have an incredibly annoying voice, Charlie. You know that. And you text far too much. And you're not that good of a cook, I don't know how you came to think you are because you truly aren't. Still, I'm glad I moved in with you. You're kind. You're good looking. And you're very funny. I should have moved out of my parents' house a long time ago. It is a toxic environment. I thought it was smart to stay there and save money. Then something happened that forced me to make a decision . . . I cannot tell you what." His expression gets somber. "You wouldn't understand—"

"I don't think I could."

"These last few months living with you . . . Well, it's been a new life! My prose has never been better."

"I'm glad to hear that," I venture.

Jignesh kisses my cheek. Then he hugs me. "You want to play *maataa* and *baapaa?*" he whispers. "I'll be *baapaa.*"

Men always assume that because I'm small, I should play the role of the woman. And I'm always too polite to point out their error.

19

Sales Manager

What is this charge of $279 for? I type to Mike on the Google chat window. *PAYPAL, January 28, 2013. No further description.*

I'm in a terrible mood today. A terrible, horrible mood that unfortunately cannot be fixed by drinking yet another cup of Irish tea.

"I bought a guitar for a friend, Jignesh," Mike replies from his desk. "She paid me cash."

I heave a deep sigh. *How am I supposed to justify the expense?* I type.

"Put it against my debt. Make it a draw."

I turn around and glower at Mike. Then start typing: *Michael, I'm trying to impose some discipline on this VERY LOUD office by making EVERYONE, including YOU, use either their phone extension or the Google chat, instead of yelling at each other from over their desks.*

I cannot stand this open space design. One feels as if inside a cage full of chickens, all of them pooping and clucking and trying to call up the farmer's attention.

Mike replies: *okay.*

My bad mood has nothing to do with the testosterone injections that I've been taking to lose weight or having quit coffee. Charlie's being stupid. I'm mad because we're already in February, I haven't finished reconciling December, and I needed to finish sending all those stupid 1099s by the end of last month. That's why I am in such a fucking bad mood.

I had to quit coffee because I'm on the cleansing stage of the Candida

Diet. Tea isn't allowed either, but I couldn't go cold turkey. Without caffeine, I'd go on a killing rampage.

I know, I should be more positive. It's been almost four months since Nina's disappearance, and the police have stopped asking questions. No one has the slightest suspicion. The detective they assigned to the case ate the soup. He thinks she must have been kidnapped and killed in Tijuana. Thank God for Mexico's senseless violence, I chuckle.

I spoke to Nina's mother over the phone. That wasn't easy, I admit. She cried. I cried. I thought of apologizing. I probably did a couple of times, but not for having killed her young daughter but because I couldn't understand what she was saying. And I thought that Nina's accent was hard to understand! We laughed too: The day she left Germany, Nina almost missed her plane because she couldn't find her passport. They looked everywhere, under the car seats, inside the trunk, until they finally found it inside her suitcase.

"How dumb of her," I said.

Clara laughed too when I told her.

Nina's brother flew down to Tijuana, and he's been living there since November, Mike told me, trying to find his little sister. Poor guy. Would I go and try to find Sita if she disappeared? I probably wouldn't. Still, I wish I could give Nina's family a body. But how am I going to take a corpse down to Mexico? She's still in the freezer, inside of Charlie's garage. Maybe I should call the brother anonymously. But what would that solve?

And what did Justin do to find her? Nada. Did he drive to Tijuana too? Of course not. What a sewage rat. It's under circumstances like these when one gets to know the best and the worst of people. I would have done the impossible to find the woman I loved. Julius Claudius deserted the Roman army, for example. Anyway—I take a spoonful of the coconut oil I keep on my desk; the Candida Diet doesn't allow for candy—I don't want to think much about Nina because I start feeling anxious.

An email notification calls my attention. A charge recently went through. A charge to . . . Mrs. Radcliff's card!

"Clara," I say aloud from my desk, after logging into the merchant site to confirm who made it. "Did you read my note?"

What note? Appears on my screen.

"The note I wrote on Mrs. Radcliff's reservation," I continue. "It clearly said not to charge her card. She's sending a wire transfer."

I didn't see any message, she types.

"It was on her reservation," I holler.

My extension rings.

"*Cariño*, I'm looking at Mrs. Radcliff's reservation right now. I see nothing about not making a charge."

"You must be looking at the wrong reservation," I say, opening Mrs. Radcliff's reservation on my computer. I find nothing about not making a charge on the notes.

I stand up and walk to the railing.

"Could the person who deleted the note on Mrs. Radcliff's reservation be a man and stand up?" I ask.

No one moves.

"Are you sure you wrote that note?" Mike asks behind me.

"I wrote it yesterday, Michael," I reply, making an effort not to throw the jar of coconut oil at Mike's head. "Who deleted the note?" I ask, louder this time.

"It might be better if you go downstairs," Mike suggests.

"They can very well hear me from where I am. Thank you."

"I know they can, Jignesh, but it would be more polite."

More polite? For fuck's sake, what does my idiot boss know about managing an office? He's never here. I am the one putting up with these morons day after day . . . Still, he's the owner, I remind myself that. It is his name the one on the articles of incorporation. I take a deep breath, adjust my shirt to make sure it covers my love-handles and climb downstairs, step by step, lips closed tight, nostrils wide opened. Everyone gawks at me.

"I am not mad," I warn the sales team. "I am just disappointed. Can I please be informed who in the world deleted my note?"

"I found your note," Rogelio says with his peculiar Mexican accent. Today he's wearing a red beret. I find it so queer that he never wears a sombrero. "You wrote it on Mrs. Radcliff's reservation from last year."

Could that be so? I bend onto Rogelio's desk and see the date on the reservation . . . Shoot. The kid is right. And I had promised Mrs. Radcliff we wouldn't touch her credit card. I feel so embarrassed!

"You see," Clara says from behind. "I'm *inocente*."

"Ha-ha," laughs Justin swiveling in his chair.

I glower at him, then enter the kitchen to make myself another tea, the seventh that morning. I don't need more tea, of course, what I need is a cup of real coffee, but if I stay near that imbecile for too long, I may pick up a chair and kill him.

Five minutes later, I return to my desk. Mike's sight follows me. I ignore him. I start typing an email, cc'ing everyone, including the cleaners.

New Rule: Before you make a charge, you must check the notes from every prior reservation, up to five years, and make sure that we—

"I've been thinking," Mike says.

I raise my hand to stop him. Cannot he see that I am busy?

"I think we need a sales manager."

A sales manager? I turn at Mike, incredulity drawn in my mien.

He tilts his head inviting me to come closer.

I use my feet to pull my chair all the way to his desk. "We don't need a sales manager," I grouse in a low voice. "What we need is more discipline. These baboons cannot be bothered to make a phone call to close a deal. They're always asking for permission to give discounts. 'Can I include a couple of bikes?' We must think of our homeowners—"

"This is becoming too much for you, Jignesh," Mike interrupts me.

"It is not. And what do you mean it's becoming too much? I am perfectly capable of handling all my responsibilities."

"You have to think big, Jiggy-boy." Mike bends down to get closer. "We want to expand, hire more people. How many properties do we have? A hundred? I want two hundred. I want to cover all of Southern California. You won't be able to handle it all. I've been talking to this guy. He has a couple of homes in Malibu and . . ."

Oh, boy. Here we go, Mike and his plans for expansion. Synergy. Disruption. Leverage. Diversification. Big words of which he does not understand the meaning. *I wrote your business plan, you dumbass!* I pulled the expected 25 percent annual revenue increase out of my butthole. I economisted it. It's all grand claims based on no evidence, so you would stop whining about why the numbers didn't make sense. The formulas didn't even add up. Between the idiots downstairs who cannot close a deal, your poor planning, and all of my stealing, we'll be bankrupt within a year.

Thankfully, I've perfected the fine art of not paying attention. While Mike babbles, I think of Princess Salmonella MacFallog. Now she's expecting.

"Don't you think?" Mike ends.

I don't know what I think, but I nod.

"Well, let's hire a sales manager."

We create an ad. Correction, *I* create an ad, Mike marks a few typos, I make the corrections, and by the end of the day, we have it up and running on Craigslist. *Sales Manager for Vacation Rental Company.*

The next morning, there are 152 resumes in my inbox.

I am of the belief that to succeed in this world, you need luck. You don't have it, you probably wouldn't be a good fit for this company. The first twenty-five emails go to the trash. Anything that came in after 10:00 a.m. is deleted too. Now, let's see, I open an email at random. This one seems to have a lot of experience. He graduated from college in 1998, though . . . Too old! *Delete* . . . This one is from Arizona, and I hate red states. *Delete* . . . This one looks smarter than me. *Delete* . . . Now, this one sounds interesting: Jamal, twenty-six, a recent graduate from Baltimore. Not much experience, but let's find Jamal on Facebook . . . Not too bad. Let's see his other profile pictures . . . *Sweet Southern Baby Jesus*, as Mr. Charlie Hayworth would say. Jamal is definitely on the yes list.

By the end of the day, I have three candidates: A woman in her mid-fifties who used to work for Hewlett Packard—Daisy, but I refer to her as *Fiorina*—my precious Jamal, and one who looks good but already got another job, and that I only include so Mike can go for Jamal. Daisy has absolutely no chance, being old and that.

I give the three resumes to Mike.

"Jamal is my favorite," I say, tapping my finger on his resume.

Mike points at a red stain on the paper.

"Pizza sauce," I chuckle.

"We better hire someone white," he says.

Pardon me? "You cannot discriminate, Mike," I say, alarmed. "And how do you know Jamal is not white?"

"Call the other two," Mike gives me back the resumes.

"You cannot eliminate Jamal simply because you suspect he's not white."

"Did you google him?" Mike replies, tilting his head and raising his eyebrows.

"I did," I admit. "Still, it's wrong. It's racist!"

"Don't be so dramatic, Jignesh. I don't mean it in a racist way. I said white, but I meant someone smart. Besides, with you here, and now Rogelio, this office is getting a little too colorful. And he just graduated from college, for God's sake. Call those two and get more resumes."

I wish Mike's aftershave didn't smell so good. It would make it easier to hate him.

I choose a few more resumes, all from males with white, Anglo-Saxon, Protestant sounding names, as my boss requires. All very cute, all under twenty-six, hair on demand. My new favorite is Ryan. Last Halloween, he dressed like Spider-Man, according to his Instagram account . . . Dylan is a fan of *Star Wars* . . . Jack is a misogynist douchebag, I can tell from his tweets, but he photographs well shirtless. Therefore, he made the cut too.

In the next few days, I interview the best candidates at the corner coffeehouse. If I believe they could be a good candidate, I call Mike so he can finalize the interview. Not with everyone, of course. My photo-based selection method isn't perfect. Dylan, for instance, was surprisingly unattractive.

"You did graduate from high school, right?" I find myself asking often.

I know, choosing by photograph isn't ethical, but if we left it to real qualifications, we could end up hiring someone ugly. Or worse: fat! And I don't want to be reminded by someone else that I'm still overweight.

I couldn't continue with the Candida Diet. The restrictions were too harsh, but thanks to the testosterone injections, I've lost almost three pounds in less than eight weeks, thank you. Now I'm only fifty-five pounds away from my ideal weight.

"Jignesh, I just can't with this shit," Mike snaps after the tenth interview. "Where are you finding all these losers?"

It's during moments like this, when my boss treats me with such disrespect, that I feel proud I've been stealing money.

"It's hard to attract qualified labor at sixteen dollars an hour, Mike," I say, sucking up on my midafternoon kale and banana smoothie.

"Then raise it to eighteen. There's a lot of desperate people out there. I can't believe you can't find better."

We end up hiring the woman from HP, the one I nicknamed *Fiorina*, for twenty-five dollars per hour.

"That's my rate!" I demand Mike.

"She wanted forty," Mike replies.

A comely, middle-aged woman, dressed as if she worked at an office in Beverly Hills, she quits by lunch, nevertheless, after she realizes that the office has only one lavatory.

Another ad. Another round of interviews. It's been three weeks already. Then, one morning I arrive at an informal staff meeting. The Spanish angel, the Mexican hipster, the blonde girl from Illinois, and Mr. Jerk A-hole Douchebag III, also known as Justin, also known as Nina's ex-boyfriend, also known as my sworn worst enemy, think that the position should be filled in internally and that they all should be allowed to apply.

"I suppose it's only fair," I say, studying a stain on my hoodie from my pork-belly sandwich. "Send me your resumes," I add, nonchalantly, knowing all too well that Mike will reject them.

"Justin will do it for eighteen dollars," Mike says to me the next morning. He speaks in a low voice, so as not to be heard downstairs. "He just wants a bigger cut of commissions. That's it. And he'll still reply to rental inquiries."

"Justin?" I cannot hide the disgust on my face. "What about Clara or Gabrielle? Both have been with us longer. Clara is our best salesperson. The homeowners love her."

"This is no job for a woman," Mike replies.

Oh, you senseless, misogynist bastard! And to believe that I was once infatuated with you. To think that I stole your sweaty gym shorts so that I could sniff them in the privacy of the bathroom . . .

"You hired Daisy," I reply.

"That was a mistake."

"This is too. You cannot hire Justin for this position."

Mike gestures me to lower my voice. "I already did, Jignesh. I'm leaving for Brazil in a week, and I don't want to worry about this while I'm on vacation. Get all his paperwork ready, and let's have our first meeting tomorrow after he moves his computer upstairs."

"We are not going to share the mezzanine with Justin, are we? He's a Republican!"

"Jignesh, I vote Republican, you know that. Justin doesn't even vote."

"That's even worse!" I burst, then bolt downstairs, to the kitchen.

I need a coffee. With extra sugar. And a biscuit. Some reduced-fat milk chocolate . . .

Justin doesn't want the job, not at all. Why would he? He constantly evades responsibility. He has no leadership skills other than being a six-foot-tall white man. But he knows that I cannot stand him. That's why he wants the job. Nothing can make him happier than to upset me.

Swallowing all my pride, a minute before 5:00 p.m., I call to Justin's extension. "I need you to please fill out a W-4 form," I say.

All this time, we've been paying Justin as an independent contractor through his LLC, *Kletter Productions of Southern California*.

"I will need a copy of your driver's license, as well," I continue. "The one we have on file is from Virginia, and we need one from California."

"My driver's license expires this month," Justin responds. "I'm having a replacement mailed here." I want to say something about not using the office's address to receive personal correspondence. However, I can't think of any sound argument. "And I prefer to stay as an independent contractor," Justin continues. "I'll take care of my own taxes."

"That cannot be the case anymore, Mr. Kletter. You need to be a W-2 employee to satisfy the requirements of this position. Besides, only full-time employees qualify for insurance. Do you not want insurance?"

"I'm fine with not having insurance."

"Okay." I hang up. I turn to Mike: "He doesn't want the job anymore. Should I repost the ad? Jamal may still be available."

"Mike," Justin calls from his desk. "Can I talk to you outside for a second?"

Justin grabs all his stuff, and the two of them go out.

Ten minutes later, Mike returns alone.

"We're going to continue paying Justin the way we've been paying him so far," he says, from the bottom of the stairs.

"Why?" I ask coldly.

"It is more convenient for him."

"Why?"

"Because it is more convenient."

"Why?"

"Because he prefers it that way."

"Okay."

The girls must know why. I'll find out.

"Also," Mike continues, "please order Justin a company credit card."

Great. Yet another account to reconcile.

"I'll need his social security number," I reply.

"Don't you have it?"

"Justin never filled out a W-4."

"Why not? Jignesh, you're supposed to have all those documents in order!" Mike cries. "How can I run a company if you're not on top of these things? Remind me tomorrow—I gotta go now."

I squint my eyes. Apparently, Mike does not have the faintest idea of what a W-4 form is for.

"Is she pretty?" I venture before he heads downstairs.

"She's gorgeous," Mike laughs, closing the door.

20

Mireille Mathieu

"D'you all mind if I play some music?" I ask the girls at work.

No one replies. They're too busy on their phones doing what they do best, being efficient.

I have been listening to a lot of Mireille Mathieu to cope with the pain of learning that Jignesh is a murderer. And to Wagner, of course. *Der Fliegende Holländer.* I'll never forgive myself for being too poor to afford Wagner's Ring Cycle when it came to Los Angeles three years ago. Now life is giving me another chance.

I cannot lie. Madame Butterfly was magnificent.

Giving the role of Sharpless to a colored man was a nice detail, I wrote on my Yelp review. *It was superfluous!*

I meant to write "superlative," of course—stupid autocorrect.

I really don't know what I'd do *sans* Spotify. Or without wine. I've been drinking almost an entire bottle of Skinny Girl's Moscato every day. Only one hundred calories per glass, but it's starting to affect my finances, as well as my professional performance.

"Are you drunk again?" Tunisha asks me.

I shake my head slightly, looking at her over my sunglasses.

"Are you high, then?" Tunisha insists.

Oh, God. I may be gay, but I'm still from the deep South. A six-foot-tall black woman with a ruthless, Yankee attitude like Tunisha's is a harsh thing to take this early in the morning.

"I'm just tired," I say in my best Melanie Griffith. "I didn't sleep too well last night."

I haven't slept well for the last three months. A few times, I've woken up screaming, which isn't good, because then Jignesh rushes into my bedroom asking "what's going on, what's the problem?" and while it may be comforting to have a strong man run to your room every time you have a nightmare, it is not so when the man in question is also the cause of your night terrors. If only I were as strong as Julia Roberts in *Sleeping with the Enemy*. You would think it would be much easier to escape since we don't live in a fabulous contemporary modern Malibu mansion with fantastic views of the Pacific Ocean, but rather in a two-bedroom craftsman in West Adams with a view of a Mexican chop-shop across the street. Still, I cannot make myself leave.

I open my bottom drawer and discreetly serve myself a glass of Moscato. I pop a Vicodin too. The bottle of Xanax that my friend left is finally over.

Jignesh's been rather generous, I must say. He let me borrow money to complete the mortgage payment last month, and last week he brought home a couple of Eames chairs from one of the houses that his company manages.

"I cannot believe that one of your homeowners wanted to get rid of these chairs," I said, immediately sitting on one of them.

Too bad he kills. And with my finances being in the state they are, I'm not sure when I'll be ready for this to be over. I'm almost thirty thousand dollars in credit card debt, one year closer to paying off my student loans, but still twenty-seven years away from paying off my little home, and in a job with no future.

I refill my glass. Music is my only consolation.

Music, wine, Vicodin, and candy. These French macarons that Lucille brought me from San Francisco are incredibly delicious . . . Hmm, Sicilian pistachio . . . Violet Cassis . . . Nom-nom . . . They're so yummy. I must have gained at least five pounds since December.

"Could you please lower your music?"

I oblige. Jade is such a stuck-up bitch. Yes, she's pretty. Yes, she's nice. Yes, she's incredibly focused, and yes, she probably will be the top-seller again this year, but what for? She's thirty-four and still single.

Tick-tock, I mutter every time I pass by her desk. *Tick-tock. Your biological clock is ticking.*

Knowing that we will attend *The Flying Dutchman's* performance this coming weekend and *La Cenerentola* next month, is the only thing that keeps me going.

"It's been already three months since we saw Madame Butterfly," I say to Sherise. She laughs politely, as she always does whenever I approach her desk and start talking. "Still, every time I recall the experience, I feel a lump form in my throat as if it had just happened this morning. And now it's happening again," I sweeten my tone, "Jignesh and I, in our best clothes, at the Dorothy Chandler Pavilion, a wonder of midcentury architecture, with its white terrazzo floors . . ." I make a gesture with my right arm. "Its honey-toned onyx fixtures"—I wave my left hand through the air—"and its massive round chandeliers"—I raise both arms—"with hand-polished crystal from Munich."

Sherise ignores me.

"What an excellent occasion to wear that purple wool jacket from Kiton you never bought!" Lucille says over the phone.

Bitch. She knows too well that I cannot afford Kiton.

"I don't know if I will have the time to go shopping," I reply to Lucille . . . I'll never forget that purple jacket. Not in a million years. How could I? One never forgets his first love, his first kiss, the first time he saw the ocean. "I wore a turtleneck with my old blazer from Liz Claiborne to *Madame Butterfly*."

"*The Flying Dutchman* is different, though."

I know Lucille is making fun of me, but she's right. Wagner is different. And I still have a few days. I may not go for a seven thousand dollar jacket, but the East Dane site has a fabulous one from Rag & Bone discounted from $695 to $371, which is totally reasonable. I lean to the left to show it to Jade. She swivels her chair and turns her back at me.

"I could totally wear this jacket with jeans to work, don't you think?" I ask Sherise, as I checkout. "Not to the Dorothy Chandler, of course," I laugh. "I couldn't bear the embarrassment of showing up to the opera wearing denim!"

For the Dorothy Chandler, I buy a pair of engineered chinos from Paige. Only $295.

"And just a plain white shirt underneath, right?" I ask Tunisha. She pulled a chair to my desk, wanting to talk about my performance. "There's no point in spending more . . . Although, before we begin, Tush," I tap her arm, "let me check what's new at Bergdorf Goodman, just out of curiosity."

Tunisha rolls her eyes, but then she approves when the site opens, and we find a pair of Wingtip Oxfords from Austen Heller on sale for only $260.

"I once saw these shoes at Cole Haan at the Westfield Mall in Century City reduced from $372 to a mere $185 . . . Did I buy them? No, Tunisha, I drove off to Off-Broadway, hoping to find them there for twelve ninety-nine. I didn't, of course. And because I was too embarrassed to leave empty-handed, and the salesperson was this rather intriguing Latino guy who probably had a wife, what do I know, but kept smiling at me as if I were a young boy fresh from the Greyhound station, I bought a pair of Skechers instead, which I never wore. Lesson learned: when it's about shoes, spend money now, worry about your debts tomorrow . . . Done. You see? It didn't take more than two minutes."

"Yes, Lucille, I'm aware I'm spending much more money on clothes than the cost of the season ticket," I explain over the phone to my bitchy friend, who, once again, is being a cruel stepmother. "However, this is an investment. Jignesh and I will return to the Dorothy Chandler for *La Cenerentola* and then for *Tosca*. And then to the Broad Stage for *Dulce*

Rosa. And, who knows, maybe Jignesh will take me to the Ahmanson Theater too, to watch a ballet, and then to the Disney Concert Hall. I'll be squeezing a lot of juice from my new wardrobe."

"Maybe he'll fly you to the Met. If you're nice."

"He may, Lucille," I reply. "Jignesh's been making a lot of money."

He may. What do you know? If I keep my mouth shut and don't stir any trouble.

21

Justin

"Why don't you run some financials, Jignesh?"

It's after 7:00 p.m., on a Thursday. Everyone else is gone, but Mike thinks we need to have a meeting with Justin to go over the company's numbers because Mike's leaving on yet another six-week-long vacation tomorrow.

The week went by with everyone congratulating Justin for his new position and Mike making stupid jokes with Justin about how different the view was from upstairs. Justin's hourly rate went up only one dollar, for fuck's sake. It adds up to two thousand more a year but still is only one more dollar per hour. And it's two-thousand dollars the company cannot afford. First, of all, because Mike won't stop using the company's credit card to pay for his personal expenses, and, second, because I haven't returned the seven hundred and twenty-five thousand dollars I took. Apple went up in price since September, but I'm still forty thousand dollars in trouble.

I print the reports that Mike wanted. Three copies. The new "sales manager" needs one too. As if. I'm not worried. Justin probably has never seen a balance sheet in his life, and Mike cannot distinguish a PNL from a cash flow statement. Patience, Jiggy-boy. This may not be how you planned to spend your Thursday evening, you should be at home with Charlie, watching *Call the Midwife*, but this will take less than half an hour. Soon the two of them will get bored, and Mike will be out for the next six weeks. We'll assign some trivial tasks to Mr. Kletter to justify his new position, and ta-ta. By the time Mike returns, Apple should have gone up in value. Worst case scenario, I'll sell with a loss and put the missing difference under "miscellaneous expenses."

Mike puts on his reading glasses. "I feel old with these," he laughs.

I found out why Justin does not want to be on the payroll. All it took was buying the girls breakfast.

"His ex-wife sued him for child support," Gabrielle explained with a mouth full of cake. "And he's afraid he would lose 60 percent of his check."

"He was married?" I couldn't believe my ears. "He's so young! And he refuses to pay child support? That's criminal!"

"He sends money to his son," Clara defended him. "He just doesn't want his ex-wife to know where he works, but he calls the kid every week. He showed us his photos."

"Why is this *Due to Clients* account so high?" Justin asks, bringing me back to the office.

Huh? I wasn't expecting that question. *Why is it so high?* I don't know. I got distracted.

"It's jacking up our liabilities," Justin adds.

Is it? Oh, yes, it is, I peruse through the numbers in my copy.

"That's the money we receive as deposits for future rents," I explain, forcing a smile.

Mike raises an eyebrow.

Yesterday, he gave me Justin's social security number to order his new credit card. I ordered the card, but I also used the number to send a form DE-34, *Report of New Employees.* Justin may get so upset when he sees the notice from the State of California ordering us to garnish part of his wages that he may quit on the spot. If only Mike had asked me not to do it . . .

"Why is the account balance so high?" Mike asks.

Why is the account balance so high? I mimic Mike's words mentally. These two dimwits don't understand the first shit of accounting. "Because we've been having a good year," I reply, forcing a grin. "It's the money paid in advance for future rentals."

"But then the bank accounts should be just as high, right?" Justin asks. "If this number is true, we should have in the bank over a million dollars—"

Oopsie-doo. Yes, we should.

"—However, we only have a hundred and seventy-two thousand."

"There have been some expenses . . ." I reply.

"What expenses?"

"Travel," I say, glaring at Mike. "Business meals. Furniture we don't need, and various other company expenses."

"But this is money that still belongs to the renters, right?" Justin continues. "These are deposits. We shouldn't be spending this money, should we?"

We shouldn't be spending this money, should we? Stupid turd.

"Ask Mike," I say, rolling my eyes, then turning to my computer and pretending to check for new emails . . . Fucketty, fuck. I underestimated Justin. I should have cooked the numbers before the meeting.

"You've been using this money to pay for company expenses?" Justin asks Mike.

"It's an investment," Mike replies, doubtful. "Right Jignesh? What did we spend the money on?"

"We?" I ask, without turning around. "*You* spent it."

"But the difference is almost seven hundred and fifty thousand dollars," Justin exclaims.

"That's a lot!" Mike says. "That cannot be right, can it?"

"Check it out," I bluff. "It's all there. Travel. Furniture. Meals and Entertainment."

The truth is that Mike's irresponsible purchases can only account for about sixty thousand.

Justin's questions continue.

"Why is the amount we pay for Time Warner so high?"

"That's the internet for the condos in Santa Monica."

"Can you show me?" He pulls his chair toward my computer. I'm forced to run a quick report. "These are thirteen charges every month," he adds. "We have only eleven properties in that building."

Fuck. Justin isn't as stupid as I thought. He's going to find out I charge Charlie's and my family's cable bill on the company's credit card. I told them it was a company benefit . . . *Fuck, fuck, fuck, fucketty fuck.* Now he takes a calculator and is adding up all the expenses . . .

"Three thousand dollars a month in meals and entertainment?"

"Mike loves to eat out."

"Mike wasn't here last December. That month it was almost five thousand."

Shit. Why did I spend so much money in December? I cannot remember. "Let me double-check," I say, opening a register at random in Quickbooks. Now Mike pulls his chair closer to my desk too. What in the world is Nakedsword Media? Oops, I may have done some unauthorized charges that month. "Oh, I know!" I say, closing the register before either one could read the name of the vendor. "Most of these are travel expenses, from Mike. I must have misclassified a few."

It's now ten before nine, and Justin is still going through the reports. He keeps asking questions. I reply as best as I can, smiling when appropriate. My underpants feel as if I had sat in a puddle. Mike asked me to print even more reports, and now Justin's going through all of the vendor payments. Mike's getting worried. He's bored too, nonetheless, I can tell. He's been texting with someone for the last twenty minutes.

His phone rings.

"Hey, babe, how are you?" Mike answers with a melodic laugh, the sort of laugh a straight man only bestows to a booty-call. He goes downstairs.

Justin continues playing with the calculator.

"If this is correct," he finally says. "We're missing seven hundred and seventy-two thousand dollars."

"What?" Mike overhears, from downstairs. "That cannot be!"

"Yes, that cannot be," I snatch the report from Justin's hands. "Oh, I see," I laugh giddily. "This is not the right bank balance. It needs to be updated."

"Jignesh, you're going to give me a heart attack!" Mike yells from the bottom of the stairs, covering up his phone. "Office stuff," he adds to whoever is on the other side of the line, then he announces: "I'll be right back," and leaves the office.

"How can the account be over seven hundred and fifty thousand dollars off?" Justin asks.

"I haven't finished reconciling last month."

"Can we then see the bank balance online?"

"We can. But the bank balance is sensitive information. I cannot show it without Mike's authorization."

Justin glares at me for a second. "What are you hiding?" He asks with a smirk.

"I beg your pardon?"

"Never mind. Let's wait for Mike to come back, so he can give his authorization. Then you can show us why you're missing so much money from this report."

"That number is wrong, I told you."

Justin's grin only grows bigger. He checks the time on his phone and then puts his arms behind the back of his head.

"I suppose I can show you," I say, opening the browser. Justin puts his arms down and pulls his chair closer. "Where did I put that thingy?" I ruffle the papers under my monitor.

"What thingy?"

"The little electronic device. The token." I open a drawer and search inside. "I cannot log in unless I enter a code. It isn't here . . . I must have left it at home. How silly of me!"

"You fucking fag—" Justin begins laughing.

"I beg your pardon?"

"You're so full of crap," Justin continues. "You cannot show me the bank balance because these numbers aren't wrong. You're three-quarters of a million dollars off. You've been stealing from Mike all this time, haven't you? I thought you were just another annoying fag, angry because no one would dare to fuck his fat, flabby ass, but now I see that you're also a thief."

"I will not tolerate any of your insults, Justin."

"I caught you, didn't I? You little piece of third-world shit."

"How dare you? You're fired, Justin. Please leave this office at once."

"You're firing me?" Justin laughs. "You're the one who's getting his ass fired. And then you'll end up in jail."

"The balance is not correct, I told you." I wipe the sweat off my face with my sleeve.

"And you conveniently forgot the electronic device, so you cannot log in, huh?"

"As a matter of fact, I just remembered where I left the device. It's in my car. If you excuse me," I stand up, "I'll go fetch it."

"Oh, no. You're not going to leave this place." Justin also stands up. "If I let you go to your car, you won't be coming back. You're not leaving this place until Mike returns and we can call the police together."

"The token is in my car," I say as calmly and as coldly as I can. "If you don't believe me, come down with me. Then we can both log in, I'll show you the correct balance, we'll see who's right, who's wrong, and then you're going to leave and never come back to this office where obscene and discriminatory language will never be tolerated."

Justin remains silent for a second.

"That's up to Mike," he calls my bluff.

"Right," I reply. "That's up to Mike."

So, we go down to my car, where I know very well we won't find any electronic device because I don't really need one to log into Bank of America. What I have in the trunk of my car is a crowbar.

I'm still washing the blood off my hands by the time Mike returns, ten minutes later.

"Where are you guys?" he asks, running upstairs.

"Justin had to leave," I say from inside the bathroom. "He got a call from one of his homies."

"His car is still outside."

"They picked him up," I open the door. I'm shaking, but I manage to smile. "He told me to tell you goodbye."

Mike looks confused. "I guess we'll have to continue tomorrow, then."

"Tomorrow is Friday. That's Justin's day off."

"But now that Justin's the sales manager, I need him during the week."

"He said he already had plans. Don't worry, Mike. We fixed it. I had half a million in *Undeposited Funds*. The rest is from checks that haven't been cashed and pending charges from the credit card company."

"For Christ's sake, Jignesh, this cannot happen!"

"I know. That's why I'm so glad we got help. You want to see what we did?"

"Nah. It's almost ten. And I'm starving. Let's continue Monday."

"You won't be here on Monday."

"Oh, shit, that's true! I'm going to Rio!" Mike dances an imaginary samba. "And I still haven't packed! Call Justin and tell him to be here tomorrow. I want to talk to him before I leave."

"I will. Go eat. I'll close the office."

"Can you? You're a jewel, Jignesh. Sorry I was a bit harsh before. I get all skittish when I think we're losing money. Don't forget to set the alarm."

"Don't worry, I won't."

22

Dream

Last night I dreamt that all this killing affair had been a misunderstanding.

"A frozen girl!" Jignesh exclaimed in my dream, partly amused, partly offended, then pulled me out of the shower, where I was trying to remove sin from my skin with a metal loofah, dragged me to the garage, and opened the freezer. We found no girl inside. Only popsicles and Jennie-O frozen dinners. We took a popsicle each. I can't recollect what flavor I had. I suppose lemon because I always choose lemon, but Jignesh had cherry. "You see?" he said, between licks. "There was no dead person inside!" And then he started laughing. I laughed too, both because of my silly mistake and because the red-colored water dripping from Jignesh's mouth looked almost like blood. Then the neighbors showed up, and each took a popsicle. We all laughed. No one cared that I was stark-naked.

Ergo, this morning, before Jignesh wakes up, I go check. What if I imagined the whole thing and had been having kittens for nothing?

Once again, I put a ladder against the wall to reach the top shelf for the toolbox, climb down, realize I chose a screwdriver with the wrong blade, go up again, come down, unscrew the latch, and open the freezer.

Yes, she's still there. And now she has a companion.

This time, I don't scream. I gently close the lid and tell myself that this second body was probably already there, that I didn't see it the first time. I open the lid again. No. I couldn't have missed a second face. It is a white guy and based on how fresh he looks, a recent kill. Maybe from yesterday evening. I should tell Jignesh to start wrapping them in plastic, to prevent

♥ 135

freezer burn. What am I thinking, giving advice to a murderer? I close the freezer, screw the latch, go inside the house, have a little brandy and a Vicodin, and sit on the couch. I need a minute or two before I get on the road.

Lucille texts: *Excited about the Dorothy Chandler on Sunday?*

I am.

I am awfully excited, and I won't let anyone ruin it.

If Hillary survived Monica, I can survive this too.

I can wait for two more days.

23

Friday

"I am so tired, it's not even funny," I announce to the office as I come out of the kitchen holding a cup of coffee, my third one this morning.

Clara laughs. I regale her a candid smile.

"Why don't you just leave, Jignesh?" Gabrielle asks. "Mike never comes on Fridays."

"He's leaving tonight," I moan. "I have to stay until six in case he calls with last-minute instructions."

Rogelio intercepts me before I can reach the staircase. "Do you have the rates for the new house?"

I look at him from the corner of my eye. Rogelio is wearing a yellow beanie with a Dragon Ball T-shirt and sneakers that must have cost his entire month allowance. Then I climb the stairs one step at a time. Halfway up, I say, without turning: "Monday."

I haven't done one thing today. I don't have the animus. I had to sell all the stock I owned to return the company's money. Now I have an overdraft in my account, and I still owe Mike thirty-six thousand dollars.

Besides, I'm a little upset about what happened last night. Whoever said that killing is easy never committed a crime. Or carried a body into a freezer. What did I yell when I hit Justin? Something rather silly. I take a sip of my coffee. Something like *Bazinga!*

What are you laughing about? Clara asks through the Google chat.

Shoot. I forgot that everyone can hear anyone's farts in this office.

Never mind, I reply. *Go back to your work, encanto.*

Tins of Christmas sweets are shrinking, 2011 vs. 2012? I've been down-voting mildly interesting links on Reddit all morning, but this one is indeed, mildly interesting. I'll upvote it . . . Justin shouldn't have called me names or questioned me about the money. I had to drive across town with his body in my trunk, put it inside the freezer, return to the office to take Justin's car, drive all the way to Compton, make sure I didn't leave a hair inside, and then take an Uber back home. I didn't make it to bed until after three.

I'm not terribly sad, however. One cannot be too sad for someone like Justin. Only a wee disappointed. At myself. As much as I hated him, I didn't want him to die. Nobody deserves to die. We should all live as friends and be careful to never stick our noses into someone else's business . . . *What is the most universally hated thing in the world?* Why do people ask all these stupid questions on Reddit? The entire site is seemingly under the control of Midwest teenagers . . . *Mosquitoes* appears as the first answer. How odd. I would have bet on children.

I maintained a doughty spirit throughout the night. Still, the moment that Uber driver arrived, I started crying. Killing is pretty stressful. I may be damn good at it, but I never wanted to become a criminal.

The driver got worried. He thought I had been assaulted.

"My mother has cancer," I said. "She's going to die."

Awful, I know, but that was the first thing that came to my mind. One doesn't plan these things. They just happen.

TVGuide's website is missing the date of Sunday, March 10, 2013? I'll up-vote this. Maybe some of the tears I shed were also for Justin, I'm not that coldhearted. The poor guy hadn't turned thirty yet. He was very good looking, and as much of a jerk as he was, he had a bright future ahead of him: White, tall, straight, male—that's enough to guarantee anyone a decent life on this planet. With no self-worth issues, like yours truly, and a good understanding of financial statements, evidently. Trained in sales too. By me. I don't think he ever realized how good of a training he had with me. Yes, I am tough, like a Spartan, but that's how it's supposed to be. One cannot win if it's not a challenge. Challenges give life meaning.

At least he is now with the woman he loved, may her soul rest in peace, sharing the same freezer, waiting for redemption.

"*Majo*," Clara says, from the bottom of the stairs, interrupting my thoughts. "I'm going to deliver a bike to a guest."

I nod. We keep the bicycles we rent to our guests in the basement.

"Then I'll go to the store," Clara continues. "Do you want anything?"

"Yes," I reply, then reach for the petty cash box. "Could you bring me one of those pecan pies from the German bakery? I'm going to break my diet. Again." I pout cheekily. "And let's open a bottle of wine when you come back. Mike brought a full box last week. I'm a bit sad."

"*¿Por qué, cariño?*" Clara pouts too.

"*No lo sé.*"

"Was someone mean to you?"

"That bitch, Justin."

I know, how disrespectful, but I cannot disclose his death just yet.

"I was meaner to him, though." I grin.

Clara laughs. "*Ustedes dos van a terminar matándose.*"

"*Sí*," I reply, and she leaves. I didn't understand one word of what she said, but I love, love, love the way Clara speaks to me in Spanish. She always puts me in a better mood. She has such a big heart. I feel sorry sometimes for stealing from her commissions. Oh, I should be like Clara and always be happy too. I should share the beauty of my pearly teeth more often. I know it's hard to believe, but underneath this facade of severity and stoicism hides a bundle of joy—I cannot allow myself to be blue. Off with the negative thinking! It's been only half a day since Justin left us, but the office already breathes a much gentler air.

"Rogelio," I say, standing up, "play some Mexican cumbia."

"I don't like cumbia," he replies, mortified.

"But you're Mexican!" I insist. "You must like cumbia and merengue. ¡*Fiesta pachanga*! ¡*Arriba, Arriba*! ¡*Mariachi*! We have to celebrate."

"Celebrate what, Jignesh?"

"That we're young. That we're alive. That it's Friday, and Mike is going on a long, long, long vacation."

Clara returns.

"The bicycles are all gone!"

"What do you mean by all gone?" asks Gabrielle.

"They're gone," Clara repeats. "Someone must have left the garage door open. They came in and broke the lock."

"Venice!" I cry. "This place is full of thieves."

The four of us go downstairs to the crime scene. The thieves broke the lock, and the chain that held all the bikes together is now on the floor as if it were a dead snake . . . Maybe it was I who didn't close the garage last night. I can't remember.

"I think we're definitely going to need that pecan pie," I say to Clara.

"¡Y el vino!" Rogelio adds.

Mike calls my extension a minute before five. I don't want to pick up. I ate too much pie, and the wine made me sleepy. He's probably already at the airport. Should I let it go to voicemail? I can't. He will keep trying or call someone else's extension.

I pick up the phone and burst: "Someone left the garage door open last night, and they stole all the bicycles."

"What?" Mike responds. He wasn't expecting this. "All of them? Bastards! How many were there?"

"At least fifteen, according to the spreadsheet which these buffoons you employ never update. Are you at the airport?"

"I'm on my way there."

"I already ordered more bikes, no point in crying. They'll bring them up tomorrow morning. Murat is going to receive them. That is, if he doesn't oversleep. It's Friday, so he must have started drinking already." I take a sip of wine. "Do you want me to write a nasty letter to the property manager asking him to install automatic doors? I already did, and I copied every tenant in this building."

I have a Master of Arts in being offensive with an emphasis on using ALL CAPS for certain words only.

"When did it happen?" Mike asks.

"Last night."

"Dammit. Did you call Justin?"

"Missing in action," I sing. "*Told ya.*" I'm watching videos of Jenna Marbles on YouTube. She's so funny! "Today's Justin's day off, remember? He never answers his phone on Fridays."

"I'll call him tomorrow from Rio. Fifteen bikes? Fuck! Anyway," Mike sighs, "we'll catch the thieves this time."

"Will we?" I can't help but impose a sarcastic tone to my words. I left Jenna Marbles, and now I'm watching *Top 10 Most Paused Movie Moments.*

"We installed cameras in the garage," Mike says.

"I beg your pardon?" I ask.

Mike is too proud of his smart idea to notice the sudden change in my tone.

"Murat and I did it last week."

"And who's watching those cameras?" I venture.

"Me. It goes directly to the cloud."

"Oh. Probably they were just kids." I pretend to laugh. "How long do they keep the footage?"

"Forever," Mike replies. "Anything that goes onto the cloud is forever. I have the app on my phone. I can check right now who stole the bikes on my cell phone. Let me put you on speaker."

"Oh, you don't want to start your vacation worrying about that."

"This is the third time they've broken in and stolen our bikes, Jignesh. This time I want to catch them."

I remind Mike of the dangers of driving and using his phone, which he disregards. I remind him that his last-minute instructions are more important. Mike agrees, reluctantly. He cannot remember the name of the app, anyhow, and, thank God, he has too many on his iPhone. While he talks, I sit at his desk and log into his email, search for "security camera," follow a link, choose *log in*, choose *forgot my password*, get a new password, then I immediately delete the email. By the time Mike is done with his list of errands, finds the app, and tries to log in, the app no longer takes his old password. At the third attempt, he gets blocked.

"Damn it!" he says at last. "Okay, Jignesh. You'll have to do it. I need to eat before I board the plane. Do you want anything from Brazil?"

"A Brazilian?" I joke.

We hang up.

"Clara?"

"¿Sí, cariño?"

"I think I'll need another slice of pecan pie. Do you mind going back to the store?"

I log in again and look for the footage from last night. I know the exact time it occurred, so it takes me a minute to find it. I can see myself opening the trunk, bending over to look inside, taking out a wrench and hitting Justin right on his temple.

I get so terrified that I let out a fart. It stinks terribly. Rogelio is coming up, probably with some silly question about a rental. He stops halfway.

"I'm leaving," he says, wrinkling his nose. "I just wanted to check if you needed anything else."

I can't force myself to utter one word. I simply shake my head.

Rogelio waves a peace sign and climbs downstairs.

24

Johohoe!

It's Sunday morning, and I'm in a terrible state, hardly in the mood for my traditional kale, oats, and cornmeal pancakes. Jignesh looks rather skittish too. His face is as pale as Meryl Streep's was in *The French Lieutenant's Woman* when she first sees Jeremy Irons at The Cobb in Lyme Regis's harbor.

"Do you still want to go to the Opera?" Jignesh asks without lifting his eyes from his plate.

I put my fork down. He must be kidding me. I'm wearing my new silk robe from Ralph Lauren—since this will be a special occasion, there was no point in buying only clothes for the evening—I haven't eaten anything but steamed broccoli for the last two weeks so I would be the skinniest man at the Dorothy Chandler—I'm having only half a pancake today and totally planning to barf it up—and I have lived for the last three months with the oppressive fear on my chest of not knowing whether the man I share a roof and sometimes a bed with is going to murder me. And after what I saw in the garage on Friday morning . . .

"I'm really looking forward to it," I say, with a sad lilt to my words like a heartbroken Kate Winslet in *Sense and Sensibility* after losing Willoughby while trying not to ruin my fifty dollar manicure from Kinara as I scratch the table from underneath.

I don't dare get mad, lest Jignesh gets mad too and kills me, the butter knife inches away from his hand and all. The disappointment on my face must be evident, however, for he doesn't insist. He briefly looks at me, then continues drinking his coffee in silence.

It's been a rather uneasy two days. A rather uneasy three months, since I discovered the first body.

Friday, I closed yet another week without having a single sale, and Tunisha had to let me go.

I did like Julianne Moore in *Safe* and started sobbing quietly. Poor Tunisha. She's an excellent boss and an awfully inspiring person, but she doesn't know what to do when white people start crying. She got all mortified like that one time when that irresponsible meth addict—what's her face? some trashy suburban name like Kimberly or Peggy—started crying too because Tunisha wouldn't approve an advance on her commissions. Kimberly had terrible skin, but her hair color was just gorgeous. And it was her natural color, I imagine, you wouldn't think that a drug addict driving a 1987 Crown Victoria full of ten years of fast-food wrappers would spend her hard-earned commissions on hair coloring, would you? Not when her teeth and skin were what needed attention. Anyway, Tunisha is such a great supervisor. She's always super considerate. She has a bright future ahead within the company. The last thing I wanted to do was to make her feel uncomfortable. After a minute, I brushed away my tears, took a deep breath, said, "thank you for everything, Tunisha," and that I would just go empty my desk and leave.

When I reached the door, all the repressed emotions came out at once, however. "I thought he was the man I would spend the rest of my life with," I think I bawled at one point. "But he kills people!" Thank God that Tunisha couldn't understand what I was saying. She called Sherise to bring me a glass of water. When I calmed down, I promised Tunisha I would do better if she just gave me another chance. I even knelt down and attempted to kiss her feet . . .

Apparently, Jignesh had problems at work too. What precisely, he wouldn't tell me, but the meal we had on Friday evening was the saddest meal we have had since he moved in. I couldn't talk and he wouldn't.

He spent the whole day yesterday at his office because of some emergency he had to deal with. I can only hope he wasn't killing more people.

I decided to visit my friend Lucille in hopes that she could, well, adopt me?

I hadn't stepped out of the car when she came running as happy as a dog on its first day at the beach: "We're pregnant!"

Lucille is a horrible, horrible person, but I could not ruin her one day of happiness, could I? She and Marco have been trying to have a baby for months—what for? It's beyond my grasp. She has such a nice figure . . . Nom-nom, today's pancakes are so good, I'm glad I added coconut oil to the batter instead of butter. Anyways, I didn't tell Lucille that I had lost my job. I simply let her talk and talk baby while I internally stewed in my private tragedy. At last, she asked: "So how are things going between you and Jignesh?"

"Oh, marvelous!" I replied.

What else could I have said? For the first time since I met Lucille, her tone didn't sound like a reprimand. I didn't want her to feel disappointed.

"And tomorrow is the big day!" She clapped.

"Oh, yes," I laughed as if I had forgotten all about it. "*Der Fliegende Holländer.*"

I'm positively looking forward to tonight's performance, I can't deny it. I know the lyrics by heart already: *Johohoe! Johohohoe! Johohohoe! Hoe! Hoe! Hoe! Hoe!* Oh, the satisfaction I know I'll get when, once more, I take a selfie donning my super expensive razor jacket from Rag & Bone at the entrance of the Dorothy Chandler Pavilion, check-in on Facebook, and then I see all those likes flowing in, especially those from all the people I left behind in Kentucky who never thought I would make it as far as Cincinnati . . . That's what keeps me alive.

"I never truly loved your father," I imagine my septuagenarian self in a rocking chair telling our grown-up children. "But that was the best night of my life."

And what a wonderful night it is, even if dinner makes me a little bit gassy. I know the Dorothy Chandler Pavilion is only a music hall, and that there are many fantastic music halls on this planet, but what an incredibly glamorous one this is. The tall concrete columns. The terrazzo floors. The gold. The mirrors. The enormous chandeliers in the lobby. Everyone looks awfully well dressed, if a little old, and mostly Jewish. The only poor people I see are all homosexuals. *Oh, yes, I know you're poor, you little Hollywood flower,* I mentally sneer at one hipster. *Your perfectly well-groomed beard and excessively tall pompadour can't fool me. Those blue jeans are from the GAP, and that blazer cries Nordstrom Rack at the Beverly Connection* . . . Jiggy is wearing a suit. He looks incredibly handsome. He's not as fabulously dressed as I am, but that's all right. Among straight power couples, the man is never as well dressed as the woman. That would make me the woman, but that's all right too. Jignesh is the strength and the aggression. I am the wits, the good taste, and discernment. I am the fertile soil. He is the seed and the tilting water.

He still looks agitated. I wish he shared my excitement. Well, who cares? This is my night, and mine only. After everything I've been through . . . At times, in the last three months, I thought that a night at the opera wasn't worth the agony of sharing my home with a murderer. Now, surrounded by all this wonderful midcentury architecture, I realize that this night is worth a thousand if not a million nights of apprehension. I can only imagine the joy I'll feel the night we get to go to the Oscars . . .

How old was Senta supposed to be? The pamphlet only refers to her as a "maiden." Couldn't they find a younger singer? I discreetly pull out my phone to google the plot, but first, I check whether I've gotten more likes since I checked-in . . . Only twelve so far. People must be watching television . . .

I never realized before because I was always on Tumblr while listening to the music, but this opera is incredibly dull. I'm falling asleep. Jignesh seems attentive to the plot, though. Even moved. Every so often, he cleans his nose on the cuff of his sleeve and brushes away a tear with his fingers . . . Maybe he didn't kill those people. Perhaps he's only hiding them for somebody else, as a favor . . .

I need to pass gas.

"I shouldn't have had pasta for dinner," I whisper to Jignesh.

I really shouldn't have, but I had been craving a delicious carbonara since that one time that Lucille took me to that restaurant on Sunset—what was the name? I cannot remember . . .

As soon as the intermission starts, I rush to the bathroom. And who do I see at the urinals there? That miserable rat, Jay. Oh, you didn't miss his name from before, this is the first time I've mentioned him. A quarter Mexican, a quarter German, half Filipino. Quintessential LA.

Jay and I had a Grindr rendezvous once before I met Jignesh. Ten minutes into our date, right before the server brought our food, Jay stood up and said: "This is not gonna work," and left me there, at the Urth café on Melrose, with two huge meals and a bill that I couldn't fit on one credit card, wondering what I had done or said to upset him.

Part of me wants him to see me. Part of me wants to hide inside a stall and wail quietly until he leaves. Which wouldn't be a bad idea since I still need to fart, but there's a long line for the stalls, and right now, there's no empty urinal but the one next to his. Maybe fate wanted us to be again next to each other. I figure I'll just go ahead with my business and pretend I didn't recognize him. If he says hi, I'll go, like, "Oh, hi—" and then look sideways, as if I couldn't recollect his name. Jay Martínez, I even remember that his favorite book is *The Alchemist*, but that will teach him. Then I'll ask, using my best Ginger Rogers' smile, "where are you seating?"

"Rear orchestra," I expect him to say. "Letter Z."

"Oh, at least, it isn't double Z, dear. Or the balcony loge," I will laugh.

"My fiancé and I are in the sixth row, letter D . . . So close that you can almost touch the performers."

I start peeing next to Jay, and, well, those urinals have no separators, so, of course, I am tempted to check real fast what I was once prevented from seeing because I failed to meet Jay's highly unrealistic expectations. I do so not in a disrespectful way, not at all, merely with the side of my eye, and to satisfy a scientific curiosity of repressed lust. A quarter Mexican, a quarter German, and a half Filipino. Unfortunately, Jay notices what I'm trying to do and, before I could say hi, or smile, or give a compliment, which I shouldn't really because all I could see was the stream coming down and not much else, he snorts, shakes vigorously, and leaves.

Well, that was just rude.

I truly don't understand people that obtain satisfaction out of making everyone else feel inappropriate.

I wash my hands and return to my seat.

"Are you having a good time?" I ask Jignesh.

He nods. He doesn't seem to be having one, however.

I offer him one bite of a strawberry macaron I snuck in. He waves his hand and mutters an inaudible, "No, thank you."

"Charlie," I hear Jignesh call my name. "Wake up. It's over."

"What?"

"The opera is over."

Everyone around me has stood up. People are clapping and cheering. Oh, boy, I slept through the whole third act. I raise up and manage to start clapping too. Jignesh is clapping louder than anyone else. He's crying too. He's not even trying to hide it.

"Why are you crying?" I ask, still groggy.

"She threw herself into the ocean, out of love. He's dead too. Now they're together, in heaven."

"She drowned?"

Jignesh nods.

"Did he drown too?"

"I think so," Jignesh responds.

"You mean you didn't kill them?" I ask, hopeful. "Good gracious, I thought the worse when I opened the freezer and saw the two—Oh," I interrupt myself. Oh, fucketty fuck, as Jignesh often says. From the expression on his face, I can infer now that he was talking about Senta and the Flying Dutchman and not about the two bodies he keeps in the freezer. I shut my mouth and continue clapping.

I don't say another word until we're on the highway.

"I saw someone at the bathroom I wish I hadn't seen," I start. I am the one driving. "Not that his name is worth mentioning."

Jignesh doesn't reply. I pull out my phone to check Facebook. *Only twenty-six likes?* By now, I would have expected at least a hundred. Oh, I forgot to tweet about it!

"Who are you texting?" Jignesh asks briskly.

Why is he so apprehensive?

"I know it isn't safe to text and drive, but I'm not texting anyone, Jiggy. I'm tweeting about our marvelous night at—Oh," I interrupt myself, realizing why he asks. I've been pretending for so long that nothing happened that I forgot that tonight something *did* happen. "Well, yes," I put my phone down and honey my tone as much as possible. "Let's address that. I said something inside the theater that maybe I shouldn't have said."

Jignesh remains silent.

"And I don't want to jump to conclusions. Maybe this is all a terrible misunderstanding, but—"

"But what?" Jignesh snaps.

Oh, boy, he's livid. I shouldn't confront a murderer while on the freeway driving at seventy miles per hour, should I? I suppose that taking the next exit, asking Jignesh politely to step out, and then speeding up is out of the question.

"—don't you think that the woman that played Senta seemed a little too old to play a teenager?" I finish my sentence.

"For Christ's sake, Charlie. Stop pretending," Jignesh bursts out. "I know what you saw. It was an accident."

"Casting can be, yes," I continue. "John Travolta comes to mind, for example. His Edna Turnblad will never be as good as Divine's. And let's not talk about Sofia Coppola as Mary Corleone—"

"I didn't mean to kill her."

"I know you didn't."

Jignesh remains silent. I pull out my phone again in an attempt to find solace in social media.

"I'm only checking if someone else liked our photo," I say. I don't want Jignesh to think that I'm texting 911 or something . . . Oh, fuck, I didn't see that semi. It almost hit me!

"She laughed at me," Jignesh continues, thick tears rolling down his cheeks. "She insulted me—she insulted my writing. I got so upset that I chased her downstairs. She fell. Then I fell too. On top of her. And then she stopped breathing. It was an accident!"

That sounds utterly rational, I reckon, staring at the semi I almost rolled under. I'd get quite emotional, too, if someone criticized me.

"And the man?" I venture, after a short period of silence. "Was he an accident too?"

Jignesh starts sobbing. And then bawling, like a Mary Magdalene, you would say, had the role of Mary Magdalene been given to an overweight Indian man with murderous tendencies instead of Yvonne Elliman.

"Now, stay calm, Jiggy-boy," I say, beginning to cry too. "I'm getting a tad nervous here, and we don't want to have an accident."

"What are we going to do?" He wails.

"We?" I shriek, then immediately regret it. I shouldn't sound too accusatory. "I mean, it's been a while since I sold you that freezer. If you're innocent, as you say you are—and I completely believe you are, Jignesh,

I don't have any doubt about that—you've had more than enough time to do something."

"But I'm not innocent," Jignesh replies. "I'm a murderer!"

"But you just said it was an accident." Now I'm crying too.

"It was. But I killed them."

"Oh, Jiggy. I don't want to lose my house! If the police find out and you end up being arrested—"

"I'm not going to get arrested." Jignesh hits the glove compartment as if it were the head of the only witness.

"Of course you won't," I say, stiffening up. "And why would the police find out? They have no reason to suspect you . . ." If I open the door and jump out of the car, what are the chances I could survive? "In any case, I wonder if you could pay the rent a few days in advance this month. Just this time, since I lost my job and—"

"You lost your job?" Jignesh interrupts me.

I nod.

"—in case anything happens."

"Nothing will happen." Jignesh cleans his nose with the back of his hand, and then his hand on his trousers. "I'll pay your part of the rent, too, if you help me."

"That would be extremely helpful."

"I'll help you pay your credit card debt too."

I clench my hands to the wheel. "Sweet Southern Baby Jesus, Jignesh, how do you know about my credit card debt?"

"You never stop talking about it."

Well, I suppose that's correct. Even so, that a confessed murderer knows so much about me is rather unsettling.

"Just keep your mouth shut, Charlie. Just for a few days more, until I can get rid of the bodies. I'll pay rent in advance for the next six months if you help me. I promise. I have the money."

I steal a quick look at Jignesh. I know he has the money. I haven't been able to check the balance on his *Charles Schwab* account since he moved in because he password-protected both his phone and his laptop, but, knock on wood, by now his three-quarters of a million dollars must have grown a little.

"But then I'll have to find a new roommate," I venture.

"I'll help you find one. One better than me. You can keep my deposit."

"Oh, Jiggy, finding a new roommate won't be easy. You know the neighborhood is in transition. The front lawn has to be reseeded. The flooring needs to be replaced. And I wanted to put wallpaper in the hallway . . ."

Jignesh cleans his face with the collar of his jacket. "I'll help with that too."

"Oh, that's not what I meant. Not at all! But now I cannot unsay it, can I? The house needs a lot of repairs, and if changing the wooden floor will make you feel a little less guilty . . ."

I know. Jesus would not have asked for a new wooden floor had he discovered that one of his apostles was a cold-blooded murderer. However, he didn't have a house of his own, to begin with, and mine is in a terrible condition.

I look inside my pockets for a Vicodin. I always carry one with me, in case I need it.

"Can I have one too?" Jignesh asks.

It is the only one I have. I bite it and give Jignesh one-half.

I'm terribly scared. I won't pretend I am not. As soon as we return home, I'm planning to lock the door to my room, put the dresser against it, wait for Jignesh to fall asleep, then escape through the back window and run down the street crying for help from the neighbors. Still, I cannot help but feel sorry for the poor oaf. He's shaking like calf foot's jelly.

Jignesh is still mopping tears by the time we reach home.

"You're not going to call the police, are you?" he asks.

I shake my head. He looks down at his feet, probably because he doesn't believe me. We enter the house and walk into our separate bedrooms.

I do as planned. I lock the door and immediately push the dresser against it. Then I sit on my bed, biting my pinkie nail, waiting for signs that Jignesh has fallen asleep to slip out of the window . . . Still only twenty-six likes, and not even one comment . . . Oh, Aunt Lou-Anne shouldn't have shared this Hillary Clinton meme. Yes, an all-purple pantsuit isn't perhaps the best choice for Madam Secretary, but that doesn't make her look like Barney. Aunt Lou-Anne is one of the meanest persons I know . . .

Lucille sends me a message: *How did it go?*

The night hasn't ended, I reply.

What else could I say?

This might be your last chance, Charlie. Don't fuck it up, Lucille replies, adding an angry emoji.

Well, that's just rude.

I open my email. My parents wrote me. How nice of them. They probably have a lot of questions. I couldn't resist telling them, too, about our visit to the Dorothy Chandler . . .

Don't fuck it up, they wrote. They didn't even sign their email.

Well, I'll be damned, I put my phone away. Now I'm upset. I didn't fuck it up. Jignesh did. By killing two people. Escaping for your dear life doesn't count as fucking it up, does it? Then again, maybe they're right. After all, Jignesh proposed to pay for half a year's mortgage. But what if they're not and I become his third victim?

I undress and put on my pajamas. Then I kneel by my bed.

Dear Jesus, I pray, *please bring the answer to my conundrum during my sleep. Amen.*

I won't be able to fall asleep without taking my melatonin, though.

I push the dresser away and open the door. I find Jignesh in the living room, sitting in complete darkness, wearing a trainer suit and sneakers.

"What are you doing?" I ask.

"Waiting for the police," Jignesh replies with the saddest face. "I thought I better wear something comfortable if I was going to spend the night in jail."

"Why would the police come?" I ask.

"You mean you didn't call them?"

I shake my head.

Jignesh breaths out. "I didn't believe you when you said you wouldn't."

"I thought it would be better if I waited a bit. You'd understand the predicament I'm in, Jiggy. Without a job and unable to afford my mortgage payments . . ."

He doesn't respond. I enter the kitchen.

"I will make every payment until you find another job," Jignesh eventually says.

I reenter the living room. "That would be awfully nice," I pop two pills. "Thank you. You're not going to kill me, are you?"

"I was planning to," Jignesh responds, raising a pillow. "But then I realized I couldn't. I may not show it often, Charlie, but I've grown used to you."

"One can get used to worse things."

"I find myself craving your company."

"That is a lovely thing to say, thank you. I appreciate everything you've done for this house too."

"I'm keen on the little moments of quietude between us as much as one can be keen on shade during a hot day of summer," Jignesh continues. "And we're more than roommates, aren't we, Charlie? We're more than friends. That's why I told Mike that I'd quit if he didn't give me the opera tickets. I knew you would love to come along. Besides, if I killed you, it would only make things more complicated—three bodies instead of just two. You're quite small, but there's barely any more space in that freezer. And the police will start asking questions about Justin's disappearance any day now. I don't want them to start asking questions about you too."

"You could just say I returned to Kentucky. Anyway, threatening Mike for those tickets was an awfully nice thing to do. Thank you."

Jignesh simpers.

I sit next to him. Then, looking at him straight in the eye, I say: "I will never call the police on you, Jiggy-boy. I promise."

At least not before la Cenerentola, I think, which is in April. Then I may think it over.

"Don't call me that," he says. "I don't like it."

I open my mouth to apologize, but then he reaches out and kisses me—a tender kiss, like that of a child expecting forgiveness. I tilt my head down, trying to resist him, but then comes a second kiss, slightly more aggressive . . . I quiver. Jignesh's tongue clumsily explores the rim of my nose. My hand runs along his thigh. I feel the way Anna Calder-Marshall must have felt in that scene in *Wuthering Heights* when she's reunited with Heathcliff. I keep my eyes closed, though. I don't want Timothy Dalton to see the guilt in my pupils . . . Jignesh's kisses grow wilder. I kiss him back, then pull away, gasping for air. Jignesh grabs my hand and bites my fingertips. I moan with pleasure. He gets underneath my shirt. I moan again . . . Timothy Dalton nailed Heathcliff like no one since, I think, feeling the roughness of Jignesh's tongue on my nipples. I think that the 1970 version has never been given the credit it's due . . . Jignesh's hand reaches down for my butthole . . . The 1992 adaptation with Juliette Binoche is positively horrid. The only part I liked was the Sinéad O'Connor cameo . . . I stick my hand inside Jignesh's pants in search of his brown soldier . . . No, I haven't forgotten that Jignesh considered killing me—the detail only makes this more exciting. I feel like Charlotte Rampling playing Lady Anne Boleyn in the arms of the king. I know this is dangerous, but I so want to become the Queen of England . . . Jignesh loses his shirt, pushes me against the couch, and pulls my pajama bottoms off, all in one movement.

"I think I have lube in my bedroom," I hear myself say.

Jignesh spits on his fingers. I say no more.

25

Deirdre

I wake up to a warm cup of coffee, brought to my bed by Charlie.

"Good morning, sunshine," he says, putting the cup on the side table. "Did you sleep well? I slept fantastically. Thank you for a delightful evening. I have the mortgage statement here. I'll leave it next to your coffee. No hurries, sugar lump. It isn't due until the fourth, next month. Now, these are my credit card statements," he holds up a sheaf of papers. "I hope you won't find it too vulgar that I bring them up this early in the morning, but yesterday you offered to help, if I may refresh your memory, and this one is already late, this one is due on Friday, and this one is a first warning from a collection agency. Do you mind calling to make at least the minimum payment? Drink your coffee first. I'm making you breakfast."

I reach for the statements the moment Charlie leaves the room . . . I should have killed him last night when I had a chance. His minimum payment is $252 on just one of his credit cards. The mortgage is $1,900!

"Do you want one or two eggs with your chilaquiles?" I hear Charlie holler from the kitchen.

I jump out of bed and log into the company's bank account on my laptop. The transfer I made on Friday hasn't cleared yet.

"Four, please," I reply.

Shortly before ten, Mike calls me. By then, I'm already on my way to the office. He asks about Justin.

"I told you he wasn't reliable," I say, feigning indignation. He asks me to call him again as soon as I make it to the office. "Did you see the photos I sent you on Saturday?" I add. I spent the entire day fast-forwarding through ten hours of footage trying to get those pictures.

"I did, but the photos weren't too clear. I asked Clara to look into it as well."

My heart stops.

Then again, why do I worry? Clara can't open a file without requesting assistance.

"How is Clara going to log in?" I ask timidly.

"I reset the password," Mike responds.

I remain silent.

"She may not be able to figure it out," I say when my heart starts beating again. "As soon as I make it to the office, I'll log in again and send you better pictures."

"She figured it out already. She's watching the video right now, with Rogelio. I want you to help them, though, so they don't spend the whole morning working on it."

I hang up and immediately call Clara. My call goes straight to her voicemail. I call the office. Voicemail again. Clara and Rogelio are the only ones at the office right now, so they're either busy with other calls, or the police are already there and have ordered them not to pick up the phones until my arrival.

I'm climbing the steps to the office door when I receive a text message from Clara: *We caught you red-handed.*

I open the door.

"We know what you did, Jignesh," Clara says, looking at me from Mike's desk.

Rogelio is standing next to her. He shakes his head to indicate I'm in trouble. Oh, God, I'm about to faint. They know. It is over. I sit on one of the chairs where we make the clients wait when they come to the office.

"I'm so sorry," I mumble. Who's going to help Charlie now pay his mortgage? "Have you called the police?" I ask.

"Not yet," Clara replies. "We're saving the evidence. We will, though, in a minute."

Not yet? There's still hope. There's an empty fire extinguisher that Murat brought on Friday by the foot of the staircase. I could grab it, rush upstairs, and break the skulls of those two dimwits. Rogelio is small, and Clara cannot be much of a fighter. Gabrielle won't be here before twelve. I have a little under two hours to dispose of their bodies . . . I just need a miniature rest before I kill for the third time . . . Fourth if we count Manuel.

"And, yes, you should be sorry," Clara continues. "Mike was blaming Rogelio."

Rogelio? What are they talking about? Could I have gotten away by blaming it on the intern? Look at him. Rocking a buzzcut that probably cost a hundred dollars. Designer jeans and new shoes every couple of weeks. How can he afford it at $10.50 an hour? He probably spends more money on hair products than he spends on rent. Why would Mike think that he killed Justin, though? Think, Jignesh, think. How can you blame it on the damn Mexican?

There's no time to elaborate. Act first, Jiggy-boy, resolve later. I snatch the fire extinguisher with one hand and creep upstairs. Clara and Rogelio are so focused behind the computer, they cannot see that I'm coming upstairs. Who should I hit first? Clara is probably stronger, but Rogelio could easily jump over the railing and zip out. He's as thin as a worm, probably as light as a bushtit's feather. I should hit him first, then Clara . . . Oh, my sweet, sweet Clara! *Tan guapa. Tan maja . . . Como una noche de verano bañada de estrellas.* We'll never again go out for Spanish tapas.

I raise the fire extinguisher over my head and aim at Rogelio. Should be one hit. I'll have no time for a second. Then one for Clara just as fast. I pray to *La Santa Muerte* to be successful. She's the protector of criminals and homosexuals, I learned from a *veladora*. One shouldn't pray to his family Gods when committing a crime. At the count of three: one . . . two . . .

The telephone rings. Both Clara and Rogelio ignore it. I feel the urge to pick up—it could be a renter for one of the houses. Then I hear the bathroom door open downstairs.

"Will no one answer that phone?" Murat boasts.

No one does, so he picks up the closest extension.

I didn't know Murat was here!

"It's a renter," Murat shouts, after greeting the caller.

"Take his telephone number and tell him we'll call him right back," Rogelio says.

So now I have to kill the Turkish beast too? I cannot do it. Murat is stronger than I am. I lower my arms.

"He wants to know if he could film inside the unit," Murat continues.

"We don't allow filming," Clara responds. She notices me. "*Jignesito. A la cárcel vas a dar, por bandido.*"

Rogelio laughs. I don't know what she said, but I understood *cárcel* and *bandito*.

I raise the fire extinguisher again. Maybe if I do it fast and not give them any time to defend themselves? Then I could throw the fire extinguisher against Murat's head, rush downstairs and finish him off.

"Why not?" Murat hollers.

I lower the extinguisher.

"Because they destroy the homes with the equipment."

"He says it will be only two actors and the cameraman," Murat replies.

"Then it's porn," Clara replies. "That is fine if there's not much equipment. Tell him it's five hundred a day, three days minimum, plus security deposit. They have to provide proof of insurance and bring their own sheets, right?" She lifts her head and sees me holding the extinguisher. "What are you doing with that fire extinguisher?"

"It's empty," I manage to respond.

"We're about to send all these photos to Mike," she replies, pointing a finger down to indicate that she simply needs to press enter. "We want fifteen thousand dollars for our silence. *Cinco pa mí, cinco pal Rogelio y cinco pal Murat.*"

"*¿Y al Murat por qué?*" asks Rogelio.

"Okay, ten for me and five for Rogelio," laughs Clara. "Murat gets nothing," she raises her voice to make sure Murat can hear her. "We know you're the one that left the garage door open, Jignesh."

What?

I put the fire extinguisher on the floor and get in front of the computer. The screen shows me exiting the parking lot in the basement and leaving the garage door wide open. That must have been less than fifteen minutes after I hit Justin. They haven't reached that part of the video yet!

"Are you going to send that to Mike?" I ask.

"Of course," Clara replies.

"No!" I cry. They both look at me as if I was crazy. "You cannot send this to him," I continue. "He will fire me."

"Oh, don't be silly," Clara continues. "He's not going to fire you. You're his right-hand man. He threatened to fire Rogelio, though, because he's the one responsible for keeping track of the bikes. I think it is only fair that he knows it was his CFO who left the gate open, so we're not blamed for it."

"He's going to fire me. He told me," I beg. "Please, leave. I'll take care of it."

"But he thought it was I who left the gate open!" Rogelio exclaims.

Murat hollers from downstairs: "Send it to Mike. Let that fatso take responsibility."

The three of them start laughing. It doesn't matter how many sacrifices I make for this company. They're always so disrespectful!

"I said I'm taking over," I wipe a tear off my face that had started to roll down. "Get off of Mike's desk. Get back to work—Murat," I call him over the railing. "You shouldn't be in the office. Go unclog some toilets" He gives me the finger. I turn to Clara: "Yes, I know it was me who left the garage door open, but I'll resolve that with Mike directly . . . Down, I said! Go back to your computers."

They reluctantly leave. I sit down at Mike's desk and breathe. His computer desktop is full of the images that Clara and Rogelio dragged from the video. Oh, God, I almost killed them. I look inside Mike's drawers for a tranquilizer. I feel another warm tear run down my cheek. I find a loose Percocet, which I immediately swallow. I would have killed them for sure if Murat hadn't interrupted us. I also find a couple of screener DVDs from last year, *Moneyball* and *The Artist*. I'm taking them home. Whoever gave them to Mike won't miss them.

I need to find out how to delete the incriminating footage.

Half an hour later, I'm still at Mike's desk. I cannot find a way to delete the video. Even if I canceled the account, the video would remain available for the next ninety days, until it gets rewritten . . . There's an option to record in high resolution, though, which reduces the storage capacity to one-half. I select it. Now I only need six and a half weeks of my coworkers' blissful ignorance . . .

I write a new email to Mike, attaching the photos that Clara and Rogelio pulled from the video and acknowledging it was I who left the garage door open. I offer to pay for the bikes, knowing too well he won't make me. *I must have been so tired*, I write. *I didn't realize what I was doing.* I copy Clara and Rogelio too, so they won't feel tempted to return to Mike's computer, then dash to the bathroom so I can weep in private for at least one minute.

Mike replies almost immediately to my email.

Don't worry about bikes. Deirdre called to ask if she could pick up her W-2. Is it ready?

Oh, Deirdre. That stupid, rambunctious witch.

I immediately call Mike. He's going to complain about the roaming charges, but I've run out of fucks to give. I'm in a troubled emotional state and cannot lose any more time writing emails.

"Of course Deirdre's W-2 is ready," I splutter before he can say a word. "It's March 18. I mailed all the forms back in January."

I actually didn't start mailing the forms till late February, but Mike doesn't have to know it.

"Okay," Mike replies. "Just don't start a fight when you talk to Deirdre. Please. Also, she's expecting a referral fee for the renter in Casa Pistola. Discount it from the taxes she owes."

"I thought you did not pay for referrals."

"Jignesh, come on. She's my friend."

An excellent friend she is, I think. She's Mike's dealer. And not start a fight? Who does he think I am? I am extremely professional. Granted, Deirdre and I have had our differences, but she's an employee, isn't she? Even if only on paper. She'll have her W-2, if not a check, and she'll be included in the biweekly payments to the state and the quarterly reports to the federal government ...

"Have you heard from Justin?" Mike asks.

"Missing in action," I sing and then hang up before he can ask anything more.

I take a deep breath. *Deirdre!* So, on top of everything else, I sob to myself, on top of Charlie's mortgage statement, his credit card debt, the video scare, and my daily tasks, which are varied and plenty, I have to deal now with that Sycorax? I need a strong coffee.

Deirdre and I see each other about once every three months. Ordinarily, our conversation goes as follows:

"You have my pay stubs, honey?" She asks.

"You have my money?" I reply, holding up the pay stubs.

"How much do I owe?" She sits down with an ear-to-ear grin that, nevertheless, is anything but friendly.

"One thousand six hundred and fifty-six dollars, with forty-two cents," I read from a Post-it at the edge of my computer screen. I enunciate every word with an even unfriendlier smile.

Deirdre studies her pay stubs, adds all the amounts with the help of a calculator, and then barks: "You're charging me two hundred and twenty-two dollars more!"

"Those are the employer taxes."

"Why should I pay the employer taxes?"

"Because that is the deal you made with Mike."

"That's bullshit!" She screams.

Oh, Deirdre Silverman. She's all hugs and kisses. She's always talking about karma and positive vibes, but she has a foul mouth. That's one important reason why I dislike her, her gratuitous use of offensive words. I also dislike her because of her hair. She's fifty-nine, but she doesn't dye it. She walks around, beaming, flaunting her long witchy skirts, her knitted shawls, her jewelry made out of wooden beads, and her medieval hag hairdo. I feel no respect for a woman her age with gray hair. I just can't even.

"You don't really work here," I insist. "Why should Mike pay the employer taxes?"

"But you already discounted taxes from here."

"*But you already discounted taxes from here*," I mimic her whiny tone. That enrages her. Not the worst thing that I do to her. Sometimes I create fake Craigslist ads with Deirdre's telephone number offering free furniture. I ask viewers to call late at night because, I write, she works night shifts.

"Those are the *employee* taxes," I explain. "The difference is what the company pays for you." Plus my twenty-five dollar commission per pay period, but we keep that a secret. "I explained that to you before, Deirdre."

"But it's so much money. And I'm poor. You're such an asshole!"

"You want paved roads, don't you, Deirdre? You want schools? You want fire protection? You want the police to—"

"Fuck the police!"

I take a deep breath. Then clean from my nose the drops of spit that came with her outburst of anger. I may be many things, among them an embezzler and a murderer, but I do fear and respect the police. I have no sympathy for demeaning commentaries toward our men in blue. I could understand why a lifelong victim of institutional racism like yours truly might state something as offensive, but coming from an old, marijuana smoking, granola hippie white woman raised in Topanga, I take offense.

"You want social security, don't you?" I add.

That does the trick. Still snorting, Deirdre opens her purse and pulls out a bunch of wrinkled bills, mostly fifties and twenties. I count the bills, put them inside the petty-cash box, and Deirdre takes her paystubs. She goes then downstairs without saying thank you, says hello to everyone else, makes herself a tea, exchanges kisses with the girls, sells them a joint, and leaves. I don't see her again until the next quarter or during tax season when she picks up her W-2.

Deirdre got paroled four years ago, after serving eight years in prison. Mike offered her a job out of pity. Nevertheless, she didn't know how to use a computer, so she couldn't work on sales, as she wanted, and she lasted less than a day as my personal assistant. She didn't want to clean or deal with the maintenance people either. The one thing Deirdre can do is sell drugs, which is the only thing she's ever done since she dropped out of high school, so Mike and Deirdre made an agreement: we would keep her on the payroll for as long as she paid for all the related expenses. The whole charade is so that she can prove to her parole officer that she has a decent job, and eventually earn enough credits to qualify for social security when she reaches retirement age. It works better for her that way. Mike introduced her to all of his yuppie friends in Venice, so here and there, Deirdre makes more money selling laced brownies than she could ever do helping at the office . . . And she gets upset about having to pay taxes! I am the one at risk. I am the one who has to issue a fake pay stub. I live in perpetual agony, fearing that we'll get audited and that I'll end up in jail for social security fraud, all for helping an unrepentant drug dealer. I bet she only works two or three days a week, from her couch, answering a cell phone.

That's why the one time Deirdre came and asked me if we could do a similar deal for her friend Jana, I looked at her right in the eye and expressing all the disapproval that exists in my heart for the sandals, the disheveled gray hair, and the smell of patchouli, I said "no." Only once, but that was a firm "no" and, therefore, sufficient. She never asked again. Which is a shame, because Deirdre must have excellent contacts with the Mexican mafia, and now, that I am still thirty-six thousand dollars in the hole, money laundering could be an incredibly profitable business.

I pull out a calculator. How much does a petty drug dealer make per month? Say that I charge fifty dollars per fake check to the small fish and one hundred dollars to the big. A year has twenty-six pay periods; that'd be $3,900 a year. Times ten people on payroll that would be thirty-nine thousand dollars. I could repay most of my debt in twelve months. And if I invest some of it in the stock market . . . Oh, I'm doing it wrong . . . It would be thirty-nine thousand dollars if I had ten small fish and ten big fish on payroll, twenty people in total. Could Deirdre have twenty friends in dire need? Maybe I wouldn't have to report everything. It wouldn't be too wrong since these people are soulless criminals.

There's no easy way to make this. Thus, at noon, when the hag comes beaming into the office, I kindly state: "Mike will pay for your taxes this time."

Deirdre looks at me as if I was a registered pedophile who had just offered her candy. Organic candy, that's it, made with real fruit coming from fair-trade, co-op farms, and agave nectar. The one that she fancies.

"What's this about?" She giggles.

"I have a business proposal," I reply.

There's no point in pretending it's about being nice.

Deirdre closes her eyes, bends backward, and guffaws as loud as if I had inadvertently put my foot inside a bucket of paint or done something just as dull-witted. I hate her stupid dippy-trippy granola laughter.

"We should talk then," she says, pushing her curls away in a coquettish fashion. "Have you had lunch already?"

"No," I say.

"Great! I could buy us lunch with the commissions you're gonna pay me."

"What commissions, I'm sorry?"

I was secretly hoping she had forgotten them so that I could pocket the money.

"The current tenants at Casa Pistola?" She giggles. "Didn't Mike tell you? You owe me 10 percent."

"He did," I laugh, pretending I just remembered. "But we pay only 5 percent for referrals, I'm sorry. I'll write you a check."

"No, honey. You pay ten. I texted Mike this morning. And I prefer cash."

"Ten percent is what we would pay to an external agency," I reply.

"And I'm not external?" Deirdre explodes laughing. "I'm supposed to work here, and I only stop by a few times a year." She bangs her palm on the table as if she had said the smartest quip in human history.

"He pays five," we hear Clara say with a monotonous tone from downstairs. "He pays ten when you collect the money and get a signed contract."

Deirdre tilts her head toward the railing and raises her voice, "He said ten, honey. As in one, zero. I spoke with him this morning."

I glare at Deirdre. She stares back. I'm sure that maintaining a smile that big must hurt. Mine is barely a simper, and it's killing me already.

"You said you texted with him."

"Same thing." She replies with another guffaw.

Evidently, this is the cost of doing business with Deirdre. I open the petty-cash box and give her the money.

"And what was that thing you wanted to talk about, love?" She asks once she's finished counting it.

We need no prying ears, so we buy two salads, and walk to one of the unoccupied studios the company has on Westminster. We sit at the kitchen bar.

"Do you have any friends close to retirement age that need social security?"

Deirdre bobs her head toward a bottle of Merlot that the previous guests left on the counter. "Should we have some wine?" she asks.

"That's for the guests checking in today."

I was actually planning to give it to Charlie.

"But, I want wine!" Deirdre cries, grabbing the bottle

I roll my eyes, then open a drawer and look for a wine opener. Deirdre looks in the cupboards for glasses.

"We need to keep this place clean," I warn her. "Someone is checking in at four."

"I won't spill a drop."

"So. Do you have any friends in a situation like yours? Friends who needed to be in payroll?" I ask after I serve the wine.

"How much are you going to charge?" Deirdre asks, lifting her glass.

"Same deal," I reply. "All deductions plus the employer taxes."

"And your commission?"

"A hundred dollars per pay stub."

She spits some wine.

"The carpet!" I cry.

"That's how much you charge me?" She screams. "YOU'RE A RAT!"

I grab a towel and get on my knees, trying to clean the spilled wine. "I charge you twenty-five, Deirdre. A hundred will be for every new client."

"Nobody will pay for that!"

"Seventy-five?"

"Fifty."

That's all right, I laugh internally. Fifty is entirely kosher.

We shake hands and make an appointment to meet all of her drug-dealing friends in need of government benefits the following evening.

26

Reservations

I'm not too at ease with this whole social security fraud and money laundering business that Jignesh has started, but I feel that I have no other choice than to be of assistance. How could I not? He's making all my credit card payments.

I laughed so hard last night when he came back home and started doffing his clothes in the middle of the living room, humming the *Ecstasy of Gold* by Ennio Morricone. For a brief instant, my perpetual flutter of anguish evaporated.

"First, we'll earn the trust of the most vulnerable among the low-level drug dealers," he said after he finished explaining the basics of his scheme in the shower. "Geriatric losers, free-spirits with no hopes of ever retiring with a government pension."

"But why would those people want to pay taxes?" I asked, with a baffled mien, seated on the vanity.

"Think about it, Charlie," Jignesh replied, handing me a loofah. I slid down. "As you approach retirement age, Medicare and the promise of a monthly check from the Social Security Administration, as miserable as the amount may be, are too tempting to resist. Especially if you're an addict."

"But how will you convince them?" I asked, scrubbing Jignesh's back.

"Word of mouth. It'll take a few weeks, maybe a couple of months, but if we work hard, soon we'll have all of the Venice gangsters on the payroll.

Everyone worries about retirement. Even criminals, Charlie." He turned off the water. "Don't you worry about retirement?"

I reluctantly agreed. I haven't contributed to my 401K since 2006.

"Then we'll go for the bigger wolves," Jignesh continued, extending his hand.

I reached for a towel and wrapped it around Jignesh's waist. Then, as he stepped out of the shower, I caringly wrapped a second one around his shoulders.

"Now, Kingpins won't be seduced by the promise of social security, of course," Jignesh went on, pouring some rubbing alcohol on a cotton ball. "To them, we'll offer a more interesting package: fake rentals. Perpetually booked nonexistent properties paid for with drug money. It's something I've been ruminating on for a while, Charlie. Give us all your hard-earned cash, all the bills you keep hidden in barrels and cannot deposit in exchange for a highly respectable electronic transfer minus a reasonable commission."

"How reasonable?"

"Twenty percent."

Jignesh put a foot on the toilet and started rubbing his crotch with the cotton ball. He does it to avoid jock itch.

"The tricky part will be to come up with apocryphal names to use as renters in the case of an audit."

"You could use old telephone listings," I ventured, reaching inside the cabinet for the hairdryer. Jignesh clapped, delighted. "Now," I added timidly, turning the dryer on, "how are you going to get away with making constant cash deposits?"

"There lies the beauty of this." Jignesh bobbed his head down so I could start drying his hair. "We won't have to make any deposits. We'll use the cash to pay for the regular staff salaries, most purchases, and our regular homeowners too. They have the opposite problem: they want to be paid in cash to lower their income. I'll delete the records for the rentals we pay in cash. The only money we'll disburse electronically will be the one that actually enters the bank system."

"But what if the police find out?"

"I'll blame Mike and say that I was merely following orders."

This last comment got me a little concerned. What if the police find the bodies in the garage too? Will Jignesh blame it on me? But then, after I finished drying Jignesh's hair and put the dryer away, Jignesh pulled me into his arms, and looking at me straight in the eyes, he asked me to clean the house, prepare food for about twenty people, and remain quiet during the meeting. I just couldn't say no.

"We could end up working for El Chapo!" he said after we went to bed.

Now we sleep in the same room. It was bound to happen.

"El Chapo?" I asked, putting my phone away.

"My plan is long-term, Charlie. Social security fraud is merely the beginning."

After Jignesh fell asleep, I looked on my phone for information about El Chapo. He's the world's biggest drug trafficker and the most wanted criminal in the Western Hemisphere, I learned. A cold-blooded murderer whose net worth, according to Forbes, is close to a billion dollars. That's a one followed by nine zeroes . . . Suddenly I got terribly excited. Twenty percent of a billion dollars is two hundred million dollars, I checked on the calculator. Even if we only took care of 10 percent of his business, the commission would be huge!

Alas, on Tuesday night Deirdre arrives at the house with only two people, two over-the-hill leftovers from the Woodstock generation like her: her friend Jana, who's not even a drugdealer, we find out, but a failed artist who sells her work on the boardwalk, and Jana's boyfriend, Cyrile, a French Canadian who overstayed his tourist visa and has been working with a fake green card since 1992.

"Deirdre has always ranked high on my shit list," Jignesh says, following me into the kitchen, "but this is ridiculous."

I try to console him: "Oh, Jiggy, Rome wasn't built in one day." My voice sounds unbelievably calm despite being also a tad disappointed. How come? Well, I thought I had run out of Xanax and took a couple of Vicodin this morning, but then I found two pills under the bed, and I took one too, just in case I couldn't handle the anxiety of this evening. "Deidre brought us two, and those two will lead us to another four," I continue, putting on a tray the smoked salmon canapés that I fixed for the occasion. "Soon those four will lead us to other eight, those eight to sixteen, and so forth. You don't build a social security scam and money laundering empire in only one evening."

That seems to calm Jignesh down a little. Back in the living room, he makes his best effort to present a friendly countenance to our guests. I stand by his side, with a permanent grin on my face, like a young Jackie Kennedy, I suppose, during those fancy dinners when her husband was only a senator for Massachusetts. I hold on to the back of a chair to not lose my equilibrium.

Cyrile and Jana fill in the forms that Jignesh brought, then we open a bottle of wine to celebrate.

"I'm very grateful," Jana says. "I never thought I would be able to get enough credits to retire."

Deirdre, God bless her, cannot stop giggling. I find her delicious. She doesn't know El Chapo, she tells me, after I ask candidly, which is, of course, disappointing, but she's good friends with Carrot Top, she adds, rolling up a celebratory joint, and she promises to get us backstage passes for one of his stand-up performances. Not that I'm a fan, but I get excited. I never forgo an opportunity to meet a celebrity.

Jignesh cannot hide how irked he is by her laughter. He refuses to smoke with us. He brings a can of Febreze and sprays a little every time one of us exhales.

Eventually, we say goodnight. The poor souls leave with the promise that, in a few years, they'll be able to retire with a small pension from the federal government, and a Tupperware full of salmon canapés each.

"I'm not even going to bother reporting Cyrile's earnings," Jignesh explodes, the moment we close the door. "Without a valid social security number, it's either us or the IRS and who needs the money most?"

"Oh, Jiggy," I begin, trying to console him, but then I don't know what else to say. I sit on the couch and finish my wine.

Earning a few million laundering money would be terribly nice, but why is Jignesh suddenly worried about money? Doesn't he have three-quarters of a million dollars in his retirement fund?

I wish I could help more now that I've been dragged into this murder catastrophe. I need to find a new job. That would be a proper way to help. But I'm so depressed, so incredibly down by this perilous situation that all I can do is waste time on Twitter and visit porn sites . . . *#Hawaii on a budget: penny-pinching in paradise* . . . Why, I can understand poor people wanting to travel, but I would be quite upset if while trying to destress, drinking a seventeen-dollar Mai Tai at Wailea, I had to tolerate a horde of millennials drinking cheap beer from the supermarket . . . I only check Craigslist for the personal listings. The things one reads there . . . *Let's have a party in pantyhose.* It's rather unsettling.

I entertain some time cleaning too. It's the least I can do for Jignesh. Dusting the shelves, fluffing the cushions. The problem is that that gets me thinking. We could use a new dining table and a bigger TV. The wood in the window frames is all rotten, and I haven't had the bravery to check, but I bet the attic is vermin-infested.

Dear God, I pray at night. I know that Jignesh is an infidel, and a sinner, and that the whole money laundering thing and social security fraud is illegal, but please help him succeed in all his business endeavors and send us the miracle we so desperately need to get rid of those bodies. Touch Mike's heart so that Jignesh gets a bonus this month too. And the next. And the next too, and so forth, at least until I find a job and can start taking care of my own expenses . . . What could I do that doesn't involve any actual effort, I wonder, scrolling down through my Tumblr newsfeed . . . Oy, nice furry peaches . . .

I don't want this to sound racist, but to think of all those black and Latinx people on welfare and me in the most complete wretchedness, with two bodies hidden in my garage and depending on a man I'm barely attracted to. I can't even enjoy wasting time on the internet without feeling a lump of anguish form in my throat. The government should send me a monthly stipend to compensate me for all my suffering. I had a rough childhood. Discriminated. Persecuted. Forced to leave my paternal home and move to Southern California to escape a reactionary life on a hyper-caloric diet, and once here, never discovered. I shouldn't have to work. I'm too meek. Too sensible. And too pretty. I'm like a Jane Austen heroine, raised by loving parents, with a handsome countenance, pleasant, old-fashioned manners, and a kind heart, but in every respect unable to provide for myself or actually willing to . . . Oy, Matteo has a 40 percent sale. Would it be too extravagant to purchase new sheets, considering our dire circumstances?

27

Casa Pistola

Mike sends me a text that includes a picture of him hugging two young Brazilian ladies. *Are you checking my voicemail?* I am not. I'll do it the moment I feel like doing it. I've been so stressed these last few days, thinking on how to erase the incriminating video and make enough money to pay Charlie's obligations, I've done nothing else at work but eat stale tortilla chips and browse forums on Reddit. I've been expelled from fifteen of them. Sarcasm doesn't do well on social media.

"Jignesh?" Gabrielle calls from the bottom of the stairs.

"I'm too busy," I dismiss her, flapping my hand. "Ask Rogelio."

"Anthony Marquez is on the phone," Gabrielle insists. "He's the guest staying at Casa Pistola. This is the fourth time he's called. He wants to talk to you."

I reluctantly pick up the phone.

"I absolutely ADORE Casa Pistola!" Anthony sings, from the other side. He has a beautiful hearty voice and a strong Mexican accent that lifts one's spirits. "I want to marry this house," he continues. "I want to make love to every chair, every rug, and every wall. I even want to fuck the refrigerator."

Well, Anthony and his boyfriend are paying $1,850 a night for Casa Pistola. If they want to bump uglies with every square inch of that house to get their money's worth, they're welcome to do so. We'll clean it thoroughly upon their departure.

"I'm glad you're having a good time," I reply.

"Tell me, Jignesh," Anthony continues. "Who's the interior designer?"

Interior designer? Of Casa Pistola? This Nellie must have no taste. Casa Pistola is the epitome of everything that is wrong with Venice: an overpriced, Dwell-inspired, minimalistic shoebox eight blocks away from the beach, with prison-like concrete washed floors, IKEA kitchen cabinets—I'm pretty sure—and decorated with junk bought at the Rose Bowl flea market. Granted, it rents exceptionally well, and it looks fantastic in all of its pictures. Still, I find it cheap and insipid.

"I need the name," Anthony insists. "Do tell me. I want her for our house in Cabos."

Cabos, he said? As in *Los Cabos*, Mexico?

"It was us," I lie.

It was the owner, I suppose. I have no idea. We got the house already furnished.

"Mike and I," I continue. "Mostly me," I correct myself. "And my assistant—Charlie. Mike was too busy with some other projects. He barely did anything," I giggle. "I came up with most of the ideas."

"You did?" Anthony exclaims. "Oh, my God, you're a genius! Where did you buy that metal sculpture in the living room? What is it? I love it! And the painting going upstairs? The yellow one with the splashes that look like mold."

I thank Anthony for his compliments but make it clear that I couldn't possibly help him, "why, with high season around the corner." That only makes him want my help more.

Eventually, he offers to fly me down to "Cabos," as he calls it, skipping the article, just so that I could see the house.

I agree to meet him at Casa Pistola after lunch.

"I LOVE what you did with the kitchen!" Anthony welcomes me into the house.

He's much better-looking than I expected. Shoulder-length, silky brown hair, cinnamon skin, a handsome nose, and eyes so green, they can only be contacts. He's so small I feel like taking him home so that he could be friends with Charlie. He's wearing jeans and a yellow hoodie without a shirt underneath so that one can see his tiny pectorals and well-defined abdominal muscles.

"I had a lot of fun working on this house," I reply, raising my voice over the *Alejandra Guzmán* playing loudly on the stereo.

"They did a fantastic good job with the kitchen countertops. Is it engineered stone?"

I have no idea if it is, but I nod.

"Did you study design?" Anthony asks.

We sit down.

"I took a summer course at Santa Monica College."

"You did?" Anthony asks, impressed. Then he confesses humbly: "I never finished *la secundaria*. I was too busy—"

Here, he makes the unambiguous gesture of a fellatio.

He laughs. I laugh too.

"Where is your boyfriend?" I ask. The boyfriend must be the one with the money. "I'd love to meet him."

"Oh, she's upstairs. She's in so much pain, my poor doggie. She got pec implants four days ago, and it hurts A LOT." Anthony rolls his eyes. "I got mine last year," he opens his hoodie. "Can you tell that they're fake?"

"I would have never known."

"The nose is new too, from three months ago. Third operation. Still not happy. I wanted it redone on this trip, but the doctor said it's too early. I'm definitely coming back in the fall." He then removes his hoodie and points at his biceps. "Fake too. Can you tell?"

I shake my head.

"Fake," he continues, pulling his pants to show me his calves. He points at his behind, then at his cleft chin, then at his eyes: "Fake. Fake. Fake. I only go to the gym to run on the treadmill . . . I didn't want to take steroids because of the pimples. The abs are real, though. Do you want to touch them?"

I do. They're as firm as a rock. His waist is as thick as a matchstick.

"You have to starve yourself to get this," he says, reaching for a can of Red Bull he had on a side table, "but with ephedrine and French cigarettes, it's so much easier. I never drink water, just energy drinks. Do you smoke?" he adds, pulling out a pack of *Gauloises*.

"I'm afraid you cannot smoke here. We have a five hundred dollar penalty per incident."

Anthony rolls his eyes, then lights up his cigarette anyway. "We'll pay the penalty, of course, don't worry."

I laugh giddily. Oh, what strange glamour has Anthony cast on me? Not even his smile is honest. The teeth are too white and straight to be real, yet all I can see is a beautiful creature with lots of money.

He shows me the photos of his five-bedroom villa inside the Cabo del Sol Ocean's Golf Course on his iPad.

"Look at this," he says. "The house isn't too bad, the views from the pool are fantastic, but the furniture yells grandma. Yuck..." He slides to the next photograph. "Yuck... Ugh! *Guácala. Caca de perro.* Look at the curtains. They make me puke."

Even a scowl of disgust looks lovely on Anthony. It is like watching a young sprite smoke. I lean forward to catch a whiff of his scent. He smells of cigarettes, of course, but also of green apples ... The house in the pictures is actually gorgeous—lots of quarry stone, lots of wood and colorful fabrics.

"I tried to make some changes myself," Anthony continues, "but I quit after half an hour. It's too much work."

"It is," I sympathize. "Oh, my," I say, putting a hand on his leg. "That chair is horrendous!"

"I bought that," Anthony laughs, pushing away my hand. I try to apologize, but he doesn't let me: "I do need help, Jignesh. I cannot do anything *por mi cuenta*. Can you help me?"

I swallow saliva. "I'm not an architect."

He puts out his cigarette. "You wouldn't have to move any walls. Just paint them. How long would that take? Half an hour? And change all the furniture." He takes a big gulp of his Red Bull. "I wish we could change the floors, though." He pouts. I make a big effort not to kiss him. "Ricky adores the Saltillo. I hate it. It reminds me of the house of *mi abuela* in Acapulco. She wasn't a nice woman, my grandma. One time she caught me playing Barbies with my cousins. She dragged me out of the room by one ear, gave me a Hot Wheels car and an old shoe box, and told me to pretend that the grout on the floor was a highway and the box was a gas station." He finishes the can. "Years later, I wiped my dirty ass on her bedcover. Anyway, I don't want anything that looks remotely Mexican for my house, nothing, but Ricky won't budge . . . I am so in love with the washed concrete in this house. I want everything modern, Jignesh. Everything. All the walls have to be white, and all the furniture has to be chrome and green and bright orange, like out of space. What do you think?"

I think of Anthony running naked through the garden of his grandmother's house in Acapulco, adorning his hair with butterflies, feeding on fruit brought by the monkeys, weaving himself some clothes from the silk produced by tarantulas.

I turn back to the pictures. Then I have an epiphany: a semi-truck full of furniture would be the perfect way to smuggle a freezer into the Baja peninsula . . .

"It won't be an easy project," I say, already considering the particulars of going through Mexican customs with two corpses. "It might take more than one trip."

"I understand," Anthony replies. He leaves the couch to go grab another energy drink from the refrigerator.

"And your budget is?" I ask, from the couch.

He shrugs, opening the can. "Forty thousand?" He takes another swig and returns to the living room. "What is your fee?"

Forty thousand dollars? I wouldn't rip a fart for that miserable amount.

"I think that might be a whit too low for a house that size," I say, clenching my teeth.

Anthony laughs. It is like hearing a fairy laughing. "I meant per room," he says. "I'm so sorry. I've been talking to so many interior designers lately that I started to use their lingo. I thought that was the standard here. Or do you charge by the square footage?"

I shake my head. Now I am excited again.

"So, what's your fee?" he insists.

How much does an interior designer charge?

"Forty percent surcharge," I hear myself say, "plus all expenses."

"Forty percent?" Anthony snorts. "Oh, my God, are you Jewish?"

"Indian. From Gujarat."

Anthony puts down the can, then reaches for a piece of nicotine gum from a package lying on the coffee table and sits down. He puts the gum in his mouth, looks around the house, then at me.

"Ricky thinks I should take care of redecorating the house myself so I would stay out of the bathhouses," he starts. "I can't. It's too much work. But everyone I've spoken to this week is either too busy, or the price is dead prohibitive. And I need to find someone before we leave."

I remain silent.

"I guess I need to make a decision," Anthony sighs. He lights up another cigarette. "I know you have to pay a fortune to have something like this, don't think I'm naive. But four hundred thousand is our entire budget. I could stretch it to four-fifty, but that's my limit. Five hundred at the most, and at 40 percent, we may be a little off. Could you do just thirty?"

"How much do you love Rick?" I burst.

"Ricky," Anthony corrects me, then adds without hesitation: "With all my heart."

"And how much does Ricky love you?"

Anthony remains silent for a second. Then he adds: "She's divorcing her wife."

"If Ricky truly loves you," I put my hand again on his lap, "then he will gladly pay 40 percent. I'll try to keep the entire bill under five hundred, I promise. I'm not a monster."

"I know you're not," Anthony replies, reaching again for his can.

"I need your help, Charlie," I cry, the moment I get home that night.

Charlie reaches for the remote and pauses his show. Then he refills his glass. There are two empty bottles of wine on the table. He's still wearing pajamas. Apparently, he hasn't moved from that spot since I left this morning.

"Four hundred and fifty thousand dollars!" he exclaims after I finish my story.

"He's willing to stretch his budget to half a million, if necessary. It's not that much money, Charlie. Not for a house that size. He's being cheap. He probably got scared by an interior designer who would charge that just for his fee."

"But you know nothing about interior design, Jiggy."

"Yet you do! Look at what you have done in this house."

"This house?" Charlie laughs bitterly. Then he burps. "Secondhand furniture from Craigslist and picked over art from garage sales?"

I swat Charlie's head. That manages to convince him of his innate talent. But then we take a look at the pictures of Casa Pistola on the company's website.

"Is this what he wants?" Charlie asks, horrified. "You cannot be serious, Jignesh. This is a project beyond my abilities. This house must have cost over a million to furnish. This house is amazing!"

"You think so? I find it rather unprepossessing."

"Oh Jiggy, that sofa must be at least fifteen thousand dollars. And look at the floor—"

"It's washed concrete!" I cry.

"That's what makes it beautiful."

I glower at Charlie.

"I'm sorry, Jignesh," he goes on, "but I don't think I can help you this time. I agreed to the money laundering business because all I needed to do was smile and fix appetizers, but my knowledge about interior design reduces to me browsing old *Architectural Digest* magazines in my cousin's attic while dreaming of one day marrying Tom Selleck . . . Look at the bathroom. My God, that vanity chair must be a Maxalto. Look at the shower."

"It's black tile and tempered glass," I say. "What's so special about it?"

"It's not black, Jignesh. It's charcoal. And it's design. Look at that table."

I give Charlie another box. "We can buy the same furniture on Craigslist."

"Craigslist? Jesus Christ, you don't know what you're talking about."

"I do. We'll look for used furniture and pass it all for midcentury antiques. For whatever needs to be new, we'll use Mike's contacts to buy floor discounts at West Elm. Then I'll Photoshop the receipts to make them look like we bought them from more expensive stores so that we can charge more money."

"I don't think we'll be able to find a sofa like this on Craigslist."

"For fuck's sake, Charlie!" I swat him again. "I've seen Mike furnish an entire house for less than ten thousand dollars. We could do it for barely a bit more and pocket the difference."

Charlie shakes his head and starts dropping Italian brand names: Cassina, Kartell, Vittorio Bonacina. He doesn't believe any of our other homes can compare to Casa Pistola.

"It's all IKEA and floor discounts from West Elm!" I insist, now with tears in my eyes.

How can he be so negative when we so desperately need the money?

"Jignesh, IKEA doesn't sell Poul Kjaerholm!" Charlie yells back at me. "And no one would advertise furniture from the Herman Miller collection on Craigslist!"

To this follows a resounding slap. That manages to convince Charlie.

The next day, we take Anthony and his boyfriend out to the art galleries in Venice.

Ricky is everything you would think he would be: a roundish hobbit with a strong Jersey accent and a shiny face full of Botox, at least thirty years older.

It goes incredibly well. Charlie has the good taste of wearing his opera jacket and rolled up slacks with no socks. His mannerisms are so overtly effeminate, either because he's too nervous or trying too hard to make a good impression, that Anthony cannot doubt his exquisite taste. We manage to make Ricky spend a few thousand dollars on a pair of 1950s mannequin legs and a Victorian death mask.

"Had I seen this in Mexico," Anthony laughs, holding on to Ricky's arm as we exit the gallery on Main Street, "I would have thought it was old junk and discard it."

Then we go out for drinks. We learn that Ricky met Anthony at a gay bar in Tijuana, I get a retainer in cash for five thousand dollars, and Ricky agrees on a first payment of two hundred and fifty thousand dollars, to be deposited directly into my bank account.

And on Friday night, Charlie and I fly to Los Cabos. Just for two nights, so that we can see the house.

"I can't imagine why he'd want to change anything in this place," I say to Charlie on Saturday morning, holding a margarita in one hand while standing butt naked on the pool terrace. I have an unobstructed view of the Sea of Cortez, framed by the striking green of the Cabo del Sol golf course and a sky as blue as one never gets to see in Los Angeles. Behind me, Charlie is naked too, lying on a lounge chair, covered in tan lotion. "This place is fabulous."

"It is," Charlie mumbles. "A twenty-first-century Spanish hacienda that Anthony Marquez wants to convert into a minimalistic midcentury California shoebox. We'll do what we can."

My phone rings.

I don't recognize the number, but the area code is from Los Angeles. A lady that sounds like she's about to invite me to a timeshare presentation asks for my name.

"Speaking," I reply. "Did I win a trip to Los Cabos?" I joke, thinking this is indeed a timeshare sales call.

"Mr. Amin, this is Detective Mora, from the LA Police Department. I have a few questions for you about Justin Kettler."

I take a long sip of my margarita.

"He works with us," I reply.

"Do you know where he is?"

I hesitate before responding. "I'm afraid not. He didn't come to the office last week."

"His mother reported him as missing this morning." Detective Mora continues. "Justin's roommate called her because no one had seen him in over a week. I called your office and talked to one of your coworkers, Clara. She told me that your boss is currently out of the country and that I should talk to you instead. It seems that you and your boss might have been the last persons that saw Justin the night he disappeared. When would it be a good time to meet with you?"

We make an appointment for Monday.

28

Craigslist

It's 10:00 a.m. Too early to start drinking wine, so I serve myself a mimosa, *sans jus d'orange*, to avoid the extra calories.

Jignesh strictly forbade me to tell anyone that we spent a weekend at Anthony's house in Los Cabos. He said he wouldn't tell anyone at his office either because no one is supposed to know we're remodeling Anthony's home. I understand. Now, how will I explain my fabulous new tan to all of my friends? They'll notice it right away, I'm afraid, and I just don't know whether I'll be able to come up with a clever enough prevarication.

The thing is, I don't have that many friends apart from Lucille and the girls from the call center, and I'll be damned, Lucille isn't picking up the phone, and at this time of the day, the girls are always busy. This Prosecco is fantastic, I'll just serve myself a little more. Sherise hasn't answered any of my texts. I could always go to the Bristol Farms around noon and stroll down the aisles, hoping to run into somebody. Let's say that bitch, Jade.

"Notice something different?" I'd say, turning toward her.

Well, no. Jade probably doesn't get her groceries at Bristol Farms during lunch hour. She probably goes to one of those tacky places for poor people, like the 99 Cent store, and after working hours. She's saving to buy a house "for her mom." These damn immigrants are draining America dry—Oh, to whom am I going to tell everything about that stunning five-bedroom, oceanfront villa in Cabo San Lucas? To whom will I describe the Jacuzzi tub in the master bedroom, the walk-in closets the size of an entire apartment, the bathroom with four showerheads, the infinity pool, the four-car garage? And the view! That fantastic view made my heart swell as if it were a hot air balloon taking me back to Paris! To whom am I going to describe the waves crashing on the rocks, the palm trees swaying against the bright indigo skies at night, the heat of the unforgiving Baja desert . . . ?

"Hi, my name is Charlie. How do you do? I'm calling about the fabulous dining room table you have listed on Craigslist, the *San Vicente Glass Top Nut Brown Wood Table* . . . It's been sold? Oh, what a pity. I wanted it for this home that my husband and I just bought down in Cabo. It's a five-bedroom, six-and-a-half bath, oceanfront villa at the Cabo del Sol Ocean's Golf Course in Cabo San Lucas. Have you ever been down to Baja? We just came back yesterday. It's gorgeous! Our home is right by the eighth hole. It has unobstructed ocean views from every room and this fabulous vaulted ceiling that . . . Oh . . . Oh . . . Oh . . . No. Don't worry . . . Yes, I understand. I'm sorry . . . I apologize. Nice talking to you. Thank you!"

I'll be damned. Well, my search brought 672 results for "dining table." Someone else will be eager to learn more about Cabo, I suppose.

"Hi. My name is Charlie. I know you prefer evening calls, it is clearly stated in the ad in capital letters, *DO NOT CALL BEFORE MID-NIGHT*, but I saw your *Fantastic Dining Set Table With Fold Away Butterfly Leaf plus Twelve Leather Chairs* that you are giving away for free on Craigslist, and I thought I had to call now and beat everyone else. We want it for a fabulous five-bedroom home that my partner and I just bought in Mexico. It is a five-bedroom, six-and-a-half bath, oceanfront villa at the Cabo—"

"Charlie? Charlie Hayworth?"

"Yes?" I reply, wondering how on Earth this random person from Craigslist knows my last name. "Who is this?"

"It's Deirdre, love. Deirdre Silverman. I don't have any table."

"Who? Oh, Deirdre, yes, Jignesh's boss's dealer. How are you? I must have dialed the wrong number, I apologize, I'm so sorry."

"You dialed the right number, honey, but I'm not offering any table. Some asshole keeps creating fake listings on Craigslist so that people call me late at night."

"Oh, my God. Who would ever do that?"

"Someone evil, honey."

"It's despicable!"

"And so cowardly."

"It makes one feel insecure about making transactions online. What kind of world do we live in? Anyhow, this is a most extraordinary coincidence. How are you, Deirdre? How's Jana doing? And her boyfriend? What was his name? Cyrile, of course. How could I forget a French name? Send them my love. Any new leads?"

"Nothing yet, honey."

"Oh, that's a bummer."

"They will come, honey. Don't worry. I'm spreading the word around."

"I had been thinking, though—let me refresh my drink. I'm having midweek Mimosas."

"Oh, that sounds nice!"

"It is nice. Anyway, I think that you and Jignesh need a more aggressive approach."

"What do you mean by aggressive, honey?" Deirdre laughs. "Threaten everyone with a gun?"

"No, of course not. But maybe you could put an ad on Craigslist. A real one that is. Not announcing our money laundering services, not with those precise words, but something that merely insinuates it. We could use euphemisms, like 'clean up your financial situation.' Or 'we can be the soap to wash your financial worries away.' I don't know."

Deirdre starts laughing again. "I love it!"

"You do?"

"It's fantastic! 'Wash your financial worries away.' You're so talented, honey. You should be a copywriter."

"You think so?"

I don't know why Jignesh doesn't like Deirdre. She's awfully charming.

"Now, tell me," Deirdre continues. "Did you buy a house in Los Cabos?"

"Oh, shoot. I cannot tell you. I swore Jignesh I wouldn't tell anyone. Especially the people he works with."

"Well, you don't need to tell me then, honey. I understand secrets."

"Oh, for Christ's sake, Deirdre. Lying to you would be like lying to my grandmother: I couldn't possibly live with the guilt. Let me refresh my drink again. I'm having mimosas . . ."

"Yes, you just said that."

I bring Deirdre up to date on our trip to Cabo. The version that doesn't include the two frozen bodies, that is. She listens attentively.

"You'll have to admit that Jignesh's plan is genius," I say after I'm finished, pouring some more Prosecco into my now again, empty glass. "I had my reserves, of course, but after meeting Anthony Marquez and his boyfriend last week, I realized it will work out just fine. Anthony's such a sweetheart, God bless him—pretty as a hundred-dollar bill, yet absolutely no taste. You should have seen him, Dee—can I call you Dee?— wearing bright red sneakers, an oversized white shirt, and Under Armour apparel, like a Britney Spears backup dancer heading to brunch with his friends on a Sunday morning, blasting Paulina Rubio in his boyfriend's red Maserati. I'm not saying that he's stupid—"

"Of course you're not, honey."

"—or that he's tacky—"

"No one is putting words in your mouth."

"—but Anthony lacks the required refinement to distinguish a Chagall from a Matisse, or a *tartelette aux fraises des bois* from a *tartelette aux framboises*," I add.

"Now you're speaking in tongues to me, love. I don't get what you're saying."

"What I mean is that he wouldn't know how to distinguish a chair bought at Urban Home from a chair by Jonathan Adler."

"I like Urban Home!"

"Exactly." I lift my glass. "I could see why Ricky's in love with him, though. Anthony could be an Abercrombie & Fitch model, assuming that the Abercrombie & Fitch marketing team weren't a bunch of white supremacists."

"But they are, love."

"Well, that's your opinion. Besides, I'm extra confident about this because Anthony and I developed a special connection I don't believe he has with Jignesh. We took them gallery shopping. You cannot force a client to buy a big-ass painting of a group of faceless men in a meeting room just because it is the most expensive item at the gallery, as Jignesh wanted. You have to ask your client a few questions, learn what he's like, what he prefers, the colors in his life, what he believes in. You need to build rapport, Dee. You would think that being Indian, Jignesh could have at least tried to read his chakras."

"You don't read chakras, love. You clean them."

"Whatever," I finish my glass. "If I have learned anything from my many years in telemarketing, it is to become the clients' best friend first. Applaud their nonexistent taste and celebrate their witticisms. Then you stab them with the bill while wearing your biggest grin . . ."

"Oh, my God, honey," Deirdre laughs. "You're killing me. You're so funny!"

"It helps to know that Anthony has a heart of gold. Shoot, we're out of Prosecco, I'm going to have to make a run to the Vons. He asked his boyfriend to tip me. Can you believe that, Dee? Two hundred and fifty dollars. 'Don't tell Jignesh,' he whispered in my ear—"

"Two hundred and fifty dollars? Rats!" Deirdre interrupts me. "Anthony's never given me more than a hundred."

"Why would Anthony tip you?" I ask. "Do you know him?"

"I'm his dealer, honey. I'm the one that referred him to Jignesh."

"Oh, my God! That's such an extraordinary coincidence. Two in a day," I laugh. "Who would have thought?"

Deirdre laughs too. Sweet Southern Baby Jesus, how can Jignesh not love this woman? Her laughter is intoxicating. She's such a doll!

29

Cupcakes

Detective Mora says yes to a cup of coffee, but no to the miniature cupcakes that I asked Clara to bring to the office this morning. And they look so delicious. They have these colorful cream cheese swirls and little hearts sprinkled on top. Some even have flags. Considering this woman's size, I would have thought she'd gobble them up before starting the interrogation.

"These are for the police," I warned everyone in advance, putting the box on top of the meeting table. "You touch them, you're dead."

God knows I was being serious.

"What time did Justin leave on Thursday?" Detective Mora asks. She's wearing a gray skirt suit that combined with her pale skin, and her tight reddish curls make her look like a KGB agent.

Everyone's eyes turn at me. Clara, Gabrielle, Rogelio, and even Murat and Juana, the head of housekeeping, decided to be at the office this morning.

"I'm not quite sure," I mutter.

"Do you know where he went?" Detective Mora takes a sip of her coffee.

I shake my head.

"With a friend?" I venture.

She didn't notice the flower arrangement I ordered either. It cost Mike almost two hundred dollars.

"What was the name of this friend?"

Oh, God. Her tone is so cold and persistent.

"I can't remember," I sob, staring at her with bewilderment.

She turns to the others.

"Maybe he went to visit his mother," Gabrielle says. "She lives in Maine."

"She's the one that reported him missing," Detective Mora replies.

Juana is following the conversation with a fretful look, covering her mouth with her fist. All the cleaners liked Justin. Of course, they did. He was always flirting with them because they brought him all the alcohol left by our guests.

"Maybe he went to visit his son," Clara says. "His ex-wife lives in Virginia."

Detective Mora raises an eyebrow. "Well, that is new information. His mother didn't mention a son." Her eyes briefly gravitate toward the box of cupcakes. "Although she did mention an ex-wife . . ."

"Please take one," Gabrielle invites her. "They're delicious."

"We bought them for you," Murat intervenes.

I glare at Murat. Detective Mora notices my look. I look away.

"Well, thank you," she replies with a controlled smile, then reaches for one with a blue topping. "I didn't want to have one, but sure they look tempting," she laughs. "You should take one too. I cannot be the only one eating."

Everyone else turns at me for permission. I mumble a "go ahead," and the five of them jump on the sweets at once, like wolves on a wounded deer. Murat takes at least three, with his dirty hands full of callouses.

"So, where does Justin's ex-wife live in Virginia?" Detective Mora grabs her pen again.

"Virginia Beach." I can barely speak with a mouth full of cake. "Right, Gabrielle?"

Gabrielle nods.

"Her father owns a building on Atlantic Avenue," I continue. "Right?"

"Do you think he could be there?" Detective Mora asks.

"Probably," I mumble, gnawing on the paper wrap. The fear makes me incredibly hungry. "You should have started your inquiry there."

"I don't think he would have gone to Virginia, though," Gabrielle interrupts me. "He and his ex-wife weren't on the best terms."

"Where else do you think he could be then?" Detective Mora asks.

"Well, dead, of course." Murat intervenes. "What?" He replies to our horrified faces.

"*Ni lo mande Dios,*" Juana crosses herself, then swats Murat on his shoulder.

"Murat is joking," I say.

"I am not," Murat continues, glaring at me. "Justin probably crossed someone and got shot. He really had a sick sense of humor this Justin, Detective, let me tell you," he adds, licking some buttercream frosting from his fingers. "I wouldn't be too surprised if you found his body parts near the Hollywood sign. I liked him, but some people didn't. You didn't." He points a finger at me.

Detective Mora turns at me with an inquisitive eye.

"Justin and I weren't—aren't—too close," I stutter.

"Not too close?" Murat asks. "You're always fighting. Justin hates your guts, and you hate his too." He turns to Detective Mora: "One time, Justin photoshopped Jignesh's face onto a gay porn picture and posted it in the laundry room for the cleaners. Remember?" he turns to Juana.

Juana titters and threatens to hit Murat again. Then she asks Clara something that I don't understand.

"Prankster," Clara replies.

"Justin is a *pranster,*" Juana says, to the detective. "*Muchas bromitas, ¿verdad?*" She asks me.

"I don't know what you're talking about," I wheeze.

Murat starts laughing. "Jignesh had a big tantrum that time," he adds to Detective Mora, pointing at me. "He threatened to fire everyone."

"I don't think this is relevant," I say.

"Personally, I like Justin a lot," Juana continues with her strong Mexican accent. "He's very charming. I must recognize, though, that he's made Jignesh's life very difficult."

"I'm not sure what you're talking about," I try to smile.

"You guys don't get along," Gabrielle intervenes.

"Don't get along? They are sworn enemies!" Murat continues. "If any-one in this room had a reason to make Justin disappear, it was him." He points at me. "And I'm not saying that Jignesh killed him," he stuffs a cupcake into his mouth. "Jignesh wouldn't hurt a flea—as far as I know. I'm just saying that he and Justin hated each other, because Justin was a complete dick, pardon my French, and this one is an Indian princess. Probably he got killed by someone else. Jignesh wouldn't have the balls," he starts laughing.

Detective Mora scribbles something on her notes. She is about to ask something else when the main door opens.

"Am I interrupting?" Asks Deirdre, peering in with a burst of giggles. "I need to have a word with Jignesh."

"You'll have to come back later, I'm afraid," I say, forcing a smile.

"I cannot come later, love, this is too important," Deirdre replies. "I'll just go up and wait at your desk. What about that?"

Before I could reply, Deirdre climbs upstairs.

"What other jokes did Justin make?" Detective Mora continues.

"Just silly jokes," I reply, hoping she cannot see the pearls of sweat on my nose. "Nothing too important."

"He was always making fun of Jignesh's size," Gabrielle continues. "And of his sexual orientation."

"What sexual orientation?" I ask.

Everyone stares at each other.

"It didn't really bother me," I try to laugh.

We hear Deidre open and close drawers upstairs.

"Justin could be mean, sometimes," Gabrielle continues. "Behind his back, he referred to Jignesh as Ganesha."

Detective Mora looks at me.

"Did you know that?" She asks.

"I thought he was being playful," I reply. "Do you need anything, Deirdre?" I raise my voice, looking up.

"I need to charge my phone, and I cannot find a connector," Deirdre yells back.

"I'll be up with you in a minute."

"Take your time, honey, I just need to connect my phone."

"If you could excuse me for one second," I say to the table, then scurry upstairs.

"What are you doing here?" I whisper in Deirdre's ear.

"I know about Anthony's house," she replies, aloud.

I shush her down. Then open a new Word document on my computer and type: *Everyone can hear you downstairs.*

Deirdre snatches the keyboard from me, then writes: *You're a rat. I want 10% of whatever you charge to Anthony.*

I get the keyboard back. *No!* I write. I underline the word and increase the font size to one hundred points.

He's my client, Deirdre types. *And I can help with the decorating.*

He's our client now. And we don't need your help. Thank you.

I want 10%, or I'll tell Mike.

He already knows.

"Oh, he does?" Deirdre says aloud. "Then you won't mind if I call him right now."

She pulls out her phone and dials Mike's number. She turns the screen at me to show that she's not bluffing. I pluck her cellphone and hang up before Mike can answer. She tries to grab it from me, but I push her. All of a sudden, my face and neck feel like they're burning. Deirdre just pepper-sprayed me!

"Why did you do that?" I cry, gasping for air.

I try to cough, but I can't. I cannot open my eyes. They feel as if somebody had wrapped them in aluminum foil. Deirdre takes back her cellphone.

I stumble my way downstairs and into the bathroom.

"What happened?" I hear Gabrielle and Clara ask behind me.

"She pepper-sprayed me," I cry, rinsing my face. My voice sounds as if I had just smoked a box of cigarettes.

"It was an accident," I hear Deirdre say, coming downstairs.

"It wasn't an accident!" I keep rubbing my face. My nose is oozing so much snot I can barely breathe.

"I felt threatened," Deidre argues.

"Did this man attack you?" This is the voice of Detective Mora. I briefly open my eyes and see that everyone has left the table and is standing by the bathroom door.

"Who are you?" Deirdre asks, with a suspicious tone.

"My name is Detective Mora. I'm from the LAPD. Did this man attack you, Ma'am?"

"No," Deidre replies after a short pause. "He startled me. And I made a mistake. That was all. You should have told me that you wanted to grab my phone, honey," she adds, to me. "I think I better leave. I have an appointment, I just recalled. I didn't mean to interrupt your meeting," she smiles at everyone. "I'll call you later," she adds to me, then walks out of the door.

30

Shopping

Shucks. It's fifteen minutes past noon. If I don't leave for the gym now, I'll miss the hot guy who hits the showers at 12:50 p.m. Well, today was a good start, I close my computer. I shopped on Craigslist today, and tomorrow I'll start visiting secondhand stores in Culver City. The last stop should be Target. Jignesh vetoed Williams-Sonoma. Too expensive, he said. I'll need to rent storage also . . . Oh, the life of a young interior designer can be so demanding. Let's have some more Prosecco before I leave. Shoot, I forgot this was the last bottle. I'll take a Myvidster break then, just for five minutes, I open up again my computer . . . *My Best Friend's Wife Gets Me Off—Twice-Creampie And Facial* sounds rather intriguing . . . I wouldn't be surprised if Anthony ends up recommending me to all of his friends, and this decorating gig becomes an ongoing business. Why, with Jignesh's brain and my artistic sensibility—

The phone rings. Area code 201. Who could that be? Probably a sales call. Or an agent that learned of my soon to be finished movie script.

"Hello, this is Charlie."

"Hello, handsome . . ."

"Anthony!" I close my computer. "What a surprise. I was just thinking of you."

"Were you?" He asks coquettishly. "That's so flattering," he laughs. "What was I wearing?"

"What were you wearing? I'm not sure. I'm not sure I was thinking of you wearing anything, Anthony."

"You mean I was naked? You're bad!" He laughs again.

"No, not that way. It wouldn't be professional. I reckon that if I thought of you wearing anything, it would be something fabulous, say, a light blue sport jacket from Rob Royson with gray corduroys from True Religion. Zanotti shoes, perhaps?"

"I'm wearing really really small white shorts and a girl's pink tank top that is far too small too. And I'm back in Los Angeles."

"Back so soon? You just left on Friday."

"Ricky flew back to New Jersey on Friday. She's attending her granddaughter's bat mitzvah, but I wasn't required at the party. After I dropped her at the airport, I drove to Palm Springs for the White Party. I just came back, and I'm here just for the night. Tomorrow I'm catching a plane back to New Jersey. Have you had lunch already? I'm staying at the Chateau Marmont. Why don't you come and tell me everything you did down in Cabos? Did you like the house?"

"Oh, dear, your house is fabulous, Anthony!"

"Isn't it? Ricky didn't want to pay for it. She said that the flight was too long and that we wouldn't use it. Have you started shopping?"

"I was working on it precisely."

"Liar," he laughs. "You just returned yesterday."

"But I was!"

"Get your ass here as fast as you can. I'm in room . . . Oh, I don't know what room I am in, it's one of the bungalows. Ask for Marquez at reception. I fucked the receptionist last time I was here, she already knows me. Well, she fucked me," he laughs. "Let's have lunch and then go out shopping. My treat."

"I don't know if Jignesh can—"

"No! Don't bring Jignesh. I don't like her. She's ugly."

"Oh, he can be really nice once you get to know him."

"Just bring yourself."

"I'll be there in thirty minutes," I say.

"Make it five."

There's no such thing as a free lunch, I learn as soon as I come into Anthony's room, forty-five minutes later. The moment I close the door, he drops his shorts.

"Make love to me." He whispers in my ear.

Not that I'm a prude, but what about his boyfriend?

"Ricky?" Anthony asks, lying on his stomach once the deed is over. He offered cocaine, and I proposed we sniff it off each other's butts. Why, we are naked and inside a 1,500 square foot bungalow suite at the Chateau Marmont. This may be the most decadent event in my life, so why not just make it dazzle? "Oh, I do love her," he continues. "How could I not when she's so sweet? She bought me a pony—that I put to sleep; I haven't told her. It's just that she wasn't here, she's with her wife, and I get terribly bored when I'm lonely. You don't?"

"I guess I do," I sniffle. Anthony's tendency to call everyone a "she" is confusing.

"Besides, you have beautiful eyes, Charlie," Anthony continues. "I can't resist men with blue eyes. They give me the shingles."

"You mean the shudders," I kiss his buttocks.

"And I didn't get laid in Palm Springs. Everyone there was too ugly."

"I can't believe that." I pinch his right buttock. If what Jignesh said is true, these peaches aren't real. Still, they look extra delicious. "Homosexual pool parties during the White Party weekend are internationally recognized as a paragon of beauty and physical perfection."

"Have you ever attended?"

I confess I haven't yet.

"There's not much to choose from, really," Anthony continued. "Everyone is on drugs, and either too old, too fat, or too ugly. The few good-looking ones are superficial queens that wouldn't look at you for a million dollars. And I don't carry that much cash in my purse. I really don't know why I keep going back every year. It's exhausting."

I cannot believe what Anthony's saying. I've seen plenty of the White

Party photos online. Everyone is tall, handsome, and hypermuscular. Then again, I cannot imagine a creature as perfect as Anthony to lie.

"It is a matter of perception, Charlie," Anthony continues, standing up to get a can of Red Bull from the mini bar, the third one since I arrived. "Fatties find everyone else beautiful, but as you climb the beauty ladder, as I did, and gain confidence in your abilities to bed anyone you set your gaze on, you realize that everyone else is simply too fat. Either in their bodies or in their minds. Even you. You're fat too, Charlie."

My first reaction is to suck up my stomach. Then I realize that Anthony is using *you* as an indefinite pronoun, and the one he's calling fat is himself.

Anthony continues: "At the end of the day, it doesn't matter what you look like; a well-timed word of praise can win you the cutest guy, especially when drugs or alcohol are involved." He guzzles his can. "The problem is when you find a mirror behind the bar and reach the conclusion that the cutest guy in the room is yourself. You can't fuck yourself, can you?"

There are methods, I think, but I choose to remain silent. That's not the point Anthony wants to make. I wipe the cocaine from my nose and rub it against my gums like they do in the movies. I gawk at Anthony. How can so much *savoir-vivre* fit in such a slender, petit body?

We order food and champagne. Then we make love again. And then again. Anthony's expert tongue artfully explores every last orifice in my body. I have to remind myself to breathe . . . Is it the champagne? The cocaine? The chickpea panisse with kale, quinoa, and a beet walnut vinaigrette that we ordered? Probably all of the above. Making love to Anthony is like making love to a ferret—a most arresting, bewitching, and knowledgeable-of-the-male's-anatomy ferret!

I feel at such ease with him that I end up sharing some of my darkest memories.

"I had my bullies, too," he replies. "But then they learned about the things I could do, and they stopped bothering me. Well, that's not entirely true," he laughs. "Some actually became very insistent."

Oh, Anthony may be incredibly rich and superficial, but I cannot take advantage of him, can I? He's like a Mexican Peter Pan bathed in fairy dust. I cannot decorate his house with cheap furniture when he deserves to live in a Palace. I will do my best to work within Jignesh's budget, but I'm putting my foot down: we'll spend where we need to spend and save only where I know it won't hurt him. I wish I hadn't tossed all those Bed Bath & Beyond 20 percent off coupons now since we're going to need them. I'll make sure the best things come from Sur La Table . . . *Oh, Anthony*, I think, watching him guzzle down his fourth Red Bull, *you'll have a Le Creuset cookware set even if I have to pay for it myself, I promise. And linens from Laura Biagiotti.*

I don't make it back home till well after midnight.

"We need to hurry up," Jignesh says, the moment I open the door. He's been waiting for me on the couch, sitting in half-darkness. "The police are suspicious."

I leave my keys on the coffee table and sit next to him, smiling condescendingly.

"What makes you say that, sugar-lump?" I ask, putting a hand on his lap.

It's probably the memory of Anthony's kisses or the champagne, but I cannot worry.

"Murat told the detective I hated Justin."

"Did he?" I say.

I cover my mouth to burp discreetly.

"And now she thinks I may have something to do with his disappearance."

"Oh, Jiggy, my little Indian treasure from Gujarat." I give him a soft kiss on his left cheek. "Haven't you watched any of the CSI shows? The most suspicious character is never the murderer—and neither is the most disagreeable. It is a good thing if the detective suspects you." I stand up and glide to the kitchen. With all the cocaine Anthony and I did, I better take my dolls now if I want to catch some sleep this evening. "You'll see. She will follow her cop instincts and think it must have been someone else who killed Justin. Maybe she'll blame Murat. He's Turkish, right?" I add, popping three pills. "Therefore, Muslim. I cannot think of a reason why the police wouldn't blame him." I wash down the pills with a sip of vodka and return to the living room. "Besides, I listened the other day on NPR that only 65 percent of homicides are solved in America. You have one out three odds you'll ever get caught."

"That's not all." Jignesh's tone suddenly turns accusatory. "Deirdre came to the office too. She wanted a cut from our commission."

I wasn't expecting this.

"You told her about our plans, Charlie."

"I told her not to tell you I told her."

"She wanted 10 percent in exchange for her silence."

"*What?* She has no soul!"

"I said it was too much."

"Of course, it is too much. It is our money."

"So, she pepper-sprayed me."

"What?" I turn to Jignesh. I notice then the wrinkles and the flush around his eyes. I turn on the lights. Jignesh seems to have aged at least twenty years since this morning.

"We talked again, not an hour ago," Jignesh continues. "We settled on twenty-five thousand."

I sit down again. Twenty-five thousand dollars is a hard blow to take. That treacherous woman!

"Ricky hasn't made the deposit yet," Jignesh says.

"But he will," I say, trying to calm myself down as well. "Anthony promised he will. We'll hurry up, Jiggy-boy. Leave the shopping to me. You take care of the truck and the paperwork and making sure that that horrible woman doesn't ruin us."

"She wants to help with the shopping too."

"And you told her she couldn't, of course."

Jignesh sniffles. "No. I told her that she should call you tomorrow."

Years of browsing *Dwell*, *Veranda*, *Azure*, and *Architectural Digest* at various reception rooms throughout the city, and of dreaming of decorating a fabulous pied-à-terre by the beach that I would never be able to afford start paying off on Wednesday after Jignesh texts me to say that he got the money and has just paid off all my credit cards.

Charge everything, he adds, *to get the miles.*

I snap photos of everything I intend to buy and send them to Anthony. Deirdre insists on modeling every piece, which is pretty annoying, but I manage to crop her out of most pictures.

Anthony replies with a heart most times or a "lovely." Occasionally he does with a "meh," and seldom with an "I don't like it. Burn it."

"Honey, we have to buy this!"

I turn around, following Deirdre's ebullient voice. She usually just points at something insipid. This time, however, my pupils dilate as I discover the most exquisite *Bellina* daybed from Baby & Child Restoration Hardware.

"Oh, Deirdre, dear, now you're being vulgar," I respond, trying to hide my enthusiasm. "What would Anthony want a little girl's bed for?"

"Don't you like it?"

"Of course not."

Have you and Ricky ever thought of adopting? I send Anthony a text accompanying a photo that I secretly snap.

Gross, no. LOL, he replies, almost an hour later. *Buy one for the dog.*

"What kind of dog do Anthony and Ricky have?" I ask Deirdre, studying the menu while at lunch at Cecconi's. I'm pretty sure Jignesh will be able to write the expense off.

She shrugs. "Why do you want to know, honey?"

"It doesn't matter," I reply coldly.

The *Bellina* daybed is so cute that after lunch we return to the store and end up buying three: one for Anthony, one for Lucille, and one for Jignesh and I, "in case something happens in the near future," Deirdre says, accompanying her words with the loudest guffaw.

I can't help but smile. I'm trying to keep it strictly professional with her, but it's hard not too warm up to a woman who keeps showering you with encouraging words about, well, getting married.

"Same-sex marriage is now in the hands of the Supreme Court, you know?" She tells me. I roll my eyes. How could I not know? "Maybe you and Jignesh won't have to elope to New York after all."

No, I haven't forgotten that Deirdre's taking our money, but she gave me a dozen Xanax, and she refilled my expired prescription of Vicodin, which was an awfully nice gesture. And no, I haven't forgotten that Jignesh kills people either, but who am I going to marry if not him? David Hasselhoff?

"You could host a reception at The Victorian," Deirdre continues.

"We could," I reply, biting my cheek to avoid laughing. I wonder how much the Victorian would cost for a hundred and fifty people.

A few days later, we return for the *Bellina* vanity mirror set too.

"A baby girl would be the pinnacle of my dreams come true," I confess to the salesperson, blushing.

Deidre claps. She's brought along her friend Jana, and she claps too.

"Can you imagine?" I continue, playing with a panel of pink gauze while the employee charges my credit card. "A little Anastasie Charlotte with my blue eyes and Jignesh's dark caramel skin tone, sleeping inside a white pram from Petit Trésor, dressed in organic apparel from Bel Bambini. We would be the envy of every gay couple having brunch at the Abbey. Everyone, absolutely everyone, would hate us."

"Oh, I would definitely hate you, honey," Deirdre laughs. "With all the bitterness of my heart."

"I'd hate you too," Jana offers.

I smile. Jana is kind of boring, but she's incredibly nice. "Of course,

Jignesh would have to propose first," I continue. "He hasn't yet. But there's time, my dearest. There's time for everything. My poor Jiggy has been in a real tizzy with the police making questions about Justin. Did you ever meet him?"

Deirdre nods. "Never liked him."

Jana shrugs.

"Neither did Jignesh." The employee returns me my card. "Oh, I asked her to give me a discount, and she did," I smile, reading the bill. "Five percent. I feel so smart. Anyway, the poor Jiggy. He keeps talking in his sleep about some silly video, flinching at the slightest sound, eating compulsively. If he continues like that, I'm afraid he won't fit in the pearl-colored suit we bought him. I, on the other hand, have significantly reduced my daily consumption of wine to one bottle, so I'm losing weight, and, despite your generosity, Dee, I haven't taken more than two Vicodin every day. Shopping is unmistakably the best therapy."

"I agree, honey. One hundred percent." Deirdre grabs a ruffled down throw pillow: "How do you like this?"

I look at the pillow for a brief moment, thinking I'd rather get skinned alive and be fed to piranhas than let that dreadful shiny thing enter Anthony's villa. Then I nod. Deirdre gives it to Jana, who holds it with the same care as if she had just received a vial with the blood of Christ, then delivers it to the same employee that just returned me my card. I hand my plastic again with a rueful laugh. It's only money, I think. I can always throw it away later . . . Notwithstanding their abhorrent color choices and complete lack of taste, Deirdre and Jana have proven to be helpful shopping companions. I wouldn't want to hurt their feelings.

And so, barely three weeks later, after lying to Jignesh about visiting every secondhand store in Los Angeles County, and spending hours instead inside every showroom on Robertson, Melrose and Beverly Boulevard, plus one embarrassing trip to the Tuesday Morning in Santa Monica because Deedee insisted—which nonetheless was fruitful because we found a tacky doll with a hand-crocheted dress to cover the toilet paper roll which I know Lucille will adore for Christmas—and after several fights during one of which I threatened Jignesh to gouge his eyes out with a fork if he didn't let me buy an eleven-thousand-dollar top-grain suede sectional from *Viesso*, the one-dollar-for-the-first-month storage space he rented is finally full. We're ready to leave for Los Cabos!

"Jignesh ended up having to borrow a little money from Mike because, altogether, we spent almost three hundred and seventy-eight thousand dollars," I explain to the girls on our way to the airport. Deidre and Jana are flying down first to take care of removing the existing furniture. "I must have maxed out my credit cards at least twelve times," I add. "We'll make a tad less than originally expected after Ricky makes the last payment. That's why Jignesh couldn't buy you first class tickets."

"I think he could have perfectly added that to the bill," Deidre replies.

This is her first trip out of the country since she got off parole, and she isn't too happy about having to fly coach. I understand. I wouldn't be either, helpful as they've been all this time.

"Anyway, who cares, honey?" Deirdre adds. "We did a fantastic job."

"We did," Jana adds, from the back seat.

"We'll load the semi tomorrow morning," Jignesh and I go over his plan that evening, at home. "Murat will drive the truck." He's paying him a little extra, to keep his mouth shut. "Loading the trailer shouldn't take more than three or four hours. We'll drive straight to San Diego, then through the border, and spend the night in Guerrero Negro, halfway down. Then we'll make another overnight stop in a smaller town, probably Mulegé."

Jana proposed Mulegé. It's an oasis in the middle of the desert, she said, and I checked pictures online. It looks absolutely fantastic, full of adobe houses and palm trees.

"We'll rent a Jeep with the excuse of wanting to explore the area," Jignesh continues. "That night, we'll drug Murat, get the bodies into the

Jeep, and bury them out in the desert. We'll come back, pretend nothing happened, then continue down the next morning."

It sounds like a plan to me. I shopped for our little nocturnal expedition too, *sans les dames*, of course. Two shovels, gloves, Valentino green camo cargo pants for me, and a pair from the GAP for Jiggy—they didn't have his size at Neiman Marcus. Hiking shoes, from Salomon Quest, 50 percent off, socks, from L.L.Bean, khaki shirts, from Banana Republic, SPF 50 sunblock from La Mer, and a mosquito repellent, just in case. Not really looking forward to that part of the trip, to be honest, but it will be fun to explore the desert, à la Peter O'Toole. I'm counting on Jignesh to do most of the digging. Why, I already took care of the most challenging part: doing all the shopping!

31

Driving

"Sir," I see a parking enforcement officer pass me and approach the only white person in sight, one of the two college students we hired to load the trailer. "Is this semi-truck yours?"

The student, more apt to be a partner at beer pong than to haul furniture, points at me.

"You need to move." The officer hands me a ticket.

"What is this for?" I cry.

"You cannot park a vehicle this big in a residential area."

Oh, fuck. Oh, fucketty, fuck. Now this. It's almost noon, I'm sweating like a pig wrapped in foil. Murat has been waiting for me since ten at the storage place, and we haven't been able to leave the house because we can't load the damn freezer into the trailer. It's too heavy! I made the mistake of filling it up with water last night so that the bodies would stay frozen for longer. The students wanted to empty it first. I said I didn't have the key for the lock, then I went inside the house to use the bathroom and almost had a heart attack when I came back to see one of them trying to remove the latch with a screwdriver.

"It's all frozen!" I screamed.

Charlie drove to Home Depot to hire more day-laborers. It took him an hour to return with just two. Still, the freezer is too heavy for six people. We end up knocking on the neighbor's doors, asking for help.

At last, between ten men, we lift the freezer and put it on a moving dolly.

As we push the dolly onto the ramp, my phone vibrates. I pull out my phone to read the text. The dolly backs up, pinching the toes of one of the students, who, of course, is wearing flip-flops instead of boots because he's a millennial idiot. He starts screaming in pain. His big toe turns purple and is bleeding as if it had exploded.

"We need to take this man to the emergency room," says Charlie.

We put the freezer back on the ground, and Charlie takes the student and his buddy to the hospital.

The text came from Murat.

Where are you? I'm starving.

Oh, God. I'm about to have a heart attack, and Murat only cares about eating. Take a deep breath, Jignesh, I sing to myself. You can't lose your patience. I would have asked Murat to come here and help, but I didn't want him to start asking questions about the freezer.

Go eat, I reply.

We manage to push the freezer onto the truck, but now I have to wait for Charlie to come back, and the two laborers he brought won't stay unless I pay them for the full day.

"It'll take a little while," Charlie calls, almost an hour later. "Why don't you go ahead to the storage unit and I'll meet you there when we're done?"

By then, the parking enforcement officer has come back and given me another ticket.

"You have to move that semi now."

The thing is that I don't know how to drive a truck. I call Murat, but he doesn't answer. The officer now threatens to have the semi towed, so I get behind the wheel. I drive so slowly that it takes me twice the time to the storage unit.

Once there, Murat is nowhere to be found. He's the only one with a key, so we cannot start loading the trailer. The workers are hungry. They leave to grab lunch. I'm starving, too, but I wait, in case Murat shows up.

"Where the fuck were you?" I bawl at Murat, one hour later. The men are already back and have been waiting idly.

"I went to the office," he yells back. "Here," he hands me a bunch of mail.

"What is this?"

"Can't you see? It's the office mail."

"Why did you bring it here? Why did you go to the office?"

"I had to go to the bathroom. I wasn't going to go here. The toilets don't have seat covers."

"Seat covers? What are you, a fucking Turkish princess?"

We continue yelling at each other while the men carry the furniture into the trailer. By sunset, we haven't loaded in half of all the things Charlie bought. My back hurts, and I'm so hungry I feel I'm about to faint. Everyone has eaten but me. Charlie calls to say that he's finally on his way. There are no places to eat around here, so I decide to wait for him, and then go have dinner.

"They took forever to let us in," he complains when he arrives, forty-five minutes later. "I'm sorry."

"Let's take a break and go eat," I reply.

"Oh," Charlie replies. "I didn't know you were hungry. I already ate. I felt so sad for the poor students that I took them to a Chipotle. I would have brought you something if you had told me."

"How did you manage to get all this furniture here?" Murat interrupts us.

"I didn't do it." Charlie looks confused. Then he laughs. "The workers did it."

"And how many TV's did you buy?" I ask, wondering why the men are carrying yet another sixty inches flat screen inside the trailer.

"Seven," Charlie replies. "They weren't too expensive."

"It's a five-bedroom."

"Yes, but it's one for each bedroom, one for the living room, and one for . . . Oh, shoot. I'm sorry. I apologize, I guess sixty inches will be a tad too big for the kitchen."

"The kitchen doesn't need a TV, Charlie."

"What are you talking about? Maybe *our* kitchen doesn't, but Anthony Marquez's certainly does. He's not going to miss *Live! With Kelly and Michael* because you thought that seven TVs were too much. Anyways, if it's too big, we can keep it and buy him a smaller one. Oh, and that doesn't go in," he tells one of the workers. "Those are bedcovers for Jana," he explains to me.

Oh, God. This must have been Charlie's plan from the very beginning. He bought furniture for Anthony's house, ours, Deirdre's, and even Jana's. "We'll put it on the bill under *accessories*," he kept saying.

"Put it back," I say to the workers. "We're going to return it. And those bedcovers too."

"But I promised Jana, Jignesh!"

I order pizza. After we eat, everyone's too tired to continue. It would be too late to leave now, anyway, so we decide to finish in the morning. However, we cannot park overnight at the storage place, so Murat takes the semi to a parking space in Compton.

I'm not able to sleep a wink that night, wondering what would happen if somebody stole the truck. Charlie, on the other hand, sleeps like a baby.

"Three weeks of shopping with the girls fixed what all those *Chicken Soup for the Soul* books couldn't in all these years," he brags over breakfast. "Now I understand rich people. Shiny things do bring you happiness."

Murat brings some extra men, and, by noon, we're done loading the trailer. We eat, then finally get on the road.

I climb up into the sleeper cab, planning to take a nap, but the mattress smells like cat pee, and I drank so much coffee this morning I simply can't. To make things worse, Charlie and Murat have been fighting about which radio station to listen to since we got on the freeway.

"Oh, shoot," Charlie says, coming back to the truck after yet another bathroom stop in Santa Ana. "I think I left our passports on the coffee table. I'm sorry."

We look all over for the passports. We even check if we left them inside the trailer. We cannot find them. Murat thinks that the truck would burn too much gas, so he suggests Charlie call an Uber. I am too tired, too angry, and too scared to object.

"I'll call a Lyft instead," Charlie replies. "They're much friendlier."

"Toodles," he waves when the car picks him up.

Murat and I drive to a truck stop. Once there, he tells me that he wants to go to a casino.

"What the fuck for?" I cry.

"What else are we going to do?"

It'll be at least three hours until Charlie gets back, so I let him go. No point on arguing with a cave dweller.

I move back to the sleeper cab and try to lie down. Not only does the mattress smell like cat pee, but I find rodent excrement too between the cushion. I sit up. I wouldn't be able to sleep, anyhow. I'm too worried about crossing the border. It is crossing into the United States that's the tricky part, I remind myself. On the way south, customs won't even look inside the trailer. And I have all the paperwork. I photoshopped the purchasing date of all the receipts, so the furniture will pass for used, and we won't have to pay import taxes. But what if the Mexican authorities decide to check, anyway? They could very well stop us, suspect that we're trying to smuggle arms, and find the two bodies . . . Maybe my plan isn't as brilliant as I initially thought.

Charlie calls up. "I cannot find them," he says. "And the Lyft cost seventy-eight dollars here. I don't think it was any cheaper."

I look again into my bag. I find the passports inside the folder with all the paperwork for the furniture.

Murat returns almost an hour later, smelling of beer and with a broken lip.

"What happened?" I ask.

"I don't want to talk about it." He crosses his arms.

I don't feel like talking about it, either, so I leave him alone. Oh, fuck. Is this a signal? We made Charlie go home in vain, and Murat got into a fight. Is this the universe telling me that we should turn around and abandon this crazy international adventure? What was I thinking? Crossing the border with two frozen bodies and making enough money to pay my debt at the same time? We're way over budget. I should have never made Charlie responsible for the shopping. We'll barely make enough to pay his debt, and I'll still be underwater. But I needed to hurry up. It's been only four weeks. If somebody sees that video . . . I can't risk waiting any longer.

"Why are you crying?" Murat asks.

"I'm not crying."

"Yes, you are. And you're moving your lips like a crazy person. Did you and your little boyfriend have a fight?"

"Charlie is not my boyfriend."

"Really? I thought you two were an item."

I look at Murat for a second. "What happened to you at the casino? Did you get into a fight?"

"Some redneck made fun of my accent."

"Mike makes fun of your accent all the time," I reply.

"Yeah, but Mike signs the checks."

"You could have been arrested."

Murat sinks in his seat. "I don't give a shit. Don't you get angry when somebody makes fun of you because you're fat?"

I glare at Murat. *Like you sometimes do?* I think. *Like most of my classmates did, growing up?* Yeah, I do get mad. I kill people.

"You need to stay out of trouble," I say, not wanting to start a discussion. "We're paying you good money."

Charlie returns, and we get on our way again. This time, I take the passenger seat, and Charlie sits in the back. He spends the next hour telling us about his Lyft adventures.

"The first driver was Italian, from Naples. 'What do you think of American pizza?' I asked him. He said he found it atrocious, which doesn't surprise me because . . ."

I no longer hear his prating. There's only one thought stuck in my mind: I cannot do this. I cannot cross into Mexico with two dead bodies inside the trailer. We're going to get caught, and I will end up in a Mexican prison . . . Would it be too selfish to jump out of the truck and let these two ding-dongs handle it? Charlie wouldn't survive a day behind bars, but how many days would I? Murat would have no problem joining a gang. He could protect Charlie, I suppose. Maybe Charlie could end up as somebody's bitch. He's the right size. Yet who would protect me? I would get killed the first time I stepped out to the prison yard. I would have to spend the rest of my life hiding in a cell the size of a closet. That is, if I get a cell of my own. Oh, God, I couldn't possibly sit on a toilet with four other people smelling my business. I'd rather get the death penalty. But that could take years! I would hang myself from the bars in the window on my first day, then . . . Does every cell have a window? I should have done some research on the matter.

How to take one's life in case you end up in prison? I type on my phone then press *Go*. I check on Charlie through the back mirror. He's still going on and on about his Italian Lyft driver. The first link takes me to a forum . . . For Christ's sake, why are the most important existential questions posted online always answered by a person with an Anime avatar? Words of wisdom coming from Sailor Moon's mouth bring no comfort . . .

"Oh, fuck." Charlie suddenly exclaims. "We forgot *La Cenerentola*."

"Was it today?" I ask.

Charlie checks the date on his phone. "Yes, it was today. Crap. Oh, mother of Christ. Motherfucker. How could I have forgotten?"

"Maybe you were too busy," I venture.

"Oh, fuck you, Jignesh," Charlie replies. "Fuck you real hard, you motherfucker eater of cum . . . I'm sorry I shouldn't have said that. I apologize. I'm just a little too flustered . . . Oh, fuck me." He slaps his forehead a couple of times. "Fuck me a hundred million times—Murat, take the next exit. We have to go back."

"We're almost in Carlsbad!" Murat replies.

"We still have time," says Charlie. "The performance starts at seven-thirty, and it's only a quarter to five."

"With this traffic? Even if we turn back now, we'll be lucky to make it to Los Angeles before nine," Murat laughs.

Charlie continues swearing for a few minutes. Eventually, he shuts down. Then he starts singing.

I wish I had a cyanide capsule to swallow right now.

I've been thinking about killing myself every day since Nina died.

"So whereabouts in Turkey are you from, Murat?" Charlie interrupts himself with a snivel. "Istanbul? I've always wanted to go there. I lived in France for a few years. Did Jignesh ever tell you?"

Correction: I've been thinking about killing myself every day for as long as I can remember. Suicide would be like pressing the reset button on your Nintendo, I used to think. You kill yourself, and, after a brief period of purification, your *jiva* starts again in a brand-new body. Hopefully, a more beautiful body. One with lighter skin and less weight to carry. And you live with another family. With luck, a much better family than the one you had.

"I went to Paris once."

"You did? Oh, Murat, wasn't it fantastic? How did you like it?"

I don't believe in reincarnation anymore. I think that when you die, you die. I'm still superstitious, one is only human, but life is meaningless, I'm convinced.

"It was all right. Too much pollution."

I robbed Nina and Justin of the one chance they had—

"Just all right? Oh, Murat, where in Paris did you go? Did you go to *Saint-German-des-Prés*? *L'Île Saint-Louis*?

I'd better make the best of the life I still have.

"I think I need to go to the bathroom," I say.

We're less than a mile now from the border.

"It's pretty bad."

"We're almost there, Jignesh," Charlie pats my shoulder. "Can't you wait to Tijuana?"

"I don't think I can hold it," I reply. "Murat, please stop."

"Where am I going to stop?"

"Take the next exit."

"That was the last exit." He points to a sign on the right.

"Get into that lane," I cry. "You can still make it."

"Are you crazy? You're going to have to wait."

"I don't want to go to a Mexican bathroom . . . There! That's a shopping mall," I point to a large building to our right just before the freeway ends turning into a four-lane. "Please stop."

"That last exit was for the shopping mall. You'll have to wait."

We drive under an overpass, then under a pedestrian bridge. I'm huffing like a bull. I can feel the bottom of my underpants pants damp from sweat. The traffic slows down. There are jersey barriers between the lanes mounted with cameras. Now we're less than a hundred feet from the Mexican checkpoint. My mouth is so dry it hurts. We pass under a large arch. I see then a sign that says, "Return to USA." I point at it, but Murat only snorts.

"You can always cover the seat with lots of toilet paper," Charlie consoles me. "That's what I used to do in France."

We reach a curve and Murat stops, because of the traffic. The left lane is closed. It's now or never. I open my courier bag and pull out the binder with all the paperwork. The mail that Murat brought yesterday is there too. *Why on Earth did he bring it?* "Charlie," I say, turning back. "I need you to pay attention to me. This is the semi-truck insurance." As I speak, I pull out each document and show it to Charlie. "These are the visas. They're called *visitante* forms. And these are the proofs of payment for you and Murat. This is the *Menaje de Casa*. It is very important. It is the list of everything we're bringing down. It has to match the contents of the trailer. This is a copy of Anthony's passport, and this is a letter stating that he's moving back to Mexico. That way we won't have to pay the import tax. It's all marked with tags. They may ask you for all of this." I reach for my passport and stick it into my pocket. I make sure I have my wallet and my cellphone with me. "Call me when you're in Tijuana," I say, passing the courier bag to Charlie, and before either he or Murat could say a word, I open the door and jump out.

"What the fuck are you doing?" Murat shouts.

"Call me when you're in Tijuana," I repeat, then shout: "American Citizen!" holding my passport up, as I rush back to the safety of the United States.

32

Tijuana

"*Buenas tardes, señor,*" I say in my best Spanish to the customs officer, trying to sound blasé. I am not, of course. Jignesh's sudden flight has left me incredibly mortified. I am shaking like a dog on his first day at the pound.

"Pull over there," the man replies in English, not trusting my bilingual abilities. He points to a space on the left, and Murat complies.

"They only want to check that we have all the paperwork, I'm sure," I say to Murat.

"What the fuck was wrong with Jignesh?" Murat startles me.

I place my hand on my chest, forcing a smile. "I guess he desperately needed to go to the bathroom."

"There must be one in there." Murat points to a building at our left. "Now, we'll have to wait for him, and it's already late."

Another officer approaches the truck on the driver's side; this one a lady in her midtwenties. I lean to Murat's side and repeat my salute, calling her "*señorita.*" She smiles. She's pretty, but she's wearing a tad too much makeup. She asks something in Spanish that I don't understand. I turn to Murat.

"*Mudanza,*" Murat says.

"*¿Sus documentos?*" She asks.

Murat grabs the binder that Jignesh left in my lap. He has manly arms. I cannot help but blush a tinch as he grazes my knee.

"*Tudo em ordem,*" he says, handing the documents to the lady officer.

Thank God he speaks perfect Spanish.

The officer asks something else that I don't understand. Murat responds and then starts laughing loudly. The lady laughs too. Me, I'm starting to sweat. Which is atrocious because I put on bronzer this morning. I wasn't going to start my vacation in Mexico looking as phantasmagoric as Tilda Swinton in *Orlando*. Well, this is not a holiday, this is work, but with all the shopping, the plans, and the excitement, it didn't feel as such until this very moment . . . Will Murat be my Billy Zane? He steps out of the truck. I espy on him talking to the customs officer through the side mirror. He certainly knows how to handle the situation. He's now flirting with the young lady, and, apparently, it is working. I recognize the look on her face. She's both pleased and taken aback by his demeanor. He's a big guy, kind of brutish, but he has a beautiful smile and a particular way with words, so as to inspire some lustful thoughts in a lady . . . He's making the young officer giggle. Now she's shaking her head. Probably he said something racy . . . I don't know what I would have done in Murat's place, I look at my terrified self in the mirror. Probably I would have started to cry and offer the officer my hands so she could handcuff me.

I receive a text from Jignesh. *Are you already in Tijuana?*

Well, technically, we are. I don't see any burros painted like zebras yet, but yes, this is Tijuana.

Murat is talking to a customs officer, I type.

Before I press send, comes another message. A notification of roaming charges. Oh, shoot. This texting back and forth is going to be expensive.

I'll let you know when you can come down, I add to my message.

Murat and the officer are now walking to the back of the trailer. I hear someone climb and open the door. Oh, God. Jignesh said they wouldn't even worry about checking!

I step out.

"Everything all right?" I ask in my best Julianne Moore interpretation, instinctively taking a hand to my ear.

Another female customs officer joins them.

"They want to check the trailer," Murat replies.

I feel my soul drop to my feet.

"Why would they want to do that?" I cry.

Oh, God, I shouldn't let them see I'm in a panic.

I start laughing. My laugh sounds terribly fake. Murat climbs atop the trailer, then helps one of the ladies on. I look to my right, toward the road we came from. Could I run back to the US and let Murat handle it?

The lady still on the ground points into the trailer and asks something else to Murat. He steps down. I should be able to understand at least one word, I took a semester of Spanish in high school, but I can't. I feel numb. I feel as if my head had grown in size tenfold.

I feel as vulnerable as that one time at the Schiphol airport, on my way to Brussels, when I handed my passport to the immigration officer, and he asked, "What is the reason for your visit?" I remained looking stupidly at him as if he had spoken in a language incomprehensible to me. What should I have said? Love? That I had sold all my possessions and crossed the Atlantic to visit the man I thought I loved but who at the last minute, just a day before boarding the plane had asked me to cancel the trip and not to come because he was already seeing someone else, someone much more convenient?

Murat starts laughing again. He shrugs and negates whatever the officer asked. The one inside of the trailer asks another question. Murat shrugs again, nods his head, and says: *"Pode."*

Pode? That's how Brazilians say, "Yes, you may." Shooks. That's why I couldn't understand a word of what Murat said. He's been talking in Portuguese all this time!

"What's going on?" I dare to ask. "What do they need to do?"

"Sir," the officer replies. "Since you didn't pack these boxes, we're going to need to check that the contents match your list.

"But we packed them," I reply.

"Your friend said you didn't pack them."

I turn to Murat. "I didn't pack them," he says, raising his hands. "I cannot take responsibility."

"But Jignesh and I did!"

"And where is he?" Murat cries. "That fatso ran away, leaving us alone with the semi. How do we know he's not smuggling something? This trailer could be full of marijuana."

He starts laughing again. The two lady officers smile politely. Oh, now I know why Jignesh doesn't like Murat. He's big, loud, and extremely vulgar, which a person like me can still find attractive, I can't deny it, but he's also selfish, whiny, and incredibly stupid!

"But I packed all this stuff," I plea, clenching my fists. "There's nothing dangerous inside the trailer."

"Did you pack all the boxes?" The officer still on the ground asks me.

"Yes, I did," I cry, but before I can add anything else, the officer inside the trailer hollers: "What's in the freezer?"

I remain silent for about two seconds. I look at Murat, begging him to come up with some astute cajolery in the tongue of Pelé that will make the officers laugh again and stop asking questions.

He says nothing.

"I'm not sure," I'm forced to reply. "I guess I didn't pack everything."

I call Jignesh from the taxicab.

"Are you guys in Tijuana?" he asks before I could say one word.

"Yes," I reply, trying to sound composed. "The streets are quite colorful."

"Oh, thank God," I hear Jignesh sigh. "Thank you, Lord Rama. I'm just across the border at a McDonald's in San Ysidro. I was so nervous I ate a Big Mac. Where should I meet you?"

"Well," I turn to Murat, seating on the left side. He's excitedly talking to the driver, not paying attention to me. "We had to leave the semi at the checkpoint. They're going to inspect the boxes and compare the contents to the list."

"What?"

"These two ladies that were helping us told us to leave and return tomorrow. It's already after six, and most of their staff were already gone, they said. They seemed exceedingly capable and were exceptionally courteous. Still, I suppose that picking up heavy boxes is not something they could handle."

I make a short pause. Jignesh says nothing.

"Murat and I are going to check this hotel they recommended," I continue. "Then Murat wants us to go out to the bars."

"They're going to find the bodies," Jignesh whispers.

"I'm afraid so."

"Do they have to inspect the whole trailer?"

"I'm afraid they do."

"Did you tell them it's only furniture? Did you show them all the receipts? Did you explain to them it's used furniture, right? We're making it pass as used so we wouldn't have to pay taxes. I photoshopped the dates on every receipt. Did you show them the receipts?"

Oh, shoot. I didn't. I completely forgot about Jignesh's little scheme. He was planning to bill Anthony for the taxes too.

"I did," I lie.

"Did you?" Jignesh cries. "What did they say? The people from whom I rented the semi told me they never check unless there's something suspicious."

Now I feel like crying too.

"We couldn't confirm that we packed every box."

"But we packed every box, Charlie. You and I did."

"There's one whose contents we couldn't confirm."

Murat interrupts me: "Where are we picking him up?"

"He hasn't crossed yet," I say.

"Why not?" Murat asks, then takes the phone off my hands: "Why haven't you crossed the border yet?" he asks Jignesh. "Do you have bad diarrhea?" He ends his sentence blowing a rather crass and explicit fart sound.

I stick my ear to the phone.

"I'm not feeling too well, Murat," I hear Jignesh respond.

"Bullshit!" Murat laughs. "We're going out tonight."

"I think I need to go to the doctor," Jignesh replies.

"Why? Get off," Murat pushes me aside and changes the phone to his other ear. "Why would you need to go to the doctor?"

They talk for a few minutes. Murat's tone gradually changes from that of a prankster to that of someone mildly concerned.

Eventually, he hands back my phone. "He wants to talk to you."

I turn to the window so that Murat can't hear what Jignesh has to say.

"I'm sorry I put you through this, Charlie," Jignesh begins.

He sounds calmer. I, on the other hand, am growing agitated.

"You don't need to apologize—"

"We only have a few hours until they find them—"

"Oh, Jiggy," I reply.

"Don't Jiggy me, please. I've told you a million times I don't like it. Listen to me: We have to vanish. Lose Murat, come back here and meet me at the San Diego airport."

"Oh, Jiggy—I mean, Jignesh. I cannot go back. They kept our passports. They didn't want us to leave the city."

Jignesh stays quiet.

"Take the next bus out of Tijuana," he eventually says, "and travel as far south as possible."

"I'm sure there's something we can still do—"

"What are we going to do, Charlie? Are you going to dress up in a black bodystocking and steal that semi?"

Well, it works in the movies. One would need to do some shopping first. Perhaps there's an American Apparel in Tijuana. And then we would need to create a distraction, maybe firecrackers, which, I suppose, one can easily find in Mexico.

"I'm getting as far away as I can. You need to do the same," Jignesh continues. "Since you cannot cross back, it will be better if we each go our own way. It was delightful to meet you, Charlie."

"Same," I reply.

"Don't let them catch you alive."

Oh, those last few words were unnecessarily dramatic . . . Although, based on what I can see of Tijuana through the cab window, a Mexican prison might not be a place where I would like to spend the rest of my life. I guess I will have to scram.

"I love you, Jiggy," I say, expecting Jignesh to say that he loves me back, but he simply hangs up. "I hope your tummy gets better," I add loudly for Murat's benefit. "Take care."

It takes all my concentration to turn back to Murat.

"I don't think I can go out with you tonight," I say, brushing a tear with the back of my hand. "I'll stay at the hotel and repose. I am upset too. Maybe it's the Mexican air? Thanks for the invitation, though. It's awfully kind. Maybe we can go out later, once we're in Cabo."

"Are you crying too?" Murat asks. "What's with you fags that everything has to be overdramatic?"

Murat's not only incredibly offensive. He sounds like that talking dog from YouTube.

"Are you on the rag?" he adds.

"Sweet Southern Baby Jesus, Murat, that's an awfully mean, vulgar, and sexist thing to say." I am mad now but still weeping. I clean my face with the collar of my shirt. "Men do not have premenstrual syndrome for your information. Not even gay men."

He starts laughing. "You're on the rag! Your boyfriend has diarrhea, and both of you start crying like pussies. He's not going to die. He said he's going to the doctor! It'll cost him a fortune in San Diego, let me tell you, he should have crossed and seen one here in Tijuana. Or he should have just farted it. That's how I cure my belly aches."

He blows another raspberry.

God, why do I even try? One cannot argue with this Anatolian troglodyte. I look away, out of the window. Tijuana sure looks unlovely. Most buildings look as if they had been made out of shoeboxes, with flat roofs, rebars sticking out, and telephones and electrical cables running everywhere. It's all pavement and plastered concrete . . . Oh, no, there's one tree. It looks so feeble. Everything looks so poor, and everyone's so garishly dressed it only makes me feel more dejected . . . I close my eyes tight so as not to cry anymore. How am I going to escape? I have no money. I maxed out all my credit cards again, thinking that Anthony would make the last payment as soon as we finished decorating his house. I have five hundred dollars in cash and two twenty-peso bills that I found at the bottom of a drawer. How far will that take me? How far will I need to go? All the way down to Guatemala?

We check in at a small hotel on Avenida Revolución. This is still a concrete jungle, but at least some small palm trees line the sidewalks, and it's a much cleaner street than the ones by the border. It looks like a Mexican Melrose, I point to Murat. Full of restaurants and trinket stores, but with pharmacies, instead of fashion boutiques. I make a mental note to go check the price of Xanax before I leave the city.

The room is clean but far from luxurious. Only one bed. We're paying twenty-three dollars for the night. Murat drops his bag and enters the bathroom to take a shower. I empty my pockets on the side table and sit down on my side of the bed. I take the remote but can't make myself turn on the TV. I see through the window that there's a Sanborns across the street. Lucille remembers that chain fondly, from the time she lived in Mexico City. She said that if we ran into one, I should order *Chiles Rellenos de flor de Jamaica*. She also said that the waitresses are dressed like piñatas, which I find hard to believe. How could they move? I recollect all this because I wrote it down on my iPhone. She's going to be disappointed when I tell her that we stayed at a hotel right across from her favorite Mexican restaurant, and I didn't have a chance to go in. Well, she's going to be disappointed anyhow because we may never see each other again.

I heart a picture of Marco kissing her belly that she posted on Instagram.

A few minutes later, Murat comes out of the bathroom wearing only his underpants.

I raise a hand to hide the offensive sight.

"What?" He asks, rubbing a towel against his armpits. "You've never seen a naked man before? Turn on the TV. I want to watch Mexican television."

I oblige. A woman wearing a ton of makeup comes on. I can't understand one word. Murat apparently does, because he laughs. He finds her pretty. I think she's merely okay.

My phone rings. I freeze. Who could be calling me? Could it be the police, telling us that they're coming to arrest us?

Murat picks up my phone. He looks at the caller ID and decides to reply: "Hello, honey. We're in Tijuana."

"Who's that?" I ask.

"Not for you," Murat replies. "We're going to have to spend the night here," he says to the person on the other side of the line. "How are you and Jana doing down there?"

"Is that Deirdre?" I ask.

Murat doesn't reply. He starts laughing. I try to grab the phone, but he pushes me away.

"I'm talking to her," he hushes me.

"Give me my phone," I demand.

After some struggle, I manage to snatch my phone back.

"Deedee?" I ask, then Murat gives me a knuckle. "Would you please stop?" I cry. "I'm not in the mood for your jokes—I'm sorry, sugar lump," I add, to Deirdre. "This mannerless oaf wouldn't give me my phone—STOP!"

"Why are you still in Tijuana?" Deirdre asks.

"We didn't leave until this morning—Sweet Southern Baby Jesus, would you please stop bothering me, Murat? This is a serious business conversation . . . I'm sorry, Dee. It's a long, sad, and incredibly disappointing story."

"Are you spending the night there?"

"We must, I'm afraid. The customs officials said that they wanted to inspect the trailer."

"Why?" Deirdre cries.

I explain to Deirdre the particulars of our little drawback, beginning from our late departure all the way through the missing passports adventure, my Italian Lyft driver, and Jignesh's sudden indisposition.

"You must be kidding me," Deirdre responds when I finish. "Do you know how long it could take until they let you go?"

"They told us to go back tomorrow," I reply.

"Tomorrow? You're in Mexico, honey. Nothing here is ever done on time. It could take weeks. Months! Have you never heard of *mañana?*"

"I know. I'm sorry, Dee, I apologize. We weren't expecting this. I don't know what to do."

Murat has finished dressing up and is now applying some horribly strong cologne all over his body. He notices the disgust on my face and sprays some at me.

"It's not your fault, sweetie," Deirdre continues. "At least, it will give us more time. My God, this house is fantastic, I could use a full week here," she laughs. "We have only finished packing one bedroom. We'll have to hire more help. This place is full of stuff, honey."

"Anthony wants it all out."

"Oh, and Jana had this fantastic idea. We found some risqué photos of Ricky and Anthony inside the master closet, and she's going to paint a mural on the master bedroom wall inspired by them. She had this vision of the two making love on the beach under a starry night, with a whale splashing water on the distance and the mountains full of cactuses and an enormous Cabo moon, and—"

"Oh, Deirdre, dear, no, no, please. I'm not sure whether Anthony could afford Jana's art."

"Honey, love, don't be silly. He can. Jana wanted to do it for free," Deirdre chuckles, "but I convinced her she had to charge."

"How much?"

"Twenty-two thousand. For the entire wall. It's not expensive, honey, it must be over two-hundred square feet. In LA she would charge double at least—"

"Oh, Deirdre, no. Please don't let her do it. I know that Jana is a fabulous artist, and I would be the first to celebrate her piece once it's finished. Still, Jignesh's going to kill me if we add twenty-two thousand dollars more to Anthony's bill, and I don't even know when, if ever, we're going to leave this place. I mean, I'm trapped in a hotel room in crime-infested Tijuana overlooking a street full of depravity with a man who clearly has never had a body wax, and I just don't know how they will treat Anthony's precious furniture at customs or if they will steal anything. I just can't!"

"Too late, honey. Jana already started. Don't worry, love, I'll talk to Jignesh. He'll be fine. And don't worry about the furniture either: I'm going to make some calls. I have connections. I met all kinds of people in prison. Did Jignesh tell you I was in prison? Of course, he did," Deirdre chuckles, "he wouldn't pass up an opportunity to dredge up my past. Leave it to me. What time is it? *Chingada madre*, in Mexico City, must be after nine. Did you know that? *Chingada madre*," Deirdre laughs. "I'm already swearing in Spanish. I learned that from the people we hired. It's pretty useful."

She promises to call all of her friends. I have no heart to tell her that it will be useless because I'll be taking the next bus out of Tijuana as soon as Murat leaves for the bars. At least now, I know that if Deirdre's right, and customs will indeed take a long time to go through the trailer, unless those bodies start to stink, Jignesh and I will have a few days to get as far as we can. Then I remember that the freezer hasn't been connected to an electric outlet in almost two days. The corpses must be floating in water now.

We hang up. I explain to Murat what Deirdre told me. Then I venture, "I may have to return to Los Angeles and leave you here to wait for the semi."

"No way!" Murat replies. "I'm supposed to be back in LA on Monday. Everyone thinks I'm in Chicago for my uncle's funeral. Mike's going to fire me when he finds out!"

"Murat, you have to understand that our client is deeply concerned about his furniture."

"You morons should have planned this better."

"We planned this to a T, mister Ali-Baba. What we didn't expect was you telling the customs officers that we didn't pack all the boxes ourselves."

My phone rings again. This time is Anthony.

"What's that thing about my furniture trapped at customs?" he snaps, when I answer.

Oh, God. Deirdre. She must have called him first. Again, I explain the particulars of our little drawback.

"You must be kidding me," Anthony replies when I finish. "Do you know how long it could take until they let you go? Years!"

"Well, that's not exactly what Deirdre said. She said it would a long time, but that she would call someone."

"She called me!"

"I know. I'm sorry, Anthony. I apologize"

"It's not your fault, Charlie. It's that stupid country I was born in. I'm going to have to ask Ricky to make a few calls, which I really didn't want to do because she warned me that something like this would probably happen, and I called her a stupid old fart."

"Well, Deirdre said she has friends."

"Deirdre is useless. Why didn't you call me earlier? Let me talk to Jignesh."

"Well, that's another thing—"

I explain to Anthony about Jignesh's sudden indisposition. He swears a couple times in Spanish. I apologize again.

"Anthony sounds especially adorable when he's angry," I whisper to Murat, putting the phone briefly on speaker so that he can hear him. Murat agrees.

Anthony ends up telling me not to worry, to stay put and be ready to wait in Tijuana for at least a few days, in case Ricky cannot figure out a way to speed up the process. As with Deirdre before, I have no heart to tell him that I'm leaving Tijuana tonight.

"I need to get drunk," Murat says, the moment I hang up.

"And I'm ravenous," I add, turning off the TV. "Let's go eat something. Then you can go to the bars."

I know, time's running out, but one cannot plan an escape on an empty stomach, and I really wanted to try those *Chiles Rellenos* from the Sanborns.

33

Trolley

"Are you all right, sir?

I've been sitting with my head down on the table for so long that people around me start to worry. "I have a tummy ache," I explain to the McDonald's employee. "Nothing to worry about."

"Do you want us to call an ambulance?"

I shake my head and stand up. "I need to leave."

What am I going to do? I brood, walking toward the trolley station. I need to get to the airport, that's obvious, but where to next?

The trolley arrives. This is the southernmost station, so apart from a few other people, the car is empty. I take a seat. Maybe I should return to Los Angeles and pick up some things. I left my suitcase inside the truck. I don't even have a change of underwear. That would take too much time, however. Time is the one thing I cannot waste. I wipe my nose against my arm. I'm sobbing again . . . Should I fly to India? I still have relatives there. Whom I haven't seen in almost forty years . . . Would that be too obvious, India? I cannot make it too easy for the police. I could go to Brazil. But what if I run into Mike? And I am not ready for a long flight, I haven't gone to the bathroom yet today . . . I better start looking for a ticket.

I pull out my phone and instinctively check my email first. It's all junk. *Goldstar, DC Shoes. Twitter* informing what's popular on my network. *Atlantis Gay Cruises* . . . I open this one and scroll down to look at the pictures of muscled white men having fun in speedos . . . How odd! An Asian fellow made it into the last picture. And a Latino . . . No Indians, of course . . . Everyone looks so happy . . . I always wanted to take a gay cruise, I sob. Cruises aren't for people like me. It says right here, in all these bright pictures: *Dusky, large, and elderly folk are not welcome.*

I close my eyes shut and pray. I pray to my family gods and to all others I know, in alphabetical order. Will they listen to me? I only pray when I'm in trouble, which lately, it seems, has been pretty much every day. The trolley stops. I hear people come in and go out. Someone sits next to me. Still, I keep my eyes shut. I feel that the longer I keep them closed and the more I pray, the closer I'll be to getting a miracle.

I'm so remorseful now! I should have never killed Nina. I should have let the poor girl go, not be so proud, take no offense at her insults. I shouldn't have killed Justin either . . .

And why did I think we could smuggle two bodies through the Mexican border? I bet those two fools didn't even try to bribe the Mexican officers. A couple hundred would have done it . . . It is not their fault, though. It is mine. It is mine for trusting a scissorbill and a birdbrain! I pull my shirt up to wipe the tears from my face.

I need to take a shower before I escape. I reek of grease from the McDonald's. Should I fly to India? My relatives won't be too supportive once they find out why I'm visiting, but where else could I go? I start looking for flights. The internet is so fucking slow . . . There are no non-stop flights from San Diego to Delhi, and the cheapest would be $3,765. Maybe it's better if I fly from LA. I wouldn't make it tonight, though. What about flying to Mumbai? They all leave tomorrow morning. Is that doable? Say that Mexican customs doesn't open till nine in the morning. If they find the bodies by ten, by the time they call the police, contact the FBI and figure out that they need to arrest me, I could already be flying over international waters . . . The Mexican police cannot be that fast, can they? I may have until noon. That's it, then. I'll stop downtown, take the next train to Los Angeles, get to the house, pack a few things and immediately leave for the airport. That's what I'll do . . .

"Fuck!" I exclaim aloud, when I realize there's no direct flight to

Mumbai from Los Angeles. Now the car is full of people. One or two passengers look at me, but the rest ignore me. I hunch down. I shouldn't call attention to myself.

The flight with the shortest stop leaves at 12:55 p.m.—do I have that much time? Not unless I want to spend the rest of my life in prison. I choose the earliest flight and enter my information . . . No, I don't want to book hotel . . . No, I don't want to rent a car either . . . Passport number? I look in one of my pants' pocket for my passport. It isn't there. I search the other pocket. It isn't there either! I feel my back pockets—where the fuck is my passport? I lost it! I stand up and examine my seat. I scan the floor . . . I must have left it at the McDonald's! Now I have to go back. I squeeze my way toward the door, ready to step down at the next stop.

When I reach for the handhold, I realize that I've been clenching my passport all this time.

I'm going to have a heart attack.

I try to go back to my seat but someone else has already taken it.

I continue the booking. Finally, I press pay . . . A message pops up, saying that my credit card was rejected. Huh? That cannot be. I enter it again. I know it has money. Rejected again? I open the Chase site and check my balance. I have seven hundred and sixty-two dollars in my regular bank account and less than five hundred dollars of credit available. They put a hold of $2,500 for the semi. I check my other credit card . . . I have forty dollars available. Oh, fucketty fuck. I shouldn't have given my card to Charlie!

I take a deep breath and wipe my tears. Maybe a flight straight to India wasn't the best idea. The police would see the charge and start looking for me there. I need to go to another country. I cannot go to Mexico, therefore I have to go to Canada. Maybe wait a few days, get a better rate . . . I'll need to borrow a few thousand from Mike too. How much money do I need to start a new life? I cannot make the transfer from my phone, and, even if I could do a transfer today, I wouldn't have the money until Monday.

Oh, what to do? I look at the people around me, begging for an answer. Please, God, give me the strength and the wisdom to make the right decision . . .

34

Disco Club Las Pulgas

The *Chiles Rellenos de flor de Jamaica* are a seasonal treat, so they don't have them at Sanborns. I have to settle on *Salbutes con Carne de Pavo*, which, nonetheless, look exquisite.

"The waitresses aren't dressed like piñatas, like my friend told me," I say to Murat.

Murat shrugs. He ordered a beer and—what is one going to do? I ordered one too.

"They look more like those Mexican rag dolls you sometimes see during Day of the Dead in Los Angeles," I continue, taking a sip from my bottle. "With colorful dresses and ribbons woven into their braids."

All the waitresses have their hair pulled back in a bun, though, and the ribbons are on their skirts, so not quite the same thing. Just similar.

The food comes and the salbutes are indeed exquisite. Overall, it's a terrific experience. If I weren't in such a terrible state of mind, all shaky and thinking that every person that walks by is a police officer coming to arrest us, I'd take the time to write a nice Yelp review.

I ask Murat how his pozole is.

"It's okay," he says.

"Did you like this place?"

"Yeah. It's like a Denny's"

I open my mouth to object. This place is a step above Denny's. I can't start an argument, though. I'm too nervous.

"So, are we going to get stupid?" Murat asks, when the check comes.

The taxi driver recommended two places. One's called *Iguanas Ranas*. Americans love it, he said, but the drinks are expensive. The other one is called *Disco Club Las Pulgas*, which is not as nice, but the girls are less choosy.

"They're in opposite directions," Murat says. "So, we have to pick one."

I don't want to go to either. I just want to run down the street crying mommy and hope that an angel will come down and rescue me from the mess I've gotten myself into. Nevertheless, the idea of a second beer sounds appealing—much more so than taking the next bus to destination God-knows-where.

"*Las Pulgas* sounds like a quaint locale," I reply. "But I cannot stay more than one hour," I add.

I'm one drink away from gaining the strength and self-confidence I so desperately need to leave this city. I'll excuse myself saying I'm incredibly tired, go back to our room, pack my things and flee from Tijuana.

By 4:00 a.m., though, I'm still hanging out with Murat.

"Ashley Judd went to prison too for a crime she didn't commit, didn't she?" I say to Bere, *ma confidente pour la nuit*, a plus-size girl with chola eyebrows who could easily break my neck with one arm, I notice. "And then, when she came out—" I pause while I reach for one of the tequila bottles Murat ordered. Bere's breasts are so big, and the cleavage of her lycra dress runs so low, I cannot help stealing a glance. *Would it be too inappropriate if I asked her to let me motor-boat her?* I wonder, as I refill both our glasses. I suspect that's one of the things you could get away with in a bar such as this and because I'm gay, she'd probably acquiesce, "—six years later, she still looked fabulous."

Bere nods. The music's so loud, and her English so poor, I doubt she understood a word. But she's pretty, and that's what counts.

"I'll be forty-three in six years," I continue. "I could perfectly go to the gym in prison. What else is one going to do in there? Well, get gang raped, I suppose, but after a few months, when the novelty of my blue eyes has worn off, I could start pumping iron and get a six pack. Then I'll remake my life."

35

Morbid Thoughts

I wake up to a telephone call from Mike.

"Jignesh, where are you? Clara said that you haven't stopped by the office in two days."

"I'm at home," I manage to mumble. Charlie's home, that is. His 950-square-foot fabulous two-bedroom craftsman in West Adams. "I'm sick."

My head feels spongy. I didn't make it on time for the last train and had to take a bus. I didn't get to Los Angeles until after midnight. I look at the time on my phone . . . It's almost ten—I had planned to be on the road by eight!

"Sick? Jignesh, this is very inconvenient," Mike cries. "I need you to be at the office when I'm not there. Clara told me that Murat is out too. Where is he?"

"He's in Chicago."

"In Chicago? Why did you let him go?"

"He went to a funeral." I start pulling clothes out of the closet. "He said that he hadn't had a vacation in over a year."

Where are my headphones? I cannot do this with one hand.

"He went to Vegas in March! I cannot run a company with everyone out. I'm on vacation! I can't relax if the company's falling apart."

"I'll be at the office tomorrow."

"No, you sound horrible," Mike replies. "I don't want everyone else to get sick. Anyway, why did you change the password for the security camera?"

I take a little longer than I should in uttering a reply.

"I didn't change any password."

"Yes, you did change it. Clara couldn't log in and I had to reset it."

I sit down. "Why would Clara need to log in?"

"Detective Mora called me. She wants to see the video."

"What video?"

"What video? Jesus, Jignesh, she's investigating Justin's disappearance. The basement video. She needs all the evidence she can collect. You cannot change my passwords without telling me! Why would you do that? I was having lunch with a friend when she called me, and after I hung up with her, I had to spend almost half an hour with Clara explaining to her how to log into my computer to download the video. I thought she already knew how. Anyway, call her, please. Last time Rogelio helped her, but today is his day off and he's nowhere to be found."

"But we already sent the photographs to the police," I squeal.

"Jignesh, are you even listening? You sent pictures about the stolen bikes. They want to see the whole tape. This is my last week of vacation, Jignesh. I shouldn't be dealing with this!"

I hang up before he could say bye.

Oh, fuck. Oh, fucketty, dickery, fuck. It's been only one, two—I count with my fingers—five weeks and two days. It's been only thirty-seven days since the night I killed Justin, and I needed six and a half weeks!

I call the office. Clara answers the phone. I ask her if she still needs help downloading the video.

"*Cariño*, you sound terrible," she replies. "Have you gone to the doctor already? Gabrielle just came in. We figured out how to download the video, but it was too big, so we called the detective and gave her the login and password, so she could do it herself. Hello?" She asks, after too long of a silence. "Jignesh . . . ? Are you still there?"

"Yes," I reply. "I just don't understand. How did she learn about the video?"

"Mike had asked me to follow up with the police on the break-in, but I couldn't find a police report in your files. So, I called Detective Mora and told her about the video. She didn't know we had security cameras in the garage. Why didn't you tell her? It's been a month, *majo*, and nobody knows anything about Justin yet."

"It's been five weeks," I correct her before hanging up.

So that's it. The Tijuana police will find the two bodies, and the Los Angeles police will see the video. How long do I have before they knock at the door? An hour? Two at the most? Maybe just minutes. I was so tired when I came home last night that I didn't even pack. I thought I had set an alarm on my phone . . . Where are my keys? I have to leave now.

Now, I stop at the door, Detective Mora has to watch the video first. Let's say that it takes her three hours. Can I cross the state line in that time? Although she knows the exact time that Mike and I last spoke to Justin. Unless she's as bad with computers as Clara is, which is always a possibility, it shouldn't take her more than a few minutes to find the part where Justin and I go downstairs, I open my car trunk and . . .

It's useless. I sit on the bed. It is too late to escape. Too late to try anything else. Justice is catching up. And where would I go? I spent the whole trip on the bus imagining the drive to Canada but never made any concrete plans . . .

Maybe Detective Mora hasn't had breakfast yet. She doesn't look the kind that would skip breakfast. Maybe she'll grab a bagel first, discuss some other case with a colleague, leave the video for later.

I reach inside my closet for a suitcase and start packing. Warm tears roll down my cheeks. I cannot stop shaking. I packed all my clean underwear for my trip to Cabo, and now I don't have any clean. We should have done laundry before we left. I don't have any clean socks either. Soon the weeping becomes a bellowing. I drop on the floor and bawl like a child.

"I don't want to spend the rest of my life in prison!"

Even if I manage to leave the city, even if I manage to make it as far as Nevada, the cops will be waiting for me. They will freeze my accounts. I wouldn't be able to withdraw any cash or use any credit cards.

I'd better kill myself.

Dying would be such a nice rest. No more suffering. No more tears.

I open the closet. The rod is quite low, but I could manage. I take out some clothes to make space, then fasten a leather belt around my neck and pass the other end over the rod. There are two possibilities. I either die, and that's it, the end of my sad existence, or I die and then reincarnate.

"I repent," I cry, pulling the belt. "I never wanted to kill Nina, I only wanted her to shut up. I didn't hate her. At least not enough to kill her . . . She was so young. And so beautiful . . . I did hate Justin, though. He was an asshole, and many times I wished him dead before. I hope he's burning in hell!"

I pull a little more.

Perhaps Justin and Nina will be waiting for me in the afterlife, ready to spit on my soul as I descend to the abyss before my next transformation. Maybe they have reincarnated already . . . Do white folks reincarnate? They must, why wouldn't they? If they're good, they reincarnate again as white people. If they're bad, into something more like myself. Maybe in a future life, I'll get to be a straight white man. They're awfully unkind, as Charlie would say, but pale skin offers lots of career advantages. One can only hope.

I bend my knees, letting my weight do the work.

Then my phone rings.

I can't resist the curiosity. I let go of the belt and stand up. The caller ID shows LAPD. Detective Mora I suppose. What for? To let me know that the police are on their way to arrest me? I let the call go to voice mail. I return to the closet and pass the belt over the rod again. She calls again. She must have seen the video already . . . Is she calling to brag, to say that I will rot in a cell? How ungenerous! But I won't go to prison. She'll find my corpse first. I bend my knees and pull. I gasp, tempted to let go of the belt, but I keep pulling firmly . . . It hurts. I'm surprised at how much. I always thought that committing suicide by strangulation would be much simpler . . . I have to take a short rest. Just one minute. Then I'll start pulling again . . .

Fuck. I forgot to write a suicide note. I stand up again.

Not that it will be hard for the police to figure out that I took my own life, but one should leave an adieu, just in case. I wouldn't want anyone else to be blamed. Especially Charlie.

I pull a notebook from a drawer, grab a pen, sit down, and start writing: *To whoever finds me* . . . No. That's too impersonal . . . I should address it to my parents and ask for their forgiveness. I rip off the sheet of paper and start again.

Pitaa, Maataa,

Please forgive me. Recent events had made my existence no longer bearable. Give my love to Sita and Amrit. I wish I had been a better son and a better brother.

Not that I care much about Sita, just thinking of that bitch infuriates me, but I know my parents will find a last proof of fraternal love comforting. And I want them to feel guilty. Why, they've made me feel guilty all of my life! I'm tempted to add something about Charlie too, but wouldn't I be incriminating my little boy if I did? I better leave the note as it is. With any luck, he may be now in Puerto Vallarta, seeking a husband.

I sign the letter, pull off the sheet and leave it on top of the bed, where I know they will easily find it. I wipe the tears off my face, step back into the closet, and once again, pass the belt over the rod and pull . . .

The rod cracks. I fall to my knees. Then I feel the shelf atop and heavy boxes full of books fall on my head.

I remain on the floor for about a minute, producing a long, doleful wail. The pain is so intense I cannot move. At last, I manage to stand up. There are books spread all over the floor. All the books I couldn't leave at my parents'. The books that made me want to be a writer. *Miss Buncle's*

Book . . . *Cousin Bette* . . . *The Adulteress!* I had forgotten about Philippa Carr . . . *To Your Scattered Bodies Go*—I wonder what happened to my friend Shahin. This book was his. I always imagined his brown face as the main character instead of Sir Richard Burton's. Of course, I never cared to find out what Sir Richard Burton looked like. Now I can just google it.

I haven't had a coffee today.

One shouldn't try to kill oneself before feeling the effects of caffeine run through his body.

I limp into the kitchen. My neck is so bruised I cannot even walk straight.

I'm filling the kettle when the phone rings again. It's Charlie.

"You'll never believe what happened," he says. "I just got a call from the Mexican customs. They're giving us back the semi."

"You got it back?" I ask, surprised.

"Not yet." His voice sounds raspy, as if he had a rough night. "But they told me we could pick it up today. They never inspected it," he adds before I could ask. "Deirdre called Anthony and Anthony told Ricky to make some calls. I just spoke with him. Ricky is friends with a Mexican senator who called the governor who must have called some officer at immigration. Can you believe it? Anthony said I should give the ladies at customs that helped us at least fifty dollars each, for all their trouble."

"Where are you?"

"Still in Tijuana," Charlie replies. "I didn't have the guts to flee last night, Jignesh, I apologize, I'm sorry. But it worked out just fine because, had I followed your advice, I would have ended up God-knows-where and with no money. I'm in a Sanborns, across the street from the hotel. I just ordered breakfast. Remember I told you how much Lucille insisted we should visit one? We came here last night. The coffee is terrible, but the salsas are to die for."

"What are you waiting for?" I finally manage to say. "Go and get the semi."

"I just ordered! And I'm too hungover to get on the road. And Murat hasn't woken up yet. We went out last night to this tawdry place called *Las Pulgas*—"

"Listen to me, Charlie. Go get the semi, and don't call me back until you have it."

I hang up. This doesn't change a thing, though. Detective Mora must have already seen the video. But now, she doesn't have a body. And if she doesn't have a body, she has no case. Isn't that how it works?

I listen to the voicemail she left.

"Mr. Amin, this is Detective Mora, from the LA Police Department. Sorry to bother you, I know you're not feeling well. Your colleague, Clara, provided me with the login and password for the security video in the building basement, and I'm looking at it right now, but I can only go as far back as the early morning of March 15. According to Mr. Ferguson's report, the last time that Justin was seen at your office was on the night of March 14, around nine o'clock. Clara mentioned that you may have saved an earlier version of this video. Do you have a copy that you could provide me? Please give me a call at—"

I put my phone down. Then I pick it up again and call Charlie.

"I canceled my huevos rancheros, Jignesh. I'm on my way to the room to wake up Murat," he says, puffing. "I'm just waiting for the stoplight to change to cross the street."

"Call me the moment you're on that truck and have left customs"

I hang up.

I guess I don't have to kill myself anymore.

I am too shocked to laugh.

I have to get to Tijuana.

First breakfast. I haven't eaten in almost twelve hours. I pour some cereal into a bowl and start eating it dry, without any milk. I have some coffee too.

Do I need to go back to Tijuana? It doesn't make sense to delay their drive south any longer. Half an hour to downtown. Catch the next train. Three-hour trip to San Diego. The trolley to San Ysidro. Crossing the border . . .

It would be faster to fly directly to Cabo.

I need to buy a plane ticket.

I return to my bedroom and turn on my computer. Everything leaving today is over six hundred dollars . . . I wouldn't need to leave today, though. They won't be there until Sunday, at the earliest. What am I going to do alone those two days?

I leave the computer and start picking up books . . . *The Clan of the Cave Bear* . . . I could just relax and read a little . . . *Little Women* . . . *Little Men*, which I liked much better. *Paul and Virginia!* A little sugary for my taste, but Virginia's modesty inspired me to become the person I am . . .

I could stay in a resort. Visit a spa. I could use some relaxation. This close encounter with death—I take a hand to my neck—left me unsettled.

I leave the books and return to my laptop. Maybe I could stay in a gay resort. I never had the courage to visit one in the desert. Do they have any in Cabo? I google *Gay Resorts in Los Cabos*. All these are gay-friendly hotels. I want to stay in a clothing-optional one . . . I search for *clothing-optional gay resorts in Los Cabos* . . . But would I dare to walk around in my birthday suit? I wore a bathrobe the few times I went to that bathhouse in Long Beach—I drove that far so that no one would recognize me. Days of yore, when I was much thinner. I would spend a whole afternoon lurking among the dark corridors, then feel wrong and dirty for an entire month, promising myself to never do it again, that I would start dating girls like my parents wanted me to, then I would drive down again, tell my parents I had gone with friends to catch a movie . . . They knew I didn't have any friends. Why did I think I could fool them? Then, one time I saw my dad's mechanic coming out of the locker room. I spent the next four hours hiding inside my room. And never returned . . .

This one doesn't look bad. The bedrooms are a bit flashy, yet very spacious. Where is it in Cabo? Oh, fuck, it's in Fort-Lauderdale. Stupid Google.

What about taking a cruise? I google *Atlantis Gay Cruises*. I see the pictures. All muscled up white men. Not one bear. Not even a twink. Occasionally a black or an Asian person. I would rather go to a place that accepts gays coming in all shades and sizes, but that doesn't exist, does it?

"What would a fatty Indian like me do running around on a boat full of scantily clothed male perfection?" I wail, closing the browser. "Well, the buffets are all you can eat." I reopen the browser. And there's one leaving today, at 5:00 p.m., from San Diego.

It could be a coincidence or a signal from heaven.

I spend the next thirty minutes looking at the pictures and reading all the descriptions about the boat. Everyone looks ridiculously attractive, but so do the men on the pages of *Advocate*, and you see all kinds of people in West Hollywood. I wouldn't be the only fatty on board, would I?

And I wouldn't even have to pack. All you need on a cruise are condoms and a pair of speedos.

My phone rings again. It's Charlie.

"We have the semi," he laughs. "We're having breakfast now. I gave the girls at customs twenty dollars. Murat didn't want to give them more. But charge Anthony fifty."

"Tell Jignesh he's a lucky bastard," I hear Murat shout in the background.

I am, I laugh. The police aren't coming to get me.

I tell Charlie not to stop until they reach Cabo, that I will meet them down there. Then I call the reservations number for Atlantis.

If I drive, I can be back in San Diego in less than three hours.

It takes me a little over two. It's a rather perilous ride; one eye on the road, one on my cell phone, trying to reserve a parking space near the ship terminal and read all about the Atlantis experience. I call Detective Mora too and apologize for the incomplete video.

"By the way," I say, before I hang up. "I was just thinking. Maybe Justin traveled to Virginia, kidnapped his son and now he's in Canada."

"The son is with his mother," Detective Mora replies. She sounds so arctic. I'm pretty sure she doesn't like me. "I spoke to his ex-wife last week and she hasn't seen him. And I doubt Justin would have travelled to Virginia. He has a warrant there for failing to pay for child support. And another one in Maine for failing to pay state taxes."

"He does? Oh, my God. I cannot believe it!"

Detective Mora snorts. I must have sounded a little too enthusiastic.

"Thank you, anyway, Mr. Amin. You've been very helpful."

"Anytime, detective."

I end up having to park a mile away from the terminal and having to run all the way down to the docks, not an easy task when you're wearing sandals, but I still make it there before four.

The sun is shining. It's unusually warm. Everyone looks excited. I'm excited. Everyone is laughing. I'm laughing too! Everyone seems blithe, free, and—what a pleasant surprise—every species of the gay zoology will be on board: from lanky, obnoxious twinks that I'd rather not see, to bears of every age, width, and color; from the palest hue of a white carnation to the darkest charcoal, passing by seals, otters, fairy queens, and objectionably dressed gym bunnies. The palette of browns wouldn't satisfy the editor of *Mother Jones*, but I must say it is far more diverse than I expected. I see plenty of Asians and Latinos sprinkled around, and more than a few African Americans. Most aren't porn material and that's comforting, I think, watching my own reflection in the glass doors. Will I see any Indian people aboard or will I be the only curry princess? Oh, there's one! And he's rather cute. We'll be best friends! We'll dance all night then sip margaritas by the pool in the morning celebrating love and diversity. I hope he's Indian, though, and not Pakistani. I don't like Pakistanis.

Now, I'm all for fair representation, of course, but I'm disappointed to see that we will share the boat with fish too. As a feminist and progressive human being it makes me happy to see women frolicking among equals, but why can't they charter their own fucking boat those effing dikes? Happily, there aren't too many.

"No luggage," I proudly say to the woman that checks me in at the terminal counter. "Just my toothbrush," which I'm holding in the same hand I'm holding my passport. She has a cute Irish accent. And slightly crooked teeth too, but I shouldn't criticize—should I? I'm too excited! This morning I was trying to kill myself with a belt, now I'm ready to embark for Los Cabos. "There are places aboard where I can buy a swimming suit, right?"

"There are," the lady explains. She pulls out a map and a pen and marks the shopping area. I wanted to save the map as a memory and now she ruined it. It doesn't matter. I'm still happy. She takes her time with me. I have so many questions! She answers each of them with a smile. There are several pools, several restaurants, night entertainment, cabaret, and there will be all these fabulous parties! I will only enjoy one-third of the trip, of course, because I'll debark in Cabo San Lucas, but two nights at sea will be sufficient to relax and be merry.

This is very irregular, I know, taking a gay cruise, but I've had months of being tense, of not sleeping through the night, of crying at every silly commercial. Who says that criminals don't suffer? We suffer intensely. My head and my neck still hurt from this morning's suicide attempt.

"Thank you, Lord Rama, for the ineptitude of the LAPD," I mutter, as I climb up the ramp. One wouldn't believe how slow detectives work from watching television. Thank you, Lord Vishnu, for the widespread corruption of the Mexican authorities. Just like in India.

I walk straight to the swimsuit boutique by the main atrium. Jesus Christ, how many stories is this place? It's like being in Vegas but no one's smoking. There's even a double glass elevator. My, the lamp hanging above the grand stairs must be the size of an automobile!

"Do you have this one in size XXL?" I ask the store clerk.

He recommends buying an aubergine scarf too, to hide the marks on my neck.

Then I go to my cabin. Windowless and tiny. Two beds. I will be sharing with someone else. Please dear God, you've been so good to me today.

Make my roommate someone incredibly handsome, I don't mind at all if he's stupid. Well, not so handsome that he will make me feel insecure, handsome enough that he's fun to look at. There's a painting from Target too, a large mirror, and a white board to hang on the front door, so you could advertise to the world your perversions. I noticed that some passengers had already hung theirs outside their cabin. The closets are tiny. All for my future best friend since I brought no luggage, which reminds me: I should have bought something too for the costume party tomorrow.

I'm trying on my new Aussiebum when my roommate enters. A tall bear in his mid-to-late-forties. Nice calves, nice arms, Oakley sunglasses, and a yellow v-neck one size too tight that hollers: *I'm from the southern provinces.*

My first reaction is to reach for my shirt. I'm on a gay cruise, I remind myself. It is okay to display oneself half naked. I choose to be friendly.

"Hi!" I say, turning around.

The bear replies with a nod. He seems disappointed. I suppose he expected a skinny person the color of boiled chicken. No biggy. I'm disappointed too. He's no wand of tuberose or as comely as one's heart's desires. Our opinions may change, though, after we have some alcohol.

"My name is Jignesh," I say, as I finish adjusting my junk, then extend my right hand. "What is yours?"

The bear doesn't answer. He drops his luggage onto his bed, mumbles something about seeing where his friends at and leaves the cabin.

Rude. Maybe he was just shy and not at all racist. Well, no. I recognized the look. Same look I always got at the bars in West Hollywood.

Deep breath, Jignesh. Relax. You're on a mini vacation. Put on your aubergine scarf, forget about wearing pants, and choo-choo your way up to the pool, as Charlie would say. Get some food and possibly a triple martini. Forget about all the traumatic experiences of the last month, forget about your entire life, forget about the fact that you're utterly unattractive, at least for the next two days. Then you can return to being miserable.

36

Baja

Mexicans, I reckon, as I observe the Tijuana landscape go by through the window, are partial to pink and pistachio green, ironwork, and unfinished constructions. The suburbs of this city are a series of flat-roofed postmodernist follies, each more unattractive than the next, from which forests of metal rods unfurl as if they were the tentacles of monsters trapped inside the concrete. I'm in a cheerful mood, I suppose, since I didn't have to become a fugitive from justice. Nevertheless, I can't help but be scared, repelled, and intrigued by the superabundance of poor architectural choices.

"What do you think all that rebar is for?" I ask Murat. He shrugs. I get distracted by another tacky detail—the plenitude of glass blocks, and the precise function of the superabundant metal rods remains uncertain.

"Poverty cannot serve as an excuse for this flagrant attack on aesthetics, can it?" I ask, with a half-anguished chortle. "It is as if a Soviet brutalist had made the initial architectural plan, then a Middle Eastern gay man from central Florida decided on the ornaments and the colors, on a John Cassavetes movie budget. Not even Armenians are this eccentric . . . Is it this bad in Turkey?" I ask Murat.

"Some places," Murat shrugs. "But Istanbul is the most beautiful city in the world."

I can't stop taking pictures. Tijuana belongs in a magazine. Probably not *Architectural Digest*, but *Vice* magazine? Bad taste is king in this godforsaken country. I can imagine a black and white exhibition at the

Getty Center and the long lines of hip Angelenos waiting to see it. Or maybe one at the LACMA, in full color. Take that house, for example. The edge of the exterior wall is a bright orange, but they painted the second-floor turquoise. The windows must come from the cheapest selection at Home Depot. One has iron bars; the other doesn't. Does that stop half the thieves? The house next door is all gray concrete, with a white picket fence, and the skeleton of a light-up plastic snowman on the roof of the front porch. There's a dog on the roof too, awfully *à propos*, barking at pedestrians as if they were the Antichrist. I take lots and lots of pictures. *We're down in Baja! #fishtacos* I update my Instagram account every five minutes.

Eventually, we say farewell to the city. The sky ahead is incredibly blue, the road like a gray tape, and in the distance, you can see the mountains.

Two hours later, we stop in Ensenada for lunch. Coca-Cola seems to be one of the local deities. We're making awfully good time. Murat has no respect for the Mexican transit laws, and he was right, beer makes him a much better driver.

"We're like Thelma and Louise," I joke when we get back on the road.

"And there's Brad Pitt." Murat points at a young ranchero waiting for the bus under the shade of a pole. "But we're not stopping to pick him up."

I laugh. He's not that bad of a travel companion. He kindly warns me to lower the window before he farts. After six months living with a man like Jignesh, I consider that an awfully nice gesture. He brought a bunch of CDs, and after our initial feud upon leaving LA we've been listening mostly to Turkish music. I've gotten used to it. I no longer feel the urge to connect my iPhone. What, ruin this trip with some old episodes of *This American Life*? No, I'm fine with Murat being in charge of our road trip soundtrack. It's colorful. And it suits Mexico.

The desert here isn't what one imagines. The landscape changes dramatically, from bushes and rocks, to tall dry grass with a few splotches of green and agricultural flatlands. Rarely we see a tree, but telephone poles abound in the territory. Staring out of the window becomes therapeutic.

My only concern is the state of the two bodies inside the freezer. Could they be floating in water now? We lost two entire days, one loading up and the other trying to cross the border. By our original plan, we should already be in Cabo. The side excursion to Mulegé is, of course, out of the question. I cannot ask for help from Murat, and I couldn't get rid of the corpses alone, could I?

.   I steal a glance at my Turkish friend. He looks manly with his ten-dollar sunglasses. He has big furry arms. Makes me wonder . . . Anyways, we've lost so much time, it wouldn't be convenient to make a stop in Mulegé if we'll spend the night in Guerrero Negro. We could always skip Guerrero Negro and drive straight, but then we wouldn't make it to Mulegé until after midnight, according to what my phone says, and one needs to rest. Getting rid of the corpses will have to wait till we get down to Cabo . . .

Murat is now singing along with the Turkish music. He turns and sings something to me. Bless his heart.

"Where do you think we should spend the night?" I ask.

"Wherever we get tired."

"Aren't you tired? I am a little."

Murat invites me to take a nap in the sleeper cabin. It smells like cat pee, but I oblige.

When I wake up, a few hours later, the landscape has changed again. Now it's all thorn bushes and cacti. It's getting dark.

"Are you hungry?" Murat asks, finishing up his beer. "I'm starving."

Intrigued by a sign at the side of the road that advertises *empanadas de panocha*, we make a stop at a charming little town called Punta Prieta. No paved streets, except for the two-lane highway. There's a big pond of stinky water across from the one place to eat, Restaurant Davis, a place so authentic it would be a success in LA. It has only one aluminum table, with a large Tecate logo on top, guarded by two sleepy dogs. We wash our hands using a large ladle to draw water out of a plastic barrel.

"I often refer to Leitchfield as the armpit of the world. It is nice to see one could have done much worse."

Murat laughs. At the table, he practices his Portuguese with the restaurant owner, a rather stout lady of indeterminate age with a penchant for Julio Iglesias. Let's say I manage to rent a jeep, I reflect, while the two of them discuss the menu. And let's say that I manage to drug Murat, as we had planned. Could I take the bodies out of the freezer myself? I could, perhaps, one at a time. The ice must have already melted. And how difficult could it be to dig a couple of graves?

A little boy playing with a naked Barbie doll approaches our table. The restaurateur's child, I presume. He must be five at the eldest. I spit on my napkin to clean a crusty bugger off of his cheek.

"¿Cómo se llama?" I ask about his doll.

The little boy hunches, trying to hide a bashful smile. His mother says something unintelligible encouraging him to answer my question. The boy wiggles, then mumbles a name I can't understand.

"¿Qué?" I ask. "What did he say?"

I turn to Murat. Murat shrugs. The smile on his face, however, reveals that he's as enchanted by the little child as I am.

"Seu pulso," he asks. "¿Cómo se llama?"

"¡Cristina!" the child eventually hollers and hands me the doll.

Poor Christina. She's sporting a rather unflattering haircut and has teeth marks on her legs.

"This little boy is gayer than an episode of the *Dukes of Hazzard*," I say to Murat after the food comes. The little boy decides to sit with us and eat one of our empanadas. Murat agrees with a snort. "I wish we could steal him," I add.

I really wish we could.

"Why would you ruin a successful career as a homosexual by raising a child?" Murat asks. "You'd be much better off with a dog."

"Oh, Murat." I take a sip of my beer. "It's not the same. You cannot dress up a dog. Or send him to school. And a dog won't get you invited to birthday parties."

I ponder my plan for a little longer, back in the semi. I see that Jignesh sent a text to confirm that he will meet us in Cabo on Sunday. That pretty much gives us an entire day to kill. We could still spend one night in Guerrero Negro, then the next one in Mulegé . . . Normally I would be terrified just by musing on this, but I feel empowered by what happened this morning. It is as if fate didn't want me to fail. This place looks so forsaken, though, I doubt I could find a car rental agency nearby. I'll check on Expedia . . .

Shoot. The closest agency is in Loreto, at least one hour south of Mulegé.

I could always call and ask them to drop a car, drug Murat, put on my fabulous Valentino camo pants and my hiking boots from Salomon Quest, carry the bodies into the car, drive to the desert, bury the bodies, and come back on time to have a little recovery nap and huevos rancheros for breakfast.

How long does it take to dig a grave? I search on Yahoo Answers.

"Murat," I say after I verify it shouldn't take much longer than two hours. "I think we should drive through Guerrero Negro and spend the night in Mulegé."

"All right." He takes a sip of his beer.

"And, while we're there, I think that we should enjoy ourselves and rent a smaller car, take a day off and maybe go hiking. How does that sound? Spend the day exploring this spectacular landscape. It looks almost handmade, don't you think?"

"I can't waste time. I need to be back in Los Angeles by Monday."

I force a laugh. "Murat. We cannot miss this. Just look at the surreal landscape. It is like being on another planet. Besides, Jignesh won't meet us until Sunday night, and he has the keys to Anthony's house. We wouldn't be able to unload the furniture anyway."

The last is a little lie. I do have the keys to Anthony's house, right in my pocket.

Nothing I say convinces Murat. He has to be back in LA on Monday morning. Still, from the comfort of the sleeper cabin I dial the number of Hotel Tranquilidad, the little motel at the end of a long dirt road on the outskirts of Mulegé with no other buildings around which Jignesh and I selected in our original plan. I ask whether they have available rooms. *They do!*

Everything goes well until I have to pay. My credit card is rejected.

Shoot. Then I recollect that, among the papers inside Jignesh's courier bag, I saw an envelope that seemed to contain a credit card. Would it be too bad if I opened it . . . ? It is a credit card, for Justin Kettler. Same Justin as frozen man? Well, he's dead now, and Jignesh reconciles the credit cards, doesn't he? He's the accountant. Only he will notice the charge, and desperate times call for desperate measures, "Right, Murat?"

"I don't think you should be using Justin's credit card."

I pat Murat's shoulder condescendingly then call again Hotel Tranquilidad and book a room under the name of Justin Kettler.

Then I call a car rental in Loreto and request a Jeep. They have a Jetta. What's a city girl going to do? I take it. It's $195 extra to deliver the car to Mulegé. "Does it come with a blow job?" Murat asks when he hears me repeat the charge. I gently tap again on Murat's arm and ask him to focus on the driving. I agree to all the charges and ask the agent if they could leave the keys at reception, because we won't make it to Mulegé until after midnight.

They cannot do that, he says. They need to see a valid driver's license and the credit card I will be using.

"Will it suffice if I text you a picture?"

It will, the agent replies after consulting with his supervisor. I had also noticed that among the mail there was a letter from the DMV with Justin Kettler's new driver's license. How convenient. Baby Jesus must be looking over after me.

"You shouldn't have used Justin's credit card," Murat says, when I hang up.

"Murat, don't be like that. Jignesh said I could, in case of an emergency. And this is an emergency. It'll be a write off, anyhow."

Murat shrugs and continues driving.

What has come over me? I'm back in the passenger's seat, staring at the road ahead, like, I don't know, Toni Collette in *Little Miss Sunshine*? I just rented a room and a car with a dead person's credit card. After the scare of Tijuana. I have to do this, though. For Jignesh. And for myself. It is time I start thinking about myself and putting my needs before those of others. I never do. I really want to succeed as an interior designer, and those two bodies inside the freezer are the one thing that's stopping me from becoming the most photographed interior designer in the three Californias. I look at Murat. Will five Vicodin be enough for him? That's all I have. Well, I have six, but I'm keeping one for myself. We should have stopped at a pharmacy in Tijuana. I'll need to take a rest, too. Digging a grave may be taxing . . . Oy, maybe this sudden fearlessness comes from the fact that Murat switched CDs, and for the last twenty minutes we've been listening to Katy Perry.

We arrive at Hotel Tranquilidad right at midnight.

"Let's park a tad further away, by those palm trees at the end of the road," I say to Murat. "That way we won't take up all the spaces."

He obliges.

"These are the keys to your room, Mr. Kettler," the receptionist says after a quick glance at Justin's identification. All white people look alike, thank God. "And these are the keys for your car. It's parked right outside."

Our room is so fabulously tawdry, with cyan walls, pink and mustard bed covers, and a Talavera pottery sun the size of a TV hanging from the wall, I have to immediately take a picture and share it on social media, *#VivaMexico #GreenDesert #Mulegé*.

On the other side of the building, there's a pool, all for ourselves, we happily discover, since everyone else has already gone to bed. The air feels so thick and warm, I suggest to Murat that we try it. Murat claims to be dead tired, but he'll sit out for a beer while I play Esther Williams in my speedo. *Perfecto.*

One fast trip to the bathroom to change and pulverize the Vicodin dolls. When it's Murat's turn to use it, I open a beer can and drop the powder inside, then stir it with my sunglasses temple tips. Murat comes out and drinks from the can without any suspicion. Thank God he's an alcoholic. He exits the room and sits on a bench in front of the pool. I will need a beer too, I reckon. I open another can. And maybe a couple of the fat burner pills that I found in Jignesh's suitcase, since the task at hand promises to be taxing. I pop the pills and jump into the pool.

"Are Turkish hotels this tacky too?" I ask my Muslim friend, pointing at the hotel's extravagant decorations.

Murat laughs, then bobs his head up and down.

As soon as he announces that he's going to bed, I'll give myself ten minutes.

37

Gay Cruise Party

One thing must be said about gay cruise parties, or any party where shirts and pants are optional but not so wigs, feathers, and leather harnesses: they're rather sticky. I dread going through the crowd to refill my mojito. People have no clothes to absorb their sweat. They stink too, despite being in the open air. Men who love men don't smell like a field of daffodils, as you would think from seeing Charlie. Not when they've been drinking and carousing for the last seven hours. They smell kind of rancid. They reek of beer, poppers, and—how else to say it?—ass. The whole boat stinks of ass. That is the most potent smell here: ass. How could it smell of anything else with three thousand men parading in their underwear, a quarter of them wearing jockstraps? Once the boat returns to its homeport, the whole crew must go through the hallways armed with bottles of Febreze, I bet, trying to get rid of the smell before the next passengers board.

In any case, I am having a good time. I suppose. Most men here aren't worth a second look, but a few are attractive. The food was good. I ate a lot. Alone. The first couple who shared a table with me didn't care to ask how I was doing. The second one did but then left as soon as they saw a whole table for themselves available. I smiled courteously and kept to myself. And the oysters.

Then I soaked in the hot tub for a good two hours, witnessed a few things that I dare not repeat, and now I'm here, at the main deck, dancing. By myself. Wearing the long sleeve shirt I wore on my way to San Diego and my Aussiebum speedo, surrounded by a crowd, that, on the face of it, is having the time of their lives. Part of me doesn't care. The other part wishes that I had made a friend already. Alas, if most men aboard aren't worth a second look, I'm not worth any. My otherwise cheerful personality and wits cannot compensate for my age, my dark complexion, and my fleshy waistline. I am invisible to this crowd.

Not that I'm often looked at, but I had forgotten what it felt like to be totally invisible. People are forced to see you at the office. Here, even the creeps get more attention. There's one I've been observing for a while. He seems to be 150 years old. He's wearing a tall hat, a blond wig, and a Miss America bikini, the bottom part of which fell long ago into the ocean. People keep asking to take a selfie with him as if his ding-dong was some kind of celebrity.

This boat evokes a few memories. Memories from the long-gone days of my youth, I munch the ice. From the time when I lacked agency, but found the smell of beer, piss, and stale poppers not so repugnant. I never accounted for much as a homosexual. Unpopular at school, unpopular at the dance clubs. I was always the first to arrive at the bar, for fear that if I were late and had to wait in line outside, a passerby would recognize me. And I was always the last to leave, hoping for a last-minute hook-up among the appropriately named "sales rack." One never had true days of glory. But I enjoyed it. A few times, I got lucky. Of course, I was much thinner.

There was this club on Santa Monica Boulevard I patronized a few times in the nineties. It burnt down. I didn't start the fire. Some skinny twat who paid no attention to the no-smoking signs, most probably. I used to climb to the stage as soon as the go-go dancers stepped down, and then, when the music started, I would close my eyes, raise my arms, and perform for the audience. My favorite piece was Madonna's *What it Feels Like for a Girl* dance remix version. I used to muse along to the lyrics, moving my arms as if they were the blades of a windmill.

I stopped doing that when I learned that the audience had given me a nickname: *Interpretasha.*

What's in a nickname, but recognition? I should have kept dancing. I should have kept going to the bars. I should have kept doing a few more stupid things, wear a red dress, smoke crack, try out the glory holes in the bathroom. Alas, I was always afraid of being caught. Always afraid of being disavowed by my parents . . . That one time when I saw my dad's mechanic, for example . . . What else would he be doing at a bathhouse but cruising for sex too? I should have said "hi," and established a friendly conversation.

"How do you do Mr. Prabhakar? How's Mrs. Prabhakar? I haven't seen her since Diwali."

"She's all right," he would have said. "How are your parents?" A gentle conversation, like the ones straight men have when they meet at a brothel. As dreary a place as a bathhouse is, a kind word would have been welcome.

I should have kept trying. I could have had a long and outstanding career out of the closet. I became much braver in my thirties. I even watched half of Stephen Fry's *Wilde* with my parents, until they thought it was too much for my eyes and asked me to go to my bedroom . . . What on Earth happened?

I miss Charlie. He's the closest thing I've ever had to a boyfriend. I wonder what he and Murat are doing now. I wish I could call them, but I won't get a signal again until we arrive in Cabo. Charlie would have liked it here. He would have liked the perverts. With him here, I wouldn't feel so lonely.

I leave my empty cup on a table nearby and head to the bathroom. It's packed. I have to wait in line before reaching a urinal, then again to wash my hands. As I wait, a young man wearing rabbit's ears and a pink tutu announces that he accidentally dropped an ecstasy pill and begs everyone else not to move until he finds it. Under the tutu, he's wearing nothing. I spend a minute or two looking at him in all fours, surveying the floor for his precious pill. He's quite young and with the right amount of hair coming out from all the right places.

I never had the thrill of having to look for an ecstasy pill dressed as a ballerina.

I didn't even wear shorts growing up. I was too modest. Revealing skin, I used to think, was a privilege of white people. Not anymore, I reckon. There are plenty of Asian, black, and Latino men here who, I can tell, aren't thinking about their poor mothers.

I should call myself fortunate. Half a century ago, I could have been killed, forced into a demeaning career, or sent to prison. Yet I'm not half as lucky as these blessed Millennials. Just look around. No sense of shame, and I'm not being judgmental. I never dared to set foot in a gay bar until I was out of college, and these men are taking their same-gender partner to prom dances. They're getting married. They're adopting babies. I never had any of that. I never dared to dream of having any of that. The generations that'll come after this will only be a million times more fortunate. They'll never have to hide or lie about who they are. They'll never feel less than others . . . Look at them smile. I never smiled. One learned to keep an inscrutable mien at all times since the wrong gesture could earn you a beating. Oh, no wonder I'm such a reprobate. One became an expert on telling lies at such an early age. One learned to keep one's heart desires to oneself and oneself only. As a result, one grew so bitter and angry.

My turn at the sink comes next. From the mirror, my reflection stares back gloomily. I look old, tired, and ridiculous.

I shut my eyes. *You're as good-looking as any other man here*, I repeat mentally, *including the druggie in the tutu . . . You is kind. You is strong. You is important.*

It doesn't work. When I open my eyes, I find myself looking as ghastly as before. I force myself to grin. A smile is the best accessory, isn't it?

This is where I always dreamed of being, and yet, I feel so out of place. This boat is full of average looking men, some fatter than me, some even darker, many of them much older, but I'm not an ordinary, middle-aged, colored fat person. I'm a murderer.

Had I been free to flutter around like a butterfly, spreading goodwill and air kisses, had I had the opportunity to be as gay as a maypole, would I have still killed people?

The unmistakable chords of *What it Feels Like for a Girl* start playing.

I scurry out of the bathroom. I need alcohol. A full bottle. I need to get drunk and dance to this song. For this is my song, mine, and mine only. I haven't danced to it for so long! I need to become once again *Interpretasha*. Where? It needs to be somewhere high, somewhere from where everyone on this boat could see me . . . She was such an innocent girl, *Interpretasha* . . . She would have not hurt a soul. She was so kind, so benign and—there are too many people! It will be impossible to make it all the way to the bar, buy a drink, then climb to the upper deck before the song finishes . . . I see an unattended cup and don't think twice: I guzzle it down in one gulp. Whiskey. A little bitter. I pull off my shirt and tie it around my waist. It's the only shirt I have. I cannot lose it.

I use my elbows to get to the nearest staircase. A few men complain. *Don't give a fuck, Interpretasha*, I say to myself. *You are out of fucks. All of your fucks have been irrevocably provided.* You have to dance . . . But I cannot get through. It's too crowded! I must get atop before the bass licks end. That's my signature dance step! I gaze around for another way up, discover another unguarded cup and snatch it—*gin and tonic!* This second drink reenergizes me. I turn back to the stairs and start climbing up from the outer part of the banister. Some good Samaritans recognize my urge to get through and move away to help me get over. I thank them with a smile, this time honest.

I find a spot where everyone on this boat can see me, close my eyes, and start dancing. I dance as if I were in 2001 again. I dance as if I were still thirty-one. I dance as if I weren't fat, ugly, old, and a murderer. I need to have fun for at least one night, well, maybe two, before I meet brainless one and brainless two down in Los Cabos.

I need to forget about the two bodies.

The song ends, and I open my eyes. I see my sister Sita standing next to me.

"What are you doing here?" she babbles.

She's as drunk as a skunk. Her friend Kim is with her.

38

Desert

There's a full-length mirror inside the room, but I don't want to turn on the lights and risk waking up Murat, so I climb atop the bathroom vanity to check how my Salomon Quest boots look with the camo pants. They are one size too small, but they look utterly fabulous, I confirm bending down with a smile. I should have bought brown socks instead of gray, but who cares, they don't show. I doubt a better dressed interior designer slash criminal ever existed . . . Oy, I'm referring to myself as a criminal. That's not good.

Whatever. I took three of Jignesh's fat-burner pills and, together with the beer I chugged, I feel brave, empowered, and fabulous, just as if I was on speed.

I apply some hand lotion. Smells like lemon—a nice gesture in a hotel as tackily decorated as this—then I tiptoe out of the bathroom, grab the semi keys, and leave the room. I spend a few moments marveling at the beautiful moonless sky. You don't get to see this many stars in Los Angeles.

I park the Jetta behind the trailer so that I can easily transfer the bodies. I feel as sexy as Michelle Rodriguez behind the wheel. Then I open the trailer doors and climb inside.

I see that Jignesh thought of everything, bless his heart. He left the bag with the shovels and the flashlights nearby so that we would not struggle in finding them. I take one lamp and climb my way over the furniture to the front . . . Shoot, I forgot a screwdriver to remove the latch. I go back to the bag and get one. It's a Phillips head, now I know that.

I put the screws in my shirt pocket and remove the latch. Now, Charlie, you just need to open the freezer. Deep breath. Remember that the last time wasn't too pleasant. Take one deep breath. I close my eyes and reach for the edge of the lid . . . Sweet Southern Baby Jesus, please prevent me from screaming like a masc-acting, forty-something bear wearing a leather harness in the presence of a spider when I open this . . . Oy, I didn't think of spiders before. I bet there must be tons outside. I can clap my way to scare the snakes, I remember that from *The Parent Trap*, but how will I scare the Baja tarantulas? Better not worry about them now. I'd need a torch to scare them. Where would I find one at this hour? Maybe I could soak a rag inside the gas tank and wrap it around a stick. I'd need a lighter. Maybe Murat has one, but before I do all that, let's open this . . . Okay, another deep breath. One . . . Sweet Baby Jesus, I promise not to ever wack off to *Swingers and Swappers* or any kind of straight porn again if I get through this. Two . . . Gay porn, I can't really promise . . . Three . . . ! Oh, my God, this is horrible, I start panting. This is awful. This is worse than I imagined. The ice didn't melt completely, as I had expected, but the man's body is almost thawed, and his looks are just sickening.

I cannot do this, I think, closing the lid. Jignesh should have been the one doing this, not me. I have to do it, though, I sob. Jignesh isn't around to help, and it may be too late by the time we reach Cabo. I'm weeping now. My lower jaw hurts as if somebody had punched me. Oh, God, I'm making the most significant effort not to run away screaming like Shelley Duvall did in *The Shining*.

I climb my way back to the door and sit on the edge of the trailer. What was I thinking? If I didn't have the guts to leave Tijuana last night, I'm not going to be able to do this either. I thought it would be much easier, that I would just need to pull each corpse to the car and drive off.

Now, what's the alternative? Keep pretending? How am I going to explain the stench to Murat, once the ice melts completely? I'm stuck with this. I cannot fail Jiggy.

I climb to the front end again and reopen the lid. There's a big blob of semi-frozen blood squirting out of the man's head. Poor guy. His face looks like a rubber mask. The lips and the eyes are completely black . . . Okay, a man has to do what a man has to do. I roll up my sleeves and stick in my hands to pull out Justin . . . The water is freezing! "I cannot do it," I pull my arms out and stomp my feet on the floor, wailing. "Jignesh should be doing this, not me!"

I try again. I cannot think too much about this; otherwise, I won't be able to finish.

This fella is heavier than I expected. I bend down. My face is almost touching his. At least he doesn't smell. I pull, and a splash of cold water wets my shirt. It's fucking cold. I'm tempted to let go, but I'm halfway through it, and my Camden shirt from Banana Republic is already ruined. At least it was only seventy-nine dollars. I close my eyes and pull again . . . Pretend that you are Nurse Jenny from *Call the Midwife*, I tell myself, hauling out a new life instead of a corpse from a freezer. I manage to pull the arms and part of his torso over the edge. I am completely drenched . . . I paid almost nine hundred dollars for these pants . . . Think about your own showroom on Melrose, Charlie. Next to Formations. Think of all those wealthy homosexuals and overly Botoxed women living in the Hollywood Hills, in dire need of a gay decorator. Think of them finding your ad in an issue of *Frontiers*, among dentists, hook-up sites, and plastic surgeons. Think on . . . My phone starts ringing. The echo inside the trailer makes it sounds thunderous, so after rapidly checking the area code and confirming it's from LA, I answer.

"Hello, this is Lisa, from your credit card company—"

A robocall? At this hour? It's after midnight! It's one in the morning. I immediately hang up. Now I'm upset. What sort of sick society have we become that one cannot keep his number private without receiving solicitation calls from scammers? This is truly the end of times. What has this world come to . . . ? Oh, God. My clothes are drenched in cold water, I'm inside a trailer with two frozen bodies five hundred miles south of home, and I still have to drive to the desert, dig a hole and leave them there. I must admit, though, that the reception of Telcel here is fabulous. Kudos to Carlos Slim. I wouldn't get the same from AT&T back in the States this far from civilization. Let's check how many hearts my Instagram pictures got . . .

I should call Jignesh too. I wanted to keep this a surprise, but I need some words of comfort before I continue, and maybe he'll be able to give them.

My call goes straight to his voicemail. He must be watching TV and put his phone off. I'll send him a message.

Murat and I are in Mulegé, I type. *I decided to go ahead with our plan and get rid of the two bodies*. Send.

Oh, shoot, I shouldn't have sent that. If anyone ever goes through his telephone records . . .

Just kidding. Having a blast. Call me tomorrow. Send.

Okay, let's put the phone away and try again . . . I'll just check really fast what's new on Facebook. Okay, not much . . . Oh, Sherise and her husband are buying a house in Mar Vista. *Congratulations!!!* I comment. Of course, that witch Jade is already asking questions . . . I wonder how they got the money for the down payment?

Okay, enough. I put my phone back in my pocket and grab Justin's body by the wrists. Then I pull . . . It doesn't move. I'll have to hug him. I close my eyes, clasp my arms around, and grasping his belt from the back with my right hand, I pull again. Oh, shoot. It's not only the body's weight. From the knee down, his right leg is still inside the ice.

Well, desperate times call for extreme measures. Like that one time at Barney's New York when I swapped tags to get a Comme des Garçons shirt for the price of a Ralph Lauren. I take some of the bungee cords holding the furniture in place and tie one around the body, then I make a chain with four more cords to reach the car. There's nowhere I could tie the end of it, so I roll down the back windows, pass the cord through and fasten the hooks.

"I'll just move forward a little," I say to myself, climbing into the Jetta. "Just enough to pull the damn frozen leg out."

I turn on the engine and slowly drive forward. I see the cords getting tighter through the rear-view mirror. I press on just a little more, less than one foot, then one of the cords snaps and a hook hits the back window. I step out of the car. I have to bite my knuckles to prevent a cry out: There's a crack the size of a tennis ball in the glass. And I declined the insurance.

Okay, calm down, Mr. Hayworth. Breathe in and breathe out. We'll put a claim on the credit card.

Oh, crap. I didn't pay with my credit card but with Justin Kletter's . . .

I climb into the trailer again. The area around the freezer is all damp. This time, I use double the number of bungee cords. Then, I get into the car and pull again. Easy and slowly, gently pressing on the accelerator, until I hear a thud and see the rope slacken. I smile devilishly, thinking that I finally made it, only to see a cascade of water come out of the semi through the rear-view mirror.

I rush out of the car and climb back into the trailer and across all the furniture. Well, I did make it. Justin's body came out and is now sprawled atop the boxes that contain the kitchen utensils. The problem is that his right leg is still trapped inside the main block of ice, which still contains the girl and is now on the floor, with her limbs sticking out because I pulled the freezer over.

The whole trailer floor is damp. And so are the boxes that contain the linens . . . And the mattresses . . . And the eleven thousand dollar sectional from Viesso. Those water stains will never come off.

I start crying again. It feels as if a metal rod had impaled me. It feels as bad as when men ask me to stop texting, and then I apologize with another text, and then they threaten a restraining order. It feels as bad as when Lucio's wife threatened to gauge my eyes out with her car keys . . . I wasn't stalking her husband! And even if I was, he never told me he was married. I suspected he was, but I thought he had lost my number and that if I waited outside his house, he would see me . . . Oh, I squeeze my fists tight and bite my own lips so that no one can hear me. It hurts as much as when the Belgian bastard asked me not to take that plane after I finally confessed I wasn't working as a stockbroker in Century City, but as a bar-back in West Hollywood and that I had just lost that job. It hurts as much as when I called him again from the Brussels airport, and he said he was not coming for me, that he had found a new boyfriend, one who didn't tell lies and had a promising career at the European Commission . . .

I brush away my tears with my sleeve. You have to do this, Charlie. You have to do it for Jignesh. He's the only man who hasn't rejected you. He's the only one who hasn't called you a fucking wacko dwarf, the only one who doesn't believe you're a loser. Well—I wipe my snot with my fingers, then on my shirt. Who cares? It's already ruined—he did call me a wacko dwarf one time, and then he hit me, but it was my fault because I wouldn't stop talking . . . Oh, I've been living all these months in fear, thinking that he's going to jump on my bed and kill me, but Jignesh's the one, I realize now. He's the love of my life, the man I want to spend the rest of my days with.

I got to do this.

If I do it, Jignesh will be in so much debt to me that he won't ever leave me.

Besides, he has a lot of money.

Did I buy an ice pick? I look around, shaking. If I did, it must be somewhere around here . . . I could use the screwdriver too, and a hammer to loosen up the leg . . . Where did I leave the toolbox?

It takes almost an hour, but I manage to break the leg loose from the ice. Then I begin the painful process of dragging the body across the heap of boxes. I have to take several rests. By the time I reach the end of the trailer, I simply drop it onto the ground. No one's around, and the night is so dark, I can't even see it myself unless I point my lamp at it directly.

I take a few minutes rest before I descend from the trailer and push the body into the car's trunk.

And now the woman.

Ten minutes later, I cease trying. There's no way I'll manage to get her out of that massive block of ice, and there's no way I could drag the whole thing across the trailer either. I better just push her back into the freezer and close the lid.

The freezer is too heavy with her inside to set it upright. I secure it with a couple of bungee cords. I'll fill it up with more ice before we get to Cabo. Tonight, I'm only going to worry about the man's corpse.

39

Love

Mostly geriatric cases in the dining room, this early in the morning. And the few lesbians aboard. They probably went to bed early.

Kim and Sita wave at me from their table.

"How did you sleep?" Kim asks when I approach the table.

Sita hides behind her mimosa.

"I slept fine," I say, pulling a chair.

This is incredibly awkward.

"I'll go get something," I add, raising a finger to excuse myself.

"Try the pancakes," Kim replies. "They're awesome."

Pancakes? I think, walking toward the food. Who would have guessed that Kim ate any carbohydrates? Who would have guessed she was a dike—or my sister?

"Of course, I knew you were gay," Sita told me last night. "It's so obvious."

She was so drunk, Kim had to hold her so she wouldn't fall.

"Do our parents know?" I asked, taking a sip of my gin and tonic.

Sita shrugged. "I suppose they do. They just don't talk about it."

I took a worried hand to my face. "Do they know about you?"

"Amrit knows."

"He's awesome," Kim intervened.

I nodded. I hate my brother, but I couldn't disagree, Amrit's awesome.

"Kim's parents know about me, of course," Sita continued. "Her mother drove us to San Diego this morning. She asked me if I'm going to marry you," she added to Kim.

Kim snorted.

"Are you?" I asked.

"Of course," Sita replied. "If it becomes legal."

"It's going to become legal," Kim intervened. "It's 2013. There's no way the Supreme Court is going to rule otherwise."

Sita reached for her neck and kissed her. I felt a knot form in my throat. And probably because of the alcohol I had so hastily drank, I couldn't help exclaiming: "Charlie and I are going to marry too."

"Who's Charlie?" Kim asked.

"His roommate," Sita responded.

"My boyfriend," I corrected her.

It felt natural to talk to them about Charlie. How he likes to call me "Sunshine" and "Sugar Lump" in the mornings. His terrible cooking. The music he has introduced me to. The way he cuddles with me when we're watching television. How beautiful he looks when he comes out of the shower, with his eyelashes still wet, smelling of his expensive shower gels.

He would have loved to be on this boat. He loves cheese, and there's quite a good selection. I put a slice of brie on my plate, in his honor. He loves figs too. And strawberries. I'll take a few. And bread. He keeps talking about how good the bread was in France. Some ham, eggs, one small quesadilla . . . a little bit of guacamole too. Pico de gallo! I'll skip all other greens . . . Where are the pancakes Kim recommended? I won't be able to eat all of this, but I'm dreading to go back to that table. What are we going to talk about now that we're sober?

"I'm disembarking tomorrow," I say when I finally join the girls at the table. "The moment we arrive in Cabo."

"Why?" Kim asks.

Sita looks relieved. I understand. She didn't expect to see me here and probably wants her space. Spend the day by the pool and the nights making love to her girlfriend . . .

I tell them about the house that Charlie and I are furnishing in Los Cabos.

"The cruise was cheaper than taking a plane," I lie. "It was so last minute."

"And where is Charlie?" Sita asks.

"He's already in Cabo," I reply, biting an English muffin.

"He doesn't mind you're on a gay cruise alone?"

I take a few seconds to respond. "Charlie said he needed some time alone." I take a bite. "With the house, I mean. To ponder the wall colors."

"The wall colors?" Sita asks. "Shouldn't you already know what color it's going to be? You already bought the furniture."

I feign a laugh, then I add, taking a bite of my quesadilla. "My dear little sister. I can tell you know nothing about how the mind of an interior designer works. One has to commune with the building."

"I'm doing a Master's in interior design," Sita responds, losing her amiable bearing. "That's why I want your junk out of the garage, so I can have a studio."

"You are?" I reply, surprised at the revelation. "Really? I could have hired you for this gig, had you told me. God knows we needed help."

"How could you not know it?"

"Well, you never mentioned it."

"But I did! My life revolves around my classes. That's how I met Kim."

"Do you also study design?" I ask Kim.

"I'm an architect. I teach a class at the Institute."

An architecture professor? How old is this Kim? She doesn't look much older than twenty-seven winters.

"Boy, you two are full of surprises," I laugh.

This isn't their first vacation together, I learn, and not even their first time on a cruise to Mexico. How come I didn't know that either?

"It shows how much you care about your sister," Sita says.

"Well, and you know lots about me, I suppose."

"I know that you like to eat."

Kim snorts.

"That's offensive."

"I know that you used to lock up in your room and dance to YouTube videos," Sita continues. "I know that you don't have any real friends, besides Charlie, and that you work as a bookkeeper."

"Do you know that I write?"

"I read two of your books. The one about the Princess who cannot fly and Mavericks something."

"*Mannikin Man*," Kim corrects Sita.

"That one."

I look at Kim. "How did you know the title?"

"She told me," she points at Sita.

Now Sita's smiling at me. Is that a smirk? No. She seems truly happy to bond with her brother.

"I'll go for seconds," Kim announces, standing up.

"I'll go too," Sita replies.

Is it possible? I ask to myself, following them with the eyes. Could my sister care about me? Now I'm smiling too. How upsetting! I have this weird pleasant sensation growing inside. I feel the urge to protect my sister. How awful! I feel happy to see her. I am pleased to know that she has a girlfriend. Suddenly, I don't think she's horrendous anymore. She's plump, all right, but so I am, and Sita has beautiful eyes and beautiful eyebrows, and her tan and those cheeks make her look lovely. Only now I notice: her hair is as curly and wild as I imagined Princess Salmonella's . . . *Horror!* I think, taking a hand to my mouth. Did my little sister inspire my beloved heroine? Now, I'm full of embarrassment . . . I've been so unfair. I used to throw her Barbies into the garbage disposal . . . I've been horribly unfair. Not only to Sita but to every woman I've ever met. I'm not a feminist! Au contraire, as Charlie would say, I'm a gay misogynist. I've never given Clara or Gabrielle the credit and respect they deserve at the office. I killed Nina, and I always assume that bad drivers are women . . . It was I, I confess, who left the turd in the toilet that scared Daisy, the woman from HP. Maybe if she hadn't quit on her first day, Justin would still be alive . . . Oh, God, one thing is to prefer cannelloni over pastrami flaps, but to dismiss an entire gender simply because they're not the dish I prefer? I am as awful as the bear I was going to share a cabin with. He preferred to find another room so that he wouldn't have to share one with me—his luggage was no longer there when I returned to the cabin last night. I am as mean as those guys who gave me the name *Interpretasha*. As mean as every straight man who ever made fun of my size, my skin color, or my sexual preference.

My sister's love and acceptance humble me. She has read two of my books. Oh, dear Lord, I ask for forgiveness for the many times I hurt Sita, especially that time I used her toothbrush to scrub the toilet, and I hereby swear not to ever cause her any harm again, to always be there, to protect her and to love her as an elder brother should love and protect his little sister.

"Which one did you like best?" I ask the moment they return to the table. "*Princess of a Lesser Kind* or *Mannikin Man?*"

"Neither," Sita replies. "They're both terrible. I didn't finish them. They're too long, too full of clichés, and too poorly written. You're just not a good writer."

Well, most siblings live lives apart, don't they? I only need to see Sita's ugly butt-face during family reunions.

"Should we meet later for lunch," Kim proposes, finishing her mimosa.

"Or back in Los Angeles," I say, standing up. "There's lots of activities to do here. Don't feel you have any obligation."

I spend the rest of the morning wandering around the boat, admiring the cabin doors' decor, reading the boards hung outside. Photographs are mandatory. Most passengers make use of classy euphemisms to express their willingness for adventure—how will the crew manage to remove all those colorful stickers? I wonder—but some have no shame in sharing their sexual perversions quite explicitly. Then I go for another meal. Alone. By midafternoon, I'm soaking in one of the hot tubs, pretending to enjoy myself while watching young fellas rest by the pool on the lounge chaises.

Like I said to my sister, there's plenty to do on the boat. Shows, bingo, even surfing, and rock climbing, but nothing truly for me. I'm either too blue or too old for all this. Not as old as that gentleman over there—I lower my shades—wearing a striped speedo that's anything but flattering considering his body mass index, but certainly not as enthusiastic either. I wish I could be that chatty. Russian, perhaps? He's tangled in conversation with two Millennials who seem to like him. They laugh at his jokes, and one even lets him rub sunblock on his shoulders.

I miss Charlie. His witty remarks and unabating babbling would have made this trip much more pleasant.

"Having a good time?" I ask the gentleman in the striped speedo after the young men leave, and he comes into the tub.

I don't really care if he is. I only want someone to talk to. Just a kind word. Some meaningful human interaction. I wouldn't mind if he decides to take some liberties under the bubbles, nevertheless. He's not too bad, after all, this Russian Grandpa. Beggars cannot be choosers. He can't be yet seventy, can he? Midsixties at most. He has nice skin, strong arms, and apparently, all of his teeth are real. He smells of alcohol, but who doesn't on this boat?

He smiles politely, then turns to the other side.

"Where do you come from?" I insist.

Maybe I misjudged him. Maybe he's shy. Maybe the young men were the ones who enticed him to talk to them in the first place . . .

"Not interested," he replies.

I remain silent for a second. Usually, I would look the other way and pretend no exchange of words ever happened. This time, however, I say, in my best Charlie Hayworth: "Thankfully, sir, I learned from a forum post that a 'dick deck' exists on this boat, where, and I quote, 'both oral and buggery sex acts are performed by random strangers in full view of any passenger who might wish to take an evening stroll.' Well, I'm certainly planning to take such a stroll tonight, sir, on the 'dick deck,' and I assume you will too, based on what I just witnessed. Rejected much? Who knows? maybe we'll meet again there, and when all the young men are either gone or occupied with each other, and alcohol, drugs, or desperation, remove all your hindrances to others' advances, I'll invite you to suck my fat Indian cock, and I'm guessing you won't refuse—will you?"

The gentleman leaves.

I do take a nightly stroll that night, and I do get myself a blowjob. From whom, I'll never know. It's dark and a little too crowded.

The next morning, I take the first tender boat to the Cabo San Lucas marina. Once I reach the dock, I turn on my cell phone. Then I get in line for customs.

I have at least thirty messages from Charlie. How adorable! Maybe he and Murat have already finished furnishing the house? Nope. Most are photographs of the Baja landscape. The last two are a bit disconcerting, however:

Murat and I are in Mulegé. I decided to go ahead with our plan and get rid of the two bodies.

Just kidding. Having a blast. Call me tomorrow.

What does he mean? I try to call him, but my call goes straight to his voicemail. I check my voicemail. He left me three messages. The most recent is from yesterday at 4:23 p.m.

I start with the first call, from Saturday at 2:46 in the morning.

"I'm lost, Jiggy," I hear Charlie cry. "I'm in the middle of the desert. It's very dark, I don't have a lamp, and my phone battery is about to die. I'm scared. I don't know Mexico's 911, and even if I did, what am I going to tell them? That I got lost trying to bury a corpse? I apologize, I'm so sorry. I thought this was going to be easier. I just wanted to help you."

He goes into elaborate details about how he managed to get Justin's body out of the trailer and into a car he rented.

"I drove for like forty minutes," he continues. "As far from the main road as I could until the path got too bumpy. Then I stopped the car and started digging. But the soil was too hard, so I had to try in several places. And then this huge spider jumped out of the hole and started to climb the shovel's handle. I threw the shovel away and ran away, screaming. But I ran too far, leaving the flashlight behind. Now I cannot find the way back to the car, and Justin's body is still inside the trunk . . . Oh, Jiggy. Where are you? Please call me. I'm afraid I'm going to die here. It's awfully dark."

I instinctively grab someone's arm.

"I just received some terrible news," I explain to the surprised stranger.

I try to call Charlie, but he doesn't answer. Then I try Murat's number. No response, either. Is Charlie alive? He must be. He left his second message yesterday at 10:50 in the morning. The tone is rather spiteful.

"I'm still alive, Jignesh. In case you wonder. Or care. You never called back. Are you already in Cabo? I never found the damn car. I wandered through the desert all night. My cell phone battery eventually died, and I kept running straight into the cacti. I should have stayed in one place, but I feared I would die eaten by giant spiders. Eventually, the moon came out, and I made it to a dirt road. I could have died, Jignesh," Charlie's voice breaks. "I would be vulture croquettes by now if it wasn't for this intriguingly rough ranchero that saw me this morning and brought me to his house. He let me charge my phone and his parents invited me for breakfast. My God, best *chorizo con huevo* burrito I've ever had. Not that it was worth all this predicament. He's going to give me a ride to the hotel later. Call me. *Toodles.*"

He's alive. But he also left Justin's body inside a car. What about Nina's? Did he bury her first?

I hear the most recent message:

"I'm afraid I have the most terrible news, Jignesh."

Charlie sounds as if he had been crying.

"There was an accident," the message continues. "Murat's dead, and the police think I have something to do with it." Charlie's voice breaks in a sob. "They're taking me with them to the *ministerio público* in Mulegé. I need you to come down and get me. Are you still in Los Angeles? Somebody needs to pay my bail."

Murat is dead? Charlie is under arrest? What on Earth happened? I redial Charlie's number. He doesn't answer.

"Are you all right?" The customs officer asks, when my turn arrives, noticing that I'm shaking.

Oh, fucketty, fuck. The police must know what I did by now. The officer will sure find my name on his computer. *Wanted for murder.* He will ask me to step out of the line while he calls two security guards . . . The building is so small, I look around . . . I could easily run into Mexican territory.

"I need a cup of coffee," I reply, giving him my passport.

"There's a Starbucks over there," the officer points to the buildings behind the pier. He doesn't even look like a real customs officer. More like a kid that got a summer job at a government office. "I hope you have a good time in Cabo," he adds, stamping my passport.

I rush out of the pier and sit on a concrete bench in the marina.

I listen to each of Charlie's messages at least three times. I still don't understand what the hell happened. How did Murat die? What did he do with Nina's body? I keep dialing Charlie's number, but every time my call goes to his voicemail. After a while, I stop calling. I remain on that bench brooding over the possibilities. Do the police know about the bodies? They probably do by now. Are they coming for me? Is Charlie all right? Maybe they tortured him . . . Oh, fucketty fuck, I shouldn't be calling his phone. If he hasn't spilled the beans already, they will see the number and think I am his accomplice!

I stand up. The Mexican police must have already contacted the FBI. The longer I keep this phone with me, the easier it'll be to track me. I walk to the edge of the dock and raise my iPhone, ready to throw it into the water. We had good times together . . . Should I delete it first? It's full of private selfies.

I'm about to erase it when it rings. The chime startles me, the phone slips off my hands and falls on the rocks that protect the dike. I reach down. The screen is broken.

It was a call from Charlie.

The phone rings again, a few seconds later.

"Charlie!" I answer, without looking at the caller ID. "What the hell happened?"

"Hey, Jignesh, it's Rogelio."

Rogelio? I check the phone screen. He's calling me from the office.

"Sorry to bug you," the kid continues, "I know you're sick, but I have a question about one reservation."

The calmness with which I respond to Rogelio, directing him through the proper procedures, strikes me as unbelievably coldhearted. I realize I thrive under pressure.

"Are you coming to the office tomorrow?" He asks, before hanging up.

"Probably not. Still feeling poorly. Have you heard from Murat?"

"Nope. He said not to bother him, so I haven't called him."

They don't know yet that he's dead.

I try calling Charlie again. This time he answers.

"Thank God I can finally reach you," I say. "Where are you?"

"Oh, Jignesh. I'm not in a nice place. Well, I am, if you don't mind the ants and the tacky Mexican decorations. And the mattress, dear Lord. I've never slept on anything harder, but overall these people have been fantastic. It would be utterly ungrateful to refer to this place as anything less than charming. I mean, it is impeccable, you could literally eat from the floor, and my host's attentions are nothing less than delightful. Anyway, what I was trying to say is that I'm not in a good emotional state. Did you hear my message, Jignesh? Murat is dead."

"Are you in jail?"

"In jail? God, no, of course not. Why would you—hold on a second, someone's at the door. Come on in—Oh, Yoli, did you bring that for me? You shouldn't have—Doña Eva made *buñuelos*, and Yoli just brought one to me. They're like a thousand calories each, fried and full of sugar. Still, they're so freaking good—Thank you, Yoli, tell doña Eva that *muchas gracias*."

"Who's Yoli?"

"Yoli is doña Eva's *muchacha*," I hear Charlie take a bite. "You'd fall in love with her, Jignesh, her cleaning is artisanal."

"And who's doña Eva?"

"Doña Eva is Johann's landlady. She's such a doll."

"Who's Johann?"

"Oh, yes, you don't know, I'm sorry. He teaches languages here in Mulegé. He's German. Between you and me, his English is not that good. His accent is horrible, but he's a doll too. He speaks Spanish, so he translated for me during the whole ordeal with the Mexican police, and now I'm renting a room at doña Eva's house, where he lives."

"But weren't you arrested?"

"No! Why do you keep asking that? Did I say so in my last message? I apologize, I'm sorry, my brain is complete pudding. They didn't arrest me, thank God. Can you imagine what would have happened to me in a Mexican jail?" Charlie's laughter sounds like a donkey braying. "I'd be dead by now. They just wanted to ask me some questions and figure out how Murat come to die—"

And that's all I can hear because then my phone dies.

40

Anthony

I wake up to the sound of the TV in the living room, Ricky's signal that it's time to get out of bed.

"Lower the volume!" I yowl.

"It's half past noon, Anthony," Ricky replies.

I roll over and look at the time on my phone. It's 12:49 p.m. I sit up but remain there for a few seconds, with my head down, breathing slowly, forcing myself to open my eyes.

I have sixteen notifications from Grindr.

I check them fast.

Fat . . . Fat . . . Lame . . . Ugly . . . Old . . . Let's see his dick . . . Yuck. Disappointing.

I need a Red Bull, I cry, putting the phone away. I would kill for some caffeine. I started the Candida diet last night, however, because I'm a fucking blob, and the diet doesn't allow for any caffeine, which means no Red Bulls, no coffee, no tea, no nada. I cannot have alcohol either, or sugar. I cannot have flour, dairy, beans, and virtually anything but meat and green-leafed vegetables. However, I will not quit the diet. Not before I lose at least two pounds.

I push the sheets away and walk across the hallway toward the living room. I nod at Emilia, the housekeeper we smuggled in from Oaxaca. She's cleaning the kitchen. *"Buenos días, Emi,"* I manage to say before I reach the couch. Emilia replies with a giggle and immediately looks away.

"Put on some clothes, Anthony," Ricky says, looking at me.

I glower at her. I've never gotten over that weird American habit of treating the help as if they were real people.

"Emilia is used to seeing me naked, ¿*Verdad Emi?*" I turn my head to her. "It doesn't bother her, Ricky." I reach for a package of cigarettes on the table and light one. "She's seen much worse. One time she caught me eating somebody's ass. ¿*Te acuerdas, Emi?*—What are you watching?"

"A Spanish movie," Ricky replies. "From the seventies."

Ricky thinks that she can learn Spanish from watching TV. As if. I've learned more Yiddish myself from hearing her fight with her children.

I don't recognize the movie, but I immediately recognize Sara Montiel, dressed like a man, complete with blue overalls and a beret, surrounded by a group of women wearing typical Spanish clothes. She starts singing *Pichi*.

"Oh," I cry in delight. "I danced to that song in kindergarten," I say to Ricky.

Ricky bobs her head in reply.

"I must have been four years old," I say with a yawn. "Because in *prepri* we did the *Danza de la Pluma*. We had this huge oval headdresses covered in feathers and a mirror in the middle, so yeah, I must have been about four when we danced *Pichi*."

Ricky takes a sip of her coffee. She's too sleepy to be engaged in a conversation.

"My mother loved that song," I continue, blowing some smoke and reaching over to catch the aroma from Ricky's cup. "We used to sing it together."

Ricky nods again.

I pay attention to the lyrics. It's been thirty-five years now . . . I only remembered the first line: "*Pichi, es el chulo que castiga . . .*"

"Oh, my God," I exclaim suddenly. "This song is about a pimp."

"She's dressed like one," Ricky says, referring to Sara Montiel.

I am so shocked that before the song is over, I put out my cigarette and go grab my phone from our bedroom to google the lyrics.

"It is about a pimp," I confirm to Ricky, returning to the couch. "Listen to this," I translate to her: "*I educate them and structure them—Them are the girls. Then I take their money to spend it on all my vices and live like a Lord.*"

Ricky chuckles. "You danced to that in kindergarten?"

"I did! And it was a Catholic school. We had nuns and priests, and there was a chapel. I have a picture of my best friend from back then, she and I dressed like Spanish procurers, wearing berets and colorful jackets. Two four-year-old boys, one brown and one blond, all smiles, oblivious that they were dancing to a revue song that glorifies beating and exploiting women . . . Oh, my God, Ricky!" I cry in realization. "This song is what fucked me up!"

"You were born gay," Ricky mumbles.

"Perhaps," I retort, "but I wasn't born a materialistic monster."

My brain starts working. All the surgeries. All the clothes. All the shoes, the trips, the drugs, the series of millionaire boyfriends . . . What am I doing in New Jersey? I could have stayed in Mexico City and lived a perfectly normal upper-middle-class life next to a man who worked for the government and whom I wouldn't have to share with a crazy wife or with her business. I could be eating carbs. I could be drinking alcohol instead of snorting it. I wouldn't have to prick my face every six weeks to keep the wrinkles away . . . I could have been a much happier person!

"If I still talked to my mother, I would call her immediately," I say later to Ricky, on our way to Newark. "What was she thinking, letting me dance to that dirty and perverted song when I was at my most impressionable? What were those nuns thinking? You saw the movie. The scene takes place inside a brothel. *Pinches monjas*, they probably made a fortune selling us the costumes. I cannot believe none of the parents ever complained."

Ricky rolls her eyes, as she typically does whenever I say something remotely contentious.

"Does your wife give you this much trouble, Sam?" she asks the driver.

I hit Ricky on her chest, and she flinches, crying in pain. No, I didn't forget about her implants. She fucking deserved it.

At the hair salon, I cannot stop thinking about the effect that that *Pichi* song must have had on me. Those words brainwashed me. Here I am, for instance, paying eighty dollars for a blowout, when I could just wrap my hair in a bun and shave the sides, like a normal person. But what am I going to do now? Go to the gym *toda desgreñada, como una* peasant? I don't even pay attention to whatever nonsense Sergio is saying to me. I'm so mad. I'm mad at her, I'm mad at Ricky, I'm mad at my mother, I'm mad at everything and everyone on this planet.

"How's Ricky doing?" Sergio asks.

"Oh, she's fine," I reply with a forced smile. "You know how it is. Worky, worky."

Sergio has a huge pimple on her chin, and every time she rolls my hair up and makes me bend down, I can see it. It's so fucking disgusting. I'm going to have to change my hairdresser. I can't believe I slept with her.

I'm so angry that I'm actually running on the treadmill. Normally I just walk for like twenty minutes, then go cruise the steam room, but I need to shake off my ill temper. Otherwise, I'm just going to chomp off somebody's dick.

That song really fucked me up. I paid two-hundred dollars for the tank top I'm wearing. Nine hundred for the Louis Vuitton sneakers. Three hundred at least for the shorts. I thought that all of these things would bring me happiness. They didn't. I didn't need any of it. I didn't need to come to this country. I could have stayed in Mexico and marry a combi driver. Or a *taquero*, I don't care. I didn't need to chain-smoke all those men, break so many hearts, and climb the corporate ladder using my body.

I get a text. It's from Charlie. There's a picture attached.

Your house is looking good.

"*¿Qué reputa chingados es esto?*" I exclaim after I zoom in the picture, so loud that half the gym patrons turn to me. "Those chairs are fucking horrendous!"

Ricky told me that the last time I stormed into her office unannounced, it cost the company half a million dollars. Thus, Ricky forbade her assistant, Sheila, to let me in when she's having a meeting. Still, I need to talk to her. Yes, right this moment, Sheila. I grab a paper-weight rock crystal from her desk and threaten to smash the window if she doesn't let me by.

"They're destroying our house," I wail, once I barge into Ricky's office. "I need to fly immediately to Cabos."

Ricky and the three men she's talking to turn toward me. The three of them are wearing polyester suits. I hate fucking New Jersey.

Ricky takes a deep breath. She apologizes to the men and walks with me out of her office. We take a seat on the couch next to Sheila's desk.

"Maybe you shouldn't have started with the Candida Diet this week," she begins.

What?

"This has nothing to do with my diet!" I yell. "Look at this," I show him the picture that Charlie sent me. "Look at those chairs! They're horrendous!"

Ricky looks at the phone for a second. "They look fine to me, baby."

"Are you fucking insane? WHAT THE FUCK IS THE MATTER WITH YOU? Did you see the cushions?"

"Anthony, a month ago, you were in love with your decorators."

"Yes. That was before I learned they would be destroying my house."

"Tony, sweetie, just have a cup of coffee, please. Have a drink. Have a Red Bull. You're not going to gain one ounce. I promise. You're not fat. You're like a matchstick. For the love of God, just do it, baby doll. You're so much nicer when you're taking your fat burners."

What? Am I hallucinating? When did the man I love turn into such an insensitive monster? Ricky knows perfectly well that I have an eating disorder. She knows my whole body is Candida infested. I showed her the pictures on the internet!

I grab Sheila's paperweight again and throw it against the window.

"DON'T BABY DOLL ME!" I scream at Ricky. "I need to go down to Cabos and save my house from those idiots. RIGHT NOW!"

The glass must be at least an inch thick because it doesn't even crack. The rock just bounces back.

"Okay," Ricky says. "How much money do you need?"

The thing that I hate the most about flying first class is watching the parade of poor people flying coach board the plane. Why can't they have their own door? Or their own planes? Why can't I have my personal private jet? I hate Ricky. She's such an asshole.

My driver is drinking cheap coffee from a Styrofoam cup. I swear to God that if she doesn't stop slurping, I'm going to stab her. As a matter of fact, I'm just going to kill her, I don't care if we end up crashing. What can I use as a weapon? I look around. Her neck is far too wide to strangle her . . .

"What the fuck are you doing to my house?" I say to Jignesh, the moment she opens the door. "And what the fuck is a semi-trailer doing in our front yard?"

41

Jignesh

"We're embellishing it!" I respond to Anthony.

He glowers at me. I step aside, and he gets in. His driver carries his luggage behind him. I hold the door open for him, then follow Anthony into the foyer.

"We weren't expecting you," I stammer. "I came to the door thinking you were one of the painters. We haven't finished, of course. You didn't tell us you were coming. When did you arrive? Just today? How are you?"

Anthony is surveying the changes we've made. He doesn't look happy.

"I don't want that semi-truck outside." He points at the door.

I nod nervously. God, what is Anthony doing here? Charlie didn't ask him to come, did he? I told him to stop sending him pictures. The house isn't ready.

Anthony enters the living room. His driver exchanges a look with me as if warning me to be careful.

"What the fuck is this?" Anthony screams. He points at the birdcage with rag dolls inside that I was planning to pass off as a piece from Betye Saar . . .

I open my mouth to explain, but he interrupts me.

"What's that stench?"

"What stench?" I mumble, following him into the living room. "I don't smell anything."

Anthony glares at me as if I had just said something insulting about his mother. "It stinks like a dead animal," he spats, then continues walking around. I look at the driver and see that he, too, can sense the odor coming from the furniture.

I guess we have gotten used to it and thought it had already dissipated.

"What the fuck happened there?" Anthony asks, pointing at the watermarks on the curtains. "And what's that?" He looks at the stains on the sectional in the living room.

"It's your new sofa," Charlie replies from his chair.

Anthony starts, surprised. He hadn't seen Charlie before. The poor thing has been sitting on that chair pretty much since we arrived in Cabo, two days ago. All this time, he's been curled up, bracing his knees, like a bird with a broken wing, his sight fixed on the Pacific Ocean.

"What?"

"Your new sofa." Charlie speaks so softly you would think he's about to faint. "It's a top-grain suede sectional from Viesso."

It's been incredibly difficult to furnish this house with Charlie in such a miserable state. He points at a piece. The men we hired hurry to pick it up with me behind to assist them, then Charlie covers his mouth as if he were thinking. He points tentatively in one direction, and the men struggle to carry it there. Then he points to another spot. Then he covers his eyes as if he were trying to hold in his tears, making us dance with the furniture all over.

"It's soiled!" Anthony screams.

Deirdre and Jana have been more of a nuisance than anything else. I don't even know where they are right now. Probably at the beach. Or smoking weed at the golf course.

"Is it?" I ask.

Anthony stares daggers at me.

"Oh, I see," I laugh nervously. "It barely shows. Charlie mentioned it. We didn't know if you would want to return it."

"We had a small accident," Charlie ventures.

"A small accident?" Anthony shrieks. "And what is that horrible smell?" He insists. "Does it come from the sea?" He walks to the terrace. "No!

It's from the inside. From the sofa." He bends down to smell it. "*¡Huele a perro muerto!* What is it?"

"We suspect a dead mouse," Charlie replies.

The stench comes, of course, from leaving a corpse inside a trailer full of damp furniture for almost three days in the desert.

My phone rings. It's Mike extension, from the office.

I reject the call. Mike dials a second time. I reject it again. He dials once more.

"Aren't you going to answer that?" Anthony hisses.

I answer the phone.

"Jignesh, I'm back at the office. Where are you? I'm about to have a heart attack."

"Just a minute, Mike—if you could excuse me for a second," I say to Anthony, then hurtle out to the terrace, around the pool, and all the way down to the fire pit.

I sit on a round stone bench. It's so big, it could comfortably seat ten people. Before I answer the phone again, I look at the azure of the Sea of Cortez, the green of the golf course, and the brown of the mountains. God, I know I've done wrong. I know that the last thing I deserve is your mercy. I know that I should go to jail and that my soul is already condemned to oblivion, but please, dear God, please help me. Let me win. Just this once. Let the colored, angry, fat, gay guy get away with it. Do it for all the times that I've been insulted, bashed, and humiliated. Do it for all the times I was called a third-world degenerate. Do it for all the hurtful jokes against Indians, for all the hatred against homosexuals, and overweight people. Do it for Charlie, the man I plan to marry, and I promise I'll never kill anyone ever again.

42

Nina

I met Jignesh at the bus station in Mulegé. We took a taxi back to the semi and got immediately on the road. We didn't know where we could start looking to hire a driver, so Jignesh sat behind the wheel.

"How could you be so fucking stupid!" Jignesh yelled at me when I confessed I had paid the hotel and the rental car with Justin's credit card.

I'm glad I didn't tell him I gave Justin's name at the police station too. He would have been really mad. As if. They typed it down as *Yostin Keller*, I saw when I signed my statement.

Then he started asking questions about Murat. I kept shaking my head, begging Jignesh not to ask for more because, well, it was painful.

"He's gone, Jignesh," I replied. "What else do you want to know? I saw his dead, lifeless body lying on a table at the morgue. Pale, like a withered flower. Like Helena Bonham Carter playing Ophelia in Mel Gibson's *Hamlet*, which I dare think is a much better version than Kenneth Branagh's, regardless of the rating on Rotten Tomatoes. However, I must say that in Branagh's version, the art direction was simply fantastic . . . Anyway, I saw him dead, and you weren't there, Jignesh. You weren't there to help me . . . You were on a cruise! And not any cruise, a freaking gay cruise full of oversexed men dancing to the latest of Katy Perry in their Andrew Christian speedos while I had to deal with two bodies . . . Three if you count Murat's."

Here, I made a dramatic pause and looked longingly through the window.

"The way that the Mexican police treated me was just horrendous," I continued. "They have no manners. They made me ride in the back of their truck, without any consideration of my wretched state. And once at their station, they made me sit down and give my *declaración* to a thick old man armed with a state-of-the-art computer running Windows 95. I asked for water. They told me that I would have to go buy a bottle from a machine outside. Then they offered me bad coffee in a Styrofoam cup. I knew very well I couldn't expect Stevia in a place so remote from God, but they laughed when I asked for half and half instead of the old Coffee-Mate creamer they offered. Then came the part where I had to identify the body. I have never felt so vulnerable and scared. My entire body shook like a little mouse in the presence of a hungry feline. Did anyone hug me and tell me it was going to be fine? No. And I needed a hug, Jignesh, I needed some reaffirmation. I had spent an entire night lost in the desert, I told them. I had wandered all morning under the unrelenting Baja sun, thinking I was fixing to die, and that no one would come to my funeral, because as picturesque as Mulegé is, full of palm trees and bougainvilleas and honeysuckle bushes flanking the streets, and with its quaint old houses with all those large verandas that invite you to spend the days watching people pass by, 'oh, there goes Ximena, the florist, and that's Margarita, she's marrying Francisco, you know, the pharmacist,' who among my many acquaintances and my two real friends would want to attend a destination funeral in a godforsaken town in the middle of nowhere IN A COUNTRY WHERE THEY HATE WHITE PEOPLE? Well, it's a love, hate relationship, I suppose," I calmed down. "Mexican television shows only white people, I noticed. Aspirational, I suppose. I, myself, would love to get a tad darker. Anyways, learning about Murat's death felt like a punch, Jignesh, right on my nose. And I've been punched before, I know exactly how it feels, it's not an exaggeration. I was punched, spat on, kicked in my privates, and repeatedly smacked against the floor all through my early twenties. I couldn't stop crying through the whole ordeal. Still, no one felt sorry for me. No one took my hand and said that everything would be okay, that I wouldn't die in prison for a crime I didn't commit. *Au contraire*, they laughed at my mannerisms, which, considering the extreme circumstances, may have been a little more effeminate than usual, but what did they expect me to do? To man-up? I'm fucking gay, and that's what gay people do. We cry. We're sentimental. We rely on the kindness of others. They kept talking in their stupid third-world language without any consideration for my wellbeing. I don't know how I would have survived without Johan, who appeared shortly after. Although let me tell you, he could improve his manners too. Germans are a tad too cold."

"What did they do to Murat's body?"

"Sweet Southern Baby Jesus, Jignesh. I don't know. I'm talking about my own suffering, and you have to turn the tables and make it all about Murat. I was lost in the desert, Jignesh. Lost. I thought I was going to die. Then I thought I would spend the rest of my days in jail. Johan said he contacted the Turkish embassy in Mexico City. I suppose someone will pick him up."

"But his whole family lives in Chicago," Jignesh exclaimed.

"And how would I know?" I screamed. "All I knew was Murat's first name and that he was Turkish. He left his wallet and passport inside the room's safe, and I didn't realize until I checked out. You should thank me that I didn't tell the police that he was driving the semi. I told them that Murat was a 'friend' that I had made at a gas station, which aroused some scornful laughter. Never have I felt more embarrassed in my entire life."

"But how did it happen?" Jignesh insisted.

I didn't know what Jignesh meant.

"How did Murat die?" he insisted.

"Well—he drowned. He was too drunk to think clearly. The Vicodin I gave him had nothing to do with it. It was a warm night. He must have gotten into the pool to cool off but couldn't swim out."

"So, you killed him?"

That did it for me.

"I did not kill Murat," I responded. "I only meant for him to fall asleep so I could take care of your business. It was an accident. He killed himself!"

Jignesh replied by giving me a cuff on the left temple.

Needless to say, I didn't open my mouth again until we reached Cabo.

Well, I must have opened my mouth once or twice again to say I needed to take a leak or to point at some picturesque item on the landscape, but other than that, I didn't even try to make conversation.

Well, no. We talked a bit when we had to open the trailer after we passed a desolate place called *El Huatamote*. Not a sign of civilization for almost thirty miles, according to Google maps. A beautiful starry night, yet dark enough so that you couldn't see your hand stretched out in front of you.

There was this homeless woman with elephantiasis who I often passed on my way to work in Santa Monica, riding a rickety wheelchair, no teeth, and all scruffy, begging with a shaky hand for a quarter. She smelled so terribly bad of poo and urine that I always crossed the street to avoid her. The stench that came from inside the trailer the moment we opened the doors was a million times worse. The air coming from inside felt ridiculously warm, too, like during the Santa Ana's. Both Jignesh and I had to vomit. Thankfully, outside the trailer.

Jignesh tied a sweatshirt around his face and got to work. He's way stronger than I am, so it took him only a few minutes to emerge with the girl's body.

I followed him five feet behind, pointing ahead with my flashlight and carrying a shovel in my other hand. I covered my face with my own shirt. We walked along a dry arroyo for a few hundred yards. Then Jignesh laid the body down, and we took turns digging.

"She was beautiful," Jignesh said with a teary eye.

I pointed the flashlight briefly at her face. I couldn't tell whether she ever was. The corpse looked all bruised and swollen.

"Maybe when the rain comes, this whole area will cover with flowers," I said, trying to cheer up Jignesh. "Her grave won't be that barren anymore . . . How often does it rain here? Let me google it . . . Shoot, I have no signal in here."

43

How Much?

"Sorry, Mike, you were saying?"

"I said: Where are you, Jignesh? I stopped at your house this morning. Are you back at your parents'?"

"Y–yes," I reply. "That's where I am."

"I need you to come to the office."

"Mike, I'm really sick."

"You cannot do this to me, Jignesh. Rogelio rented Alman's house to a guy that showed up with two dogs. Alman is furious. And the cleaners threatened to quit because you were short with their hours. You know how feisty Juana gets. She stirred them all up. I cannot deal with this shit."

"I left signed checks with Gabrielle," I stammer. "She just needed to run a report. I explained to her how to calculate the amount. Did she do it wrong?"

"Yes. She confused the Marías and underpaid Juana."

From where I am, I can see Anthony walking around the house, going on and on about the furniture. I turn the other way around, facing the ocean.

"How could she do that?" I ask Mike.

"Because that's not her job. It is yours. You need to fucking be here."

"I have bronchitis." I cough. "It's highly contagious."

"Dammit, Jignesh, your timing is just precious. Anyway, that's not everything. I found out what you did, and I'm really disappointed. I expected better from you. Why did you do it? Was it because you were jealous? Was it because you felt threatened by Justin? Why did you do it?"

I remain silent.

"So, you found out," I finally say.

"Of course, I found out. You're a fucking weasel, Jignesh."

"You don't need to get offensive, Mike."

"I cannot say it otherwise. It was a low move. Did you think I was so stupid that I would never find out? I have the withholding order from the EDD in my hands. You knew that Justin couldn't become an employee because his ex-wife had sued him for child support, and even after I explicitly told you not to, you reported him as a new hire. The ex-wife is rich. She didn't need the money as much as Justin did. Her father owns hundreds of condominiums! They just wanted to squeeze every last penny from the poor guy. And now, thanks to you, he's gone. We lost one good, trustworthy employee because he had no other choice but to disappear. I should fire you, Jignesh. It was a cowardly move. I would if I could, but I need you here to fix this mess. Justin's in Mexico now, poor guy."

"In Mexico?" I gasp. "How do you know? Did he call you?"

"He's not going to call. I know because he used the company credit card to book a hotel and rent a car that he never returned. The rental agency tried to charge nine hundred dollars in late fees, and they called from the bank because they thought that the charge was suspicious. I rejected the charges and canceled the credit card."

"Are you going to press charges?"

"Jesus Christ, Jignesh, don't you get it? He's desperate. Have some compassion. I won't even tell the police that he's in Mexico. He has another warrant in Massachusetts because he owes taxes. He might end up in jail if they catch him. It's really fucked up, Jignesh. Congratulations. You fucked Justin real bad."

"It's Maine. He owes taxes in Maine."

"Whatever," Mike snorts. "To make things worse, Murat disappeared too. He was supposed to be back on Monday. It's Wednesday now. But you know what? I'm sick of him too. He's my buddy and all, but he's a fucking drunk. He's rude, he's unreliable, and always ends up pissing everyone off. I'm okay if he never comes back. I'm up to the neck with irresponsible people. I cannot take a vacation without this place falling apart. Things are going to change. I'm not going to take any time off until the summer, except for this Friday, I have to drive to San Luis Obispo for a friend's wedding, but that was already planned. For now, I need you to call Alman, I don't care if you're sick. If you cannot convince him to be cool with the dogs, you need to find another property for this guy. I don't care how. I'll write the checks for Juana and for the Marías, and you better fix payroll as soon as you can. When do you think you will be back?"

I sound as humble as a two-year-old child: "Next Monday, perhaps?"

Mike sighs. "I'll call Detective Mora too and tell her about the withholding order from the EDD. I'm not going to tell her that Justin's in Mexico, and if you talk to her, you better don't either, please. Do it as a favor to me. Please. He wanted to disappear. That's it. Anyway, get better. Let me know what Alman says."

I return inside. Anthony is sitting on the sectional sofa, crying.

Charlie hasn't moved from his place. He's looking at Anthony with pitiful eyes.

"Everything all right?" I ask.

"No, everything is not all right," Anthony sobs. "You were supposed to make this house fabulous. It isn't fabulous. The furniture is damaged, the linens are all damaged, I hate those fucking chairs, the dining table is scratched, and I saw what happened to the china. It's all broken because you didn't secure the boxes."

"Anthony, dear," Charlie begins. "What did you expect with a budget of only four hundred and fifty thousand dollars? You have to understand that we did our best considering how limited our resources were."

"Only four hundred and fifty thousand dollars?" Anthony shrieks. "Do you have any idea of money's worth? A family of four survives two decades with that amount of money in this country!"

"Well, that wouldn't last that long in Los Angeles," Charlie responds with a forced grin. I see a tear roll down his cheek that he immediately brushes off. "Can you imagine?" He snickers. "How much does that amount to in a year? Forty-five thousand dollars—no, half of that. About Twenty-three thousand dollars, right?" He looks at me for confirmation. "That wouldn't pay for a year subscription to a decent gym in Beverly Hills. Not for one person, much less for four. You cannot compare. I mean, this is a fabulous house. It's large and grandiose, and the view is absolutely fantastic. A house like this, oceanfront and right on a golf course, could easily go for ten million back in LA. You couldn't be cheap. But you were. We did our best effort, Anthony, considering your circumstances—"

"Honey, you're here!"

The three of us turn toward the pool. Deidre and Jana are back from the beach.

"When did you arrive?" Deirdre asks, taking off her sandals and dropping her beach bag by the sliding door before rushing to hug Anthony. "Jana, this is Anthony."

"Oh, nice to meet you," Jana says, trailing behind. She has stopped by the door to take off her sandals too. "I've heard a lot about you, Anthony. All good things—You haven't shown him the mural yet, have you?" She asks Charlie and me.

"What mural?" Anthony asks, horrified.

"You haven't seen it? Come outside," Jana replies.

Anthony stands up and walks out to the terrace. His gaze follows Jana's finger pointing at the wall left to the sliding doors. He sees a twelve-foot spray-painted mural of a naked young man seen from behind. The buttocks are impossibly round, and his ballsack and the tip of his penis can be clearly seen hanging between the legs.

"It's you, honey," Deidre says, clapping her hands. "How do you like it?"

Anthony flinches, then drops into a chair.

"I haven't finished, of course," Jana explains. "I still have to paint the waves and the sand and the stars and this X here," she points at a brown mark, "will be Ricky waiting for you to take him. Like a bride."

Anthony tries to stand up but immediately falls back into the chair. He takes a hand to his throat, gasps, and then his body contorts as if he were about to have a stroke. This time he begs, rather than command: "I need coffee."

"What's that, honey?" Deirdre asks, bending down.

"Coffee," Anthony wheezes. "Please."

Unable to understand him, Deirdre lifts her arms, asking for help.

"I think he wants coffee," Jana says.

Deirdre rushes into the kitchen. She frantically opens every cabinet looking for the coffee maker.

"Where are the filters?" She asks after she finds the coffee carafe.

I point at one of the cupboards.

"I think he's having a seizure," Jana exclaims.

Deirdre leaves the carafe and opens the refrigerator.

"Will a Red Bull do?" She asks, finding an open can that somebody left inside.

Anthony nods.

"He says yes," Jana hollers.

Deirdre runs back outside. She offers Anthony the can, but he can't lift his hands to hold it, so she puts the can to his mouth and presses his cheeks so that he can chug the liquid down, just like Sally Field does to Julia Roberts in *Steel Magnolias*, I suppose Charlie would say.

"Should we call a doctor?" Jana asks.

"No, honey, it'll be all right," Deirdre replies. "Could you finish making the coffee?" She asks Charlie. Charlie, however, remained transfixed in his place.

"I'll do it," I volunteer.

"No, Jignesh," Deirdre adds. "Jana will do it. You help me bring Anthony inside."

"It is a beautiful painting," Anthony mumbles, a moment later, laying on the couch. Jana couldn't figure out how the coffeemaker worked, so he's eating coffee grains with a spoon, straight from the can. "Thank you."

"Did you like it?" Jana asks.

Anthony nods.

"How much will it cost to fix this?" He snivels, looking at the upholstery.

I can't believe Charlie's cold blood when he replies: "At least another hundred and fifty thousand. On top of your balance, that is."

Anthony takes a hand to his temple and bends down.

"How much was my balance?" He asks with a stifled laugh.

I can't believe mine, either, when I hear myself add "Ninety-four thousand."

"Plus twenty-five thousand for Jana's mural," Deirdre adds, after me. "That's after a twenty percent discount, of course."

ACKNOWLEDGMENTS

This book would have never come to life had I not been a coffee addict and had I not moved to the City of Angels in 2009. Thanks must be first given then to the goats who discovered caffeine and to the good people of L.A., who provided material to an author with no imagination. Then, I must thank Writer's Blok at the Church of the Nazarene, where I wrote the first draft. Many complained about the uncomfortable chairs. I never noticed: The whole experience was fabulous. Thanks, of course, to my husband and social secretary, Mr. Terry McFadden, who read the entire manuscript twice. Finally, I must thank the Quill Prose Award final judge, Uzodinma Iweala (hopefully, he didn't mean it as a joke), and the people at Red Hen Press: Tobi, Kate, Monica, Natasha, and Rebeccah, you have been nothing but utterly and incredibly fantastic. My little ugly baby (this book) couldn't have fallen into better hands!

Biographical Note

Carlos Allende is a media psychology scholar and a writer of fiction. He has written two previous novels: *Cuadrillas y Contradanzas*, a historical melodrama set during the War of Reform in Mexico, and *Love, or the Witches of Windward Circle*, a horror farce set in Venice, California. Based on his research on narrative persuasion and audience engagement, he developed the course The Psychology of Compelling Storytelling, which he teaches in the Writers' Program at UCLA Extension. He lives in Santa Monica with his husband.